Heartwood

Donald L. Ball

iUniverse, Inc.
Bloomington

Heartwood

This is a work of fiction. All of the characters, names, incidents, organizations, and dialogue in this novel are either the products of the author's imagination or are used fictitiously.

iUniverse books may be ordered through booksellers or by contacting:

iUniverse
1663 Liberty Drive
Bloomington, IN 47403
www.iuniverse.com
1-800-Authors (1-800-288-4677)

Because of the dynamic nature of the Internet, any web addresses or links contained in this book may have changed since publication and may no longer be valid. The views expressed in this work are solely those of the author and do not necessarily reflect the views of the publisher, and the publisher hereby disclaims any responsibility for them.

Any people depicted in stock imagery provided by Thinkstock are models, and such images are being used for illustrative purposes only.

Certain stock imagery © Thinkstock.

ISBN: 978-1-4620-1224-4 (sc)
ISBN: 978-1-4620-1225-1 (ebk)

Printed in the United States of America

iUniverse rev. date: 4/19/2011

Acknowledgements:

My wife Bev for her continued support and patience.

◊

Sergeant Matt Zelinsky of the Tuolumne County Sheriff's Office, (California)

&

Sergeant Jim Kemmerle of the Ashtabula County Sheriff's Office, (Ohio)

for their insight and making me dig even deeper.

◊

Arleen Kovats, quintessential over-achiever of Grand Valley High School in Orwell, Ohio for her verbal and photographic history of the school, and local knowledge.

◊

Greg Hudson for being my go-to guy for weapons data.

"Many wealthy people are little more than janitors of their possessions."
~ Frank Lloyd Wright ~

CHAPTER 1

The enterprising trio was young, full of spirit, and agile enough to outrun any pot-bellied bank security guard. They had a good plan. Well thought-out on a late summer afternoon while lounging around a family swimming pool in an upscale neighborhood near Fresno, California. One newspaper article unwittingly furnished them with an answer to a critical element of their timetable—two minutes max to a crime scene by local police once the report was received. Young and one-dimensional, they overlooked the word, *max*, in their plans.

They could do it. Arrive at the bank in mid-afternoon when the crowd was the thinnest. Burst in with masks in place, brandish the handgun, create havoc and confusion, demand money from tellers and have the cash placed in nondescript plastic bags available from any supermarket. They would wear latex gloves so no fingerprints would remain behind to act as a homing beacon. Money was inconsequential to them. Overindulgent parents willingly supplied them with enough money and free time to do whatever they wanted during the hot, lazy summer months. Their goal was to grab just enough to have bragging rights, at least within their close circle of trusted friends. It was the challenge.

Poised at the loading-only curb, painted a brilliant yellow just two days ago, was a tricked out, '71 Dodge Charger R/T hardtop waiting to whisk them away to one of their homes where they could hide the vintage muscle car and high-five each other. To avoid arousing suspicion on the drive to the bank, the group had installed Velcro clips to keep the license plates in plain view. While his two companions were inside, the plan was for the driver to leap out, rip off the tags, and wait in the idling car with his foot hovering over the accelerator ready to punch life into the 426 Hemi. The plates could be refastened later when out of sight of the bank and nosy witnesses.

Inside the bank, all went according to plan until one fell prey to a sudden case of adrenalin overload. Logic and planning became a blur. People no longer existed, only shadowy smudges crouching in corners or behind desks, some shielding their frightened children behind them. The two-minute drill went into slo-mo. A long piercing cry of, "No-o," echoed through the vaulted room when a gun was pointed in their direction. Two hurried shots were fired. As they sprinted for the door, one woman was face down in a pool of blood with her children crying at her side.

The solitary, faded, window curtain in the bedroom was drawn back to let in the morning sun. So there would be no squeak or sound of wood rubbing on wood, Elizabeth eased a dresser drawer open. A hurried glance out the window guaranteed no one would be watching. From under a pile of blankets stored in anticipation of the freezing winter months, she withdrew a large white envelope and held it in her trembling hands.

One end was torn and ragged where she'd stuck her finger under the lip to rip it open so many years ago. Inside was a folded document. She bit at her lip as she slid the papers out, placed them on top of the dresser and with tender strokes, smoothed out the creases. "This is all I have," she whispered as she agonized through the pages, but her dark and hollow eyes always gravitated to the last page. "I promise you, I will never forget."

"You can do whatever you want with me, but I will not accept responsibility for locating this last asshole." Jason Carmichael stood face to face with the sheriff of Fresno County.

Sheriff Yacek Szabo sat behind his desk and studied a current topographical map of Fresno County complete with yellow Post-it pads secured in place by stick pins showing the numerous types of crimes needing immediate attention in the county.

"I'm out of options, Jason," Szabo barked. "You know damn well we're short-handed. All the counties are understaffed. That's why you were loaned out to solve the Griffen case up in Tuolumne County." Szabo took a deep breath. "It's all a matter of timing, and sharing of personnel. You are one hell of a detective. Now, please. Don't force me to order you to do anything."

"Are you aware of who this victim was?"

"Marie Gallagher. I know you developed feelings for this woman during her daughter's kidnapping case, but I'm not sure how far it went from there."

Jason's hollow eyes burrowed deep into his boss. "Yeah. Feelings," he sighed. The walls of the sheriff's office were closing in fast. He felt he could rip every award and certificate from them and never even care. "I loved her children as my own. And three punk ass kids out for a prank thought they could rob a bank like they see on TV...they became nervous...and one innocent woman is shot dead. Marie is dead, Sheriff. The courts have turned her children over to their biological father who is a total ego-driven piece of crap and could care less about them."

Szabo's eyes drifted to an older map of the county on the far wall. This ragged-edged copy of an antiquated local map dated back to the 1800s. Its brown and sepia hues were highlighted by a sliver of light that filtered into the office through a small four-pane window in desperate need of cleaning. "Sometimes the law is never just."

Jason snickered. "If that was supposed to make me feel better, it didn't work. I was at Marie's funeral, and I watched this douche bag walk in with his latest conquest...some ditsy blonde with false eyelashes out to here." Jason held his hands about a foot in front of his face. "I tried talking to them, but I'm positive their cumulative IQ's wouldn't add up to two digits. When the ceremony was over, he started to walk away with the blonde. He hadn't even held his kids' hands while they stood at his side during the burial service. I was the one who inched over and held their shaking hands. Afterward, this moron took a few steps to leave, but John had to yell out to his dad, who finally managed to turn around and acknowledge his and Kathy's existence. A moment ago, you alluded to justice, but ya'know what? When you take the *just* out of justice, you're left with *ice*…and that's exactly how I feel. And you want *me* to find the other punk? That ain't gonna go down by any set of rules you'd agree with."

"You are above this, Jason," Szabo said. "City managed to take out the shooter during the firefight at the scene—he was the only one carrying. The second insider was last seen running away on foot down the alley leading to a wooded area behind the bank. Probably scared shitless. The driver evidently panicked and took off when he heard the sirens. He wasn't even around."

"So much for any *semper fi* to your buddies, huh?"

"Yeah. We have a good indicator of where the other suspect lives after they ID'd the shooter's body. That's why the DA asked the county to pursue this matter. You know, the media is all over this botched holdup and they expect results. The internal security cameras at the bank captured some pretty decent images of the inside guys…even though they were wearing ski masks. Other witnesses have attested to the language they used, and the pitches of their voices indicate they're just kids, and nervous, too."

"Yeah. Just kids. Poor, poor kids. With a weapon. And if we find this other guy, his parents will hire some slick ass lawyer to try to make us feel sorry for him because he was tip-toeing through some grass at the time. And they'll moan, *It was his first offense,* or, *It was just an accident.* And they'll undoubtedly claim use of excessive force by law enforcement." When Jason slammed his fist down on the table, the sound ricocheted off the walls of the narrow corridor like the report from a high-powered rifle. "I'm so sick of this crap. There's always a reason for their actions—a stupid reason. Nobody assumes responsibility anymore."

"You know what I think, Jason? This will bring closure to you if you nab this moron."

"Sorry. No buy-in." Jason drew in a long breath. "When is it my turn, Sheriff? When is it my turn to watch some smart-ass punk's eyeballs roll back in their sockets just before he takes his last breath?"

The only thing separating them was a desk stacked ten inches high in paperwork. Pointing to Jason's shoulder, the sheriff asked, "How's the wound healing?"

"The wound is healing fine." Jason recalled his encounter with pot growers up in the mountains east of Sonora, and how a very special woman not only saved him from certain death, but took on an unexpected role in his jumbled-up life. The intensity of Jason's voice softened. "The doctor had the shoulder X-rayed, and the bone is mending well. The bullet wound is history. It feels good to be able to put a shirt on by myself." He didn't mean this last comment. It did feel comforting to have Dena Manning stop by each morning to maneuver the few shirt buttons into those defiant little slots while his left arm was immobilized against his chest by bandages and endless wraps of tape.

"You're leaving me with very few options, Detective."

"I'm sorry. I have to go somewhere to get my head screwed back on."

"How long do you need?"

"A day, a month…I don't have a clue." Jason's eyes went blank as he stared at the sheriff while placing his badge and sidearm on Szabo's desk.

"You keep in touch. That's not an order. It's a request from someone who cares about you." He extended his hand to Jason. "Any idea where you're gonna go?"

"Oh, probably back to a place I used to live when things were a little more innocent. I may just lie down in a corn field and stare up at the clouds and imagine animals drifting by. Don't know for sure, but it's a good place to start."

For a moment, the sheriff studied Jason's hardware staring up at him from the desk, and then slid them into his top drawer. "I am not accepting these…officially."

◊   ◊   ◊

In the rolling hills east of Cleveland, Ohio, there's a town where, with the exception of a few cars passing through the main intersection, life seems destined to remain forever unchanged. Amish buggies, whose only adornment is a triangular, luminescent placard on the back as a means of warning automobile traffic of their presence, still ply the roads in the same traditional, unhurried method as those which had been driven by their parents, and their parents before them.

It was on this quiet, muggy autumn morning when Jason Carmichael turned onto a familiar, dusty road. Behind him, through his rearview mirror, he studied the main road and the cement bridge he'd just crossed over, now crusty brown and pock-marked from years of being battered by the elements and occasional gouges from the blades of snowplows.

Less than a year before he graduated, this had been the site of an Amish girl's death. At the time, Friedel Mueller was a senior in high school—quite a departure from the norm for a culture where anything beyond the eighth grade was considered not only unnecessary, but irresponsible as well. Some in the local population whispered suicide, some whispered murder. The whispers within the Amish community were never heard. Maybe he would ask around to find out if anything ever came of the investigation.

Ahead of him, the narrow road led to an old covered bridge. Since his reluctant departure from this little community almost twenty-five years ago, the old road had taken on a different appearance. He stepped out of his rental Chevy and gazed down the slight grade toward the wooden bridge. It appeared as though the Ohio DOT, at one time, had made a half-hearted attempt to pave the dirt road, although by the number of potholes and ruts, it looked like nature was beginning to reclaim its territory. When he kicked his toe into the hardened layer of dirt, it broke up like delicate chunks of dried concrete. He scuffed his shoe over a few of the clumps and ground them into fine powder.

Gazing in the direction of the covered bridge, Jason wondered why it appeared much closer to the main road than it did when he was in high school. He climbed back into the van and eased it closer to the side of the road, shut the engine off, and stepped out to draw in the fresh morning air. When Jason closed his eyes, he could taste the warm moisture and enticing flavor of sweet corn on his lips.

The smell of freshly tilled soil and cornfields brought back memories of walking through neighbors' fields and playing hide-and-seek, then getting yelled at for knocking down a few stalks by farmers who took their crop-raising seriously. Then as he grew, playing in those fields became a test on how *not* to be noticed as farm boys and farm girls began to embrace the isolation those fields afforded on balmy summer evenings.

Out of habit, he locked his car before starting down the road.

Near the fan-like approach to the aged structure, he eased his 210 pound frame onto one of the retainer stumps and gazed at the entrance, now locked and boarded-over. He swiped his hand across his forehead, blew the dust from his sunglasses and examined the sign fastened to the right of the temporary door.

Modern analysis by local officials and the state's historical bridge association saw fit to condemn the structure and close it to all types of travel. Even lightweight buggies had to travel longer distances to reach their destinations. A fact either overlooked or ignored by those who lacked the same commitment to tradition as their Amish neighbors.

The barrier, although padlocked, had not blocked off the entire bridge, at least not to the eye. Jason looked through the formidable slat work which afforded shadowy viewing at best. Allowing a few moments for his eyes to acclimate themselves to the blackness inside, he cupped his hands around his eyes and began to examine whatever he could. Cobwebs and sawdust abounded, along with random piles of shriveled up leaves and soggy twigs probably blown in by a stray wind before the closing. The pungent odor of rotting wood stung at his senses as if he'd stuffed his head into a watery jar filled with fertilizer. "That's strange. I don't ever remember seeing those before."

He leaned forward and ran his fingertips around the perimeter of an adjoining stump to feel the chamfered edges, roughly cut not by an automated machine, but by an axe at the hands of a long forgotten craftsman.

Jason yawned, stretched his arms wide and paced back and forth in front of the bridge. With every passing, he walked a little further in the opposite direction until he could grasp a better sense of the span of the bridge through the elm trees.

His eyes again focused on the retainer stumps, whose purpose was to keep vehicles from sliding down the embankment as they approached the entrance, especially after a summer downpour or when the narrow road was covered with snow or ice.

Carvings could still be seen on those stumps and the timber at the entrance to the dark and secluded wooden tunnel, painstakingly put there by teenagers long ago as they found another use for the wood by engraving proclamations of their affection for each other. Initials, most often joined with a plus sign between them, represented someone's declaration of undying love, sometimes fulfilled, but most times, they just drifted off, unnoticed, into obscurity.

KR ♥ *DE* still stood out after all these years. Kathleen Rogers was Jason's secret passion throughout high school, whereas David Ellison was his prime adversary for her affection. A point never overlooked by David as he used every opportunity to rub it in Jason's face that Jason was the loser. A short kiss between Kathleen and David in his presence, or an arm around her drawing her close never failed to annoy Jason to the point where he'd walk away so he'd not have to endure the omnipresent smirk on David's face.

David was never shy about bragging about his many achievements, both on the field or in the back seat of the car his father had purchased for him as a reward for his abilities on the various fields of sport. His father was a well-respected cabinetmaker in the area rivaling those of the nearby Amish craftsmen. Some of those traits evidently spilled over onto David who, with the help of his father's prized tools, was able to carve intricate curves in his letters in the wood rather than the awkward series of straight slashes seen in the other professions of love. His proud father often cited distorted sayings which declared winning was, in fact, everything. All else was to justifiably fall by the wayside.

On a stump on the far side of the road, the amateurish initials, NC + JC were still visible. Those inscriptions were one of Jason's futile attempts to entice Kathleen away from David, hoping she would be jealous when she saw Jason's initials associated with those of Nicole Carsten. Another misconception added to his long list of delusional ploys which failed miserably.

David would brag about his wood-carving abilities while never failing to point out the shortcomings of all others. Of course, all this was done with a feigned sense of humility. When David was in one of his look-at-me modes, he never failed to point out the heart between the letters in place of the humdrum *plus* sign used by others.

Up close, Jason recalled the blood he'd wiped from the post as his pocketknife slipped a few times while trying to impress Kathleen.

An Amish carriage approached from the direction where Jason parked his rental. The sound of a single horse's hooves as they crackled the dirt and sand was as soothing as a distant train's whistle echoing through the night. When the buggy passed, the man, with his wife sitting dutifully on his left, nodded a courteous hello. A reserved smile could be seen beneath the man's bearded face. The woman dipped her head to acknowledge the meeting.

Jason offered a cordial smile and nodded in return as he watched the carriage disappear over a small knoll. The wheels and clopping sound faded into silence.

So many times, he and his friends had ventured into the dark cavern of this bridge fashioned from Northern Spruce to peer through the missing slats on the sides into the river below, hoping to catch a glimpse of the mysterious, giant fish they all were certain lurked down there somewhere. That elusive bass, some referred to it as a mutated perch caused by a top secret military project—no one really knew for sure— continued to stir their youthful imaginations year after year until one day other activities magically crept into their lives, most often centered around cars, cheerleaders, hormones, and the omnipresent cornfields.

The temporary door again caught his attention. What he'd noticed inside the foul-smelling interior of the bridge stirred his imagination.

◊　　◊　　◊

The following day, while visiting the one and only fast-food restaurant in the area, Jason recognized the markings of an Ashtabula County Sheriff's vehicle parked out front. Its gold accent stripes and five-point star stood out against the solid black exterior.

Through the large front window of the renovated building, Jason noticed a deputy devouring a burger guaranteed to clog the largest of arteries, all the while managing to chat with the local girls who, by the expressions on their faces, took great delight in having someone from out of town pay a visit—especially a young, broad-shouldered type who probably shaved every other day.

At first, Jason hesitated, but then approached just as the deputy started for the door. "Excuse me. If you don't mind, I'd like to ask you a question?"

"Certainly," the deputy replied, as he shoved his trash into the *Thank you* bin.

Jason noticed the deputy was squinting as if studying this stranger, so he identified himself as a county detective from California. "Do you know anything about the death of an Amish girl about twenty-five years ago not far from here?" After getting a better look at the deputy,

Jason wondered how old this deputy could have been when the incident occurred. With a sheepish look and a scratch of his graying hair, Jason said, "I know I'm kind of grasping at straws here."

"Can't say as I do." The deputy continued to scrutinize Jason as he handed him a card with his name and department on it.

Jason glanced at the card and read, *Deputy Ken Hutchinson, Ashtabula County Sheriff's Office*, then asked, "Do you have a few minutes?"

"Sure," the deputy said with an apprehensive crinkling of his brow.

They both squeaked into the plastic-coated seats of a booth near the entrance.

"Almost twenty-five years ago, there was an Amish girl named Friedel Mueller who was found dead under the concrete bridge on 322 just west of town. As far as I know, no one was ever found accountable for her death. I was just wondering if anything has ever been resolved regarding the incident."

"Why do you ask?" The deputy cast Jason a suspicious look.

"I've been away for a long time, and I noticed something yesterday I'd never seen before."

"Like what?"

"A set of initials."

"Initials?"

"Yeah. You know the old covered bridge on Avery Road?"

"Uh-huh. Boarded up now."

With every short, non-committal answer Ken Hutchinson made, Jason sensed how feeble or ludicrous his observation seemed. "There's a lot of initials carved around that old bridge…mine included. A couple who used to go together carved their initials into one of the inside braces…and this guy prided himself with everything…and as far as I know, he only dated one girl seriously. Their initials are still there…but just inside the barricades the DOT put up, kind of out of the way, there is another set of initials with *FM* plus this same guy's initials."

"So?" After a feeble attempt to contain a snicker, Hutchinson offered, "More than one person could have the same initials."

"Except for one thing. This guy could carve wood like no one else I knew. His signature font was script. The *F* in Friedel was rounded… beautifully. Just like the *D* in his name."

"What's the other set of initials?"

"*DE*...for David Ellison."

Ken Hutchinson's eyes widened. "The same David Ellison?"

"The same as what?"

"Our Lieutenant Governor."

CHAPTER 2

After a late breakfast, Jason rolled his cell around in his hand and debated whether or not to call Dena Manning. Eleven-thirty here would be eight-thirty out in California. She would probably be coaxing a bowl of shredded wheat down her son's throat to prepare him for another bus ride to school, and then she would be alone. As he held the phone, he envisioned what he would say to her. Would he talk about her brother's death? Would they talk about Marie's death? Would the topic get around to the fact that she was married? What he really wanted to do was talk…just talk to someone with whom he'd grown to feel a sense of comfort and trust. He slipped the phone back into his pocket.

◊　　◊　　◊

Pulling his van up near the entrance to the bridge, Jason retrieved his camera from a spot he'd chosen under the seat to keep his valuables out of sight from curious onlookers…the kind who presumed out-of-state plates meant lucrative pickings. His car bore Indiana plates even though the vehicle was picked up at Cleveland Hopkins airport—a probable result of a one-way rental. As he walked down the secluded road, he heard a car approaching and turned to see Ken Hutchinson drive up in a county Crown Vic, its lower panels dirtied from a light morning rain.

They exchanged greetings while walking over to where Jason discovered the intriguing initials.

"I checked the files last night up in Jefferson," Hutchinson said. "It seems there was a Mueller girl who met her maker from something many might interpret as an accident, but nothing ever came of the case, and it has been lying dormant ever since."

"No follow-up?"

"Nothing. There were notes suggesting it may have been an accident, but then someone scribbled in *possible suicide*. It's been filed as pending ever since," he added with a shrug of his massive shoulders. "I checked with my boss man and asked if he minded if I looked into this. At first, he seemed reluctant, but what else could he say?"

"It may be nothing," Jason offered.

"Who knows? Nothing else has surfaced after all these years. What harm could it do?"

Jason pointed out the area to Ken as he directed his flashlight through the weather-beaten slats.

Ken seemed indifferent as he rattled a set of keys. "Let's see if one of these bad boys work. We all have master keys…in case some nosy kid finds a way to get stuck in one of these things." He fumbled with the set until he found one that popped the lock open. The makeshift door creaked as he swung it inward. In a casual tone of voice, he said, "I guess these doors weren't built to last too long."

"Certainly not up for any design awards either," Jason added with a wry grin.

They examined one of the support posts at the end of the bridge's roof while Jason pointed to the meticulous carvings. Jason pulled his camera out and took a snapshot of the handiwork.

"Good idea." Ken studied the initials for a moment, and then asked Jason to take a photo with him standing next to them. After Jason had taken the first shot, Ken asked for another with his hand next to the initials to give an idea of perspective for any other potential viewers in the future. Ken rubbed his fingers in the channels of the wood. "Smooth, and they sure look like they've been here for a while, don't they?"

"They're about as weathered as everything else in here." Focusing on the creaking noises of the aged timber, Jason asked, "How strong is this bridge anyhow?" Even on this brilliant, clear afternoon, it was an eerie, but perfect sound suited for a movie, except the Hollywood heavyweights would probably set this scene in the dead of night accompanied with claps of thunder and howling wolves in the background.

"Well, somebody smarter than us saw fit to close it, so my guess is our asses aren't too safe in here. Let's take a few more shots and get the hell out." Ken used the camera to shoot the interior from different angles to prove this was the bridge in question, and asked Jason to stand in a particular location…for perspective. A technique his boss insisted on from any of his deputies during an investigation.

Outside, Ken asked to see the other set of initials for comparison.

"See?" Jason pointed out. "The girl's name was Kathleen Rogers. See how uniform the curved lines are? And scope out the heart instead of a crude plus sign. Then look at the rest of this stuff here." With outstretched arms, Jason gestured around the entire area and pointed to another stump closer to the bridge. "These are mine—still have the scars to prove it. But what I wonder is, what was David Ellison doing messing around with an Amish girl?"

"If, in fact, those initials really do stand for David Ellison. Otherwise, these initials don't prove squat." Ken emphasized his remark by a nonchalant shrug. "And, the set of initials out here have the heart symbol, but the one inside uses the plus sign. Not very consistent if it was, in fact, the same carver."

"Yeah…yeah, you're right," Jason admitted with a grudge. "I just can't seem to recall anyone else who had the knack for doing such quality carving…unless it was done by some Amish guy. So neat… ya know what I mean?" Jason again scanned the various declarations around the area.

"You're not too familiar with their customs, are you?" Ken asked with a charitable smile.

"I've been gone for quite a while."

"Look. I really appreciate you coming forward with something after all this time, but you know what I wonder? Why hadn't someone looked into this at the time?" Ken began to fill out several sheets of paperwork on an internal departmental form.

"This bridge is here," Jason said, using his head as a gesturing device, "concrete bridge way up there. Who'd think to go looking for clues down here? And besides, unless you knew David, how many trees or bridges would you have to go looking for to find out if he'd just happened to carve something in them?"

"Hmm. How long are you going to be in the area?" Ken snapped the lock shut.

"I'm...uuh...I'm here for a different reason. My schedule is pretty much my own."

"Where are you staying?"

"A local B & B. Owned by the Loomis family. Ya know 'em?"

"Can't say as I do." Ken handed Jason his note pad. "Would you please write down their address and how I can get in touch with you?"

"Sure. No problem." Jason thought for a second and decided against giving Hutchinson his cell number. While Ken jotted down the Loomis' phone number, Jason added, "When someone answers, just ask for me. I'm the only one staying there. They gave their names as Loomis, just Mr. and Mrs. is all they told me. Kinda strange, y'know what I mean?"

Ken looked up from the notepad and offered a slight frown. "No. I don't know what you mean."

"Oh. Usually, these B & Bs are user-friendly. They like everyone to call them by their first names—like you're old friends or something. But they introduced themselves as Mr. and Mrs. Loomis...and let it drop."

"You're a stranger," Ken said with an icy tone. "Anyone else in the house except them?"

"They have a son, Douglas. About sixteen, or thereabouts."

CHAPTER 3

Jason floated through the night with thoughts of seeing Dena again. Sleep had not come easy. It was all he could do to keep from calling her. What would he say if her husband answered the phone? He'd propped his cell against the base of a lamp on the nightstand so with the slightest light, her picture and number would be visible, and he swore he could smell her scent on the phone, but she never wore perfume. She just had the refreshing smell of clean.

He erased thoughts of Dena's engaging smile as he turned into the driveway of the Mueller farm. He was not sure if he was doing the right thing, but the initials in the wood still intrigued him. Having a classmate die under strange circumstances at a time when his own private world was filled with nothing more than dreams of the future and where he could go to have fun, was particularly devastating. For the first time, it made him question his own mortality, long before those thoughts should ever cross anyone's mind.

Fine dirt lined the entranceway with the occasional intrusive clumps of grass appearing every so often just as in any driveway in the world. There were narrow tracks and the prints of horses in the powdery dust. With each step, the hooves had displaced a small amount of dirt, forcing it outward to form minute ridges around the perimeter that resembled miniature craters.

Remnants of harvested rows of corn gave way to the last vestige of the season. Silky tassels glistened in the light breeze of this one last section planted in hopes the cold weather would not set in early. The progressive planting was a custom ingrained through generations to accommodate the problematic consequences of having them all reach maturity at the same time.

The meticulously maintained house itself was located in the shade of an ancient beech tree which looked like it could have been planted for an old Hitchcock movie. Its branches extended out about twenty-five feet on each side to offer temporary relief from the relentless summer heat. The house was painted white, and had a substantial front porch to sit on during those humid summer days and evenings where entertainment may have consisted of catching fireflies or reading the Bible. All the stables and out-buildings were white also, their trim being a blue/gray hue.

Barn doors were opened to allow as much of a cross breeze as possible to cool the interior. Around the perimeter, plows, mowers, and riding rakes with well-worn unpadded metal seats and large curved tines could be seen waiting for the next harvest. One section of the barn just near the entrance was dedicated to the storage of various tack for the draft horses. All organized and lined up as neatly as you'd expect to see in the rope locker on the proudest of naval vessels. Or was it the other way around?

Modern conveniences an outsider would deem an absolute necessity were never on the agenda as the Amish lived their lives according to the old established tenets of the *Ordnung*.

Jason marveled at the continuity of the community, where time seemed to have stalled out so many generations ago. He'd been by the Mueller farm hundreds of times but never really stopped for a visit since, even at an early age, it was drummed into him the Amish craved isolation, especially from a world in which they had no interest. Maybe it was respect that kept him away.

In each window, a traditional single curtain hung pulled to one side, fulfilling their utilitarian, simplistic approach to life where worldly goods were tenaciously frowned upon. For balance, most decorators would have hung two curtains for symmetry and drawn them gracefully to each side, held in place by two equally stylish tie-backs. To the Amish, one curtain represented shade and protection. Two would have been considered ostentatious.

Men in wide-brimmed hats watched as Jason eased up the driveway. The young, unmarried ones were clean-shaven. As he stepped from his van, one bearded man approached.

"Good morning, friend," the bearded man said, wiping his brow with a large handkerchief.

"Good morning to you too, sir," Jason said, as he reached for the man's hand. "I'm looking for Mr. or Mrs. Mueller."

"Which Mr. or Mrs. Mueller might that be?" the man replied, with a commanding, resonant voice which could easily carry across open fields.

Jason suddenly felt very awkward and embarrassed. "I'm looking for the parents of Friedel Mueller."

The man stared at Jason for a few moments, took off his hat, and wiped at his brow again. Stains of perspiration darkened his armpits. "There is no Friedel Mueller here."

"I realize that," Jason stammered. "I'm sorry...but...I knew Friedel from Grand Valley High School...over in Orwell. I know she died about twenty-five years ago. This is rather difficult for me. I'd just like to talk to them...if I could."

"The elder Mr. Mueller died a few years back. My mother's still alive, but she's getting on."

"You're Friedel's br....?"

"My name is Isaac. Friedel was two years my junior when she left us." The man continued to cast Jason a suspicious eye.

"I'm sorry, Isaac. I checked county records as well as old news from the Cleveland Plain Dealer and found nothing ever happened to resolve Friedel's death. As far as I could tell, no one has ever followed through with any sort of investigation."

"And what would it be that you intend to do about it?" Isaac asked with an icy tone.

Jason shrugged his shoulders. "I don't really know. All I know is I have a feeling I may be of some help...and that's what I'd like to do."

A young boy about six years old ran out of the house and hung at Isaac's side. He kept looking up at this strange man who'd driven onto their farm in a piece of machinery he'd never really gotten close to before. He offered a shy smile while keeping an inquisitive eye on the shiny white van.

Isaac patted the boy on his head. "Go find your grandmother, son. Ask her to meet us on the front porch."

The boy sped off to do as he was told.

Jason stood facing Isaac. Neither of them spoke as they waited for Friedel's mother to appear. After a few awkward minutes, a gray-haired lady came out to the steps, wiped her hands with a light blue cloth, brushed away a few wrinkles from her apron, and then eased herself onto the edge of the porch. Eyeing the stranger, she waved them over. Her white prayer covering gleamed as if it had just been washed and bleached.

"Mother. This man is here about Friedel," Isaac said, lightly touching his mother's hand.

"Mrs. Mueller. My name is Jason Carmichael. Friedel and I went to school together. I'd like to tell you how sorry I am about what happened." He reached for her weathered hand. "I was just talking to your son about what happened that night, and from what he's said, nothing has ever been resolved. It isn't right to not know the truth."

"And what truth will you be trying to determine, sir?" Elizabeth Mueller asked.

"Was it an accident? Was it something…else?" Jason's face reddened as he couldn't force the word, murder, from his mouth.

Isaac remained silent.

A horse-drawn carriage entered the driveway and pulled up under the shade of the old beech tree. A gray-haired man stepped out and looped the reins of his horse around a weathered, but sturdy post. He was introduced as Joshua Stoudt, the elder of the congregation. "A good morning to you, friend," he said in a weary voice.

"This man's here to talk about Friedel," Isaac announced. "Name's Jason Carmichael." He rocked from one leg to the other, sometimes leaning on the fork he kept at his side. Turning to his son, he leaned over and whispered, "Please see to Mr. Stoudt's horse."

The lad darted off and returned dragging a bucket half full of water, placed it in front of the horse and stroked his head as it bent down to take in a long drink.

"Hmm." The cynicism in Joshua's voice was hard to miss.

Jason glanced around and noticed the curious looks in each of their faces. It had been a long time since he'd talked to anyone in an Amish community and wondered if he was doing the right thing, especially since he had nothing more to offer than a glimmer of hope. Turning to address both Friedel's aging mother and the elder, Jason grasped for something to say to convey to them, that the reason he was here was because he had been a classmate of Friedel and left before anything was resolved. All at once, he felt selfish. Who was he really indulging? "Like I said before—I went to school with Friedel. She was well-liked by a lot of people." As he shook Mr. Stoudt's hand, it felt as though he was grasping a chamois cloth, wadded up and left to dry in the hot sun… coarse and hard.

"We saw very little justification for her to be in high school." Mrs. Mueller's eyes became hollow and dark as she spoke. "If she hadn't been there, this would probably not have happened, but," she sighed heavily, "Friedel did have her…determined…side."

"She was smart. I'll give her credit for that," Jason said. "Many times, she had answers to questions before we even understood what was being asked." Jason's subtle smile was met with detached stares.

"What is it that you would want of us, Mr. Carmichael?" Joshua asked.

Jason could not help but notice the boy gravitating toward his white van. Its chrome alloy wheels, now dusty, were still able to reflect a curious face in the shiny surface. As a matter of habit, Jason automatically locked his doors when he'd gotten out. With a flick of a button on his remote entry system, he unlocked the doors. The sudden chirping sound caused the boy to turn and face the scrutinizing faces of the elders, each of whom were eyeing the vehicle with a traditional sense of trepidation. "Would it be okay if he looked inside?" Jason asked Isaac.

Isaac faced the boy and with an officious wave of his hand, said he could look, but was not to climb inside. "Do not touch anything, Benjamin."

Jason opened the sliding door and made sure it was in the locked position.

Benjamin scurried to the opened door and seemed captivated with the tan leather seats and rear area which housed a makeshift bed as well as a small closet for hanging a few clothes. Overhead, a black net was hung for storing a few items, which if wrinkled, would go unnoticed.

"You asked what I'd like from you, Mr. Stoudt?" Jason continued. "Probably information about…Friedel, like was she seeing anyone, especially outside your congregation. Things like that?"

"Tis not allowed," Joshua stated in an authoritarian voice.

"I didn't think so," Jason admitted, realizing he'd overstepped an obvious cultural boundary.

"What is it you do for a living, Mr. Carmichael?" Elizabeth Mueller asked.

"I'm a detective…out in California. My parents moved from here right after I graduated from high school."

"What makes you believe you can discover something that even the local police could not, after Friedel was taken from us?" she asked. "It's been such a long time."

"Yes, it has." Jason gave a lengthy sigh, and his voice took on an ethereal, almost dreamlike quality as he stared off into the distance. "You know what's strange about growing up? When I graduated from high school, I thought I was one of the smartest people around. So savvy. Yet during all those years, I passed your farm every day, and I never stopped by to say hello." He faced the Mueller clan and offered an apologetic smile. "And now I regret that. At the time, I thought I knew Friedel, but in fact, I did *not* really know her. I knew her in name only, and I regret that, also. From what I can remember of her, she was soft spoken. She was courteous to everyone. She never spoke ill of anyone. She was intelligent, curious about the world, ambitious, and she always listened to what others said. She didn't talk too much, but when she did…well, others should have listened."

"She did have her rebellious side," Elizabeth said with a sense of reserved pride.

Jason nodded. "And a bit of a philosopher, too, I might add. I remember once, she said to me, *you never learn by talking*. That saying stuck with me all these years. After all this time, I realized what I *did* know didn't compare to what I *should* know. A few seconds ago, you asked what I can bring to the table after all this time. I can offer you the services of someone who truly cares about what happened to Friedel." Jason forced another smile.

All eyes turned to Joshua.

"I would consider it a privilege," Jason added.

No one spoke as eyes remained fixed on the elder. After a long penetrating look at Elizabeth and much stroking of his dense gray beard, Joshua whispered, "You said you didn't really know Friedel, Mr. Carmichael, but from what you've just said, you knew her quite well. Do not think less of yourself."

"Thank you."

Elizabeth abruptly turned her back on Jason and extended her arm to Isaac. With his help, she managed the short step onto the porch. "Would you care to sit with us, Mr. Carmichael?" She insisted Jason sit in one of the straight-back chairs next to her. Joshua maneuvered his chair around to face Jason. Still clutching the hayfork in his hand, Isaac sat sideways on the floor with his back propped against a support post and dangled one foot over the edge.

"I believe this man to be sincere," Joshua said.

"I appreciate that, Mr. Stoudt."

"We discussed Friedel's desires many times at great length," Joshua continued. "She wanted to be more knowledgeable about mathematics and business. Friedel was offered a chance to experience the outside world…we call it *rumspringa*…before we asked her to commit. We want you to understand, Mr. Carmichael, we are not totally ignorant of the need to somehow integrate ourselves with another culture we do not believe in, but cannot justifiably condemn. We do have to earn money to pay taxes, as you do. We have to buy certain supplies as do you. We try to earn money through selling our cabinetry skills, or through selling cheeses, milk, or quilts. Friedel considered what she was doing as a future investment in the ability to preserve our culture, at least from a financial perspective."

"Friedel made some substantial arguments for her continued education," Elizabeth added. "Whatever she was, I will never forget her vitality."

Jason responded with a courteous nod. "After the incident, can you recall talking to the police?"

"Yes. Certainly," Mrs. Mueller replied. "They didn't know whether it was an accident or…something else. One even hinted at suicide. We could not understand why Friedel would want to end her own life, so that left us with the other two options."

"And nothing more was said?" Jason asked.

"It kind of faded away," Mrs. Mueller sighed.

Isaac stepped off the porch, faced Jason, and folded his arms over the handle of the fork. "I know you think you're doing something good here, Mr. Carmichael, and don't think we are not grateful for your kind thoughts, but our whole family has had to put this behind us. It's been a long time and what you've done is open up old wounds. I'm sorry." He then turned his back to Jason and stared across the fields.

Seeing the anguish in the faces of Friedel's family, Jason now knew he'd made the right decision, the only things at fault were his tactics.

As Jason started to leave, Joshua stopped him with a gentle hand. "You have to understand, Mr. Carmichael. It is our belief to forgive those who err against us. We must follow those tenets...no matter what."

Jason bit at his lips for an instant. "To your knowledge, did the county perform an autopsy on Friedel's body?"

Mrs. Mueller pinched her eyes shut. A tear rolled onto her cheek as she gave an almost imperceptible nod.

"In the case of a questionable death," Jason continued in a gentle voice, "a good investigator would ask for a Medico-legal analysis to be performed in conjunction with a coroner's exam. By law, the immediate family has a right to a copy of that document. By any chance, did the police, the medical examiner, or anyone else ask you if you wanted a copy of the report?"

Isaac and Joshua rolled their heads from side to side.

"The police asked if I wanted it," Mrs. Mueller whispered in a hesitant, almost apologetic voice. "I didn't know what good it would do, but I did keep it...somewhere." Through sunken eyes, she gave Isaac a pleading look. "Actually, I know exactly where it is. I take it out every so often and stare at it." She continued to stare into Isaac's eyes. "I'm sorry, but I do remember so much."

Isaac dropped his fork and knelt at his mother's side.

"With your permission, I would like to see it," Jason whispered.

Mrs. Mueller held on to Isaac's shoulder and with her eyes, asked his approval. She then turned to Joshua and gave him the same plaintive look.

"Elizabeth. Are you sure you want to open these old wounds?" Mr. Stoudt asked.

"Yes."

Joshua and Isaac glanced at each other for a moment before giving her an understanding smile.

It was but a few minutes for Elizabeth to return with the envelope containing the report. The white envelope was clutched to her chest as she came out the door. Looking to her son, she whispered, "I'm sorry. I have kept this to myself all these years," and then handed her private treasure to Jason.

Seeing the torment in her eyes as she divulged such a secret to her family made Jason treat the envelope as one might expect an archeologist would do when unfurling an ancient papyrus scroll for the first time. Jason quickly scanned through the contents of each sheet, then flipped back to page one and read the analysis of the investigator. One by one, he examined the words, but it was the accompanying sketches of Friedel's bodily injuries which drew his attention. Some were referred to as bruises, others were termed abrasions. Yet another view highlighted the black discoloration around her left eye. Jason had seen this before on others when they'd been struck by a fist during a fight. From his experience, an injury to the left eye meant the victim was probably struck by a right-handed person. He would keep this in mind. When he'd finished his examination of the Medico-legal report, he carefully folded it up and slipped it back in the envelope. "Thank you," he whispered to Elizabeth. "I know it took a lot for you to let me examine this."

Elizabeth cast a nervous glance at her son. With a quivering voice, she added, "It was all I had of Friedel."

Isaac gave a polite nod.

Clutching Elizabeth's hands, Jason said, "I will ask Mr. Stoudt's question again. Are you sure you want to open these old wounds?"

"We will discuss it within our fold."

CHAPTER 4

As was the custom in their community, a meeting was held to discuss the news the stranger had brought to them this day. Chairs were lined up in the gathering room of the house where bi-weekly religious services were sometimes held. A few candles were placed around the open room to furnish a semblance of light. Reverting to the use of high German, Joshua was first to speak.

"I've invited you here to speak of Mr. Jason Carmichael's interest in the death of Friedel Mueller twenty-five years ago," he began in a solemn tone. "Elizabeth Mueller, her family and the congregation have lived with this loss for so very long, but with no results, or anyone held accountable, it appears we have been placed in a position of capitulation." He looked out over the group and stroked his silvery beard. "Does anyone have any thoughts?"

One man stood. "This Jason Carmichael you talk of. Exactly who is he, and why are we considering allowing him into our lives?"

"You are right to question my proposal. All I can offer is this; I have talked to this man and I believe he is sincere in his quest to resolve a situation others seem to want to forget."

"But where did he come from? And why now?" the same man asked.

Joshua leaned against a window sill and studied the man for a few seconds. "We can not question why someone appears in our lives no more than we can question when and why God appeared in our lives.

This man is not a god, but I believe there is a difference between this Jason Carmichael and those who came before him."

"How so?" another voice asked.

"He has nothing to gain from his offer," Joshua continued. "I believe Jason Carmichael's purpose originates from within his heart, whereas those who preceded him came because it was their job, or obligation. Who would you want on your side?"

No one spoke immediately, but instead focused their attention on Elizabeth Mueller for her reaction. Elizabeth looked at the faces of her family as well as those who looked to the elders for guidance. Young men, with their clean-shaven faces, had probably wondered what had happened, but never openly sought answers. Instead, they relied on occasional conversations between aunts and uncles as to the incident which had claimed the life of a young and intelligent woman so many years past.

"We all believe in God's ideals of forgiveness," Elizabeth whispered. "But try as we've done through many generations, can we continue to turn our heads away?"

Joshua pointed at a friend who indicated he had something to contribute.

"Our children go from our homes to school every day…and are often held up for ridicule because of our beliefs. If we are to function within a society who demands our taxes, and imposes its values upon the minds of our children, then why shouldn't we hold someone accountable for something that represents much more than just an imposition to us?"

As the bearded man sat down, a few heads in the congregation offered a subtle nod of approval.

"We have always looked out for each other," Isaac said. "If we allow someone to help us, are we not admitting that we are unable to take care of ourselves?"

"I believe God intended us to be separate," added another neighbor, "but I do not believe He intended us to be at the mercy of anyone who would use us as they would cattle. We belong to God, our children belong to God, but not to another human who would arbitrarily nullify our very existence. Not even if the person be one of us." The speaker waved his finger in the air in an authoritative manner before he sat back down.

Joshua listened intently to the comments from all the members of the congregation, most of whom advocated cooperation with authorities from outside. And all nodded an agreement with him as he added a supplementary cautionary note he would impart to local law enforcement agencies, and that was; whatever they contributed was not to be construed as weakness. Nor was this grant to be construed as an open invitation for any sort of permanence as to any intrusion into their choice to continue their lives as they saw fit.

Another bearded man asked, "What shall we do if it is found that the guilty person is within our own congregation?"

The question instantly drew stares, whispers, and even a hint of animosity from almost everyone present.

Joshua waited for the murmuring to die down. "If we abide by the laws of the state by helping find this person, then we must abide by those same laws to punish him. Bearing in mind that although this procedure may be alien to us, it does have our best interests at heart, and therefore I do not feel we can selectively choose where we support the process, but reject the consequences."

"Shall we abide by God's justice, or the state's justice?" the same man scoffed.

Elizabeth Mueller stood, brushed at her apron and folded her frail hands in front of herself, then faced the man. "I do not believe they have to be different."

CHAPTER 5

"Good morning, Jason," Deputy Hutchinson said as he leaned out the window of his Crown Vic. Ken removed his hat and placed it on the seat, keyed his mike and informed dispatch he was 10-62, the local code for meeting with a citizen. "Why did you choose to hook up at this bridge instead of in town, or where you're staying?"

Jason leaned on the rail of the old cement bridge and brushed a few particles of road debris from it before resting his weight on his forearms. He gazed down into the slow moving water and rocks, some of which were coated with green, slimy moss. "You always have to go through the owner of the place to get to me, and besides…I like this bridge. I used to stand here as a kid…look down into the water and wonder where it was going. I guess I always wanted to go where the water went."

Ken pulled a notepad from his shirt pocket. "Want to hear something interesting?"

"Sure."

"I talked to my boss man again. Told him about the unique carvings, and he seemed interested, especially since the files are technically still open. Usually, these types of cases are handled by detectives, but he gave me the green light to see what I could come up with. I'm really trying to make detective, so now all I have to do is wait for an opening. Of course, I have to have approval of the sheriff. This may be my chance."

Jason nodded.

"So…what I did was," Ken continued, "I looked up birth records for the county, but a lot of the Amish births are not recorded there anyway. It was a shot in the dark," he added. "We know Friedel Mueller was seventeen when she died, and the covered bridge closure wasn't too long after that, so I checked all listings for anyone with the initials *FM* that might have fallen into that age range. There was only one other *FM* even close, but she would have been around twenty-six at the time." He looked Jason squarely in the eyes. "And you stated you'd never seen those initials there before?"

"That's right."

"So that leaves us with those initials you spotted, in all probability, belonging to the Mueller girl."

"So-o-o…?"

"My deductive reasoning says it would also have us believe that *DE*, in all probability, would stand for our illustrious lieutenant governor."

"I sense a certain amount of disdain for David?"

"He's a politician. What more can I say?"

"I looked back through the archives of the Cleveland Plain Dealer plus Ashtabula's Star Beacon and the general consensus was the crime rate dropped dramatically when David was on the county payroll. That's gotta count for something." The easiest thing for Jason to do now would be to encourage some sort of inquisition in hopes of bringing down the one person who'd badgered him through most of his school years and subconsciously haunted his adult life.

"Yeah…you might think." Ken now leaned on the bridge railing, too. "I was about ten when the mills began shutting down and all the manufacturing was being transferred to Japan…or some other places. Pittsburgh, Lorain, Cleveland…and all the peripheral businesses in the area that thrived on those mills shriveled up over night. Yeah, the crime rate did shoot up…but it also tapered off as people began moving out. For all his campaign bravados, our David Ellison always compared the inflated post-closure stats with what happened after a hefty percentage moved away, but if you looked at stats from a per capita viewpoint, it hadn't really changed at all."

"I think that's usually referred to in political circles as statistical manipulation."

"Bullshit works, too."

Jason snickered at Ken's candor. "Uuh…did you also check for anyone born in…"

"Early seventies?" Ken asked. "Yeah, yeah, I did. Checked births... and school registration, too. Just because someone wasn't born around here doesn't mean they didn't move here from some place else. Seems there was an Ellison family moved here from Richland County, down near Lexington, but there is no record of any first name beginning with *D*." Ken closed his notepad and raised his eyebrows as he looked at Jason. "Seems you may have stumbled onto something rather big, Jason. We may be in for a rough ride...a really rough ride."

"A rough political ride," Jason added.

"You bet. And I should caution you. We appreciate your observation, but from now on, this is a local police matter. You're about three-thousand miles away from your jurisdiction."

Jason squirmed as he rubbed his toe into the gritty debris and some larger chunks of weathered, brownish cement along the edge of the bridge. "I'm on a self-imposed sabbatical anyhow. Not anyone's business. When I came here, I didn't mean to involve myself with anything except some serious therapeutic drinking."

There was a momentary look of exasperation on Ken's face followed by a skyward glance as if wondering, *Why me?*

"I, uuh, talked to some of the Mueller clan yesterday."

"I don't have to tell you if we don't do these things by the numbers, we might blow the whole case...if we even have one." Ken held his finger in the air, as any attentive parent might do to keep their child from rambling on, and retrieved his notepad. "Who did you talk to?"

"Elizabeth Mueller...she's a widow now, and Friedel's older brother, Isaac...probably in his forties. Also, the clan elder, a Joshua Stoudt," Jason confessed, then continued to relay the gist of the conversations they'd had, including the perceived hostility by Isaac.

"That's to be expected. Don't take it personally though. They have their ways, and to tell you the truth, I'm not so sure they're wrong to resent us for getting involved with their activities. They're pretty much dedicated to *gelassenheit*." Ken quickly explained, "The will of God."

"Yeah, but if someone is murdered, that shouldn't fall under their exclusive jurisdiction, do you think?"

"It's hard to tell what their spin on anything is...but I'll be talking to them, too. You didn't happen to ask who Friedel may have been attracted to, did you? I mean, the Amish lad."

"Who said she was involved with anyone?"

"The girl was seventeen, Jason. Usually, by the time they're sixteen, the girls have chosen someone, or are seriously looking—even have their *newehockers* picked out." Ken used near perfect pronunciation for the Pennsylvania Dutch term for attendants or *side-sitters*. "Did you ask that question?"

Thinking back on the awkward meeting, Jason responded, "No, no, I didn't."

"According to the report and by most calculations at the time, the incident happened around ten at night. Did you happen to ask if anyone knew what a good Amish girl was doing out that late at night? And by herself?"

"Yes, I thought about it, but believed the question would border on argumentative or insensitive."

"You may have a point. By any chance, you didn't mention David Ellison by name, or anything about the existence of those initials on the bridge, did you?" The expression on Ken's face looked as if he was deep in prayer.

Jason sighed and rolled his head from side to side. "No."

"Did you ask if anyone knew about her social standing with other kids, even the non-Amish?"

"No, but I knew her in school, so I felt the question was immaterial. I relied on my own experience."

Ken leafed through the pages of his notepad. "How do you feel about keeping the media out of this?"

Subconsciously, Jason's mental reflexes kicked in as he recalled the circumstances of how he'd met Dena Manning, and what she'd struggled through as a result of an ill-reported newspaper article with its idiotic speculation of her brother's death. "No one saw fit to follow up with it twenty-plus years ago, so I suppose there could be no valid reason to involve them now."

"Good. That's the sheriff's spin, too." Ken started for his car.

"Uuh. We're not done yet."

Ken strolled back to the edge of the bridge and leaned on the cement barrier, but not before brushing the surface with his hands. "Fire."

Jason joined him with a few brushing strokes of his own, but saw no reason to keep his sleeves clean. All he wore was an old t-shirt while

Ken probably wanted to keep the black sleeves of his uniform spotless. After all, most counties are not in the laundry business. "You will be interested to know, Elizabeth Mueller was given a copy of a Medico-legal report when Friedel's body was examined. I know technology has changed in the last twenty-five years, but how anyone could have overlooked the descriptions and markings on the body defies logic."

"Do you have that report?"

"Nope. I know the Amish frown upon images of themselves, but from what I gathered from Elizabeth's tone of voice and watching how she handled the document, it was a personal treasure. To her, it was probably the only thing she had where her daughter's name appeared, and the last sheet was a body sketch showing locations of bruises and abrasions. When she showed it to me, I believe she wanted to cry, especially when she focused her eyes on the body diagram. Maybe to her, this was as close to a picture as she would ever get."

"You said bruises and abrasions. Was there any indication of puncture wounds?"

"No."

"So, Mrs. Mueller still has the report."

"For sure."

"Would she give it to you if you asked?"

Jason focused his eyes on this young deputy. He knew the document would be safe in Elizabeth's care and could think of no valid reason to ask such an insensitive question. If the time ever came when it was needed, he could probably obtain an official copy through the county, but for now, just having the information was good enough for him. Jason chose to ignore Ken's question and gazed down into the gentle stream below.

"Would she?"

"No," Jason shot back, "and I wouldn't ask her."

"What was in the contents?"

"The medical examiner's findings and a sketch showing bodily injuries. Have you ever seen one?"

"No." Ken fidgeted for a moment and then began to brush his fingers across the cement guard rails as if on a cleaning detail aboard ship.

"I'll tell you what was interesting, and why I think whoever looked at it from an LE perspective was in la-la land. Let me ask you a question. Pretend you're a woman on this bridge, alone, at night." Jason motioned for Ken to lean over and look down. "If it was an accident, how could she have fallen off? I seriously doubt she was stupid enough to try to balance herself on this cement barrier to see if she could walk across. This was a smart woman. Could she have fallen off by standing where you and I are right now? No way, unless she was stupid enough to lean out so far that she lost her footing...but again, this was a smart woman. Let's eliminate accident. Suicide? From everything I know about her, she had every reason to live. That's why she was so committed to attend school past the eighth grade."

"Was there a toxicology exam done as part of this report?"

"Yep. No indication of any foreign substances."

"Blunt trauma. Blood spatter?"

"Done."

"So, that leaves..."

"Foul play. Here's where it gets interesting for me. If someone fell from here and landed down there, where do you think bruises, fractured or broken bones would occur?"

"On the side where she landed?"

"Exactly. But on this report, the examiner indicated Friedel had multiple abrasions on the side where she landed—face down by the way—plus on her back, arms, and sides of her rib cage. From the exam, it was determined Friedel had a few compressed and broken vertebrae in her neck, the kind indicative of landing head first. These were not the marks you'd expect from a simple fall, either by accident or suicide. Correct me if I'm wrong, but unless Friedel hit the bottom, head first, and then bounced high enough to come down a second time with enough force to generate even more bruising on another side, I believe she was attacked before she went over or was dead before someone pushed her over the edge."

"Beaten to death? But why?"

The morning sun had moved higher in the sky and the bridge's cement was beginning to act as a storage unit for heat. To the naked eye, the heat waves created the illusion that the bridge was in a constant state of flux and out of focus. Using his left hand, Jason shielded his eyes from the wavy patterns and focused on Ken. "This may sound sick, but Friedel was a very beautiful young woman. Even her modest clothes didn't do a good job of hiding what was underneath. Some of the guys would look at her and give serious consideration to changing religions."

"Rape? Attempted rape?"

"Yeah. But another puzzle. In the report, it states Friedel's hair was loose and hung down below her shoulders."

"Amish girls don't…"

"That's what I thought. They keep their hair in a tight bun and never cut it. Plus in the clothing inventory, there was no mention of a black prayer covering."

"Was there a mention of sexual penetration?"

"Nope. So, I believe Friedel may have been seeing someone outside the congregation. And she must have trusted this person for multiple reasons. Hair down. No bonnet. Ten o'clock at night. Secluded location. Little or no traffic. I didn't think of her as a risk taker. At least not at school."

"DE?"

"DE." Jason rattled off his cell number to Ken. "One other interesting tidbit of info," Jason continued. "Whoever performs an examination of this nature is obligated to include their credentials. But…the person who signed this document gave no indication they were qualified by any of the three recognized accreditation organizations. So, for all we know, this person could have been a technician, but in all probability, not a licensed forensic or anatomical specialist."

"Why does shit like this happen?"

"Ya know? There are certain groups of people who will always form a rigid envelope around anyone who would be considered a threat to their political aspirations. You think your lieutenant governor would want something like this to go public? No way in hell. They're gonna try to keep a lid on this thing…big time. Once political alliances are made, they are cast in concrete. This kind of exposure could bring down more than just David Ellison."

Ken glanced down at the pile of dirt Jason had scuffed together with his shoes, then, with piercing eyes, asked, "You sure you want to stick around the area?"

A light blue van turned onto the narrow dirt road leading to the covered bridge and slowed down as the driver approached the rear of a black carriage. The man in the carriage reined his horse close to the side of the road, then stuck his arm out and waved the van around. Instead, the driver of the van gave a courteous wave, flashed his headlights and remained well behind, almost coming to a stop until the buggy turned left in front of the covered bridge to continue on its way. The driver of the van then stopped at the entranceway. A small cloud of dust drifted past his opened window.

After a few minutes, the man stepped out, surveyed the scene, then slid open the side door and started taking a few black plastic cases from the rear, placing them near the locked door to the bridge.

The morning air was already beginning to feel muggy with the heavy kind of air that made you feel as if someone was putting a warm, woolen blanket around your entire body. The absence of any breeze only compounded the effect. The man wiped at his forehead with a large red handkerchief.

He unlocked the door to the bridge, stepped inside and began to shine a flashlight around. A few moments passed before he reappeared and shifted some of the black boxes inside. Flashes of light streamed through the slats at the entrance, if only for an instant.

After some disconcerting bouts with creaking floors, potential breakthroughs, as well as spiders that went unnoticed until walking face-first into the gooey webs, the man emerged and sat on one of the stumps in the shade. Bowing his head, he again wiped at the back of his neck and forehead.

His attention became focused on another stump across the way. In a slow deliberate move, he stood, arched his back, and then went back inside and began to haul out the equipment he'd taken in earlier. In a well-choreographed routine, he set up near the stump with the controversial markings, bent down and examined them with some sort of high powered viewing device he wore strapped around his head as would a surgeon performing a delicate operation. He then carefully scraped at a portion of them with a tiny stiff brush and transferred the fine dust into small paper bags, then wrote down the date, time and weather conditions.

After taking a few more pictures, the man repackaged all his equipment, loaded the van, took a few hefty swallows of water from a bright orange cooler, and left.

CHAPTER 6

Each morning, the proprietor of the B & B made Jason a generous breakfast, complete with potatoes to accompany eggs and spicy homemade sausages. Jars of jams and preserves, each having their own spoon so as not to taint the flavors of the others, were placed in a wicker style basket on his table. Loaves of fresh bread were made available for toast or just plain eating pleasure. And Jason loved to eat.

A copy of the Cleveland Plain Dealer was on the table every morning. With no one around to encroach upon his days of relaxation, Jason enjoyed his cups of Italian Roast coffee while thumbing through the morning newspaper, often remembering times many years ago when, as a child barely able to grasp the paper himself, his dad would sit him on his lap and read the funnies to him.

Since the conversation with Ken Hutchinson, he perused the paper with added interest, hoping he would not spot some kind of official announcement from the sheriff's office about the long overdue reopening of the investigation into Friedel Mueller's death. As part of his sociological conditioning in LA, he'd grown accustomed to rampant displays of indifference for pursuing perpetrators of vicious crimes, supposedly based on availability of detectives, but probably dealt more with an underlying habit of sweeping away what was considered an undesirable element of the community. Jason hoped this kind of fanaticism was not a prevailing factor here, especially in regards to people whose only crime was the desire to live a moral, close-knit, and religious way of life.

As he scanned the front page of the paper, he noticed a *filler* in the lower corner. He almost passed it over, but something caught his attention. He flipped to the next page and read an article about the expansion of a maritime museum in Vermilion, a picturesque town on the shores of Lake Erie. What caught his attention was the name of the curator; Kathleen Ellison.

"Hmm," he murmured. Speed-reading through the piece, he wished there had been some sort of picture to verify it was the same Kathleen who'd not only tugged at his heart, but his jockstrap as well back in high school. It was Kathleen Rogers then, and she and David seemed destined to be together, so who else could it be?

Jason was not of the mindset to dwell on the past nor did he have any inclination to relive his high school days. He knew life only had one direction, but couldn't help but wonder what had happened to all those people who were so important to him then. His stalwart buddies who seemed destined to be forever shoulder to shoulder, ready to tackle any and all opponents whether on the field or not. Or the luckless classmates who found themselves the brunt of many a joke as they elbowed their way through the line of jocks on their way to math classes or the weekly meeting of the chess club. He was never proud of what he did, but it seemed rational at the time, and there'd always been this gnawing cynicism within him, that if he didn't join in, he himself may have been labeled the outcast. So often, he wanted to find everyone he'd ever badgered, sit down with them, and apologize to them, hoping they could forgive and forget. All the while knowing that to receive forgiveness would only make him feel better about himself, but could never erase how those people were made to feel about themselves.

Driving to Vermilion in the pounding rain didn't seem to be the most logical thing to do, but Jason had to find out if the article in the Plain Dealer was really about the same Kathleen with whom he'd gone to so many parties, or to the beaches at Geneva on hot summer days. Okay, so she was with David and he was with Nicole, but they still engaged in playful games of touch football in the sand which always escalated into tackle since that was the only justifiable excuse for wrestling a member of the opposite sex to the ground…as opposed to a date at the local passion-pit where back seats were revered as hallowed empires.

As he drove into the small community, he spotted a sign carved from what appeared to be a grayish, weathered plank to attract attention to the newest addition to town. The scrollwork at the top of the sign formed a border highlighting where to turn. Just after that, there was a makeshift sign supported by two metal posts proclaiming, "Go Sailors!"—as a motivational tool for an upcoming football game between Vermilion High School and another regional foe.

The narrow street offered angled parking for the visitors, and another sign suggesting a short walk to the shore to look northward at the placid lake.

Brilliant beams of light streamed through the dark broken clouds, forming what looked like a gigantic stage prepared just for his arrival. Jason took a moment to enjoy the temporary break in the weather by rolling his window down and breathing in the refreshing smell of the lake. It was one of those things people always did after a downpour.

Taking a moment to read the placard posting the hours, Jason climbed the wide beige-colored cement steps leading to the front door. Once inside, he scanned the various rooms of what had obviously been an old mansion, now converted to hold its own slice of the past—where tribute was paid to the lives of so many who'd toiled to make the ships run and the steel mills produce.

A docent approached him asking if she could be of some assistance.

"I was wondering if Kathleen Ellison might be here." His voice sounded as if he was in some grand cavern.

"Yes, she is, but she may be busy. Is there something I can help you with?"

"Kinda," Jason said. "I read an article in the newspaper and I think I may know her…from school…a long time ago."

"Ooh?" The docent scanned Jason as if she was attempting to estimate his age. "I'll go see if she's available. May I have your name?"

"Jason. Jason Carmichael. Class of '85." He pumped his arm into the air as he'd done so many times at pep rallies, and in a dopey kind of voice, added, "Go Mustangs."

The sneaker clad docent gave him a suspicious look and disappeared around a corner. In a few moments, one shriek burst from the next room, and footsteps hurried in his direction.

"Jason? Oh, my God…Jason." A woman dressed in a less-than-modest skirt and white blouse came directly over and gave him a warm embrace. "Let me take a look at you." She stood back and grasped Jason by his shoulders.

The docent smiled and left.

"Hi," Jason said with a bright smile. Kathleen had matured in a most captivating way. Her dark mysterious eyes had always been a feature that drew men to her as if they were an intimation of things to come, and hair that had often been described in high school as being *dirty* blonde was now sprinkled with tinges of gray. "I hope you don't mind me coming here…but I saw your name in the Plain Dealer and…"

"Mind? No. Absolutely not. It's great to see you. God, it's been…"

"A lot of years. Let's just leave it at that," Jason suggested as he stroked his graying temples. He couldn't help but notice the absence of a wedding ring on her finger. "What ever happened between you and David, anyway?"

"Long story. You probably don't want to know about it." Kathleen motioned to a wooden bench sitting diagonally in a corner facing a large window which provided a commanding view of Lake Erie.

"Try me."

"College…married…to David…a little girl…tears…divorce."

"You seemed to have left out quite a bit of information." With raised eyebrows, Jason asked, "Care to fill in any of the blanks?"

"For you, yes. Where should I start?"

"Anywhere you want. Just do me a favor and leave out anything to do with the honeymoon."

Kathleen leaned forward and rested her arms on her still delicious looking legs. Her dress, almost too bold for an area known for its propensity for modesty and decorum, rose a few inches as she crossed her legs to face Jason. "You left pretty soon after graduation, didn't you?"

"I didn't think you'd even noticed."

Kathleen gave a short, feminine laugh which might have gone unnoticed had it not been for the vibrant acoustics of the paneled room—something an audio engineer would term...*live*. "I notice everything," she assured him with a touch of her hand. "Anyway... David and I both attended Kent State together. You could say we were basically together for most of our lives. I majored in history, he majored in Poli-Sci and public speaking—like he needed any coaching in that," she added with a not-too-subtle bite in her voice. "As he became more involved in the political arena, he changed...he changed a lot."

"How so?"

"Attitude for the most part...toward me. We had a little girl... name's Jennifer. Then he had to travel around the county at first, but then he wormed his way into state politics, and was away more and more. When he'd come home, we'd have to give lots of parties to entertain and make those necessary contacts with important people. Jason, I was just as educated as he was, but he treated me as if I was his possession, or an ornament...an ornament that had to be coached before every social event. He'd tell me who to talk to, what to say, topics to steer away from, what each person liked to talk about...to snuggle up to their good side, you know?"

Jason nodded.

"I didn't feel as if I was married to anyone. I felt as if I was in a perpetual state of being *briefed*."

"So when did you divorce?"

"About three years ago. Jennifer lives with me. David fits her into his schedule every so often," Kathleen said with an icy tone. "Then I applied for this job. They needed a curator, I needed an income of my own, and Jennifer needed stability." With a sense of resignation in her voice, she added, "It all worked out okay."

"That's great."

"What about you, Jason? Where have you been since you dropped off the face of the earth?"

"California. My dad landed a pretty good offer at an aerospace firm, so we moved. I think he really wanted out of this area."

"What did he do in the space industry? I thought he was into philosophy."

"That was a minor interest. He really liked abstract logic. Somebody evidently appreciated his wild ramblings about time and space continuums."

"I suppose," she said with an unpretentious shrug. "How do you like it out there?"

"Oh, it was kind of fun for a while…until you find out you have no real friends. Or should I say, you have no friends who are *real*." In his mind, he quickly retracted the last statement when his thoughts drifted to Dena Manning and what they'd been through together.

"That's sad. So what brought you back here to this quiet little town…all by yourself? You are by yourself, aren't you?"

Jason looked down and mumbled, "Have to get over some stuff."

"Like what? Were you married, too?" she asked as she stole a peak at his barren ring finger.

He still avoided locking eyes with Kathleen. "We were talking of marriage." Jason's voice seemed to drift off into space. "She was killed during a botched-up bank robbery."

"Oh, my God. I'm so sorry." Kathleen reached over and cradled his hands in hers. "If you don't want to talk about it…"

"It's okay, I suppose." He looked up into Kathleen's eyes, then down at their clasped hands. So many times, earlier in his life, he'd dreamed of being this close to Kathleen. Now, here he was, sitting on a bench face to face with a woman he'd tried so hard to erase from his memory, but never failed to remember when reflections of his malleable school years crept back into his thoughts. "It was pretty difficult to swallow."

"Did the cops find out who did it?"

"Yeah, everyone except the driver of the getaway car. I'm assuming by now, the locals probably have him—kids weren't all that sophisticated. The down side is, even if the police have caught up with this last moron, in today's world, people get away with so much, and they attribute it to crowded prison conditions. Like I give a crap."

"That exact topic is what endeared David to a lot of the constituents in our county and the state as well. He really attacked the penalization process in Ashtabula County…to the point where crime dropped almost thirty-five percent. Most of the reduction was attributed to the closing of the steel mills in Lorain, which pretty much put the screws to the port in Conneaut and cities like Pittsburgh, PA. Things got pretty ugly for a while up along the lake."

"Hmm. I imagine. Cleveland, too?"

"You bet. You just can't close down facilities that have been the bread and butter of an entire region for generations and expect no ripple effect throughout the rest of the state. Like I said, people were hurting, and they did whatever they could to survive." Kathleen sighed and arched her eyebrows. "Anyway, David's initiatives made headlines all over the state. He knew he was on his way up."

"He always was pretty aggressive, wasn't he?"

"David seldom took *no* for an answer," Kathleen said, letting out a lengthy sigh.

"Hmmm." Jason nodded while he gazed around the room at the paintings and pictures portraying a seafarer's life, complete with contrasting moments of tranquility and monstrous storms. Paintings depicting aged limestone and bulk ore-carriers plunging off what must have been an enormous wave, their bows barely visible through the blowing spray, hung in dusty gray frames fashioned from weathered wood.

"Care for a personal tour?" Her voice, laced with warmth, did not reverberate around the paneled walls as did most others. It was almost as if the walls were engaged in some obligatory mission to retain not only the physical artifacts within, but the words spoken in reverence to all those for whom the facility existed. She turned her head in the direction of another room and called out, "Sue. I'm out for the rest of the day."

From around the corner, the docent's voice replied with a crusty, "Okie-Dokie."

"I'd like that," Jason whispered.

Some of the exhibits were constructed so they furnished visitors with a feeling of what it might be like to stand on the bridge of a ship. White paint covered the cold steel railings installed for visitors to grasp as the imaginary ship swayed dangerously from side to side in massive seas caused by winds registering eleven or greater on the Beaufort scale. A condition so severe that most seamen would be haunted by the memory until the day they died. The only ingredients left out of the exhibits were the visitor's own imagination and desire to survive.

Another room was dedicated to archival pictures of anything to do with the now defunct steel industry. Racks of mostly black and white pictures of every size illustrated the many factors in the steel production cycle—from the Mesabi ore range, where a bulk of the iron ore was mined to the loading docks at Duluth where the red, powdery rock was transferred to waiting bulk carriers. Scenes of the locks at Sault Ste. Marie depicted these working vessels in every type of weather. A colorful map hung on the wall showed why the locks at Sault Ste. Marie were the gating items which defined the Great Lakes shipping season.

When the water in the locks froze, the shipping season was over and the men could return home to enjoy meals not served on stainless steel tables edged with fiddles. Although the fiddles served the purpose of restraining one's food on the table while the ship rolled precariously in heavy seas, they also fostered the uncanny ability to create a make-shift reservoir which deposited its hybrid contents onto the lap of any unfortunate seamen foolish enough to sit at the end—much like sitting at one end of a wobbly ice-cube tray.

Ships from the Wyandotte and Pittsburgh lines were recorded at sea, entering the various unloading ports, or tied up at docks where the claws of the massive electric Hulett unloaders were maneuvered into the cavernous holds to extract the precious ore with their enormous buckets and then deposit the load into waiting rail cars.

One could almost hear the whining of the reddish, ore-encrusted cables as the bucket was lowered again and again. Its claws grasping enough in one load to fill half a rail car, then the whining started again as the bucket was hoisted from the hold, moved back along the track to the dirty rail cars. As each portion of the hold was emptied, the Huletts would grind to one side or the other on train-like wheels to position themselves over the next opening. With each movement, dust and stray chunks of iron ore would crackle and pop under the enormous weight of the wheels and their mobilized structure. Looking at the vintage photographs, one could almost taste the fine ore dust that usually coated the lips of all within shouting distance of the unloading operation.

Kathleen told Jason how she'd canvassed the general population through newspaper ads asking for any pictorial records anyone had and would like to contribute to the museum. From that meager beginning, inputs poured in from sons and daughters, or relatives of all sorts, anxious to preserve a way of life reluctantly stripped from them.

Kathleen and Jason sat on one of the many benches in the museum while she described what the facility looked like before she'd taken over the helm. "The previous curator had his heart in the right place, but unfortunately desire was transcended by inexperience. This is backyard history, Jason—the kind of history that has a direct effect on a lot of people."

"You've certainly accomplished your goal," Jason said as he again concentrated his attention on all the exhibits and her attention to detail within the facility.

"Part of my goal was to not only remember a local past, but to honor the people who spent their entire lives in it, raised families, and often spent holidays away from their loved ones because of it." Kathleen glanced at her watch and reached for Jason's hand. "I was on my way to a meeting. I'm late now, but you were worth it." She searched his eyes for a moment. "I was wondering if…maybe…you'd like to have dinner… or something? I think we have a lot to catch up on." Her voice sounded like a gentle breeze.

"Tonight?" God, he hoped he didn't sound too desperate.

"Tonight is perfect, Jason. I'll ask my neighbor to watch Jennifer for the evening."

"How old is she?"

"My neighbor?" Kathleen asked with an impish silliness in her voice.

"No-o." He'd no sooner answered before he realized he'd just been had.

"Jennifer's eleven…going on forty. She's a little mother who thinks of herself as more than capable of staying home alone, but if I treat it as a sleepover with my neighbor, it's much easier."

"Does she look like you?" Jason had visions of what her and David's children would look like. Something he'd been burdened with most of his adult life.

"I knew you'd ask," she teased. "She looks more like me every day. Blonde hair…blue eyes…great complexion, boys standing in line just to talk to her." Kathleen's voice took on a dreamy quality as if she'd been carefully thinking about exactly what to say and how to say it. "You cannot imagine what a thrill it was for me to see you today. If you don't mind, I'd like to introduce you to Jennifer before we go."

"Are you sure we shouldn't take her with us? I wouldn't mind."

"We've waited this long for a first date. I think she'll understand, but thanks for asking. That was very thoughtful."

"Can't argue with your logic," Jason whispered.

"Six-thirty, okay?"

"Fine."

"Good. Here's my card." She jotted down her address and home phone number. "Also…I don't want you to have any excuses for not calling, so I'm in the phone book under Rogers-Ellison in case you happen to lose the card." There was a wry twinkle in her eyes. "It's kind of hard to miss. Seems like the entire county listing is but twenty pages long, especially with all the Amish people around." She tapped her fingers on Jason's chest as a gentle reminder. "No excuses."

CHAPTER 7

Since leaving California, Jason had eaten at a hodgepodge of restaurants, some of which could have qualified as gourmet while others may best have qualified for disaster relief funding. Hints at the category into which these establishments fell could generally be evidenced if the menu had detailed instructions describing the Heimlich Maneuver.

Through a rain-streaked windshield kept reasonably clear by wipers set on *Max*, Jason peered out trying to read any address that might give him a clue as to how close he was to Kathleen's house. It was bad enough the street signs were almost obliterated by trees and bushes, but he did manage to locate the street where she lived. Now all he had to do was find the house.

He leaned forward in his seat as most do during strenuous driving conditions, thinking the extra few inches will enable them to see more clearly. "Aha." He caught sight of a lighted address on a fence post with an even number on his right. Kathleen was at 1651, "So that should be on the left," he mumbled while rolling down his window to get a better view. A home with a front porch light on gave him the clue he needed to know he may have arrived. He made a U-turn in the street and ventured out to verify the address before embarrassing himself by knocking on the wrong door. "1651. This is good."

Kathleen's home was cradled between two older homes, each bearing a slight resemblance to a house which could have been located on some windswept prairie for years with no indication of a paint store for hundreds of miles. Her landscaped lawn was separated from the street and sidewalk by a waist-high wrought iron fence. A mature willow tree stood centered in the yard, its branches, which under normal circumstances would have drooped gracefully as would the arms of a ballerina, now waved wildly in the blowing wind. Brass lamps on each side of the front door pierced the darkness like a beacon to guide sailors safely on their course.

Kathleen clutched her jacket tight to her neck as she greeted Jason on the porch. "Hi. I'm glad you could find the place in this weather."

"It was a challenge," he said, trying to overcome the sound of low, rumbling thunder. "Boy. I forgot how nasty these electrical storms can be."

"I apologize, Jason," Kathleen yelled back. "I should have had you follow me here."

"That's okay, I've driven in worst." Jason scuffed his feet on a brown welcome mat before going in.

Kathleen reached around Jason to close the door.

What he expected to find was an array of artsy-crafty knick-knacks adorning every wall and table, and where pastels would be a predictable ingredient of the landscape. Instinctively, he scanned the living room for the sign plugging *Baskin-Robbins - 31 flavors*. All those lectures he'd attended during various art classes in college, which he'd reluctantly taken to fulfill some obscure fine arts requirement, finally made some sense. As he recalled those lessons, it reminded him that all history was filled with varying examples of decoration as a primal sociological instinct whose sole purpose was to create a sense of individualism. Jason concluded this period of mind-paralyzing decor fit somewhere between rococo and early ice-cream parlor.

But in Kathleen's home, he felt an overwhelming feeling of warmth. The walls were textured—an obvious upgrade from the outdated lath and plaster style so prevalent of the era in which the house was built. Windows were framed in solid oak with sills to match, each carefully stained in golden tones with colorful curtains gracefully draped at each side. Her furniture was situated facing the front window to take advantage of the view of the lawn and willow tree.

The only thing out of place was the absence of a stair railing leading upstairs. Each tread had a distinct mark where spindles had once been located, but now were nothing more than a series of square holes waiting for some carpenter's finishing touches.

A pair of feet could barely be seen on the first landing.

Kathleen waved for the feet to come closer. "Jason, I'd like you to meet Jennifer. Honey, this is Jason Carmichael…the man I was telling you about." Kathleen looped her arm around her daughter's shoulder.

Jennifer raised her head. Until now, it appeared she'd been examining every wrinkle and blemish on the tops of her well-worn shoes. She reached for Jason's hand. A gawky smile appeared on her lips, and her deep blue eyes squinted while she studied Jason as if he was a Petri dish under a microscope.

Kathleen was right…she did look like her as a little child. He'd known Kathleen since the fifth grade, and remembered how the boys seemed to gravitate toward her at recess. Then as time went by, the reason boys were attracted to her became more and more obvious, and all the while, she seemed to bask in the attention. "Hi, Jennifer," Jason said, as he bent down to grasp her hand in his.

She looked up at her mother as if asking if her duties were over and could she now go over to her friend's house.

"Why don't you get your sleeping bag," Kathleen suggested. "I'll let Beth know you're on your way over." She watched Jennifer leave the room before turning to Jason. "She's had a rough time of it. She sees her father on TV more than she'd ever seen him at home. She doesn't ask, but I know she wonders about the divorce a lot, and it's a little difficult to explain to someone her age why people aren't together anymore."

"It's a little hard to explain to some adults, too."

Jennifer came back into the living room with a large green bag slung over her shoulder and another canvas bag with what Jason perceived were all the necessities for an overnight outing between girls.

To Jason, the bag translated to scads of makeup, exchanges of notes which had been passed between friends at school, and maybe there'd be a few entries into those shrouded diaries. He was certain there would be some interesting entries made in those pages tonight regarding the mysterious stranger from her mother's past.

A flash of light through the window interrupted their first meeting as Jason instinctively counted the number of seconds until he heard the distant rumble of thunder. The howling wind had picked up to the point where whistling sounds much like miniature sirens could be heard coming in through tiny orifices no one knew about nor cared about when the house was built. As the thunder grew closer, the house reverberated like a giant loudspeaker reacting to sympathetic vibrations.

Feigning a theatrical pose and accompanied by a dramatist's voice, Kathleen pointed at the side door and pronounced, "Be gone, my child."

"Oh, okay," Jennifer grumbled and gathered her canvas bag she'd dropped on the floor.

"Do we get a good-bye?" Kathleen asked.

"Bye, Mom. Bye, Jason."

Kathleen peered through a side curtain until a light next door blinked on and off. That was their private signal to ensure the arduous journey between houses had successfully been completed.

When the signal light went dark, Kathleen glanced at her watch. "We'd better be going. I'd like to take you to one of my favorite restaurants. I eat there a lot." She retrieved Jason's jacket hung from one of those rustic little pegboards stained to make it appear old and weathered—this convenient knick-knack obviously being the precursor to guest closets. Slipping into her leather jacket, she remarked, "I hope we don't lose power."

The booming thunder now sounded as if it was directly overhead. Windows rattled and dishes seemed to be dancing on the shelves. Kathleen glanced up as she reached for her umbrella, casting a wary eye on her treasured possessions.

They drove to the side of town near the lake where, years ago, a cozy little boat harbor sat hidden amongst some bushes and majestic oaks, almost isolated from the public's eye traveling the lake's shore highway. From what started out as a sport fisherman's haven, had now expanded to include a proliferation of much larger boats, some in the forty-foot range. By the looks of their arrangement, side-ties could accommodate even larger vessels. Jason wondered what they did with these boats when the lake froze over. There had to be a major boat yard nearby.

As a child, every time his father would take him to Vermilion on business, he'd ask to be dropped off there to sit on the lawn near the gate. Jason never forgot the hours he'd spent under those trees of the little marina dreaming of what lie just over the horizon.

Not far from the harbor was a modest looking building designed to look like a Spanish hacienda, complete with graceful archways leading to a patio decorated with huge flowerpots. The arched front door, stained with a dark tint to resemble the aged entry into some isolated frontier fort, was bordered by wrought iron lamps. All these features were incorporated by an imaginative designer to create an alluring golden glow as customers entered the courtyard.

As soon as they'd entered the lobby, Kathleen removed her jacket and folded it over her arms as she guided Jason to the area near the hostess' station. "I've already called in for a reservation. How's that for efficiency?"

In the subdued lighting, Jason couldn't help but notice how Kathleen's dark expressive eyes seemed to capture the attention of anyone who happened to glance in her direction. When he was in high school, he'd unconsciously formulated a rudimentary, albeit adolescent, philosophy regarding the difference between his girlfriend and Kathleen. He'd thought of Kathleen as *clean* sexy and Nicole as *dirty* sexy. As time passed, he'd refined his perspective from that of *dirty* versus *clean* to that of unwavering puritanical innocence versus innocence laced with vulnerability. Vulnerable was good. Such were the mental gymnastics of the adolescent mind. "Fine." Jason looked around the lobby at the Mexican décor, complete with colorful *sarapes* hung for affect on the rough textured stucco walls. "Did they say how long a wait there'd be?"

"About fifteen minutes. They don't look that busy, but they're a little short on help, so they said."

"That's okay. Want a drink? Maybe a Margarita? I'll buy," Jason asked, as he reached for his wallet.

"Okay, blended…and with salt. You don't have to pay. I have money, too, y'know."

Seeing a cocktail waitress inching her way through the lobby, he raised his hand to get her attention.

"Would you like something from the bar while you wait?" the waitress asked.

"One Margarita, with salt, and blended, please…and a Dos Equis." Jason spoke a little louder than normal to be heard over the PA system.

The music only ceased when the hostess broke in to announce the names of the next party to be seated.

"I'll be right back." The waitress smiled and inched her way back through waiting customers to the bar.

The music droned on as Kathleen and Jason tried to engage in more conversation, and with each word, they'd lean into each other so they could hear what the other was saying and instinctively pressed closer together. At one time, Kathleen, in a coquettish display of affection, leaned her head onto Jason's chest as he spoke.

"Who gets the Margarita?" the waitress interrupted. Kathleen reached for the glass. The waitress handed Jason the beer from her carefully balanced tray. "Would you like this added to your dinner tab?"

"On the tab would be fine...and this is for you." Jason handed her a five dollar bill. Both Jason and Kathleen nodded a thank you as the waitress responded to another raised hand in the lobby.

At first, Jason concentrated his attention on Kathleen's captivating eyes, but became distracted by the slow, deliberate motion she made with her tongue as it moved around the rim to gather a taste of salt before taking a sip. "Mmm. This is my favorite part," she purred.

"Kathleen....party of two. Kathleen....party of two."

"That's us. Let's go." There was a slight downturn in her voice.

"Whew. That didn't take as long as I thought."

The hostess showed them to a cozy booth with comfortable cloth seats and handed each a glossy fold-out menu filled with myriad tempting appetizers and main courses.

"I already know what I want," Kathleen said, while pushing the menu to the edge of the table.

Jason studied his for awhile as if it were a homework assignment.

When their waiter showed up, he took their orders and departed with very little extraneous dialog.

"I see what you mean about this place," Jason said as he surveyed the dining area. "They have so many tables...and yet they're not filled."

"Well, the Margaritas are good, huh?" Kathleen continued to lick the rim of the glass as she teased Jason with her seductive eyes. Switching to an impish grin, she added, "They want you to wait...so you drink more. That's where the money is. You want to hear how I landed this position at the museum?"

Jason nodded and took another sip of his Dos Equis.

"Remember back at the museum, I said the effort should focus on the personal history of all the people who counted on the steel industry so they could maintain a vital part of their lives? That's all these people knew, Jason…both at the mills and aboard those freighters. I kind of hinted at it earlier, but my minor in school was psychology…specializing in industrial/organizational practices, not only working conditions and the effects of automation, but the introduction of women into leadership roles."

"Sounds like that last one could be interpreted as rather judgmental… or at least, controversial."

"True," Kathleen said in a matter-of-fact voice. "Unfortunately, resolutions to those problems are being wrought by either individuals or via committees who are marginally qualified to formulate any definitive action, and that has a profound effect on the general workforce and, ultimately, on the minds of the people who are the backbone of success for any company…or in this case, the entire steel industry."

"Let's see. Who has the beef tostada?" asked the waiter who stood facing Kathleen. Jason gestured with a slight wave of his hand and sat back in his chair as the food was set down, not so much because of his gesture, but because Kathleen had nodded in Jason's direction. After the meals were carefully placed, the waiter asked if they needed anything else.

"Ice water, please." Kathleen leaned toward Jason and whispered, "I can't guzzle Margaritas, or I get a friggin' brain freeze."

"Same for me." Jason looked at the waiter, who seemed entranced with Kathleen. "Water?" Jason reiterated his request while tapping the waiter's wrist.

"Oh? Okay. Two waters," the waiter said as he turned to leave.

Jason and Kathleen shared a quiet laugh as the waiter departed. Jason hinted that if Kathleen were to make it obvious she was *available*…and then he stopped talking long enough to let her fill in the blanks.

"No, thanks. And don't go trying to fix me up. I know exactly what I want." Kathleen took a sip of her drink, licked her lips, then continued, "Corporate philosophies change quickly with the globalization of economies, especially with every changing of the guard. With that change comes the voiding of policies and remedies that used to have validity and merit for generations." Kathleen gave a satirical chuckle—the kind where you laugh while wondering why you are laughing. "You've seen the job scene go from a place where you spent many years at one company, to where you spend fewer and fewer years at more companies….you move so much. Not just the *you*, you, but the *everybody* you."

"Technology changes. You have to keep up," Jason added.

"That's right. That's why keeping this museum afloat was so important to me—as a symbol of recognition, and respect, and as a tribute to a way of life that's been forever changed." Kathleen dabbed at her mouth with a napkin while she glanced around the room.

Jason noticed the slight reddening of Kathleen's eyes as she spoke so reverently of people whom she'd probably never met.

"How's things going here?" asked the waiter while gesturing at their plates. "Are you both through with these?"

Jason glanced at Kathleen's plate. "Yeah. We're through. Thanks."

Eyeing Kathleen's ring finger, the waiter removed the plates and silverware. "Anything else?"

"No, thanks." Kathleen cast Jason a hurried look. "Sorry. Did you want another beer?"

Jason smiled back at her since the waiter remained transfixed on Kathleen. He shook his head from side to side.

"Check?" the waiter asked.

"That'd be good," Jason said, aiming his comment at the back of the waiter's head.

"Oh. Okay," the waiter responded while still staring at Kathleen. "I'll be right back with your check for you and your-r-r…?"

Kathleen looked up at him and grinned. "Gynecologist."

When the waiter returned with the check, he gawked at Kathleen again. "I work here every Thursday and Friday."

"What a coincidence." Kathleen slid out from behind the table. "You and I have the exact same work schedule. Too-o-o bad."

Jason glanced at the bill and handed the waiter sixty dollars. "Keep the change."

"That's not much of a tip for a doctor," the waiter remarked.

"Well…y'see?" Jason snickered. "I'm just an *amateur* gynecologist."

Kathleen stood off to the side shaking her head. As they left, she glanced over her shoulder to see if the egotistical waiter was out of earshot. "That was great, Jason. Did you notice the look on his face?"

"Yeah. Finally."

With a devilish gleam in her eyes, Kathleen giggled, "That was fun, wasn't it?"

After taking a hurried glance out the window, they decided it might be better to wait the storm out. The thunder and lightning had lessened, but the rain kept up its relentless barrage leaving the parking lot and street a virtual river. Emergency vehicles with their light bars flashing plied the streets trying to create enough of a wake to free the few cars whose engines had stalled. Sometimes, it even worked.

Kathleen guided him to the lounge and found a cozy seat near the fireplace. "We've spent almost the entire day talking about me and the museum. Now, it's your turn. I want to hear about you."

"Okay…change of subject. I've been putting this off all night. I don't know how to ask you this, so I guess I'll just come right out and ask it. When we were in high school, did David ever date anyone else?"

"What? Why would you ask me this?"

"There's a reason I'd like to know. To your knowledge, was there anyone, even a passing interest in anyone else?"

"No. Not that I know of. Why all the questions about David? This is making me feel a little uncomfortable."

"Do you remember how David bragged about…?"

"Everything?"

"I wasn't going to put it that way," Jason said, "but I suppose…never mind. When he carved your initials and heart shape into that stump at the covered bridge, remember he boasted about how he could shape those nice little curves when the rest of us could barely manage some blood-letting slashes?"

"Yes?" Kathleen's brow furrowed.

"The other day, I was at the bridge. I was nosing around, and I found another set of initials just inside the barricade. His—plus *FM*."

"*FM*?"

"Friedel Mueller."

"Oh, my God. The girl who was found under the highway bridge?"

"Yeah. At first I didn't know what to make of it, so I got in touch with a county deputy."

"What happened? You think David had something to do with her death?" Kathleen's elbows rested on her knees and her hands were cupped to her mouth.

"I'm sorry. Maybe I shouldn't have brought this up."

"What? And let me find out only if there's some sort of investigation? No…damn it, you did the right thing. Are you sure?"

"About the carving? Yeah. The deputy who came out agreed they sure looked like they'd been carved by the same hand. I never noticed those initials before."

"I never saw them either, but then again, I never looked for anyone else's."

"That's probably true of everybody…including me."

"This can't be possible." Kathleen rocked her head from side to side. "Do you think there's any connection?"

"Records indicate Friedel's file has never been officially closed, which means the sheriff may very well reopen this case…if those initials really mean anything."

Kathleen sat on the couch rubbing at her forehead with her fingertips. "After all this time, I felt something was going right for Jennifer and me. The museum, and moving back to my own, private little town. Then you show up. Even that had all the earmarks of another success story. This can't be happening, Jason. What you're suggesting…is…David could have had something to do with that girl's death."

"This finding could amount to nothing more than a coincidence. Or wishful thinking." Jason threw his arms up.

"Let's hope you're wrong about those initials."

Jason gave a slight nod. "Did you ever hear anything about the man Friedel was supposed to marry? Especially his name. 'Cause I sure didn't. She was seventeen when she died, and by sixteen, their lives are pretty much cast in concrete."

Kathleen gazed out the window. "I seem to remember David talking about a guy named Ditmann. Yeah…Jonathon Ditmann. I don't know why I remember the first name, but the Ditmann clan is quite prominent in the area."

"Thanks. This is a big help."

"Hmmf." Her eyes now had a pleading look in them as she searched Jason's eyes for an answer. "Should I wish that you'd have stayed away?"

After prying her hands away from her face, Jason clasped them and looked into her eyes. "For your sake, maybe. For Friedel Mueller's sake…no."

"Ya know? All day, I've never asked what you do to earn a living out in California."

"I'm in law enforcement in Fresno County."

"You're a cop?"

Jason nodded.

"Hmm. Interesting."

CHAPTER 8

A bearded man appeared on the front porch of the Ditmann farmhouse to greet his unexpected guest. The man stood, feet spread wide and his massive arms folded across his chest perhaps as a demonstration of bravado as Jason brought the muddy white van to a stop. The man's wide brimmed hat was dripping wet from tending his chores before the brunt of a storm moved in.

Lightning on the black horizon resembled a flash from a camera being dispersed through a pane of translucent glass.

Stepping out of his car, Jason smiled at the man. "Are you Mr. Ditmann?"

"Yes?"

"Mr. Jonathon Ditmann?" The snarling thunder rumbled toward them.

"That be me. What is it you want?" the man answered, accompanied with a diplomatic nod.

"I'd like to ask you some questions about Friedel Mueller. May I come on the porch, sir?"

"You're welcome to sit." There was a dryness to Jonathon's answer. As Jason approached the porch, Jonathon removed his hat and tapped it against his leg to remove the bulk of the water before sitting in a wooden framed chair. He then gestured to the chair next to him. "Been a long time...about Friedel," his voice weary and strained. "Word around here is you or your kind would be paying me a visit."

Jason attributed Jonathon's reserved greeting to a kind of wariness the Amish might feel toward the presence of an outsider, and who would generally be regarded as either an intrusion or a threat. After Jason formally introduced himself, he whispered, "Is it okay if we talk about Friedel out here, or would you rather talk someplace else…privately?"

"There are no secrets here."

Jason bit at his lower lip and fixed his eyes on Jonathon. "After Friedel's death, did anyone talk to you about how, or why she may have been on the bridge that night?"

"Yes."

Jason waited for some follow-through, but sensed any information he needed would have to be dragged from Jonathon. "Ya see? I didn't notice anything in the reports that addressed this question…or at least recorded it for future reference."

"You think she was murdered, don't you?"

"I believe it was not an accident."

"Why are you dredging this up after all this time? Is it not enough that families have suffered through this, and I lost a good wife?"

"Do you have any idea what she was doing on the bridge that night?"

"No."

"Were you, in fact, going to be married to Friedel?"

"I was eighteen at the time. We had discussed marriage. Are you familiar with our traditions?"

"No, sir. Well…some, but not all of them."

"We do not do as you do in your world. You offer jewelry. We offer clocks or eating utensils as an expression of our commitment to each other." Puffing his chest out, he added, "I made a clock for Friedel… fashioned from solid walnut."

"Did she accept it? As a commitment."

Jonathon rolled his head from side to side. "She felt she had to."

"So, she didn't accept it?"

"I said she felt she had to. It was not accepted with the spirit that we would expect."

"Did she ever tell you she wanted to back out of this arrangement?"

"There were discussions."

"Were you embarrassed by this…ambivalence?"

"It is our custom to abide by our commitments."

"Did Friedel make any commitment to you?"

"In words only."

"Excuse me for asking this, Mr. Ditmann. Did you feel any resentment or humiliation within your congregation because of Friedel's hesitancy to carry through with your marriage proposal?"

"We place community above personal gratification."

"Am I to assume you'd both gone through the *publishing* ceremony?"

"That we did. Our names were read by the deacon as is customary to get published, but because of Friedel's…continual reluctance, my father was not able to name a date and time for the wedding. It became awkward."

"But you were there…at the publishing?"

"No. And Friedel was supposed to be at her home preparing a meal for us. Tis the custom."

"Do you know where she was that day?"

Jonathon looked down and rolled his lips under. "Studying. In her room. She told me she'd been crying."

Jason scratched his head, looked out into the rolling black clouds, and then faced Jonathon again. "Were you angered by Friedel's ambivalence?"

"Anger is not part of our beliefs. God teaches us to believe that all things happen for a reason," Jonathon answered in a defensive tone. "Did you come here because you believe I was involved with Friedel's death?" He drummed his fingers on the edge of the wood chair.

"I believe I have to pursue all options. That's all."

"We had discussed the choosing of our ushers for the wedding. We call them *forgeher*."

"Did Friedel actively participate in these choices?"

"No. She often sat there. Her eyes were not looking where her heart was looking."

"What do you mean by that?" Jason asked.

"She wanted more. More education, more opportunities, more… changes in her life," Jonathon explained as his brow wrinkled.

"Was she considering leaving the community?"

"I couldn't possibly know the answer to your question with any certainty."

"I assume you have great pride in your community?"

"It is our life."

"Do you know if she was seeing anyone…from outside?"

"That is not permitted." Jonathon's eyes were cast downward.

"Yes or no, Mr. Ditmann?"

"I do not know." Jonathon locked eyes with Jason as he answered with a brief raising of his voice. "That is all I can say. Friedel was… different."

Rain was now pelting down onto the dusty arc in front of the house creating a belt of mud around the frame of the Chevy. Thunderous sounds made conversation much more difficult to understand as well as lessening the concentration level necessary to formulate any logical sequence of inquiries.

Jonathon seemed to have a flair for putting every statement into a matter-of-fact tone of voice. Jason figured it either allowed him to detach himself from any emotion, or make him appear non-committal. "You said you made a clock for Friedel…as an overture to your marriage proposal?"

"That I did."

"In my culture, had I bought a ring for someone I wanted to marry and they said no, I'd probably return it to the jeweler. But then again, that's our custom. I don't have a clue what you'd do with something that was hand-made…plus I'll bet you had a lot of BST invested in it, huh?"

"BST?"

"Blood, sweat and tears. It's a saying," Jason explained with a persuasive grin.

"Yes. A lot of effort was put into the gift."

Jason leaned against a hitching rail, and spread his legs apart for balance. "So? Did you sell the clock, destroy it, burn it?"

"Changed it."

"Whoa. I never thought of that. Howdya do that?"

"Added some things."

After a few awkward moments waiting for more clarification, Jason prodded, "Such as?"

"Care to see it? Better at pointing than explaining."

"I'd like that. Thank you."

Tall and lanky, Jonathon had an enormous stride as he started for the front door. He never slowed down to accommodate Jason, who now felt like a child trying to keep up with his father. Once inside the front door, Jonathon removed his broad-rimmed hat and motioned at the wall containing the clock.

Jason glanced not only at the clock, but around the Spartan room with its plain wooden chairs, hardwood floors, and the solitary curtain hung at each window.

"It was little plainer when I first did it," Isaac explained as he wiped the clock's highly polished surface with a soft white cloth. "I added some more scroll work…here. And here." He pointed out some fine lines of a lighter-colored wood which formed a border just inside the perimeter. "This is what's called *purfling* if someone was making violins." Jonathon ran his weathered fingertips around the outside edge of the clock as if he were caressing it. "I used elm."

"This is gorgeous, Mr. Ditmann. Did you ever make violins?"

"No need."

"How is this…installed? I don't have a clue of how you would do something this beautiful…or intricate."

"Special tools. You cut a small channel just inside the outer edges. Depth is important, as is the width. Then I cut small strips of elm to fit inside those grooves. Kind of time consuming, but it makes for a nice effect…and interesting contrast with the walnut."

"Boy, I'm impressed. Did you ever think about selling these? You really have a talent for doing so much with wood."

"Thank you, Mr. Carmichael, but this is not my business. We're farmers, and that is what I know. I see no reason to change."

Jason rose to shake Jonathon's hand and excuse himself.

"You have not addressed my concerns, Mr. Carmichael," Jonathon added with an air of defiance. "Why, after all these years have you chosen to open something we feel was nothing more than a token gesture at finding out who did this act?"

"A token gesture? Sir…it may have been handled poorly then, but rest assured, it is not being handled poorly now. Why would you feel this way?"

"It is no mystery to me how we are looked upon by others."

"Like maybe, someone hates you enough to not aggressively pursue whoever did this?"

"It seems a rather logical assumption."

"Let's look at it another way, Mr. Ditmann. If someone had no animosity for your culture, they would most assuredly have pursued the criminal just as they would for anyone...of any religious belief. If on the other hand, the investigator did as you implied, hate your culture, and could find reason to discover the criminal to be within your own ranks, they would have gone out of their way to pursue the criminal for no other reason than to discredit the Amish."

"But," Jonathon pointed out, "had the criminal not been of the Amish faith, would they be pursued with equal vigor?"

Jason studied Jonathon's square jaw and piercing eyes now firmly set in a leathery face. "That is where our mutual faiths have to merge."

◊   ◊   ◊

When Ken Hutchinson entered the fast food restaurant, Jason spotted him and nodded to the seat next to the window.

Ken waved and stood in line at the order counter. After he finished, he slipped into the booth opposite Jason. "You already order?" His voice sounded too polite.

Jason nodded.

"Why didn't you tell me you were seeing the lieutenant governor's ex-wife?" Ken's words had all the bite of the staccato report from a high-powered automatic.

The abruptness made Jason feel uncomfortable to the point where he could actually feel tiny beads of perspiration appear on his forehead. *Who the hell does this guy think he's talking to?* He toyed with the idea of easing the tension by answering, *Because you didn't ask,* but quickly dismissed the idea. "I'm sorry. I didn't think it was important."

"Damn it." Ken's whisper carried enough force to extinguish a candle. He scanned the room to see if anyone was within hearing distance. "Anything to do with politics is important. If this somehow gets blown out of proportion, my ass is gonna be in a sling. Have you discussed finding the initials with her?"

"Yes. But I wouldn't consider what we're doing as seeing each other. And how'd you find out I was in contact with Kathleen anyhow?"

"Pretty easy stuff. White van. Indiana plates. Plus I know your number. We know just about where anybody of importance is in the state, and we have our ways of keeping tabs on them." Ken took a deep breath. "Did she seem surprised when you told her?"

"More like worried."

"Hmmpf. There are a multitude of reasons why people worry."

They were interrupted by a female voice announcing two numbers over the PA system. Jason and Ken eased out of the booth to retrieve their orders.

"Am I to assume I'm under surveillance, too?" Jason asked when they slid back into their booth.

"I thought we had an agreement that the information you and I discussed would go no further than us," Ken said between bites of his bacon-burger.

"I'd already told her when you and I talked. So, answer my question. Am I under surveillance?" Jason shot the deputy a curious look over the top of his burger.

"Look, Jason. I'm under the gun here. We're spread pretty thin throughout the county, so this is my chance to do something...let's say, a little more significant...than issuing traffic citations all day long. Do you understand what I'm saying?"

Mulling over what the deputy had just shared with him, Jason wondered if Ken's main agenda had, from the beginning, been nothing more than an opportunistic move on his part to make a name for himself within the department. "You're the expert."

"If you're gonna stay around the area, then please don't make it any harder than it already is...okay? All the pieces have to fit, and they have to fit in some sort of order, or we could trigger a whole slug of cover-up activities by the people involved. And these are powerful people." Ken wadded up his napkin into a tight spiral with the pointed end aimed at Jason. "I like you, Jason. I think you're smart...and I think you did the right thing when you got me involved after noticing those initials, especially since this case has been left open all these years. Somebody out there knows the truth about Friedel Mueller."

"The family deserves to know someone is following through with a loss of life, even if they don't agree with their lifestyle."

Ken dabbed his mouth with another napkin from the small stack the restaurant furnished at each table. "Or…agree with someone wanting to *leave* a way of life." Ken finished his milkshake accompanied by the traditional slurping sound as he tried to suck up every last drop of the ice-cold liquid. "About those initials. I had a lab guy from forensics in Columbus take a look at those. He took some close-ups of the marks and examined them at the scene as well." Ken pursed his lips, and the corners of his eyes appeared to droop. "It wasn't what I was hoping for."

"I don't understand."

"Under magnification, one set of marks was done with a rounded type of chisel. He could tell by the tiny scalloped pattern left around the curved edges in the *D* and the *R* as the carver worked his way around the letters. In the second set…the one bearing Friedel's initials, the carver used a square or flat style of chisel."

"Hmmph. Can I see the report?"

"Don't have a hard copy yet. The only info I got was from a telephone conversation with the tech—kinda informal. I wish he could have verified the initials were done by the same person. Then we'd know we were looking for one guy. Now we may be looking for two different cutters."

Jason rubbed at his hair and rolled his eyes from side to side. "One would have been convenient…two could mean two people…or one person using different tools."

"So the lab work never really proved anything?"

"Yeah, it did…in a negative way. Had there been one carver, the technique used to make the marks could have proved it. And we would be pursuing one individual whose initials we think we know. Now we may still be pursuing one individual…but not the one we thought. Expanding our possibilities is the only thing we've just accomplished."

"Shit. I hoped we could be closing in on someone."

"No one ever said this was gonna be easy, my friend. If *solving* crimes was easy, there'd be no more crime." Jason tapped his fingers to the side of his head and remembered Joshua Stoudt's words. "A very wise man said to me…recently. *Do not think less of yourself.*"

"Thanks. What's next?"

"To your knowledge, has there ever been a murder within the Amish community committed by another Amish?"

"Not that I know of, but….who knows?" Ken shrugged his shoulders. "Why would you ask?" Ken gazed out the window at his Crown Vic parked in front of the gas station.

"I had a talk with a Jonathon Ditmann…the man jilted by Friedel. This is what I read into the conversation we had. Jonathon was not terribly pleased with Friedel's attitude toward his wedding proposal. Friedel dragged the whole thing out until it became an embarrassment to him. Eventually he was forced to renege on his offer and make another choice. A choice I'm not sure was easy for either party to stomach after losing face in the close-knit community."

"Hmm. There was mention of him in the cold file. Losing face… leads to jealousy…leads to anger."

"Yeah, but here's the cool part. As per their tradition, he made a beautiful wall clock for Friedel to formalize his intentions of marriage. After they'd been officially *published* by the deacon, Jonathon visited her house as was customary…and instead of having a family meal prepped, she was in her room doing homework. With that slap in the face, it came as no surprise the marriage plans had gone belly up, so Jonathon modified the clock to present to his new future wife. You want to know what he did to it? He added decorative moldings along the edges—he called it *purfling*. Very fancy. Very intricate. Very time-consuming. Very demanding in technique."

"How'd you find out about this clock?"

"A trans-cultural phenomena called pride. He was very proud of what he'd done, and was quite willing to do a little show-boating. He opened the door, I just entered."

"So? We've just expanded our suspect list from DE to JD. And wouldn't that mean Friedel really was seeing someone outside the congregation? Assuming Jonathon was trying to frame David, how do you suppose he found out about Friedel and David? And if Jonathon was capable of committing murder, why wouldn't he have killed David instead? Then he could have had Friedel…maybe. Doesn't this scenario have a rather sophisticated plot line?"

"You're right. I didn't say it was an easy out, it just allows us to focus on someone other than David Ellison."

"We aren't ruling David out, are we?"

"No way. Being as though I'm visiting back here for awhile, maybe it was time I paid him a visit…just for old times sake."

"While you're at it, let me share this with you. And I mean *you*, as in you only." Ken's eyes were drilling holes into Jason. "Since you felt uncomfortable asking Elizabeth Mueller for the Medico-legal document she has, I tried to obtain a copy for myself. Guess what?" He leaned forward, and whispered, "It doesn't… fucking…exist."

"What?"

"Not in hard copy. Not in the county data base. Not in the state data base."

"You're not strokin' me, are you?"

"I just found this out. These records go back a ways. In time, most of the docs are channeled into the private sector where they are collated, coded, and indexed for future retrieval." Ken rolled his head from side to side. "What the Mueller clan has…is priceless."

"When you fill out your daily report, is it done via computer, orally, hand-written?"

"Computerized. It's instantly forwarded to my road lieutenant, or since I've been working on this case, the lieutenant in charge of the detective division. And yes, I entered the elements of our conversation the other day before I tried to get a copy. I wish I hadn't done that."

"Looking backward, it was wrong, but what you did at the time was absolutely right. I would have done the same thing. Whoever was responsible for trashing the original doc and purging the data base is, or was, clever."

"And probably has connections." Ken gave a sardonic laugh while he piled the immortal remains of his lunch onto his gray plastic serving tray. "Not too indicative of an Amish farmer, huh?"

"But think about this. What are politicians really good at?" Jason tapped his forefinger to his temple. "They're good at getting others to believe in them, and to believe in their cause, or believe in their agenda, or their philosophy. What we have here could very well amount to a conspiracy between David Ellison and Jonathon Ditmann."

"With JD being the dupe."

"Exactly. David wanted into Friedel's pants. Didn't happen. Jonathon wanted to marry Friedel. Couldn't get her. They're both pissed." Jason reached for Ken's hand. "I believe what you've discovered amounts to an incredible find. Brilliant…but scary and possibly deadly for whoever is in possession of that doc." Jason scratched his graying temples. "Beyond your normal chain of command, let's hope there aren't too many people who have access to your daily log."

CHAPTER 9

Visiting the Mueller farm was becoming routine for Jason. First, he came as an envoy to ask a question of a culture he only thought he knew, then to offer his services to resolve a wrong. But he didn't like the purpose of this visit. "Good afternoon, Isaac. I'm glad I caught you here."

"Tis been a difficult morning, Mr. Carmichael. We've been scraping mud from our field equipment. Nothing moves in this weather." Isaac's overalls were more brown than blue and could have stood up in a corner by themselves.

Jason nosed his shoes into what had been a dusty driveway, but now had the texture of over-worked cookie dough. He looked at the wide pneumatic tires on his van, then at the thin, steel wheels of the Mueller's mechanical horse-drawn rake. Pounds-per-square-inch was one of the many problems he had to solve to squeak through college mathematics, but he never had such a graphic example of its application. Looking back at the grooves he'd created in the driveway, Jason said, "I hope I can get out, too."

"In time, it will dry and everything will be back to normal. It is His will."

"Is your mother here?"

"Yes. She is in the kitchen preparing our evening meal."

"How hard would it be to contact Mr. Stoudt, also? What I have to say will have an impact on all of you."

Isaac faced into the screen door and yelled out, "Benjamin. Will you please come here?"

A few moments passed before the sounds of footsteps hurried toward the door. Benjamin peered through the screen, and in his high-pitched voice, asked, "What?"

"Will you slip your boots on and ask Mr. Stoudt to come over. Tell him Mr. Carmichael would like to talk with us."

The front door flew open and Benjamin plopped down on the stoop to slip his boots on, all the while looking up at the beardless Jason. "Hi."

It hadn't taken Jason long to grow accustomed to the formal greetings within this culture, but it was definitely refreshing to hear a casual, *Hi*, once in awhile. "Back at ya." The boy looked confused, or was it a look of sympathy? Jason reminded himself to not try so hard to be cool again.

Benjamin headed across the road to another farm.

Elizabeth came to the door and greeted Jason with a warm smile. "Care for a biscuit? Fresh from the oven."

"No, but thank you very much." It was the first time he'd seen her smile. "I'm sure they're delicious."

Elizabeth swung the front door open. Before she eased herself into one of the chairs, she draped a plain white shawl around her shoulders and drew the cloth tightly to her throat. "Feels chilly in the shade."

Across the field, Jason saw Benjamin and Joshua Stoudt headed for the porch. He waited until everyone was situated and had greeted each other. The seating arrangement was just like the last time they'd sat on the porch. Elizabeth in the center, Joshua in a chair facing her, and Isaac sat on the edge, except this time, he held a shovel rather than a fork. Six year old Benjamin was the new addition.

"Uuh. What I have to say might not be appropriate for the young man," Jason said.

"Does this involve Friedel?" Mr. Stoudt asked Jason.

"Kinda. Well, yes...in a way."

"Benjamin will be a man in a few years, Mr. Carmichael," Joshua said. "Maybe 'tis time for him to engage in the experiences of our world."

"Okay then. This is not the kind of visit I would hope for." Jason inhaled deeply. "I believe your lives may be in danger."

"What? Why, Mr. Carmichael?" Elizabeth gasped.

"It has to do with the document you showed me a couple of days ago, Mrs. Mueller. I'm sorry, but somehow, all accounting of that document has been purged from the state's electronic data bases, the original signed certificate, and any of what we would call hard copies—photographic reproductions of the original. That Medico-legal piece of paper you have been saving all these years is…invaluable to law enforcement."

"I don't understand," Elizabeth said.

"You allowed me to read the report, and it shows multiple views of Friedel's body from each side and all the wounds as they appeared on the body at the time of her death. In a court of law, those pieces of paper would be irrefutable evidence of wounds not directly attributable to an accident or a simple fall." Jason knelt in front of Mrs. Mueller and held her hands. "Your daughter was murdered, Mrs. Mueller. I wish there was some other way to tell you this, but I can think of nothing other than telling you the truth. I'm sorry."

"And now, whoever did this knows my mother kept a copy?" Isaac picked up his muddy shovel and waved it Jason's direction. "How would they know this if you hadn't told them, Mr. Carmichael?"

"*They* wouldn't have," Jason admitted. "But it was a fact that had to be logged in. It's a policy all law enforcement personnel must abide by. Otherwise, if someone kept the information to themselves, what would happen to a case if something happened to the investigator? The bad guy is awarded with a complimentary ticket to freedom."

"Let's listen to what Mr. Carmichael has to say before we make any hasty decisions," Joshua said.

"It seems a hasty decision has already been made," Isaac fired back.

For late September, Jason was beginning to feel the same kind of heat he'd grown up with. Hot, sticky, and definitely uncomfortable. "Look. The damage is done. What we have to figure out between all of us is; how are we going to protect a key piece of evidence in order to bring Friedel's killer to justice?" Jason had not let go of Elizabeth's hands. "Are you still in possession of the Medico-legal document?"

Elizabeth looked to Joshua for counsel.

Joshua rose from his chair, stared across the fields of corn and toward a pasture where Holstein cattle were grazing. With his back turned, he whispered, "We trusted you, Mr. Carmichael."

"I cannot blame you for questioning me," Jason whispered back. "If I may, I would like to add this before you make a decision. The fact that this document was considered so important to someone who then recognized the need to obliterate its very existence is proof enough for me that we are on the right track to finding out who killed Friedel. These are but stepping stones to finding this person."

Joshua turned to face Jason and Elizabeth. "I still believe Mr. Carmichael has our best interests at heart. We may not like what he's done, but he is the only one who has come forth to sacrifice anything in order for Friedel to find peace." Joshua folded his hands as if in prayer. "A few days ago, when we met to decide whether we could trust in Mr. Carmichael, one man asked whether we should abide by God's justice, or the state's justice. It was you, Elizabeth, who said, *I do not believe they have to be different.* I believe we all have a price to pay to find the truth. And our price should be to bear part of the burden to find this truth." He nodded his decision to Elizabeth.

"Yes," she said. "I still have the document of which you speak."

Jason breathed a deep sigh of relief. "Good. We…all of us…have a decision to make right now. Either I can take the report and keep it in a safe place where no one has access to it, or you can hide it somewhere where only one person knows where it is."

"Why only one of us?" Isaac asked.

"I've been in this business for many years, and I have a good idea of what kind of person we're dealing with. I also know what these types are capable of doing to get their hands on that document. It ain't pretty."

"You're saying someone might invade our property?" Elizabeth asked.

"Worse."

"These are but scare tactics," Isaac said in a bitter voice.

"These are not scare tactics, Isaac," Jason shot back. "This is a definite possibility. I've seen people killed for a dime's worth of nose candy." Jason thought for a second. "Ten dollars worth of drugs."

Joshua scanned the out-buildings and fields. "I believe we have the means to hide the document. I also believe it should be Isaac who will determine where the place shall be. He is very strong."

It wasn't physical strength Jason was concerned with. In his years of law enforcement, he'd seen too many examples of the lengths desperate men and women would go to pry information from an unwilling human being. "I will abide by your decision."

"It is done. Is there anything else you wish to discuss with us, Mr. Carmichael?"

"Yeah. Yeah, there is. Do you have any weapons on your property?"

Isaac and Joshua nodded in unison.

"What exactly are we talking about?"

"Rifles." In a matter-of-fact voice, Joshua added. "We do hunt, you know. And the deer compete for the same fodder as our cattle, especially during certain seasons."

"No hand guns?" Jason asked.

"No," Joshua said. "A shotgun or two...for pheasant."

Jason locked eyes with Joshua. "Would you kill to save one of your own?"

◊ ◊ ◊

The two day thunderstorm had turned Kathleen's front yard into a clutter of leaves and small branches from not only her willow tree, but from other trees blocks away. A few of her neighbors were raking up what they could and stuffing them into black plastic bags waiting for the county disposal truck to haul them away.

Jason had no sooner stopped his van when Kathleen came onto the front porch to greet him. Jason froze for a moment. The other day at the museum, she looked professional, neat, trim and businesslike. Tonight, she looked elegant, her hair pulled to one side and wearing a dress which Jason envisioned fell half way between the two literal interpretations of the term *working girl*.

Gone were the awkward high school days and coy looks. She stood to one side as she invited him in, discreetly touching his arm as he entered. "Hi," she whispered in a velvety voice. "Come on in. Jennifer's here."

"So. Groping is off limits?"

Kathleen chuckled and waved a friendly greeting to her neighbors before she led Jason inside.

"Uuh…have you talked to David?"

"Yes…briefly. He wanted to know if we were okay."

"Did you by any chance mention the initials at the bridge?"

"No. Absolutely…not. Jason, I was actually afraid to ask him. Had he said he didn't know anything, I'd have thought he was lying. If he'd said *yes*, I'd be scared to death that his survival instincts would kick in… and…I mean, I would be scared to death."

"Why is it so easy to believe the worst about someone?"

"I hope you're not talking about some semblance of faith here, Jason. Because if you are, when it comes to faith, I know exactly what David believes in. When he started his career, he was the one who was pursuing people of influence. But as time passed by, he became higher up in the political arena, then something strange happened…people started pursuing him. It's not about faith, Jason, and it's not about money…it's about power, and control…and influence."

"You were smart to not bring anything up. No use launching a flare."

Kathleen grasped Jason's hands. "Thanks…I think," and gave Jason a short kiss.

"There is an outside chance that David had nothing to do with Friedel's death."

Kathleen's furrowed brows and squinty eyes had *why?* written all over them.

"When I was talking to the deputy in charge of the investigation, he mentioned some tests conducted by a forensic unit on those initials. And the gist of the report is; the ones with Friedel's initials were done differently from yours."

Kathleen settled back into the sofa and lowered her head into her hands. "Jason, I'm not very good at this kind of stuff," she admitted. "I really hope what you say is true."

"Does Jennifer ever visit with her dad down in Columbus?"

"Yeah, but it's kinda sad," Kathleen said with a heaviness in her voice. "Just two days, and David couldn't divorce himself from his job for even a few hours to be just a father to her. Y'know? Maybe push her on a swing, hold her hand and walk with her, buy an ice cream cone, maybe even allow himself to spill a little on himself so they could laugh about it. I caught a glimpse of his new...*interest*. She dresses very well... very well indeed. She'll be a big asset to him."

"Hi, Jason," Jennifer said in a bubbly voice as she entered the room. She stood next to her mom and looked up at Jason. "You know what?"

"What."

Kathleen reached around Jennifer's shoulders and squeezed. Both giggled a little. "You're not going to tell, are you?"

"Uh-huh. My mom talks about you a lot." There was a definite new-found sense of pride and gusto in Jennifer's voice as she rocked back and forth on her feet.

Jason knelt down in front of Jennifer. "Well, do you know what?"

"Uh-uh," Jennifer answered with a curious grin.

"I'm glad your mom talked about me a lot. If I was with some of my friends, I'd sure talk about her a lot...and I'd certainly make sure to talk about you, too."

"Really?"

"Count on it."

The three of them sat on the sofa together—Jennifer in the middle with Kathleen's and Jason's hands around the back of her. As the evening wore on, Jason and Kathleen stole glimpses of each other over the top of Jennifer's head.

"What do you do when you visit your dad in Columbus?" Jason asked Jennifer.

"Stuff." Her voice tapered off into a void. "Went to a park...with my dad and a lot of other people. They wore suits a lot."

"You don't like suits?"

"You can't have fun in suits." Jennifer glanced down at the floor, then back at her mother.

Kathleen stuck her nose in the air and took several deep sniffs as she tugged Jennifer to her feet. "What about our meatloaf?"

"Yeah, Jason. We made one of mom's special dinners just for you."

This night, Kathleen's meatloaf was the first meal he'd actually enjoyed. Not only because it included all the necessary ingredients for a well-rounded meal, or possibly because of the inclusion of Jennifer, but most probably, it could have been the fact that he had any company at all.

Jennifer's presence took on the role of a calculating and vigilant observer. One who seemed to be continually looking down into her plate and toying with her food, all the while slyly peering over the top of the rims on her tiny designer glasses. Jason had already been briefed by Kathleen that those glasses were more a fashion statement than a necessity since fashion was slowly creeping into Jennifer's life, and heaven forbid if she could not keep up with what the rest of her class was doing or wearing. When Kathleen whispered this tidbit of information to Jason, she also confided to him how she hoped this was as far as the lemming craze would progress. Both grinned anxiously at the implication.

After dinner, and with no prodding from her mother, Jennifer began to remove dishes from the table. She stacked a few articles into a neat pile and headed for the kitchen. On her second trip, Jennifer, her mouth hanging open in awe, looked at Jason and asked, "Like... what...are you doing?" She leaned on the table and stroked her fingers through her hair.

"I'm not supposed to do anything?" Jason asked with a feigned air of innocence.

Jennifer waved her hands, while emitting one of those long drawn out adolescent sighs and headed for the kitchen with more dishes. The first time, she'd used her arms to push against the swinging door. This time, she used her rear end to bump the door enough for her to scoot through.

After the door stopped swinging, Kathleen whispered, "It must be something rare indeed for her to have you join in."

"I thought I did something wrong." Jason glanced at the door, waiting for it to burst open again.

"Don't worry. She never had a man help around here." Kathleen began to gather the silverware in one hand and some scrunched-up paper napkins in the other. "You know what David always did after supper? His customary end to the evening meal was to mumble a brief, hollow compliment to me, then retire to the small office in the back of the house to carry on with his political contacts and aspirations. So often, the last view Jennifer ever had of her father was when he'd enter his room and close the door after himself. There was never any tucking-in or any bedtime stories, but if she was lucky, there might be an obligatory good-night kiss."

"Let me handle this," Jason said with a mischievous grin. He picked up two plates, one in each hand and nudged the door open. "Hi," he said while ignoring Jennifer's quirky stare. He set the plates on the counter, side by side. "Don't move those."

Jennifer was wiping out some remaining gravy from one of the dishes with a paper towel, and gave him a sideways glance, then stared at the plates Jason had so carefully placed.

A few seconds later, Jason returned with two more plates, one in each hand, and just as carefully, set those on the counter in their own little space. "Don't stack those," he whispered.

After more trips in and out of the kitchen, carrying two of everything, saucers, cups, or salad plates, Jason never said a word. He just motioned to Jennifer, pointed to the utensils and officiously waved his finger cautioning her not to stack anything.

With each successive trip, Jennifer grew fidgety, but never asked why he was taking such great pains to situate everything on the counter into its own special spot. She squinted her eyes so much, Jason was unable to tell what color those beady little eyes were, but she never said a word.

On his last trip to the dining room, Jason whispered to Kathleen, "I get to wash." When she took a deep breath to ask why, he put his finger to his lips, "Shh."

Following Jason into the kitchen, Kathleen leaned against the doorjamb and with a satisfied grin, said, "This is my lucky day. All I had to do was cook. You guys do all the rest." Kathleen kept glancing at Jason as he stood next to Jennifer at the sink.

When the sponge was fully saturated with soap, Jason made a few fast swirls in the water. "Ready?" he asked Jennifer, who stood poised with a towel and a quirky look of curiosity.

"Why do you, like, do that?" Jennifer asked. Her gaze scanned the counter, where every square inch was now filled to capacity with dirty dishes, some hanging precariously near the edge.

"Do what?"

"Mom-m," Jennifer whined. "Look at the counter. Like...there's dishes all over the place. They're almost, like, falling off the edge." Jennifer was waving the towel around in gigantic circles over her head.

"Hey. Don't ask me. Jason's the expert." Kathleen turned away from her daughter.

"Oh? That's what's bothering you," Jason said as if he'd just discovered a fundamental law of nature. "Were those dishes clean when you set the table?"

"Duuuh," Jennifer responded with a heavy sigh of frustration.

"How many sides of the plates did we eat on?"

"Mom-m." Jennifer stomped her foot on the vinyl floor.

Kathleen smiled warmly, raised her eyebrow and motioned in Jason's direction.

Jennifer pointed at the top of the plate Jason held in his hand.

"See? That's why you never stack dishes. When you stack them, they get dirty on both sides." Jason demonstrated his theory by swishing the soapy sponge over the top surface only. "You finish twice as fast. Brilliant, huh?" Jason tapped his forefinger to his temple and grinned.

The evening remained sultry and validated the reason front porches were ever invented. The three of them sat on the porch watching for any sign of life in the small town. Had it not been for small get-togethers at someone's home, social life would have gone entirely unnoticed by the casual observer.

Jason removed his shoes and propped his feet on the railing. Kathleen sat at his side with Jennifer snuggling next to her, continuing her suspicious gaze at this strange person who'd entered her mom's life.

"It's peaceful here," Jason whispered, as if the sound of his voice might disturb the neighbors.

"It has its moments," Kathleen added. "But for the most part, you're right. Tell me about California."

Jason glanced at Jennifer, who was now leaning forward and staring at him, and by the look in her eyes, was probably entertaining hopes of hearing something exciting.

"Oh, my God. Do you, like, know any movie stars?" Jennifer blurted out.

"Absolutely…none."

Kathleen grasped Jason's hand and squeezed it.

"How about a fast car? Do you, like, have a fast car? Like a Ferrari?" Jennifer continued.

"I've driven some really fast cars, but I don't own one."

Jennifer resumed her position next to her mom. "I thought everybody out there had, like, a really fast car."

Kathleen was softly chuckling about Jason's comment. "Isn't it close to bed time, honey?" Kathleen asked as she gently tapped her fingertips on Jennifer's shoulder.

"I suppo-o-o-o-se." Jennifer sat up and started to get off the porch swing. "What are you guys gonna do?"

Kathleen touched her shoulder to Jason's. "I think we have a little catching up do to." Her voice sounded warm and inviting.

After giving her mother a quick good-night kiss, Jennifer gave Jason a bashful hug.

Jason leaned forward and returned the gesture, saying, "Boy, that was nice. Can I have one every time I come over?"

Jennifer looked up and nodded, then darted into the house. A short time later, she yelled out from her upstairs window, "Good night, Mom…and Jason. And yes, I brushed my teeth."

"Was it difficult to come back?" Jason gave the swing a little nudge with his foot. The gentle rocking motion felt good.

"In what way?"

"Ooh…like turning the clock back. Coming back to a small town."

"No…but I understand what you're getting at. I wasn't trying to relive any part of my past so much as I had this…uncontrollable urge to go back and start doing the things I should have done differently in the first place. There's a difference between reliving and rebuilding."

"Yeah. I suppose," Jason murmured.

"C'mon, Jason. You can't tell me you came all this way to look at some old bridges." With no warning, she stood, walked off the porch and glanced up at the window to Jennifer's bedroom. "Good. The lights out," she whispered as she returned to Jason's side. "Y'know? Every time we're together, the conversation seems to steer around to what my marriage to David was like, or to what you discovered at the bridge. Tonight, can we talk about what happened to you?"

"I'm not sure there's a lot to talk about."

"There's a story in there, Jason," she teased, while gently tapping her fingers on his forehead. "So. Open up." Kathleen curled her legs up and sat facing Jason.

Jason hesitated a few moments before whispering, "So many things happen in the early stages of your life that influence the direction your life will take, and you don't even realize those things are happening. It takes years of looking backward to find out where you messed up… and then, one day, it finally dawns on you that you've done so many things…but you've accomplished nothing."

"You have accomplished many things. How many bad guys are in jail because of you? How many lives were saved because those guys are not free to kill again?" Kathleen edged closer to Jason and looped her arm through his. With a teasing voice, she whispered, "But that's not what I wanted you to share with me."

"Oka-a-y? What's the topic?"

"Well, for a starter—I know, you told me about the woman who'd been killed during a robbery attempt—you never told me her name— but other than her, is there anyone else in your life I should know about?"

"No." There was a kind of hesitancy in his voice. "Not really."

"Don't mess with me, Jason. An answer like that could only mean there is, but you don't want to tell me about it."

"It's complicated."

"It's always complicated. That's what relationships are all about."

"There's another one."

"Whoa. This rings of intrigue. Am I gonna have to drag this out of you?"

"Marie. Marie Gallagher. She's the one who was killed."

"Jason. I'm so sorry." Kathleen's voice sounded soft and velvety. "I didn't mean to sound so callous. Do you want to talk about her?"

"Not really. Maybe some other time when I'm hammered."

"What about the second one?"

"The other is a woman who saved my life…in more ways than one."

"Whoa. This puts a whole new spin on it. Is she attractive?"

"Very…and married."

"Everything has its remedy."

"I've never heard it put so bluntly before."

"I'm sorry. Do you keep in touch with her? I mean, since you've been back here."

"No. I did leave a message for her telling her I arrived in one piece, but I feel a little uncomfortable sometimes." Jason flipped open his cell phone and showed Kathleen a picture of Dena with her arms wrapped around her German shepherd, Annie.

"Because?" Kathleen grabbed the cell from Jason and studied the photo of Dena.

"Duh…married. Personal conversations. Plus it's difficult for other reasons."

"Because?"

Jason pried the phone from Kathleen's hands. "Okay, damn it. There is something down deep within me that keeps tapping me on the shoulder. I feel we were brought together by death. First, her brother. Then Marie. And that's not how I want to think about it." Jason ran his fingers through his hair.

"What's her name?"

"Dena. Dena Manning."

Kathleen rested her hand on Jason's arm and gave it a tender squeeze. "So, this is my competition, huh?"

The tranquil evening was interrupted by the sound of wheels coming slowly down the pastoral road. Kathleen's street was situated on a fine dividing line between the vast farm land to the south and Vermilion's expanding urban boundaries. It was not uncommon to hear a carriage make its way home after an evening of prayer or possibly the settling of some internal disharmony. Usually, the Amish tried to ride either on or as close to the shoulder as possible to keep the horses hooves from being injured by the prolonged impact with the blacktop. Neither Jason nor Kathleen noticed the absence of the sound of hooves.

As the crunching noise on the gravel grew nearer, Kathleen, her eyes half closed, peered into the dim light for an indication of the source of the sound.

80

Just as the sound came close to the front of her house, the squeal of a starter motor shattered the still air, followed by an engine revving to what must have been close to six grand. A flash came through the front window of a car accompanied by a deafening report from a high powered rifle. Then another, and another.

Startled, Jason and Kathleen leapt up from the swing. Before either could manage a word, the car sped off into the night, not turning its lights on until well away from the house. The last sound they heard was the screech of tires as the vehicle swerved around the corner and disappeared from sight.

Shaken by the mysterious intrusion, Jason asked Kathleen if she was all right.

"Yeah…yeah." Unnerved by the gunfire, she brushed at her hair and pulled it away from the side of her face.

Jennifer leaned out the window and called down to her mother.

"Are you okay, honey?" Kathleen asked with a slight quiver in her voice.

"Yes. What was that?" Jennifer asked. Her voice sounded remarkably more controlled than either of the adults huddled on the porch.

Lights from nearby houses instantly lit up the neighborhood as their owners cautiously ventured onto their porches and peered into the night. Some addressed their neighbors while quietly voicing the same concern Jennifer had just asked.

"I don't know, Jennifer," Kathleen said. "Oh, God. Nothing like this has ever happened around here."

CHAPTER 10

Something about the visit with Kathleen bothered Jason as he drove the lonely road back to Windsor. Who would fire a high-powered weapon so close to her home? Was his presence just a coincidence? Was the barrage a warning shot across the bow for him? Kathleen is smart... and she cares. She cares not only about her community, but those who have preceded her and been forced out of a way of life by people she so brilliantly described as remote, uncaring, unsympathetic, and oft times ill-qualified to make life-altering decisions.

His mind drifted to the painting of the wolf in her living room, its eyes piercing into the viewer's very being as if it was right in front of you, staring you down in a challenge to the death. Whoever flinched first, lost.

The Loomis family was beginning to treat this visitor as one of their own. It did help a bit when he told them he'd spent his formative years here instead of an exclusive engagement on the fast-paced west coast. Another factor for his welcome may have been what had begun as a few days stay had turned into a week, something practically unheard of in such a hard-pressed area of the county.

It was late when Jason returned from Kathleen's house. He parked his van in the short gravel driveway next to the B & B, punched his remote and listened for the high-pitched chirping sound to indicate his alarm was activated.

The screen door to the main living area of the inn was unlatched—something which would be unheard of where he lived. The owners asked him to secure the latch if he came in late, not because of any danger from a criminal element, but for protection from the critters who thrived on nighttime activity. More than once, they'd been awakened to find a raccoon or two enjoying themselves near the counters after they'd managed to tease the cabinet doors open the same way they'd jimmied the front door. Innocent stares from those big brown eyes never compensated for the hours it took to clean up the mess.

As he climbed the stairs to his room, he mumbled, "This place must be a hundred years old, and none of these steps squeak. I bet I could bounce up and down on these things and nobody would even know I was here." He did bounce up and down a few times…and he was right.

Even though the sultry air hung heavily on his skin, he pulled a light sheet up around his neck to ward off any chill that might pierce deep into the night.

Crickets chirped loudly as the night wore on. Then as if controlled by a universal switch, they suddenly stopped. Jason enjoyed the quiet.

Long after the crickets had ceased their nightly serenade, Jason rolled around in his bed mulling over exactly what he'd been through since he'd come back, and with each thought, he'd switch positions, reshape his pillow with a few punches, then plop his head down and breath in the night air.

Just as he dropped off from sheer exhaustion, a blast from a firearm pierced the air, followed by yet another. His heart instantly raced as he bolted to the window and threw the curtains aside. He knew the sound was from a shotgun. The report from the rifle at Kathleen's had more of a sharp cracking sound when fired…this was more of a rounded tone peculiar to a different type of shell and charge. He peered out into the night and saw nothing, but heard the roar of an engine speeding off. Just as at Kathleen's, he noticed the driver turn on his driving lamps only after getting far enough from the scene. Jason sat on the edge of the bed knowing these two events were too similar and too interrelated to be written off as a mere coincidence. This was a warning shot across the bow.

AC/DC's driving intro to *Thunderstruck* was the ring tone he'd assigned to Ken Hutchinson. Jason rolled over in bed and studied the pattern, made by the morning sun and lacy curtains, on the wall. It looked like a 60's psychedelic, mono-toned version of a tie-die shirt. "Morning," he managed.

"You still in bed?"

Jason flung the covers off and leaped out of bed. "Nope. What's up?"

"You been down to the old wooden bridge lately?"

"No."

"So you didn't see the sign?"

"No."

"Hmmpf. It's been years since that old bridge has been considered impassable. For years, it's just been sitting there rotting away. Suddenly, it seems the historic bridge committee has declared it a priority."

"What do you mean?"

"It seems, my friend, that someone has gotten the ear of whoever makes decisions in that committee to begin renovation now—as in yesterday"

"Whoa. How'd that happen?"

"Well, according to routine policy, the Avery bridge has been a low priority. You know what dictates what bridges get first attention? Traffic. If any of those old bridges are on some major artery where traffic movement is a major concern, it happens. If it's even visible from a major roadway, it happens because it's a tourist attraction. The Avery bridge falls under none-of-the-above. So, who would you guess has the horsepower to jump start the bridge renovation?"

"DE?"

"Definite possibility."

"So, what happens from here on?"

"Historically, they could legitimize a different spin on any of these bridges, depending on its state of deterioration. That's where it gets tricky."

"Go."

"Sometimes, bridge renovation amounts to nothing more than upgrading key components in the support beams and trusses, especially the ones where they come in direct contact with the ground. That's when the responsible engineers determine there's not too much structurally wrong with the bridge itself. The other end of the spectrum is to have it declared structurally unsound from head to toe, draw up detailed diagrams of the way it was originally built...then demolish the entire bridge and start from scratch."

"What's the sign say?"

"Take a wild guess."

"What happens to all the wood?"

"Probably winds up in someone's fireplace."

"Evidence goes up in smoke, huh?"

"Except for one important fact. We still have those pictures we took inside the bridge. You still have the *pics*, right?"

"Sure do. Stored them on my thumb drive."

"Good. You hang on to those. No matter what happens to that bridge, those *pics* are our only proof those initials exist...or existed. Anyone else know about those pictures?"

"No." Jason felt in his pockets since he had a propensity for shoving little electronic devices in them and forgetting they were there. "What about the forensic expert from Columbus you told me about? The one who examined the initials."

"That was an official request, Jason, filled through official channels. If someone has the horsepower to trigger any activity on that particular bridge, then maybe those reports and pictures can conveniently become lost, too. Connections, Jason...connections. That's what it's all about."

"You don't have a copy of the forensic report?"

"Hmmpf...no. It was a verbal over the phone. He said he'd send the stuff, but I never received anything."

"Does stuff come to you directly or through...?"

"Usually through what we call an evidence clerk, but I've never received a hard copy."

Since coming back to the area, Jason felt as if he'd been skating though life on slick ice just as he'd done years ago, when challenges arose and dares were thrown down, and caution meant nothing. But life is more like getting a large box on your birthday, and when opened, you find there are no instructions inside, only miscellaneous panels and a wide assortment of confusing hardware. Only then do you notice the warning on the outside proclaiming *some assembly required* accompanied by a no-return policy. "Doesn't it seem rather odd that so much official documentation is finding its way into the trash bin?"

"Sure does. Hey, I'd better be going. The sheriff has me doing some standard patrol duty. Seems law enforcement is not immune from budgetary constraints, either. We've had a substantial cutback in personnel of late. Anyhow…I just wanted to touch bases with you regarding the bridge. I honestly don't know how to stop this renovation project. Once those gears are set in motion, it's a bureaucratic nightmare to even find out who's actually in charge."

"Humor me on this one. Have there been any reports of random gunshots in the last few days around this area?"

"Yeah…yeah, there has. Why would you ask?"

Jason fumbled for some well-chosen words. "I was at Kathleen Ellison's house last night, and someone fired three rounds from a high-powered rifle directly in front of her house—scared the crap out of all of us, and probably the neighbors, too. Then last night, someone fired a shotgun, both barrels, where I'm staying. I didn't think too much about it at Kathleen's, but it was too coincidental the second time on the same night."

"We did receive a report of suspicious activity last night out your way."

"Yeah. Since I first contacted you, did you happen to enter my name in your *dailies*?"

"On the first one, I did, but once the boss man set me loose on the Mueller case, I don't recall entering it again. Why?"

"I just wonder how visible I am on someone's radar."

"Does Kathleen Ellison know where you're staying?"

"Kinda."

"That's not a good answer."

"She knows I'm staying in Windsor, okay? But she doesn't know exactly where."

"Yeah, that's up for grabs," Ken said with restrained sarcasm. "I hope I don't have to spell this out for you…but I believe you're being sent a message. And whoever's sending that message, knows where you are, and they know when you're there. We haven't had a single incident like this in years, or as long as I can remember, then you show up and bingo, cold files are reopened, bridge priorities get magically upgraded, and people start using county roads as firing ranges. Someone has connections."

"DE?"

"I don't believe what's been going on around here is random gunfire, Jason. Someone who has a lot of clout doesn't want you around."

◊　　◊　　◊

Recent budgetary issues brought forth by the county commissioners placed an unbalanced burden on Sheriff Phelps' department. After the cutbacks, the sheriff had no other alternative than to temporarily reassign Ken Hutchinson to patrol duty. Ken understood this had not been an easy decision for the sheriff, but at least he still had a source of income. Ken still kept his note pad in the front seat of the Crown Vic. For awhile, at least, he'd had the opportunity to wear civilian clothes rather than the black shirt, gray pants, and the matching gray tie of the Ashtabula County Sheriff's Office. "Oh well, I saved myself some hefty cleaning bills," he mumbled to himself. Soon, he would be back on the Mueller case.

His first assignment from the Road Lieutenant was to nab after-work partiers who tried to navigate the narrow country roads using diminished driving skills. After so many citations and DUI indictments had been logged, statisticians at the local rag wondered, in bold print no less, how certain people managed to find enough money to drink every night, but then had the nerve to complain because they couldn't afford health insurance.

That's where Ken fit the sheriff's objective now. Waiting.

Just outside the town of Jefferson, Ken tucked in amongst a small grove of maple trees on a section of road a columnist for the same rag had satirically labeled as an *alternate means of population control.*

Ken kept his windows rolled up to retain a semblance of warmth. An Amish carriage plodded down the shoulder with a man and woman inside the protective canopy. She wore a black prayer covering. Could this unmarried woman have been Friedel Mueller twenty-five years ago on the way home from a meeting with Jonathon Ditmann? Ken gave a subtle wave at the couple, but received no bowing of the head in return.

A few seconds later, two sets of headlights appeared from the north. The first cruised by at a reasonable speed—even swung into the far lane to give the Amish couple ample clearance. The second slowed down considerably when the luminescent placard of the buggy came into view. Both disappeared from sight beyond the trees.

It was quiet. Ken leaned his head on the headrest and stared at the stitching in the ceiling panel. "Now I remember why stakeouts are so boring," he grumbled. A tapping sound on his window brought him back into the real world. Ken lowered his driver's side window and broke out into a casual smile. "Whoa. I never expected to see you out here?"

A flash lit up the area for a split second. When the bullet struck Hutchinson in the temple, he crumpled sideways in the seat. Through the window, the business end of a 9mm Glock probed the body for signs of life. Two more shots were fired.

CHAPTER 11

A little after noon, Jason pulled his Chevy alongside the edge of the road in front of Kathleen's house. Wet leaves were scattered on the ground, some driven into small piles as they were hurled up against the raised edging of the cement walkway.

She was waiting for him on the small stone porch while briskly rubbing her hands up and down her exposed skin. Grasping his hands, Kathleen said, "Hi. I'm glad you're back."

"Me, too."

"You know? It wasn't very nice of me last night…"

"What do you mean?"

Kathleen slipped her arm through Jason's and guided him into the living room. "Last night, I would have felt safer knowing you were close to me…us."

"About last night…" Jason began.

"We have so much to talk about." She put her fingers to his lips and whispered she'd be right back. When she returned, she was wearing a flimsy black dress perfect for this type of weather, and perfect if the wearer was not intending to venture out into public. She looked stunning. Her dark eyes glistened as she slowly pivoted around in front of Jason, anxiously awaiting his approval. "What do you think?"

With a slight reddening of his face, Jason muttered a breathy, "Who-oa."

When Kathleen laughed, she had a flair for turning what might be considered a humorous moment into a provocative moment. She slipped down next to Jason and whispered in his ear, "Anything special you'd like for lunch?"

Jason mustered up all the fortitude he could, and in a shaky voice, responded with a feeble "Whatever." In an instant, Jason experienced a flashback to his Navy days when he'd slip his thumbs inside the belt loops of his pants and grin when his shipmates referred to him as the *walking tripod*.

"Am I being too obvious?" Kathleen whispered with pouted lips.

With a sheepish look, Jason said, "I…uuh…feel a bit awkward." Jason resisted the impulse to mention Dena Manning's name, what she meant to him, and the fact that he'd been resisting every impulse to call her. He backed away.

"I'm sorry. I'm so sorry." Kathleen curled her legs up under her and faced Jason. "It's been so long since I've seen you. I thought maybe…"

"It's a visit, Kathleen. That's all," Jason explained as he looked into her eyes, now slightly reddened from embarrassment. "Can we talk?"

"Sure…sure." Her whisper tapered off into a dark, cryptic void. There was a kind of coldness to her voice as she moved to the opposite end of the couch and leaned against a decorator pillow. Her black satin dress hid very little of her legs, which she amplified by crossing them… slowly. "What would you like to talk about?"

Jason couldn't help it when his eyes gravitated south. She looked good in lavender, too. "Your life maybe?"

After letting out a long sigh, Kathleen muttered, "You want to know something about my life? It sucks. Big time. I'm college educated— that was my success story. Beyond college…let's see. We have a failed marriage…small nondescript house in a small nondescript, going nowhere town…position in a museum where we're blessed with a hundred visitors a year…no man in my life worth a damn…and the closest thing I have to a family is my stupid cousin in Jefferson who hasn't had an original thought as long as I've known him."

"I would consider Jennifer a huge part of your family."

Kathleen brushed the comment away as if swatting flies. "Yeah. She *has* to stay with me." She stared out the window for a few seconds. "I'm sorry. I didn't mean to appear hostile or self-centered, but what I'm feeling is scared. Really scared, Jason. Naturally, Jennifer is part of my life. When you told me you were a cop, I thought about this…

situation…you've put us all in, and if any of this leads to David, then it means it will also find its way back to Jennifer. I'm not sure I know how to deal with this. I feel like I'm losing control."

Jason wondered how many people look back at their lives and wonder what would have happened had they opted for the *other* road. His thoughts bounced back and forth between Kathleen and Dena. With both, he wished the relationship could have been founded under entirely different circumstances. "Will you let me help?"

"Yeah. Answer this for me. If those are truly David's initials at the old bridge, then what the hell was he doing with me? Do you remember Friedel? I mean, really remember her."

"I think I do. What are you getting at?"

Kathleen told Jason about an incident when Friedel happened by while David had his arm around her. "She seemed to be glaring at both David and me, but she kept on walking. At first I wondered why the stinging look, but quickly wrote it off as maybe she was passing judgment about someone else's concept of social respectability." Kathleen brushed at her hair with her fingertips and made a semicircular move around her ear as if she was trying to persuade her hair to stay wedged behind it. "Don't you wonder why the media hasn't jumped at this revelation of yours? It has headlines written all over it."

"Funny you should mention that. I've been in contact with a county deputy who's been looking into this case…"

"Because of you," Kathleen added.

"Guilty. The point is; we both agreed it would be best to keep the investigation quiet. If the media ever did grab hold of this, it would become Ohio's answer to the OJ trial. So, until we feel we've latched onto some solid information, this is all speculative."

"I suppose I'm glad there's no…*breaking news*…regarding David. And it would be breaking news. Our illustrious governor wouldn't take kindly to a member of his inner circle being paraded before his constituents as a suspected murderer."

It was decision time for Jason. Years can do much for numbing the senses to the point where rational thoughts are heard only by the ear and not by the soul—much like those who go to a concert and listen to all the notes, but never hear the melody. "I have something to tell you, so please try to understand. The gunfire we experienced out front last night was only the beginning." He reached for Kathleen's hands. "When I got back to where I'm staying, there was more."

Kathleen let out a short gasp.

"I believe I have become a target. Those shots were a warning to me to get the hell away from here. Anyone I come in contact with is a potential victim-by-association. I could never do this to you or Jennifer."

"What are you saying?"

"I intend to stay away from here until this thing is put to bed."

"Don't do this to me, Jason."

"Listen. Right now, there are very few people I trust, and the ones I do trust are not exactly the Rambo type. I've made a commitment to resolve this thing with Friedel. And I have to follow through with this."

Kathleen shifted closer to Jason and rested her hand on his leg. "You want to hear something sweet? When Jennifer spent the night at Beth's, she had a major conversation with the other kids about you."

"This is good. Right?"

"She confessed to me how handsome she thought you were… worldly, I think is what she said…and that I was all googly-eyed when you came in."

"You weren't all googly-eyed, were you?"

Her voice sparkled. "Somewhat…maybe…probably." When Kathleen placed her hand on Jason's arm, she didn't look at him. Instead, she stared over his shoulder into the distance for a moment, but then in a slow deliberate manner, she fixed her eyes on Jason. "Do you ever wonder why certain people are together? When I was with David, I felt like I was a valued commodity who could help him get where he wanted to go. I never hated David for being what he is, but now I find myself on the verge of having to hate him…if what you've brought up is true."

"It's like having to cope with questions, isn't it?" The dimmed lamp on the end table illuminated her sad eyes. "What I mean is; questions others ask you are never as painful as the questions you ask yourself."

◊　　◊　　◊

On the way back to the B & B, Jason drove through town past the old Grange hall, its white paint now peeled and chipped, and its black-trimmed windows boarded over. Many times, he'd sat in on town meetings there, either as an interested member of the community, or as part of an assignment for a civics class. As he surveyed the neglected building, he thought maybe a few things really had changed.

So rare it was, to be afforded the opportunity to return to a time in his life which seemed so much simpler. Where walking to school on a quiet country road was commonplace. Where talking to a stranger was not life-threatening, or where shopping meant going to a small store owned by the relatives of a classmate, and your name was your credit line. At least, that had been his goal until he noticed the initials at the bridge.

As he approached the Loomis' B & B, he noticed the lights in the parlor were still lit. This was rather unusual. Jason chuckled to himself when he recalled them using the term, *parlor*, when he first came there. He would have said *living room*, but after looking at the dedication to their restoration of crown moldings and oak framed archways, all highly varnished, he changed his mindset and honored their term. Besides, it had a certain nostalgic ring to it he'd grown accustomed to.

Since the incident with the late-night gunfire, they'd grown close, even looking to Jason as a kind of protector in this bizarre chain of events. The ritual he'd come to consider normal when he arrived was, the Loomis' would quickly withdraw into their own rooms or into the basement where they'd set up temporary living quarters. After all, this was *his* house for the time being. Tonight was not one of those nights.

Somewhat embarrassed, they confided in Jason of their son's involvement with other boys his age getting into some minor scrapes with the law as a result of boring summer evenings with nothing to do. Sitting around an old mahogany coffee table covered with outdated magazines fanned out for an interesting effect, they asked Jason for his advice, and about what he'd done to be productive when faced with those same challenges years ago.

Doug Loomis sat across from Jason, while irritating his parents with the traditional eye-rolling routine.

Jason lied through his teeth. Although he'd been a good student and capable of semi-rational thought processes, Jason shared a kind of bond with Doug when he saw the same gleam in his eyes he'd had so often when he first thought of himself as a walking tripod. He talked of family-ordered chores that kept him busy long into the night, or tutoring the mentally challenged fringe element of the jocks he hung out with. That is, "If I wasn't burdened enough with homework of my own." And then there were the sports. He loved basketball and football, but he purposely skirted tales of his favorite game of all, the one where he and Nicole played hide-the-weenie.

Doug fidgeted while ignoring the penetrating looks from his parents.

"There's only one way to gain maturity," Jason said, "and that's to wait it out. But in the meantime…"

A shotgun burst rattled the decorative dishes so carefully positioned in an antique hutch. Then the other barrel cut loose. Outside, the roar of a powerful V8 pierced the night and the squeal of tires ripped through the walls like paper.

Mr. Loomis raced to the window, while his wife screamed at him to stay away from it. "Son's of bitches," he yelled out.

Doug pumped his arm in the air and shouted, "Du-ude."

The gunfire was like an earthquake for Jason. By the time you realize what's happening, it's all over. "Let's back away from the window, everyone, okay?" He slipped his hand under Mr. Loomis's arm and coaxed him back to the sofa. "We have no idea what this is all about." Again, Jason knew he was lying through his teeth, but seeing the look of panic on Mrs. Loomis' face, he believed it was for a good cause. The first time this happened here, he couldn't even write it off as a bizarre coincidence, but this time it validated his belief that someone knew exactly who he was, where he was living, and more importantly, his intent to stay.

Mrs. Loomis sat with her face buried in her hands. "First, the deputy, then this," she moaned.

"What? What's this about a deputy?" Jason asked.

Mrs. Loomis waved her hands in front of her face. "Oh, it was on the news this evening. One of our deputies was found shot to death up near Jefferson."

"Details," Jason said as he waved his hands around in small circles. "Details."

"I don't remember too much, do you, honey?" Mrs. Loomis said.

"I'll settle for a name," Jason said.

"Oh, golly," Mr. Loomis said. "It was Len, or Ken, or something like that."

"Was it Ken? Ken Hutchinson?"

"Yes. That was the name," Mr. Loomis said. "Seems he was found by some of the Amish folk who happened by—said they became a little suspicious when they noticed the window open, and no one around."

"Hmmph. I'd 'a kept on goin'," Doug said in a blasé tone of voice. "Guy was probably out takin' a leak behind some trees."

"You think this is funny?" Jason barked at Doug.

"Well, probably not, I suppose," Doug said, almost whimpering as Jason stood nose to nose with him.

"Did they mention exactly where this deputy was found?" Jason asked the Loomis'.

"Not really. Just outside Jefferson someplace," Mr. Loomis said, and then spun around to face Doug. "I think you owe Mr. Carmichael an apology, son."

"Sorry," Doug said in a drawn-out, dull tone.

The prescriptive apology was a nice touch, but Jason knew it was just a practical scheme to avoid having to endure some sort of punishment by the parents. "Did you hear about this on TV or the radio?"

"On the radio. We heard it while we were fixing supper," Mrs. Loomis said. "Why?"

"Just a thought." Jason cast a hard look at Doug. "Did the news report describe the scene where the body was found?"

"Nope," Mrs. Loomis said. "It was probably kinda gruesome, anyhow. Glad they didn't."

Jason pulled the drapes open and looked up and down the little two-lane blacktop in front of the B & B. Reflections from the porch light made the slick parts of the tar on the roadway glisten like puddles of water. Everything else looked dark. "Look. I'm gonna go upstairs and get some sleep. I suggest you do the same."

The Loomis' said a worried "Good night," to Jason. Doug gave a short, emotionless wave.

"Good night," Jason mumbled and climbed the steps.

While brushing his teeth, Jason stared into the mirror, knowing he would have to find out more about the site where Ken was killed.

What had he gotten himself into? Jason spit into the sink and rinsed it down the drain. "I'm so stupid," he muttered to his reflection. "I've gotten myself into this shit and all my hardware is sitting in Szabo's desk back in Fresno. And who am I going to trust here?"

◊　　◊　　◊

Now here he was, sitting on the edge of the bed gazing at the streaks of morning light as it filtered through the lace curtains. Jason looked out the window at the fields and woods that seemed to be in a perpetual state of production. In early spring, taps would be driven into the maple trees, and onto those shiny spigots, galvanized buckets would be hung to collect the sweet sap which dripped ever so slowly. The contents of those buckets would later fill vats in sheds and when cured, embellish many stacks of pancakes or French toast, or become the essence for many candies to be formed into different shapes and sold at local festivals, much to the delight of every dentist within a hundred miles.

Outside his door was the Saturday morning Cleveland Plain Dealer. Wearing only his shorts, he stuck his head out to see if anyone was around before he opened the door any wider. Seeing no one, he quickly reached for the paper and retreated to a small table near the window. The incident about Ken made headlines—ASHTABULA DEPUTY FOUND DEAD. Beside the header was a picture of Ken wearing the class-A uniform of the Sheriff's Office.

He hadn't had his coffee yet, but there were more important things to think about. The article gave a detailed description of the scene. It even featured a shot taken from about fifty feet away, by a staff photographer, of the county's black Crown Vic.

Jason focused on the blown-up photo of the car, pointed business end out, amongst some trees in the background. The second thing he noticed was the apparent lack of glass fragments near the car which meant his window was probably rolled down when the assault took place. But why would his window have been lowered? The article cited the police estimated time of death to be around eight last night. From recent experience, Jason knew the temps would have been in the low sixties at best. Definitely not the type of weather you'd sit around in, especially with a window lowered, waiting to see if someone comes zipping by.

Jason repositioned the Plain Dealer under the light streaming in the window to get a better look at the photo. Another feature in the photo which struck him as odd was the lack of tangential holes in the door or support posts. This indicated Ken had been shot at close range with a hand gun or rifle, definitely not a shotgun pattern here, nor was this the result of an ambush style assault. In all probability, Jason guessed Ken had been killed by someone he not only knew, but knew well enough to allow the shooter to get so close.

With a heartfelt apology to the Loomis family, Jason skipped his usual prepared breakfast. Before exiting through the kitchen door, he took another look at Doug and his unkempt morning *look*, hoping to spot anything that may have gone unnoticed last night. Nothing. A blank stare through eyes at half mast. Jason wondered if this kid ever did any homework.

Before pushing the screen door open, Jason patted his shirt pocket to make sure he had his cell with him.

It took him only about fifteen minutes to drive to the old covered bridge. Traffic? What traffic? This was prime time commute hours. Most of the traffic here was in fields, far from being an obstruction on the two-lane blacktop.

Stumps at the bridge were covered with a light layer of morning dew. Jason parked facing the entrance and focused his attention on the sign attached to the wood framing announcing the start of the renovation project. Contained on the ornate placard was a detailed breakdown of what percentage of the total expenditures would be covered by various state and county agencies, as well as contributions from numerous private donors who felt not only a responsibility, but a sense of civic pride to not allow a slice of their world to fade uncaringly into oblivion.

On the placard, Jason noticed an apparent lack of monetary involvement by the state's historical bridge society. Maybe it was buried in the internal politicizing within the counties bureaucracy. Nevertheless, there was no specific breakout of funding on the notice. He could use this to his advantage later, if need be. How and under what circumstances, he didn't quite know...yet.

Jason was surprised the name David Ellison did not appear at the bottom of the edict, but it was the governor who was eulogized. "Oh, well, David, ol' buddy. We're gonna have a little talk."

Before exiting the van, Jason stared at the covered bridge wondering what kind of trouble he'd gotten himself into. Had he made the right decision about Kathleen and Jennifer yesterday? Hell, yes. He didn't think of himself as the bravest of men, but neither had he ever run away from a fight. His father's words about confrontations always stuck with him. *Never fight for pride alone, for the very essence of pride is fraught with contradictions,* he'd remind him over and over.

After Jason had been subjected to enough back-street philosophy to make him puke, he'd jibe his dad about the use of the word, fraught. *No one ever uses fraught in a sentence,* he'd say as he'd take a friendly swing at his dad's arm. *They do too use fraught,* his father would counter. It never took long before they'd be engaged in a wrestling match to try to disprove the other's point of view until his mom would toss them both outside.

Jason climbed out of the Chevy and entered a number on his cell. "Hi," he said. "Can you talk?"

"Can I talk? Hell yes, I can talk. Where have you been? What have you been up to? Why haven't you called me?"

Dena's voice was more refreshing than the smell of the nearby cornfields. Her words rang of smiles, and the memories of her squinty eyes when she'd become excited or upset made the distance seem so much closer. He wished she was sitting next to him right now. "I…I've been kinda busy."

"Busy? You were going back there to relax. Why can't you relax? What's so damned important to get you all tensed up? You sound tense, you know that? Why haven't you returned any of my calls? All I hear is your stupid voice saying, *Yo. You know the drill,* followed by the stupid beep. I've called you a jillion times."

"You called three times."

"Okay. Maybe I exaggerated a little."

"Which one of your questions should I answer first?"

"Oka-ay. Let's slow down."

Jason waited through the lengthy sound of a deep breath being taken. He could almost feel her gentle breath on his face.

"Hi. Where are you?" Her voice sounded like velvet.

"A little town called Windsor," he whispered back.

"Would it have been so difficult to give me a call?" Dena's flame was lit again. "No-o-o. You have to make me worry myself sick. You know what my fingernails look like? Do you? They're down to nubs. I'm gonna have to spend a fortune to get them back to normal. God, I can't believe you, Jason."

Jason chuckled. "Nice to hear from you. I wish you were here. Sorry about the nails. I need you to do me a favor." He thought he'd slip this last one in before she rearmed.

"What?"

"I need you to go talk to my boss in Fresno. Name's Yacek Szabo. Your friend, Owen Wheeler will vouch for you if there's any problem."

"What do you want me to do?"

"I'd like my badge back, and my credentials, too. I'd like my sidearm, but that ain't gonna happen through the mail."

"What good is your badge going to do back there? You're slightly out of your jurisdiction, aren't you?"

"It's a hell of a lot better than flashing my driver's license at someone."

"Why do you need this stuff? The last time we talked, you were going to go lie in some cornfields and stare at clouds."

"There's a...a kind of situation here, and I sort of involved myself with a kinda investigation, and I would kinda like to see it through."

"Jason. Are you in trouble?"

"No. I think. Kinda."

"Are you in danger?"

"No. I think."

"Stop stroking me, Jason. What have you gotten yourself into?"

Jason filled Dena in about the initials at the bridge, the contact with Ken Hutchinson, and the discovery of the Medico-legal form that disappeared from all official record keepers—either by private firms or as a matter of course at the site where the report was originated, the Mueller clan and especially, Friedel's death. He deliberately left out the details of Ken's untimely demise yesterday.

"When do you need this stuff?"

"Soon," Jason said. "I don't have too much time to waste. I have a feeling things are going to get nasty around here...soon."

"Do you want me to come back there? I will, you know. I'm your partner, in case you've forgotten."

"No. Absolutely not, But thanks for the thought." He rattled off the Loomis' address. "Just make sure the package is addressed to me."

"I will. I'll get on this first thing Monday. Okay?"

"Okay. How's Dave doing?"

"He misses his uncle a lot." Her voice softened. "He doesn't talk too much about what happened. Truthfully, I don't know if he can comprehend all that happened, but he looks at pictures of Jerry we have around the house and just stares. It breaks my heart."

"Does your husband try to...?"

"Clay doesn't do too much of anything except work. But that's a whole other story I don't want to go into."

Her voice had a callous ring to it.

"Can I ask you a question?"

"Anything."

"When you were with Marie, I know you bonded with her children..."

"John and Kathy."

"Yeah. This may sound cruel of me to ask, but here goes. Did you ever ask yourself whether you were in love with Marie, or were you in love with the thought of having a family?"

"Say again. You're breaking up." He checked the bars on his cell. Three.

"I asked you a question about..."

"I'm getting near a dead zone. Please send the package. Bye."

Gazing at the bridge, he again focused on the present and wondered if Ken had been right about someone wanting him out of the way. If that was true, then how long would it be before those gun barrels were lowered from the vertical to the horizontal?

CHAPTER 12

The last time Jason visited the Mueller farm, he'd experienced a slight agitation in Isaac's demeanor. There was a positive side to this minor confrontation. Under most circumstances, people who have something to hide lean heavily into congeniality in hopes they can remain off the radar.

He parked under the ancient beech tree in front of the Mueller home. This time, there was no rain or soggy ruts to negotiate around. He tapped on the front door.

"Good afternoon, Mr. Carmichael," Elizabeth said with a weary smile.

"I'm really sorry to just show up like this, but I don't know how else to get in contact with you...and Joshua Stoudt...and Isaac."

"You could call Joshua if you wish. He has our community telephone at his house. We are permitted some modern conveniences," she added with a brighter smile, "although the device is available to all of us."

"Thanks. Might you know the number?"

"No, but I will send my grandson to fetch him." She swung the front door open and stepped onto the porch. A dusting of powder floated to the deck when she slapped her hands on her dress.

"Yes, please...and Isaac, too, if you don't mind."

Elizabeth called for Benjamin who seemed to be the right age to assume the roll of *gofer*—too young to lift anything heavy—too old to be considered useless. Gofer fit.

The boy could really run. Jason watched him charge off across the front yard. Well trained, he waited before dashing across the road. In a few minutes, he returned while reversing all the safety procedures he'd been taught. Jason thanked him with a firm handshake.

"Now, Benjamin," Mrs. Mueller added. "Please find your father. I think he may be in the main barn."

Again, the lad pulled his wide-brimmed hat tightly to his long golden hair and lit out for the barn, taking care to run in front of a horse tethered to a post near the barn's entrance. Benjamin stopped short, gave the horse a quick pat on the under side of his neck, and scurried inside.

"He's an energetic young man, Mrs. Mueller."

"Yes, he is. Thank you. He is so anxious to help in the fields, but he'll get his wish in time."

Isaac appeared in the shadows of the double doors leading into the barn. He slapped at his coveralls with his hat and started for the house, wearing the same determined look Jason encountered the last time he was here.

Joshua arrived in his carriage and hitched the horse to the weathered post under the shade tree. "Good afternoon, Mr. Carmichael," he said while offering Jason an outstretched hand.

Jason studied the carriage for a moment before he ran his fingers along its surface. "Good afternoon to you." With furrowed brow, he asked, "Fiberglass?"

"Oh, yes. Lasts much longer than wood. You seem puzzled."

"Uh, yeah. I suppose I've always thought of these as wood."

"We do not categorically reject modern technology." Joshua grasped Jason's hand again and offered him a confident smile.

To Jason, Joshua's hand not only felt like a brick, but had the texture of number-ten sandpaper. "I'm glad you're all here. There is something I'd like to share with you, and it's not pretty." He looked into each of their faces. "Have you heard the news about the county deputy who was killed Thursday night?"

"No, we haven't," Joshua said. "We try to keep our distance."

Jason studied the three sitting on the edge of the porch. "I feel the distance you speak of is going to become a lot closer very quickly. The deputy who was killed was working with me on Friedel's case. I was the one who contacted him. I was the one who found and pointed out suspicious initials at the covered bridge. And I was the one who mentioned the Medico-legal document you have in your possession." Jason took a deep breath. "At this moment, I have no idea why I'm still alive."

They all let out a short gasp, but it was Elizabeth who rested her hand on Jason's arm.

"Look. I've stirred up some things in this county. That's the good part. The bad part is; I've put you people in danger. That document you have hidden somewhere is a crucial piece of evidence, and I know the person responsible for Friedel's death does not want this investigation to continue. And this person will stop at nothing. Deputy Ken Hutchinson was a good man. He cared about what he was doing, and he cared about all of you."

"I know this to be true," Elizabeth said. "The man who came here yesterday was very sympathetic to finding Friedel's killer. And he…"

"There was a man here yesterday?" Jason asked. "Did he give you his name?"

"No. Well, maybe he did," Elizabeth said in a low voice. "I just don't remember it."

"Was this man wearing a uniform?" Jason knelt in front of the trio.

"Why didn't you tell me of this?" Joshua asked Elizabeth.

"I didn't know what to do. The man seemed concerned."

"Was the man wearing a uniform?" Jason repeated.

"No," Elizabeth said. "He was wearing a suit. And he drove a big car—a big white car."

"Did you happen to notice what kind of car it was, Mrs. Mueller? The manufacturer's name or logo is usually on the trunk or the hood."

"No. I didn't think to look."

"How did he introduce himself?"

"I don't think he gave me a name. He just said he was here to verify we still have the legal document in our possession. I didn't trust him. I don't know why."

"Did he try to persuade you to release the document to him?"

"No. Not really. He mentioned that it was technically property of the state and I had no legal right to have it."

"That is bul…!" Jason bit at his lip. "That is not true. Trust me. That report is yours. Did he make any threats, veiled or otherwise?"

"I don't understand," Elizabeth said.

"A direct threat means give it to me now or you die. A veiled threat is where words are carefully chosen to appear less threatening. Such as, *You don't have to give me the document, but if you were to hand it over now, I can recommend you not be held accountable for a federal offense.* They try to make you think they're doing you a favor."

"The second one," Elizabeth said.

"Yeah. That's what a politician would do." Jason reached into his rear pocket. "Most people will show you their badge, some sort of credentials, or ID to prove who they are and what branch of law enforcement they represent. Did he furnish you with a business card? They look kinda like this." Jason showed the last of his own personal cards from the Fresno County Sheriff's Office he'd kept in his wallet. It wasn't official, but it was better than nothing. "Keep it."

"No. He just wanted to know if we still have the document." Elizabeth began to fidget. "Did I do something wrong?" She first looked at Jason and then to Isaac.

Under normal circumstances, Jason would have uttered a muted, *Oh shit*, but kept the remark to himself. This man knows the doc exists. Obviously, he was priming the pump before turning the water on. "Did he ask you where you keep the report?"

"Yes," Elizabeth whispered.

Another, *Oh shit*, would normally surface here. "You didn't…"

"My mother is not stupid, Mr. Carmichael."

"Sorry, but I have to ask the question." He turned to Elizabeth again. "Did you tell him?"

"No, I didn't…because I don't know where it is. You told us before to let only one person know of its whereabouts. I am not that person."

Jason breathed deeply. He felt the Muellers would be safe, but whoever this person was would undoubtedly try the same tactic on others. It was just a question of getting to the right person, and getting to them quickly. Who would be next? "Can you give me a general description of what this man looked like?"

Elizabeth studied Isaac for moment. "A little shorter than my son. Stocky build. Kind of gray hair…cut very short on the sides. Looked rather athletic. Big shoulders—like he'd been working in the fields, but no tan face. I can't recall much more. To be honest with you, when I don't trust someone, I cannot look at them."

"Do you think you would recognize this person if you saw him again?"

"Probably. Oh...and he parted his hair right in the middle, not to the side like others."

Jason jotted the general description in his notepad.

"You said this deputy who was helping you has been killed," Joshua said. "What makes you think his death has anything to do with Friedel?"

"Too coincidental, Mr. Stoudt. You're right to question my opinion, but from my experience, when things seem too coincidental, they're not." Jason felt all three of them were analyzing him as a prospective car buyer would do just before signing on the dotted line, wondering whether this purchase is really worth it. In this case, a used detective is worth much more than one right off the assembly line.

"What should we do about this stranger, Mr. Carmichael?" Joshua asked. "The one who Elizabeth distrusts."

"Good question. In all probability, there will be a funeral for Deputy Hutchinson. I firmly believe he was killed by someone he knew, or knew of. If this is the case, then this person could possibly be present at the funeral. If this person stayed away, it would be a giveaway. Usually, when a member of law enforcement is killed, the community shows up to honor him or her. It wouldn't seem too farfetched for a member of the Amish community to attend. Would you be willing to go to the funeral?"

Elizabeth scanned her son and Joshua. The nods were slow, but positive.

While she dabbed at her eyes, Jason whispered, "For the funeral, we can all go together, if you feel you need support from those close to you, Mrs. Mueller." Jason extended his arm in the direction of his van. "It seats at least four in the back."

"We can do this," Joshua said. "If this will help, then we must do our share."

"Then it's settled," Jason said. "When I find out when and where, I will give you a call, or stop by. Your choice."

"A call will be sufficient, Mr. Carmichael." Joshua rattled off the communal phone number. "But you are welcome to stop by, if you so choose."

After jotting the number down in his notepad, Jason faced the group again. "I have one more question. Do you ever associate with Jonathon Ditmann?"

"We attend the same services," Joshua said.

"Do you have any negative feelings for him?"

"Why would you ask such a question?" Isaac fired back. "He is one of us."

"Have you seen any of his woodworking projects? From what I've seen, they are pure works of art."

"So?"

"It was just a question, Isaac. I'm interested to know what the general feeling was in the community when Friedel turned him down. Was it considered an insult? Was he humiliated in front of his community?"

"Well, of course he was hurt, in a mental kind of way," Isaac said. "Who wouldn't be? He'd made a beautiful clock for her. He'd done everything right and proper."

"Did he ever show any anger toward Friedel because of her decision?" Jason asked Isaac.

"He shot one of his herd. That's all."

"Why would he...?"

"We are dairy people, Mr. Carmichael. If a cow gives birth to a male, some within our society believe it is perfectly acceptable to kill it. It was a young bull. Males do not produce milk, they only consume food—food for those who can supply us with milk." Isaac shrugged his shoulders. "Simple."

"Thank you all for your help. I will be in touch regarding the funeral for Deputy Hutchinson. And I am concerned about this visitor you had. If I were you, I would keep my guns loaded...and handy." He patted Mrs. Mueller's hand. "I don't have to tell you this, but look after each other."

CHAPTER 13

A perfect day for shopping. Monday afternoon, gloomy, overcast, mild temps. What Jason needed couldn't be found at the local mall, nor purchased with a credit card. This was a strictly cash-only acquisition. What Jason needed was protection from Friedel's killer, who he was now convinced knew all his intentions, his whereabouts, and his resolve to pursue this problem until the end. Jason was the threat who had to be eliminated.

Twenty-five years later, the bad part of Cleveland was still the bad part of Cleveland. Jason eased the Chevy van down a street where cars fell into two classifications—dilapidated and pristine. Missing fenders, graffiti, broken windows with plywood duct-taped in place, and bald tires defined most. The one which would be defined as pristine was owned by the one person feared most by all the others. He was the one who owned the territory. This was his world and everyone knew it. His car was both a symbol and a tribute to his place in this tiny corner of a merciless world where outsiders could disappear with no witnesses. Even the people who lived here didn't want to come here.

Garbage cans did not exist in this area, only black plastic bags dumped at the curb, most of which were split open creating a virtual amusement park for flies and roaches. The shiny white van with Indiana plates and chrome alloy wheels made a statement to those who gathered on the street drinking and smoking. As Jason passed, he made sure to never make eye contact with anyone. He knew what he was looking for.

Just past the halfway mark, he spotted a tricked out, bright red Shelby Mustang GT-500 lowered to about four inches off the ground, sporting oversize chrome tail pipes—the kind that emit a deep, throaty sound when the engine is revved. Jason could see the gleaming white leather upholstery through the open windows. Chrome spinner hubcaps reflected whatever sunlight managed to find its way between the soot blackened bricks of the apartment buildings.

With the attention he'd attracted, Jason felt like the celebrity float in a parade. Behind the Shelby was a parking spot—the one no one wanted in case there was ever a scratch on the Pony car. Jason pulled in carefully. This was no time for an accidental slip on the accelerator.

When he ventured out, he strolled around to the front of the van and blew a few particles of dust from the grille. With no eye contact yet, Jason leaned against the front of the van and looked in the direction of six men who'd yet to move from the throne they'd claimed as their own. One man sat in the middle of the cement steps. The rest gathered around like the entourage the man demanded. Jason folded his arms across his chest in a defiant pose and held his ground. It was his way of saying, *Here I am, what are you gonna do about it?* He was definitely the cream in an Oreo cookie.

The man sitting on the steps rose slowly and stared at Jason while blowing smoke in his direction. Wearing a sleeveless shirt, the tattoos on his muscular arms represented his badge of authority. He took two steps toward Jason and cocked his head to the side. "Whutchu doin' here, man?"

"Shoppin'."

The man gave a coarse laugh, turned to his friends and extended his arms out to his side. "Da man thinks we sell whut? Groceries?" He turned back to face Jason. His breath reeked of cheap whiskey and stale smoke. "I said, whutchu want? And don't go fuckin' with me. I don't like nobody fuckin' with me."

"I need something I think you can provide." Jason showed him his fist, extended his fingers, then slowly curled the two lower ones inward so they touched his palm. It was the distinct image of a handgun. His eyes never left the man.

"Whatchu think we are? We don't do no shit like that." He faced his lieutenants and gave a subtle bow. "Now, do we?"

The others chuckled. It was one of those sounds that would make most people reach for the closest roll of toilet paper.

"We be honest hard working men here, y'know what I'm sayin'? This is an insult to me and my bloods. I don't know if I wantchu around here." He stood nose to nose with Jason. "And if I don't want you around…you not gonna be around."

"What's that tucked under your shirt? A trashy novel?"

"None of your fuckin' business, Mister Shopper man."

Jason looked at the group of men and hoped like hell he was not showing any signs of sweating. "You got a name?"

"You a cop?"

"As a matter of fact, I am. But I'm so far from my jurisdiction, it doesn't count for squat."

"Why don't you go buy whatchu want at the store? You not a rogue kinda cop, huh? Y'know? Like you're out killin' some bad ass mother fuckers."

"I can't wait for a permit, and I'm not local."

"So? You just one law-abidin' fucker who needs a gun, huh? I'm touched."

"You got a name?"

"My friends calls me Tigre," the man sneered.

"What do your enemies call you?"

"*Mister* Tigre." He gave his coarse laugh again. "Just before they get a serious case of the horizontals."

"What should I call you?"

"Well, you ain't like no friend of mine, and you ain't no enemy. I guess I never knew some dude in the middle. You in the middle, Mister Shopper man, y'know what I sayin'?" Tigre looked at Jason's van and then scrutinized his body. "You wearin'?"

"Nope." Jason lifted his shirt to show Tigre he was not hooked up for sound.

"What's your name, Mister Shopper man?"

"Jason."

"No last name?"

"You didn't give me yours."

"Are we gonna have problems here, Jay-sohn?"

"Nope. As long as I get what I came for."

"Ooo. Jay-sohn sounded like he made me a threat. You threat me, Jay-sohn?"

Jason rolled his head from side to side, but never broke eye contact with the man.

"Good. Tigre don't like no threats, y'understand what I'm sayin'? Tigre thinks you got balls to come here." With a cocky raised eyebrow, he scanned his friends who had edged closer to Tigre as a sign of support. "You can call me Tigre."

"Well, Tee-gray." Jason hoped he wasn't pressing his luck. "Can you do me some good?"

"What makes you think I got whatchu want?"

"Check me out, Tee-gray." Jason lifted his shirt again and turned his head to the side. "See? No wire, no ear plugs. Nothing. Check out my van if you want. Look up and down the street. Do you see any other suspicious cars? Look at the roofs. You see anyone peering over the tops. Look at the windows around here. You see any curtains that don't look right? I need a couple of pieces now, and I don't give a damn how I get them."

"Get the fuck outta here. You think I'm gonna take a chance on some white dude just shows up outta fuckin' nowhere. Tigre look stupid to you?"

"Tigre looks suspicious, maybe even a little nervous, but not stupid enough to turn this down." Jason flashed a wad of twenty dollar bills.

"How much?" Tigre nodded toward the roll of cash.

"Two hundred, maybe two-hundred and fifty. New. No sequential bill numbers. Care to check it out?" When Tigre reached for the cash, Jason quickly withdrew his hand. "Look enticing enough to consider selling me my groceries?"

"You good. You really good, Jay-sohn. Let me talk it over with my bloods, y'know what I'm sayin'?"

Just as Jason leaned back against the grille of the van, a Cleveland PD unit came by. Through an opened window, an officer asked, "Everything okay here?" The question was obviously directed at Jason.

"Everything is fine, officer." Jason waved him off. When he did, the unit raised their windows and eased down the street, but not before taking a moment to stop next to the Shelby Mustang. In a few seconds, the police accelerated to the end of the block, ducked around the corner and disappeared.

The group of men laughed and slapped Tigre on his back.

"They don't come around much," Tigre said. "Fuckers don't have the nerve to even roll their windows down around Tigre. But they sure check out my ride." When he rubbed his hand over the trunk lid, it was more of a caress than a simple touch.

"You make a decision, Tigre?"

"My boys say you come back in two hours. We have your groceries for you."

Jason nodded, and eased out of the spot behind Tigre's Mustang. In a few seconds, he rounded the corner and was out of sight. He looked in his rear view mirror and mumbled, "I gotta pee."

◊　　◊　　◊

Cleveland's waterfront drive offered Jason a way to kill two hours and enjoy a much needed change of scenery from what he'd encountered this morning. His day began with a leisurely breakfast in pastoral settings, and then in the span of one hour, he'd experienced the underbelly of society. He wasn't a philosopher, but it did make him wonder what it is about civilization that, although society at large would not openly condone it or even admit to it, dictates a need for sociological stratification. Much like Jose Ortega's words would remind us: *If nature automatically lit a fire for us as soon as we were cold, we should be unaware of the necessity of keeping warm.*

As Jason was about to turn onto the section of town claimed by Tigre, a CPD pulled in behind him and gave him a short chirp of the siren. Another pulled alongside and waved him to pull over. As Jason slowed, the vehicle on his left pulled in diagonally in front of the van, effectively blocking him from escaping.

One officer from the lead vehicle leaped out and stood poised with his hand on his gun. He didn't withdraw it, but it was an obvious move on his part to let Jason know this was going to be more than a traffic stop. He stayed in this position as the officer in the rear car approached the passenger side window. Before the second officer tapped on the window, he scanned the rear of the van.

Jason lowered the window. "What's up gentlemen?"

"I need you to step out of the car, sir," the second officer said in a deep, authoritative voice.

The other two officers from the lead vehicle moved to Jason's side and motioned for him to step out.

"Driver's license and vehicle registration, please," one ordered.

Being a member of LE, Jason knew better than to question, just comply. "This is a rental. My rental agreement is in the glove box, and my license is in my wallet—in my jacket pocket."

"Please get them now."

They all kept an eye on Jason as he reached back inside the van. When Jason handed them the documents, they passed them between themselves, nodded and gave them back to Jason. "What were you doing in this part of town?" one asked in a blunt tone of voice.

"Visiting. For your information, I am a detective with the Fresno County Sheriff's Department—in California."

"Uh-huh. Have any ID?" the same officer asked.

"No. It's being sent to me."

"Right. Seems like you have some rather unique friends in this neighborhood to be just visiting. You want to change your mind?"

"No."

Gazing through the tinted windows of the van, another officer asked, "Mind if look inside?"

"Go ahead," Jason said, "but I haven't done my laundry in a few days."

The officer slid the side door open and pulled open a few covered pockets usually dedicated to the storage of videos or snacks for kids if this van had been a family rental. "Clean," he said to the others, and slid the door shut. He then opened the passenger side door and checked the same glove box Jason had just reached into, plus removed his hat and ducked his head to look under the seats.

With a staccato rhythm in his voice, Jason asked, "The reason you pulled me over is?"

"We were a little concerned for your safety when we saw you earlier. Who were you visiting?"

"A man named Tigre."

"Hmmph. Nobody visits Tigre. If Tigre wants to see you, he will send for you. Why were you talking to Tigre?"

"I assume you have issues with the man."

"Just answer the question."

Jason leaned back against the door panel. Just as he was about to exercise his stalling skills, Tigre and his friends walked around the corner. When they eyed the cops, they started to turn and walk the other direction. Jason yelled out, "Tigre. It's all right. I told them why I was visiting you."

The group stopped when Tigre stopped. He waved at them to stay put while he swaggered toward Jason and the police. "Whutchu stop this man for?" he asked the police. His belligerent attitude was still intact.

Jason scanned the area where his sleeveless t-shirt was tucked into his pants. Neat and flat. Tigre was shrewd. He knew how and when to accessorize. "I was about to tell these gentlemen how I promised your father I would check in on you." Jason turned to the police. "His father served with me in the Navy." Jason hoped he wouldn't be nailed for a little street *improv.* "His dad lives on the west coast. Been having some hard times."

Tigre gave a cocky grin, and nodded an affirmative.

"Back away, Tigre," one officer ordered. "We'll handle this." Then in his own cocky way, added, "We won't be needing your help."

The sergeant who seemed to be in charge watched Tigre round the corner with his disciples. "I don't know what you're up to, but you don't belong in this part of town. Watch yourself."

They all climbed back into their respective vehicles and left.

Sitting behind the wheel of the van, Jason scanned the street ahead and wondered why, all of a sudden, he knew what it was like to be on the receiving end of an interrogation—not that it wasn't justified. Maybe these guys really did want nothing more than to protect him. He did have out-of-state plates. But so far, in his *vacation*, except for the Amish, there were few he could trust. And why the hell did he think he could trust Tigre?

The van rounded the corner where he'd first met Tigre. Nothing had changed. There he was, sitting on his self-proclaimed throne with his constituents leaning with their backs against the brick siding. His forearms looked even more muscular as they were propped on his knees. Jason saw the Mustang sitting in the same spot. With a few hours difference, the sun ducked behind the buildings on the far side of the street. Without the sun, the chrome spinners on the car were just another set of hubcaps.

Jason eased his Chevy into an empty spot a few car lengths ahead and started to walk back.

Tigre leaped up. "Stay there, mother fucker."

Jason opened the passenger side door and sat on the seat with his legs dangling out.

"Whutchu think you're doin', mother fucker? Police know me. You don't have to do no alibi'n for me. In case you didn't notice, them fuckers didn't stop you in plain sight of me. They had to pull you over where I wasn't around. They weak, man, y'know what I'm talkin' about? They know where Tigre is, is peace. I take care of everybody here. You just ask."

Jason watched as Tigre swung his arms out to the side as if he was embracing the entire block. It was his way of proclaiming his territory. "I just thought…"

"Dontchu go thinkin', Jay-sohn. Around here, I do the thinkin'." He glanced over his shoulder at his comrades who—had this been the military—would appear to be standing at parade rest, except their arms were folded defiantly across their chests. It was a pose with one purpose—to intimidate. Their presence was very persuasive.

"You got what I need?" Jason asked in a soft voice.

"You got the green?"

Jason started to reach into his pocket to retrieve the wad of cash.

Tigre grabbed him by the arm and jerked him from the van.

In that split second, Jason's immediate reaction was to fight back with all the skills he'd acquired in the military and as a member of LE, but knowing he was one shout-out from being encircled by a half-dozen men who might look at him as an alternative to a workout at a local fitness club, he opted for his second choice—listen.

"Walk with me, Jay-sohn."

A few steps later, the hold was released, but just as Jason was beginning to feel good about the transaction going down as planned, Tigre shoved him into an alley filled with battered trash cans. There was a conspicuous bulge under his shirt.

Jason flung his arm back and faced Tigre. At this point, he had no idea of where this transaction was headed. If Tigre thought he could take him out to set an example for his followers, Jason was determined there would be more blood spilled on the street other than his own.

"Don't go trippin' on me, Jay-sohn." Tigre cocked his head in the direction of his lieutenants. "Be cool. You understand? Be cool."

Jason nodded while casting a hurried glance toward the end of the alley looking for the reinforcements. "Talk then."

"Don't you ever, ever, stand up for me in front of my friends. It makes me look weak. You understand what I'm sayin'? Around here, the only thing that keeps you alive is strength...and one of these." He pulled a black, 9mm Makarov from his belt and held it to Jason's face. When Jason reached for it, Tigre yanked the Mak back and held out his hand. "Money...Jay-sohn."

"You got two?"

"I ain't seen no money. You show me cash, I show you groceries."

Jason handed him the rolled up wad of twenties and reached for the weapon.

"How much in here?" Tigre whispered.

"Two-hundred and fifty."

"Not good enough. Four-hundred."

"Three," Jason countered.

There was an evil, threatening look in Tigre's narrow eyes. "Three, then. For the sake of my father."

"Count it," Jason said.

The wad of bills was fanned out like a deck of cards. Tigre thumbed through them with the precision of a seasoned bank teller. "Three straight up." He chuckled, "You good. You really good, Jay-sohn." There was a hint of a smile on his face. Distorted, but nevertheless, a definite upturn. He handed Jason the two Makarovs.

With the swift, calculated move of a combat veteran, Jason ejected the magazine of the first gun and held it up—empty. After pulling the slide back, he watched to see if anything flew out of the ejection chamber, gave a quick visual into the opening to make sure there was nothing hiding in there waiting for an accident to happen. He took a quick sniff of the barrel to determine if it had been fired recently. Clean. A quick pull of the trigger completed the inspection. Jason rolled the weapon over in his hands, and then performed the same inspection on the second Mak. "Nice feel."

"It's a twelve-plus-one. Enjoy."

While the transaction was going down, Tigre's cohorts had assumed ownership of the van. One sat in the passenger seat with his legs dangling out to the side. Two more had slid the side door open, perched on the entry carpet and were smoking cigarettes. The others leaned against the car. Maybe it was the cleanest thing they'd leaned against in months. Jason looked at the nasty bunch and thought, nobody else is gonna mess with the car with these guys around.

Tigre pulled Jason back and pinned him to the wall and hissed, "Why you make comments about my father?"

"It, uuh…it just came to me."

"Listen to me close. Don't you never make no comments to me like that. My father was killed. Happen when I was fifteen. I been on the street ever since."

"I'm sorry."

"Don't you feel sorry for me, Jay-sohn. For a second, I thought you really knew him. I wanted to know more about my father." He jammed his arm across Jason's throat, and with a booming voice, added, "Now, get your fuckin' white ass back to your white ass car."

Tigre did not walk anywhere. He strutted. He swaggered. It was a shoulder-rolling, arm-clenching show of muscle.

Jason yielded to Tigre's demand, and started to ease the van out into the street. Before he could maneuver out of the tight parking spot, Tigre leaned his hands on the open window frame and locked eyes with Jason. "I don't know why you want these pieces, but I hope I do you some good."

"They will be put to good use. I have a lot to make up for with a very special group of people."

"Here." Tigre handed Jason an extra magazine and one bullet. "The first one is on me."

Jason rolled the bullet around in his fingertips. It was a hollow tip point—perfect for going in at 9mm and ripping out the other side in excess of 60mm.

"Y'know? You may not realize it, but we have a lot in common," Jason whispered.

Tigre's brow furrowed. "Whatchu mean, man?"

"We both do what we have to do to survive."

As Jason pulled away from the curb, Tigre gave a slight head wave to one of his lieutenants sitting behind the wheel of an old green Buick parked three spots behind Jason's van.

◊　　◊　　◊

All the way back to the B & B, Jason never crossed a double line or sped, and made sure he came to a complete stop at every stop sign. The last thing he needed was to be pulled over for a minor infraction and have the police do a search of his car. He'd have a hard time explaining the two 9mm Makarovs in his glove box.

In most states, the term *search and seizure* is defined in a very generous or what some might label as, *inspired,* language. This looseness has the potential to have either a positive or negative impact on society at large. There is a distinct difference between an automobile and a home.

For a home, a search warrant would have to be issued by a judge, and on the request, a list of specific items would have to be included that the police were looking for, as well as the reason.

The automobile is an entirely different matter. The term *search and seizure* might be interpreted at the discretion of the member of law enforcement present at the scene. The up side is; it allows LE to gather on-the-spot evidence against a suspected criminal which would be considered perfectly legal. Another subtle nuance would include the authorization to generate an *inventory list* of everything in the car in case the car must be towed away and not in the continuous possession of the owner. It is this gradation of authority which concerned Jason. If someone chose to arrest him on the most minor of infractions, they could take stock of everything in the car…and he could never explain the handguns—at least not without exposing his intention to solve the Friedel Mueller killing.

He wished he knew the area better. He wished he knew who he could trust. What began as a favor had become an exercise in operating just outside the law. He didn't care to be labeled as a loose cannon, but he'd made the commitment. What he was doing wasn't wrong, but was it defeating the purpose of local law enforcement? He needed to talk to more people, especially David Ellison.

When he drove into the Loomis' driveway, he stared out the window wondering if there was going to be any more gunshots this night. Only a few distant lights from non-Amish farm houses penetrated the darkness. It was so peaceful here. He never took his clothes off. He simply rolled over and closed his eyes.

As the lights in the house were doused for the night, the driver of the green Buick from Tigre's neighborhood stopped out front for a few seconds, and then drove off into the darkness.

CHAPTER 14

The Loomis' prepared another breakfast feast for Jason. At first glance, the presentation was detailed and extensive, but how much variation can one family do with eggs, toast, pancakes, potatoes, waffles, French toast, or the various kinds of meat available. These meals were destined for consumption by a few who may stay one or two days, and the obligation would disappear, but when the same guest went into a holding pattern for an extended length of time…well, it got to be a challenge. Lately, at every offering, he was a served a side dish of apology.

Each time, Jason brushed the comment away in a good natured manner. But the appearance of their son, Doug, gave Jason the reason he fell just short of bolting from the homey kitchen every morning. Doug's attitude and messy attire bordered on rebellious social comment. Jason wondered if he'd ever sat through one of Ken Hutchinson's presentations at school, because if he had, it sure hadn't sunk in.

The morning Plain Dealer, placed at his door this morning, featured a lengthy article about Ken Hutchinson's personal life, his start in law enforcement, and accomplishments. He was not married, so there were no photos or testaments from a grieving wife and children. However, his parents were interviewed and gave a recounting of his life beginning with the early years, high school, and the police academy. A tearful remembrance was included about why he chose to go into law enforcement.

His was not a lofty goal designed to save the world, the article stated, but to use his position of authority to help others, especially when it came to the problem of drug abuse…or usage at all. He wanted to portray a different image to the people of Ashtabula County and transmit that image to students beginning in middle school. His message had always been clear from the get-go—stay away from all the temptations heaped upon the shoulders of those people during the most malleable time of their lives.

The article also gave all the particulars for his funeral, including the time the procession would begin, and the route to the cemetery.

Jason expressed his usual cheerful thanks to the Loomis' and left for another meeting with the Mueller clan, but not before stashing one of the Maks in his room. He deliberated about giving Joshua Stoudt a call on the communal phone, but opted to simply show up as he'd done so many times before. They didn't seem to mind.

When he drove in the driveway, he caught a glimpse of Elizabeth coming from the barn, her hands cupped under her apron. When Jason approached her, he noticed her struggling with a load of eggs, and was thankful she chose not to wave her usual hello.

"Morning, Mrs. Mueller. Can I give you a hand with those?"

"Ahh. You are just what I needed, Mr. Carmichael. My back seems a little out of sorts this morning."

As soon as Jason made his offer, he wondered how he was going to carry all those eggs in. He quickly zipped up his jacket and cupped his hand underneath. With his free hand, he began to transfer one egg at a time onto his make-shift basket. When the transfer was complete, Elizabeth led the way into the rear of the house and into the kitchen. It was comfortably large by any standards, but then again, there were many mouths to feed, and those mouths would be there even during the winter months when snow drifts would pile up against the house making the entire region look like an unforgiving white desert. "Better?"

"Much. Thank you. Why the visit?"

"Would it be possible to call Isaac and Mister Stoudt in here? There's something I'd like to share with them."

"Of course." She rang a tiny bell and Benjamin came running across the weathered wooden floor. When he spotted Jason and his egg-filled jacket, he gave a shy smile and brushed at his hair. Elizabeth wasted no time asking her grandson to do as Jason asked. Benjamin was out the door like a bullet. "Here. Let me take those now." She carefully made a barrier from two knives on top of the table and placed the eggs against them so they would not spin off onto the floor. "Biscuit?"

"Yes. I'd like that very much." Jason scanned the Spartan kitchen with its black iron wood-burning stove and oven. Next to that antiquated appliance, sat a propane powered stove—probably used when weather was good. The wood burner would come in handy when the propane truck could not make house calls during the harsh wintry days when snow might be driven up against the building by bone-chilling winds. He took a few moments to grasp the lack of lights and microwave oven. Features outsiders would treat with disdain had they been looking to buy the house. An oak ice box with polished brass handles in the corner served as their refrigerator. Before Jason bit into the huge biscuit he'd been offered, Elizabeth offered him a knife and plate of whipped butter. Jason could barely contain his enthusiasm.

Elizabeth then offered him a jar of homemade blackberry preserves. The kind with huge berries packed inside rather than the pulverized store-bought concoctions.

Wide-eyed and drooling over the chunky sweet paste, Jason knew he'd just entered heaven.

The front door opened and staccato sounds of two sets of footsteps clumped across the floor leading to the kitchen.

"Mr. Carmichael," Isaac said with a watchful, inquisitive eye.

"Mr. Carmichael," Joshua said, but with a more generous look of tolerance.

With an outstretched hand, Jason responded, "Gentlemen."

They all sat down at the kitchen table.

"When I was here last time," Jason began, "you seemed amenable to going to Ken Hutchinson's funeral…to see if you could recognize the man who tried to…?"

"We remember," Isaac said.

"Good. Deputy Hutchinson's funeral is being held tomorrow. I'm not sure what your customs are regarding funerals, but I see no reason to go to the service—it's at a local Lutheran church in Jefferson—or to the procession. I kinda lean toward going to the burial site. What do you think?"

"The same man came by again yesterday," Elizabeth said. "He was quite different than the first time."

"How so?" Jason asked.

"He came close to threatening me," she said. "And he only stayed for…maybe a minute."

"Good. Did he give you his name this time?" Jason asked. "Or who he represented—like a person, group, or law enforcement agency?"

"No. He seemed more…determined…this time," Elizabeth said with a nervous quiver in her voice.

"What did he say?"

"He knew I had the document he wanted, and it was just a matter of time before he would get it, no matter how."

"So much for the use of veiled threats," Jason mumbled. "This could only be interpreted one way—a direct hit." As far as Jason was concerned, time was running out for niceties when it came to the safety of the Muellers or anyone who was openly supportive of them.

"Did you notice what kind of car he was driving this time?"

"I remember you asked last time," Elizabeth said, "so I tried to get a look at it, but he kept stepping in front of me. I think he realized what I was doing. All I could see was…it was white, with four doors." She brushed at her apron and then pressed her hands to it to eliminate any signs of wrinkles. "Is that right? Two on each side?"

"Yes," Jason said. "This is why I think we should all attend the funeral tomorrow. My gut feeling says that whoever this person is, will be there. If I could find out who this person is, we all stand a better chance of getting through this alive."

"We will all go," Elizabeth announced in a gritty voice.

Joshua and Isaac looked a little surprised by the abrupt declaration, but both quickly offered their assent.

"I will pick you up at three-thirty tomorrow." Jason thanked them all and hopped into the Chevy. He had to find an ammo store as soon as possible. An extra magazine or two wouldn't hurt either. The twelve-plus-one—as Tigre so succinctly pointed out—could carry twelve rounds in the mag with one in the chamber. This was another one of those frustrating times when Jason wished he could be as well armed as the criminals.

The biscuit Jason had devoured at the Mueller farm came close to filling him up. Instead of his normal bacon, double cheeseburger supreme at the local fast-food burger joint, he opted for a plain half-pounder...with fries...and a milkshake.

He'd just deposited the remains of his afternoon meal when his cell buzzed. He glanced at the photo of the caller. "Dena. Glad to hear from you." And he was. "Did Sheriff Szabo give you the things I needed?"

"Sure did. Got a hold of Owen Saturday. He contacted Szabo. I picked up the stuff yesterday."

There was that bubbly sound of pride in her voice. "Great. Did you mail it?"

"Nope."

"Oh, that's right. Yesterday was Sunday. So you mailed it this morning?"

"Nope."

"Dang. I was hoping I'd have this stuff ASAP."

"You are."

"What do you mean?"

"Come and get it, you big dummy." Her words were softened by her feminine laugh.

With a suspicious voice, Jason ventured, "Where are you?"

"Baggage carousel at Cleveland airport."

"You're joking."

"No joke, partner. Get your ass over here. I'm exhausted."

"I can't believe you, Dena. What the hell prompted you to come to Cleveland?"

For a few seconds, there was nothing. Then came her airy response. "You."

◊　◊　◊

Jason's resolve to obey all the traffic rules were flushed down the toilet. All the way to Cleveland Hopkins, he kept thinking if he was to be stopped now, all he would stand to lose would be one of the Maks and his squeaky clean driving record. He could live with that.

When he drove up the concourse dedicated for arriving flights, he saw Dena sitting on her luggage staring at the ground. He shut his engine off and coasted in. She looked...attractive. Jason always thought the word *beautiful* was a quantifier for superficiality—a word with undertones of having all the right features in the right places and in the right proportions. Using that boorish criteria, even Paris Hilton would be considered beautiful, but Jason could think of nothing else of substance about a person that others would simply describe as beautiful. To be attractive meant there was much more underneath. There would be a sense of humor, warmth, sensitivity, an intellect, expressive eyes, spirit…and it would help if the person wasn't butt ugly. Dena was definitely attractive.

He rolled to a stop about ten feet from her and stepped out. "Hi."

Dena leaped to her feet and reached for Jason. The hug lasted longer than when they'd said good-bye to each other back in California. Of course her husband, standing nearby, kind of stifled whatever feeling there was at the time. "Hi."

Their lips were close again and he could feel her warm breath drift past him. It felt good. "What's with you showing up out of nowhere?"

Dena had not let go of Jason. "You told me what you wanted, but you never said how I should get it to you." She handed him his badge and credentials from the Fresno County Sheriff's Office

"Thanks. You ar-r-e…"

"What? Incredible? Unpredictable? Strong? Gorgeous? Needed?"

Jason was tempted to say *all of the above*, but hadn't formulated a definition for the word gorgeous yet. It'd taken him years to define the difference between beautiful and attractive. Okay, he could concede to gorgeous. Levi Strauss was missing the boat when their marketers overlooked the quintessential body to advertise their product. "How did you arrange a flight so quickly?"

"Y'see? There's this thing called a phone."

"What did Clay say when you told him you wanted to go to Cleveland?"

"We can talk about him some other time." Dena gave Jason another long hug. "When we talked, you sounded so stressed out. What's happening?"

Jason picked up her luggage and guided her back to the van. "Let's talk on our way back to where I'm staying."

"Where *we* are staying. Right?"

Jason chuckled. "The people who own this place were so happy to have me for a guest at this time of year. They'll be ecstatic to have another guest."

"Do they know I'm coming?"

"Sure do. Called them on my cell." Jason maneuvered the van through traffic and found his way back to route 322. Once that hurdle had been conquered, it was a straight shot to Windsor. On the way, Jason explained what he'd seen at the covered bridge, and how an innocent inquiry evolved into an unofficial investigation. And he knew of no one he could turn to. He told her of David Ellison, and of Friedel and the Mueller family. What he'd never expected was the importance of the Medico-legal document and to what lengths someone was going through to make sure the last known copy went the way of the dinosaurs. "I have to add one more thing, and you don't have to go if you don't want to."

"What's this all about?"

"I have to go to a funeral tomorrow." He looked into her eyes for a moment. He wished he hadn't been driving, because he knew this would be a touchy situation for her and didn't want his comment to come across as insensitive.

Dena pinched her lips and gazed straight ahead through tearing eyes. "First, my brother, then Marie. Is this the season for funerals or what?"

"I'm sorry." He reached for Dena's hand.

"If it will help you find out who killed the Amish girl, I'll go." She squeezed Jason's hand tightly for a moment, but did not let go. Her touch remained tender.

The last few miles before reaching the Loomis' B & B, Dena perked up and began to talk about how neat all the farms seemed to be. There were no twisted piles of debris that someone might use…someday, or dilapidated machinery waiting for an antique dealer's visit…someday.

The gravel driveway made its familiar crunching sound as Jason nudged the Chevy into a small row of bushes. Switching off the ignition, he glanced at Dena's eyes, which seemed to be focused on the gingerbread decorative siding of the Swiss-inspired inn. All that was missing was a snow covered mountain in the background and Julie Andrews strolling over a hilltop.

"How positively quaint."

As Jason was dragging her bags out of the rear of the van, the Loomis family came out to greet them. "Here, let me take those," Mr. Loomis said.

After a quick glance at Dena, Doug rushed over and gushed, "No, Dad, I'll get these." He almost stumbled backward trying to walk and keep his eyes glued to Dena at the same time. In a moment of pure adolescent inspiration, the young man blurted out, "You can call me, Doug."

Jason was sure Doug wished he'd have brushed his teeth and put on a clean shirt.

Navigating the stairs up to the second floor was challenging for Doug. Jason watched him bang the suitcases into the wood paneling and painted drywall. By the look on Mr. Loomis' face, the word, *touchup*, was sure to enter Doug's vocabulary very soon.

There were only four rooms to let out during the summer months, but Jason made sure Dena's room was next door to his. Each had their own bathrooms, with showers. The rooms had a rustic look—the kind which would offend neither the female nor male who might occupy the room. Jason referred to them as gender neutral.

When the Loomis' left, they smiled and quietly shut the door behind them.

"On the phone," Jason began, "you said you were tired. You want to lie down for awhile?"

"I'd like that. I had very little sleep on the plane." She sat on the edge of the bed.

"I...uuh, I'd better go check out some places to eat. When I'm alone, I tend to eat anywhere. I'm pretty much of a pig when it comes to eating out."

"No, you're not. Remember the delta restaurant we ate at after we questioned the girl up in Stockton? I wouldn't call that a place a pig would go. I will always trust your judgment."

Jason looked at the spot next to Dena and stammered, "I guess I should go." He glanced at the time on his cell. "How does one hour sound?"

"One hour will be fine."

CHAPTER 15

"How was your sleep last night?" Mrs. Loomis asked Dena, while pouring a hearty cup of coffee for her. There was always a warm, grandmotherly smile to accompany her words.

"Oh, I could never have slept better. Thanks." Dena had spent the last fifteen minutes gazing out the window in the rear door at the cattle grazing in the fields. "It was so peaceful."

Jason was glad there were no gunshots last night to welcome Dena to the neighborhood. He'd taken advantage of Dena's comatose state to duck into Orwell and pick up a spare magazine for the Makarovs plus enough ammo to make it through a major firefight…at least, that was his plan. He'd spent the rest of the evening cleaning both handguns and making sure their firing mechanisms functioned smoothly…while trying to allow Dena her well-deserved sleep. He figured out, for her to accomplish what she'd done over the weekend, she'd probably gotten more Z's on the flight out. And with her knees tucked under her seat, she was lucky she could walk.

"I'm so sorry, Jason. When I hit that bed, it was all over."

"No problem." Oh, well. He would make up for missing a meal by over-indulging today.

"Am I dressed okay for what we're going to do today?" Dena asked.

"You look fine." Rather than the usual Levi's, Dena chose a modest length skirt—blue, to match her eyes, and an off-white long-sleeved blouse. He'd never seen her in high heels, which accentuated her

127

legs—all ten feet of them. He made sure to look elsewhere at every opportunity.

Too bad the same didn't hold true for Doug. This morning, he arrived in the serving area with his hair combed, shined shoes, and fresh clothes. There wasn't a moment when his eyes strayed away from Dena. He'd never been so anxious to set the table, serve the food, clear the table, pour more coffee, and even resorted to offer his services if her clothes needed ironing—after the long trek confined in an over-stuffed suitcase. Jason was sure there were more kinds of stuffing on his mind. More than once, he was heard whispering, "You can call me, Doug."

"Where will the graveside services be held?" Dena asked.

"County seat," Jason said. "A few miles north of here. A nice little town."

"It's called Jefferson," Doug blurted out in a forced, deep voice as if reciting from the imaginary Ashtabula Encyclopedia. "It's the county seat."

Dena smiled and thanked Doug.

"What time will the procession arrive there?" Mr. Loomis asked.

"About three—so it said in yesterday's Plain Dealer. And, thanks for the heads up on the ammo shop in Orwell. They had exactly what I needed."

Dena's head jerked slightly at Jason's statement.

"Needed a couple of extra mags and a box of 9mm's," Jason explained to her.

"Good place to buy whatever you need," Mr. Loomis added. "Family owned. I've known them for years."

Not missing any opportunity, Doug leaped in with, "I could take you there."

Jason tapped him on the shoulder and gave him a charitable smile while he chuckled to himself, *Doug's robust offer would have carried more sincerity had it not been directed at Dena's blouse.* "Thanks. I found my way there quite easily." He wiped his mouth and pushed the chair back from the table. "I'm gonna brush my teeth and then we should be able to meet up with the Muellers." He grabbed the back of Dena's chair before Doug took a shot at it.

"We'll see you this evening," Dena said with a generous smile. Then with a bubbly voice, she pinched Doug's cheeks and whispered, "You are so-o, so cute."

For the first time this morning, Doug was at a loss for words.

◊   ◊   ◊

Elizabeth wore a fresh apron and prayer covering for Ken Hutchinson's burial ceremony. Hopefully, the man who'd paid her two visits would be there for her to identify. Jason hadn't devised a solid Plan B if he wasn't. From there, it would be a long overdue confrontation with David Ellison to see where that led. All he could do was exert pressure on him to make him slip...just once. In his diverse arsenal of tactics, when he'd been confronted with little or nothing to go on, he found a full frontal assault worked best. No subtleties. Just come right at them. Make them nervous. Rattle them until they lost control. That's when the slip-ups happened.

Although ties are worn by men only for special occasions such as weddings, today, Isaac and Joshua wore ties to accompany their dark suits. In place of the straw hats they normally wore to protect them from the sun while working the fields, they wore formal black hats.

They looked very proud standing on the front porch as Jason and Dena drove up the driveway.

"How am I supposed to act around these people?" Dena asked as Jason pulled up under the shade of the huge beech tree in the front yard.

"Don't *act* any way," Jason said. "These are normal people who are probably just as nervous about meeting you as you are of them."

"Do they know I am coming?"

"Yeah. I talked to Mr. Stoudt yesterday on the phone."

"They have a ph...?"

Jason popped his door open to greet the Muellers and Joshua. Elizabeth stayed on the porch until the dust settled from Jason's van. He tried to enter slowly, but without the previous rains to dampen and compact the soil, it didn't take long for the dirt to become powdery again. "Sorry about the dust."

Isaac waved his arms around—not a flamboyant gesture on his part, but just enough to let everyone know this annoyance was not appreciated.

Elizabeth closed the front door and came down the two steps into the front yard.

"It's okay," Joshua said while casting a discourteous glance in Isaac's direction.

"Elizabeth, Isaac, Mr. Stoudt," Jason began. "I'd like you to meet Dena Manning. I would not be here today had it not been for this woman." He stood at Dena's side.

With a surprised look and a hint of a smile, Elizabeth said, "This can't be your mother."

Everyone laughed as they all shook Dena's hand and gave a warm smile.

"Is she a part of the investigation you're conducting, Mr. Carmichael?" Elizabeth continued.

Jason shot Dena a quirky grin. "She is now." He slid the side door of the van open and quickly checked to make sure he'd cleared out whatever debris there was in the van in preparation for today's visitors. He knew Elizabeth would sit dutifully on the man's left if the man happened to be her husband, but was not sure where she would sit now that her husband was no longer part of her life.

The bench seat, behind the two captain's chairs in front, accommodated three across and this would work out perfectly. Joshua slid in first, followed by Elizabeth. When she started to step up into the van, Isaac offered his mother his hand to steady her.

When all were settled in, Jason reached in and showed them how to fasten the seat belts. He was not sure if they'd ever seen these types of restraints before. They fumbled with the belts and metal clips. Once all were properly secured, Jason popped into the driver's seat and headed out the driveway.

"My, my," Elizabeth said while tugging on her seat belt. "These are quite the items to keep us safe. Maybe we should install some in our carriage, Isaac."

After studying Elizabeth's mischievous eyes and subtle upturned lips in his rear view mirror, Jason thought he was beginning to understand where Friedel had gotten her refreshing sense of individualism.

Every time Jason scanned his rear view mirror, he noticed the men as they rubbed their fingertips over the leather. They seemed to find the soft contoured seats and fine stitching very attractive. He also knew they were not about to comment on how comfortable the ride was.

The trip to the cemetery was quiet…for awhile…until Dena blurted out, "So. In weather like this, how do you guys keep cool underneath all those clothes?"

◊   ◊   ◊

The formal procession was beginning to flow onto the cemetery grounds after a long route which began at a Lutheran church in Jefferson, and past the county courthouse with its four-story center spire reaching skyward. Along the way, citizens, who wished to acknowledge the memory of a local member of their community, planted an American flag alongside their property, or held a flag in their hands if they were in the city limits.

When Jason drove in, there were a few cars already parked on the grassy shoulder of the narrow access road. Nearby, there was an area reserved for immediate family and the attending vehicles, all cordoned off by a dark blue velvet rope.

Grass was trimmed to a uniform height. About twenty feet from the driveway was a mound of dirt covered by a blue tarp held down at the corners with velvet-covered weights. In front of the fill, was a set of brass rails waiting for its precious cargo to arrive. Except for the chirping of Robins scavenging for worms released by the disturbance of the soil, it was quiet.

Both Jason and Dena clenched their lips as they exited the van. It seemed their summer had been like a tumor growing inside each of them where no amount of treatment could alleviate the pain or suffering. First, it was the death of her brother at the hands of a trusted lover. Then came the frivolous act of teenage morons and the death of Marie Gallagher—who was to become Marie Carmichael. Maybe not. It all became jumbled up by the investigation of Dena's brother's death. It was a convoluted relationship for Jason and Dena. They automatically held hands as they looked at the setting. So serene. So comforting. The very essence of finality.

It was a few moments before they realized Elizabeth, Isaac and Joshua had not gotten out of the van. When they turned, the three of them were struggling to unlatch their seat belts.

"Oh. I'm so sorry," Jason said in a soft voice. He reached in to show them the little red tab to press which released the restraint mechanism, and it took a few more moments for them to disentangle themselves from the straps.

Jason scanned the people who'd already arrived hoping to capture a glimpse of David. This had been his district when he first entered politics. It seemed appropriate for him to be there. But there was always the possibility he would be needed elsewhere...like at a campaign fund-raiser.

The hearse was the first to enter the grounds, followed by four limousines carrying family members and the clergy. Soon, Ashtabula County deputies, the Ohio Highway Patrol, other contingents of law enforcement personnel from neighboring communities, arrived and lined up in their well-rehearsed routine. All wore their class-A uniforms. The Ashtabula County chaplain stood at the head of the plot in front of a special wreath from the department containing Deputy Hutchinson's shield as a center piece. This shield would later be removed and presented to the family by the sheriff.

The solitary click of a drum stick on the rim of a tenor drum furnished the tempo and mood for the arrival of the bagpipe brigade. Each member marched in a slow gliding step until they reached a position to the right of an awning set up to protect family members from whatever the weather had to offer. Once in position, they remained at a rest posture with their hands crossed in front of themselves waiting for the command from the drum major to do what they do best...pay tribute...and bring others to tears.

As the limos arrived, Jason gathered his group together. "We have two purposes here today. One is to see if Elizabeth can identify the man who's been badgering her, because I firmly believe he will be someone of importance...someone with connections. The other, for me, is to see if David Ellison shows up. If he does, I do not intend to confront him in this environment. I will deal with him at another time." He ushered them to the shade of an elm tree where they could remain somewhat hidden in the shadows. He could even duck behind the tree if David did show and happened to venture too close. "Until then, let's stay together."

People filtered past the rows of elm trees and began to gather around the burial plot. No one seemed to notice the isolated group in the shadows. Just as everyone was beginning to settle in for the ceremony, a limo arrived and double parked outside the area reserved for family.

Jason leaned against the tree and studied the figure who strutted from the long white vehicle. The man wore a tailored black suit with a dark blue tie. His cufflinks sparkled in the sunlight. Before venturing too far from the limo, the man surveyed the site as if looking for the perfect place to make himself available for a much-deserved photo-op. It was David.

"You okay?" Jason asked Dena. It dawned on him that he'd yet to let go of her hand.

"Yeah. You?"

A few people acknowledged the Amish with a smile as they passed. Jason was sure many of the people in attendance were not personal friends of Ken, but concerned enough to make sure the family knew a member of law enforcement would not pass without knowing others in the community were also saddened. Jason's first urge was to introduce himself to the family and share his brief history with them, but it was neither the place nor a smart move when he was trying his best to remain anonymous. If he had the opportunity, this gesture could come later.

As David passed the elm tree, Jason stood behind Joshua and Isaac, their hats forming a convenient screen. It appeared David had put on a little weight around the middle. Jason smiled.

The crowd had all gathered around the burial site and the ceremony began. The Chaplain was first to welcome all who came to honor the memory of a man who had passed long before his time. It was very similar to the Tuolumne County chaplain's compassionate tribute to Dena's brother back in July. Jason had let go of her hand when he ducked behind his temporary shield when David passed, but now, she was standing next to him with her arm slipped under his. Jason was not sure who was supporting who.

"Did you notice anyone familiar?" Jason whispered to Elizabeth.

"No. No, I didn't."

Jason glanced at Joshua and, with his eyes, asked the same question.

Joshua rolled his lips under and rolled his head from side to side.

"What was this guy wearing when he showed up at your place?" Jason asked Elizabeth.

"Suits. First dark blue. Last time…black."

Pretty generic. Anyone here could fit that description. Jason then pointed to David, who stood out from all the others…because he chose to by maneuvering himself away from the crowd. Jason figured if the local media were to document the ceremony, David was sure to stand out. Come election time, a teary-eyed lieutenant governor standing in the vicinity of a flag-draped casket of a dedicated public servant would surely generate a positive impression in the voters' minds. Pointing to David, he asked, "How about him?"

Elizabeth studied the man. "Sorry."

As the ceremony progressed, there came the time for the pipers to play Amazing Grace. It was one of those gut-wrenching songs which has the capacity to elicit the same emotion regardless of anyone's culture, religion, or heritage. Dena grasped Jason's arm so tightly when she heard the haunting melody again, it let Jason know she needed him more than anything else at this moment in her life.

The ceremony concluded with the folding of the flag draped over the coffin. The color guard performed the routine with military-like precision. It was handed to the chaplain by the head of the color guard, who then handed it to the sheriff with the pointed end of the flag facing outward. The sheriff approached the family, smartly pivoted the flat side toward the mother, while he whispered his condolences. She accepted the national ensign with a forced smile. Underneath the sunglasses, Jason was sure her eyes were as red as the stripes on the flag.

Quietly, mourners began to file away from the site. Some remained for awhile to gaze at the casket, now covered in flowers and mementoes tenderly placed there by family members. They, too, began to steal away to leave the family to their own special kind of suffering.

"Anyone look familiar?" Jason asked while keeping an eye on David.

Elizabeth whispered, "No."

After the crowd had thinned, David approached the sheriff on his way to visit the family. As he passed, he patted the sheriff on his shoulder in a very casual way. Not the kind of gesture one might expect at such a solemn moment. David's head was bowed as if he'd whispered something, but it was over before he'd taken another step. Continuing on his way, David's pace slowed as he approached the awning where family members were still clutching each other and passing tissues around.

As he reached for their hands, another man accompanying David stepped to the side quickly and snapped a photo with a digital camera. The move seemed carefully choreographed since David was bending at the waist, grasping the mother's hands. David finished by shaking hands with other family members before retreating to the comfort of his limo. Jason was sure David had some kind of alcoholic beverage waiting for him. Probably a little more sophisticated drink than the usual beer he wanted after a game back in the days when anything would do if you happened to be a desperate teenager.

The limo exited the cemetery and sped off.

The windows of the van had been left open to keep the interior as cool as possible. In his side view mirror, Jason noticed the sheriff walking in their direction. The sheriff's campaign hat was tilted down, apparently to shield his eyes from the afternoon sun. And the two sets of four stars he wore on his formal uniform glistened like beacons in a night sky. Instead of looking directly at the sheriff, Jason kept him in sight by framing him in the mirror.

As the sheriff closed in on the van, Jason noticed his attention was not fixed on him, but on Dena, who was bending into the van to help the Muellers fasten their seat belts again. With her around, Jason didn't need to hide.

Without missing a stride, the sheriff passed the van and with the kind of sound you'd expect from a coiled rattler, whispered, "Carmichael."

Jason watched him climb into a county Crown Vic emblazoned with "Sheriff," and a five-pointed star on the side panels.

"What was that all about?" Dena whispered.

"I don't have a clue," Jason said. What he wanted to say was; he didn't have a clue of what was in store for him. Or worse—for Dena. Why had he agreed to let her be part of this? "Let's get these people home where they'll be safe." He sped out of the cemetery onto the blacktop leading back to Windsor. As a final check of the scene, he scanned the grove of trees he was passing. Nestled among the trees was the unmistakable bright red Special Edition Shelby Mustang. By the vanity plate, there was no doubt this was Tigre's ride. The last time he'd seen the car, all the windows were rolled down, but now the windows were raised and with the darkly tinted coating, he was unable to tell who was behind the wheel. What the hell is going on?

CHAPTER 16

After the funeral, Jason gathered the group together on the Mueller's front porch. The evening turned pleasant. Temps had dropped a few degrees and the humidity hovered below the eighty percent saturation level. Although Joshua's horse had been tended to by a small boy during his absence, the need evidently presented itself and being an animal, the horse left a very large wet spot in the dirt.

Joshua removed his hat for a moment, dipped his head to Dena and Elizabeth, and climbed into his carriage.

"It was a pleasure to meet you." Dena extended her hand to Joshua.

Joshua returned the warm smile and gesture. With a soft voice and gentle snap of the reins, Joshua chided his horse away from the post where he'd been tethered. Before leaving, he gave Jason one of his subtle waves that one might miss had they glanced away for a second.

The horse seemed to enjoy being released from the afternoon's inactivity. He held his head high and pranced out into the driveway leading to the paved two-lane road. Half way out, he let out with one of those vocalizations of excitement which sounded like a baritone fluttering his lips to loosen up before a concert.

Standing on the front porch, Isaac stood next to his mother while glancing toward the barn. His eyes had grown distant, maybe even a tad edgy. When Dena offered her hand to him and whispered how nice it had been to meet him, he glanced down at the polished nails and muttered, "You, too," then excused himself, saying he had chores to attend to. He removed his formal black hat and jacket, and then hung them on the back of a chair. A few seconds later, he disappeared into the barn.

"I suppose we'd better be going, too, Dena," Jason said.

Elizabeth let out a long sigh as she watched her son disappear from sight. "Before you go, Mr. Carmichael. I am saddened that Joshua and I failed to recognize anyone at Deputy Hutchinson's service. I feel we have let you down."

"Please don't feel that way." Until the funeral, Jason seemed to have a pat answer about who was involved with Friedel's death, but all those preconceived notions were developing serious leaks, especially after observing the casual contact between the sheriff and David Ellison. What was their relationship? And even more, it was becoming abundantly clear that whoever killed Ken Hutchinson was certainly somehow linked to Friedel. He grasped Elizabeth's hand.

"Do you have a few moments?" Elizabeth asked.

When Jason glanced at Dena, she gave him a quick nod of assent. "Sure."

"Once in a while, I visit Friedel's grave. But, other than saying I love her and I miss her, I never have anything to share about finding who was responsible for her leaving us…until you came here. It would mean a lot to me if you and Dena would join me."

"It would be our pleasure, Mrs. Mueller," Dena said. She sandwiched Elizabeth between herself and Jason.

"It's a little walk through the fields," Elizabeth said. "I hope you don't mind."

They rounded the corner of the house and headed for an open pasture where the Holsteins were grazing. On the far side of the field was a stand of maple trees, whose leaves were at the magic point of changing into their fall colors. Hints of red and orange fluttered in the gentle breeze and created a pleasant color palate for the eye.

No matter how clean the farms were, there were still the inevitable clumps of droppings from the cattle. Elizabeth cautioned them to keep looking down and to the front. If the spacing was too narrow between clumps, they would let go of each other for an instant, and then link arms again on the other side.

"There. Over there," Elizabeth said, pointing to a series of wood plaques nestled in the shade of the trees just inside the perimeter. She knelt down in front of one of the markers with an intricately carved, *FRIEDEL MUELLER*. "You don't have to kneel if you don't want to. It's just something I do."

"I will join you," Dena said as she dropped to her knees next to Elizabeth.

Jason followed close behind.

Elizabeth folded her hands in her lap and stared at the marker. In the softest of whispers, she began, "Most often, I sit here by myself and don't even talk. I like to think of it as being beside Friedel and holding her hand."

"What a beautiful thought," Jason said.

"After Friedel died," Elizabeth continued, "I would come to the woods to sit here with her. She was so young, so vibrant, with an entire life waiting for her…and then she was gone. I kept waiting for someone to come and tell us what happened and who was responsible for doing such a thing. But it never happened. I prayed a lot, but it did little good. I suppose the Lord has chosen to include Friedel in His grand plan. Do I sound like a pathetic old woman?"

"No. Absolutely not," Dena said.

Jason rested his hand on Elizabeth's shoulder.

"While we were at the service today, I tried to put her out of my mind." Whenever Elizabeth began to speak, she always raised her right forefinger in the air as if she was telling you this is the point she wished to make. The gesture conveyed a very divine subtext. "We have certain beliefs, or rituals you might call them, that may be quite different from yours. While we were there, I noticed how many people came, and I'm not sure how many of them were family. When one of us passes on, we are surrounded by family and members of the congregation only."

"I suppose it's another way to let the close family know that the person was well-thought of by others, too," Jason said.

Elizabeth nodded her understanding. "May I ask if you believe in a god?"

Jason whispered, "No. I'm sorry."

"Nor do I," Dena said. "But please don't think of us as bad people. We try to do the right things."

Elizabeth caressed the top of Friedel's marker with her fingertips. "From an early age, we are raised to believe in someone greater than ourselves, and we try to do the right things, also. So, I suppose doing what's right has nothing to do with religion. Let me assure you…both of you…I do not think less of either of you for not believing, because until Mr. Carmichael showed up last week, no one seemed to want to do the right thing. In the few days we've been together, I feel my spirit lifted like I've never felt it lifted before. Is Mr. Carmichael a god? No. But every day, I find myself putting in a few good words for him." She grasped Dena's hand. "I'll be sure to include you, too, my dear."

"I appreciate the thought." Dena's voice tapered off into a void.

In the shade of the maples, three people sat on the ground quietly sharing stories of their pasts. Dena told Elizabeth of how her brother was killed, and by someone very close to him. So trust meant not only a physical bond, but a spiritual bond as well. It meant being able to say things out loud to another someone who cares. And to know, with absolute certainty, the person was listening to her inner thoughts, and not brushing them away as if they were a series of words strung together for the benefit of hearing her own voice.

Jason found himself at Dena's side as she opened up to Elizabeth and marveled at how quickly the two bonded. And this was only Dena's first day here.

Dena buried her face in her hands. "Here I am talking about my loss, and we came here to let you talk of yours. I'm sorry."

"'Tis all right, my dear. It matters not where we choose to mourn. 'Tis only important that we do mourn. Healing can take place anywhere."

"But this was my brother. Your loss was for your child—someone who was inside you. A person you cared for and nursed through all the runny noses and colds and…and attitudes."

"I would gladly welcome those back into my life, but the Lord must have had other plans for Friedel." Elizabeth never took her eyes off the wooden plaque. "Do you have children, Dena?"

"Yes," Dena said in a somber tone as she confessed how guilty she felt for leaving her son with a trusted neighbor so she could be at Jason's side for his latest case.

Elizabeth frowned and edged closer to Dena. "I don't understand why you feel this way. Do you feel you are not being a good mother?"

"That pretty much sums it up," Dena said.

"Do you love your son?"

"Yes."

"Does your son know how much you love him?"

"I'd like to think he does."

"Do you spend time with him?"

Dena nodded.

"Have you communicated with him since you're away?"

"Yes. I called this morning about ten-thirty here—that's seven-thirty there—just as he's getting ready for school. We made a pact—we called it a pinky swear—to assure him I'd talk to him every day."

"I know the pinky swear," Elizabeth said with a big grin. "Friedel told me of this cute little game children play." She and Dena curled their little fingers together and shared a comfortable laugh while saying, *I swear,* back and forth.

"Evidently, the child teaches the adult," Jason added.

"Oh, come on, Jason," Dena teased. "Don't tell me you never pinky swore with anyone."

"Well, there was this one time…back when you swore to me you'd stay out of the action and you just showed up out of nowhere—you could have been killed."

"That's because we didn't pinky swear." She and Elizabeth shared another comfortable laugh.

Elizabeth adjusted her weight by leaning over on her elbow. "If your son has any spare time, how does he spend it?"

"Oh. He plays with his friends. He keeps our dog entertained and out of mischief…Annie loves to chew things. He helps out around our property." Dena gazed around the farm at the cattle and crops. "We don't have nearly as much as you do, but enough to keep him busy."

"These are the important things, Dena. Every day, you hear of mothers, and fathers too, who are *with* their children, but don't give them, or are incapable of giving them, what you have already given to your son. He is blessed to have you as his mother. Some parents abuse their charges, show them disgust or anger, and in so doing, teach them how to hate. In the long run, who do you think will be the better child?" Then came Elizabeth's familiar finger-in-the-air routine again.

"I like how you think," Dena sniffled.

"Over the generations," Elizabeth continued, "we are blessed, or cursed, with more innovations which make our lives easier. And that leaves us with excess time. But time to do what? Remember this, child, and remember it well. The true test of a person's character can be judged on how they spend their free time." Elizabeth tapped her finger to her temple and offered a mischievous grin. "I read a lot...and not just our Bible."

"Will you share some stories about Friedel with us?" Dena asked as she ran her fingers over the carvings on the wooden marker.

Elizabeth stared into Dena's eyes, then into Jason's. A hint of red appeared around her lids. With the tenderness of a mother stroking her child's hair, she pulled out a light blue handkerchief from her apron pocket and stared at it. "In our culture, a bride makes a special apron for their wedding ceremony. I made this from a remnant of Friedel's apron. She is buried in the garment she made, but never used."

"It is beautiful," Dena said.

"I cannot bring myself to treat this as a rag," Elizabeth whispered. "I have very little to hold in my hands. This helps me." Still neatly folded, she extended the hand-stitched keepsake to Jason.

"I, uh, I can't take this from you, Mrs. Mueller."

"I don't want you to, Mr. Carmichael. I just want you to touch it." Tears began to well up in her eyes. "Maybe it will bring you closer."

Jason rested his hand on the handkerchief. He assumed they never had a use for fabric conditioners, but this felt soft and delicate, as if it had been soaked in a softener for days. In a gentle motion, he eased the handkerchief back into Elizabeth's hands.

She clasped her hands around the handkerchief, then lowered them onto her apron and whispered, "We all have an image of how our lives should be, and whether or not we openly admit it, one of those images is about death." She raised that one special finger on her right hand again. "Don't we all feel that we, the parents, should go first? When a child is taken from us, we feel life has cheated us. As if something wrong has happened in the natural cycle of the universe. Our children should bury us, not the other way around. When we heard of Friedel's...accident, we were devastated. But as time passed and nothing ever got resolved, we felt as if society was telling us, in a rather callous voice, *Oh, by the way. You used to have a daughter. The weather for tomorrow will be sunny and warm.*" Elizabeth forced a smile. "Oh, my. You asked for a story about Friedel, not the petty meanderings of an old woman."

Leaning back against a maple tree, Jason said, "Please, this is all important." Jason watched Elizabeth narrow her eyes as she studied the faces of these strangers who'd abruptly entered her life.

"We...our family when my husband was alive...tried to convince Friedel how frivolous and egotistical she was being by demanding to continue on with her education. Did we ever tell you Friedel was on the verge of being officially shunned by the congregation?"

"No," Jason said.

"She was. In German, we call it *meidung*. No one will speak to this person, or conduct business, or utter a simple hello. It is the worst thing that can happen to us, so we are told. But there *was* something worse. She was taken from us, permanently. All she wanted to do was make a better life for our community. She even wanted to buy a small computer to hold on her lap. She said we could learn how to be more efficient. When we said it used electricity, she told us she could use the twelve-volt system we use in our barns." As an afterthought, Elizabeth added, "We have to use some form of electricity to maintain our milk at thirty-eight degrees Fahrenheit, plus process our milk in bulk containers instead of the old milk cans. Otherwise, no one would buy our milk for public consumption. Some of us own diesel generators to serve the same purpose and to charge batteries. That's all I know. I leave the rest up to the men."

"I didn't realize you had generators," Dena said. "I feel very ignorant sometimes...about your customs. I only knew you couldn't own cars or phones. And you use horses for plowing and harvesting...stuff like that."

Elizabeth gave Dena a wide smile. "Times change us, my dear. Yes, we use horses, but did you know, our congregation has a tractor? Did you see it on our way out here?" Elizabeth used the word *tractor* with the same gusto a corporate executive would boast about owning a Lear Jet.

"No."

"The men use the engine to generate twelve volts to power our equipment. But," she added, "our tractors have steel wheels in place of the rubber ones you would use. This eliminates the temptation to use them on the roads as a means of transportation. It would be illegal, and against the tenets of the *Ordnung*." She quickly added, "I only know what I hear from the men."

"That's so sad," Dena said. "About Friedel...and the *meidung*... shunning."

"We had so many talks, but Friedel had always been aware that, for us to exist at all, we had to accept a certain amount of differences within other cultures, and that is how she tried to convince us she should better herself. She and I would walk in these very same fields and talk of a better life. But when the elders became more aware of her goals, they threatened to exercise *meidung*. It only strengthened her resolve. She could be quite contrary at times."

"But you loved her," Dena added with a warm smile.

"As any mother would. So, you see, we are not too different from your world. We just get there slower."

Dena chuckled. "We all have to live with our cages, don't we?"

"Yes, but you should try to not bring your cages with you when you visit others."

Dena gave her an inquisitive look. "Are we back to talking about me and my son again?"

Elizabeth's smile was contagious. It wasn't long before the three of them were strolling back to the farmhouse—Elizabeth's arms linked through Jason's and Dena's.

"I noticed the carving on Friedel's marker," Jason said. "Do you remember who did that?"

"Oh, yes. It was Jonathon Ditmann. Even though he was quite upset by Friedel's rejection of his marriage proposal, he did it as a favor to us."

"Even though he'd married someone else?" Jason asked.

"Jonathon? Oh, yes. He harbored no ill feelings."

"Did this *someone else* know she was the runner-up?" Jason asked.

"I don't understand."

"Runner-up means came in second," Jason said. "Jonathon's second choice. Was she hurt by this change of events?"

"She would never had said anything if she was...I think."

Jason opened a gate which led to another pasture where the cattle could graze on mature grass while not disturbing the grass growing in another field. Cows were roamers. They kept their heads down and ate…and walked…and ate. They didn't care if they were trampling fresh sprouts of grass. It was a tried and proven method used by many generations. The farmers didn't need a computer to tell them this. It reminded him of a tale about an old wise Indian who stood on a hill in the newly-populated Oklahoma plains years after the opening of the west. The Indian watched the white man plow and till the soil to make it ready for a non-indigenous crop. In a dry, emotionless tone, the Indian grumbled, *Wrong side up*, which was his way of saying these people had no clue about what the unpredictable seasonal winds would do to the land that had sustained others for centuries. And he was right. The infamous and devastating dust bowl of the mid-nineteen thirties followed close behind. Jason latched the gate shut.

The only sounds were from three pairs of feet crunching through the grass, and then there was the occasional hand gesture from Elizabeth pointing to a cow plop to avoid. They'd just passed through another gate when a series of shots rang out. Its staccato report echoed back from the woods where they'd just been.

Elizabeth pressed her fingers to her lips and looked toward the farmhouse. "There should be no hunting at this time of year."

"That wasn't a hunting rifle," Jason cautioned, "That was an automatic." He patted under his shoulder where he kept his newly acquired *Mak* in a shoulder holster, and began a slow trot to the Mueller's home.

Dena joined him for a few steps, but opted to stay at Elizabeth's side.

As he approached the barn, he saw Isaac running back from a pasture near the road.

"They shot one of our cows," he yelled. "Somebody just killed her outright." His hands were squarely on his hips facing the road. "Who would do such a thing?"

Jason sprinted up next to him, grabbed his shoulder, and pushed him into the barn, knowing it was possible the shooter might be interested in taking a clear shot at a two-legged target. "Stay in there."

Lagging behind Jason, Dena yelled for Isaac to keep down. "Jason knows what he's doing." She led Elizabeth into the barn, forced her to the straw floor, and crouched over her.

Using the cover of the last remaining rows of corn as cover, Jason inched toward the road, being careful to stop and listen. All the times he and some high school date spent in those fields were a precursor to today. He didn't realize it then, but knowing what footsteps in amongst an aging cornfield sounded like could be a distinct advantage. He hoped the shooter didn't have the same level of insight.

Keep low, he kept reminding himself…almost crawling to not disturb the leaves on the stalks, all the while looking through the stalks toward the road. He could see the cow lying on her side. There was no movement. "Son-of-a-bitch." Jason listened for sounds of an engine revving. He was sure he could remember the distinct sound outside the B & B when those shots were fired. Would the sound be the same as at Kathleen's? It was definitely a beefy V-8. He positioned himself far to the side of the cow, knowing that if someone was lying-in-wait, they would expect someone to check the animal to determine how much damage was done. He wasn't gonna fall for that crap.

The sun was almost setting. Visibility sucked. What kind of weapon had this person used? It was definitely an automatic. He heard no sound of a car. The person was probably long gone by the time Jason managed to make his way into the pasture. But what if the shooter hadn't left yet? The cow wasn't going to get any better. He knew killing the cow meant one of two things; it was either bait for him to bite on…or a warning. Well, there was a third; some irresponsible drunken slob out to make a social statement about the Amish community. He liked to think that kind of mentality had died a natural death decades ago.

Keeping his eye on the road, Jason inched back into the shelter of the corn. Certainly, Joshua Stoudt had heard the shots. Jason hoped he had the presence of mind to stay put. The last thing he needed was to see Joshua walking down the road toward the Mueller farm. This is where a phone call would be deemed an absolute necessity.

Once away from the road, Jason sprinted for the barn to see if everyone was all right.

Isaac pushed the door open as Jason neared. "I was watching you through the window. Thought you'd like a little help."

Dena's arms were still wrapped around Elizabeth.

"Thanks." Jason peered out the window into the setting sun. "Y'know what's interesting?"

"Other than a dead cow?" Dena yelled out.

"No. Look where my van is parked. It's under the shade of the beech tree…in the shadows. I wonder if whoever did this didn't notice it, and would it have made a difference?"

"What difference does it make Mr. Carmichael?" Elizabeth added. "We were attacked."

Jason knelt at Elizabeth's side. "I don't think this was an attack on you. It was a warning. You have a piece of paper someone wants. This person's goal is to make sure no one sees that document and he could care less about how his goal is achieved. He could have killed you long before tonight. He could have burned your place to the ground to destroy the document. Instead, he is trying to intimidate you in order to pry the document from your hands."

"Didn't you say this David character was getting all chummy with the sheriff at the cemetery?" Dena asked.

"Yeah. Unfortunately, I don't have a clue of what they may have said to each other. My gut feeling says they both know something." Jason was glued to the window in the barn searching the field between the barn and the road. "We can't stay in here forever. Let me go out first. Dena, you come with me, but drop down by the tractor or rake over there. If everything looks okay, I'll wave to you. Deal?"

"Deal."

The correlation of the setting sun, the dead animal, and the probable location of the shooter gave Jason an advantage. The sun would be at his back, so anyone who might entertain a notion of using him as a target would be looking directly into it. For every positive thought he had, he also knew the odds were not totally in his favor. With new technology, and the right set of combat goggles, this someone could find him if looking into a blast furnace. Jason kept low. For some reason, tonight, the sun seemed to be setting faster than normal. He made sure Dena had positioned herself next to the large forked rake the Amish used to gather straw into long rows where it could later be loaded onto a wagon for the tedious trudge back to the barn.

As he grew closer to the dead cow, Jason scanned the road in each direction. With no real mountains or high terrain to hide behind, he felt whoever was responsible for this kill was long gone. Just to make sure, he took a long breath and rose…and waited.

Nothing. He studied the distinctive black and white hide of the Holstein and how close to camouflage it looked. But it did her no good this evening. Her head had almost been severed from the body by multiple, high caliber hits to the neck, the worst of which were focused around the spinal column. Jason waved to Dena, who came running to his side.

Looking down at the carcass, she muttered a breathy, "Some asshole is goin' down for this." Then she knelt beside the animal and stroked her like she'd done many times before for any animal who'd been hurt. Still wearing the dress from today's ceremony, Dena failed to notice she'd chosen a pool of blood to kneel in.

Jason slipped his Mak into his shoulder harness. "Let's get Isaac out here. He probably has plans for her."

"What do you mean?"

"She'll probably be quite a few evening meals."

"Jason. You can't be serious."

"These cattle are bred as a dual purpose animal." Jason kept looking up and down the road for any suspicious activity. His military background taught him to keep an eye on grasses, especially tall grass. If there was any movement in the field across the road, the grass would telegraph the position, and since the air was still, he would have no doubt what caused the rippling within the field. "I know it sounds cruel, but Holsteins are used for milk…and as a source of food."

"O-o-oh."

"This really sucks. These people have done nothing wrong. All they wanted to do was live their own life."

"What are we going to do? We can't just walk away from this tonight?"

"These people do have rifles at their disposal, but I'm sure they're no match for the caliber of people who would do this." As he knelt down next to Dena, he spotted Isaac had taken it upon himself to join in. He was about fifty feet away in the open field and was approaching fast. Jason held his breath.

"Is a piece of paper worth all this, Mr. Carmichael?" Isaac was panting from doing his one and only hundred-yard dash. "This is our livelihood."

Jason's mouth dropped. What happened was deplorable, but was Isaac placing his sister's death below that of a range animal? It was only Dena's first day with the Muellers. When he glanced at Dena's piercing eyes and clenched lips, it was evident she'd picked up the not-so-subtle nuance in Isaac's statement and tone of voice. He hoped she wouldn't let out with one of her well-meaning tirades. Good. She hadn't opened her mouth yet.

"What's wrong with you, Isaac?" Dena had been on her knees next to Jason, but in a flash, she was bending over Isaac like an irritable mother with a terminal case of PMS. "We risk our asses to come out here, and you are upset…"

Good. At least she didn't say, *pissed off.*

"…because a cow has been killed? Don't you want to find out who killed your sister? Jeez." A few clumps of blood-soaked mud dripped from her knees.

Isaac's eyes widened and his head snapped back. "Yes, I do. I suppose I have grown immune to sadness after twenty-five years."

"Well, don't grow immune to sadness," Dena continued, "because without it, someone out there in this world is flipping you and your mother off."

Oh, oh. He won't know what that means. Turning to Isaac, Jason suggested they call it a night. "You do what you have to do with the cow. I'm sorry she was killed, but I want you to understand something. This is a message from someone who seems willing to intensify their tactics to get what they want from you. So, I have to deal with this the only way I know how, and unfortunately, it seems I can't call in the sheriff's office for any assistance. Do you understand?"

Isaac nodded. "I will take care of the animal. We will meet with the others tomorrow to discuss how far this will continue."

"Do me a favor, Isaac," Jason said. "Go into your house, load your rifles and keep them handy."

"I have another idea," Dena added.

◊　　◊　　◊

The woolen blanket furnished Jason with protection from the nightly chill. Elizabeth gave him another…just in case, which he kept on the chair next to him. He was sure he could make it through the night out on the front porch. At least that's what he said to Elizabeth before urging her to go back inside. Under the blanket, he wore a down jacket he'd kept in his van.

Dena needed no coaxing. As soon as Jason was settled in, she disappeared into the room Isaac had suggested she use. It was her idea for Jason to stand guard out front with the help of two Marlin lever-action rifles supplied by Isaac. Isaac promised Jason he'd come out every so often. *Yeah, right.* Both rifles were loaded with Remington 35s. All Jason had to do was cock the rifles if the occasion arose. The remainder of the ammo sat in a box on the other chair. Jason hoped he had enough if he needed them, but knew if this mysterious someone showed up again, he'd be out-gunned. He kept his Mak at his side in case there was any up-front-and-personal action.

He didn't do it in front of Dena, but he guessed at how many shots the shooter had taken to bring the Holstein down. The neck was almost severed, but the body also contained no less than ten entry wounds. And the burst he'd heard hadn't lasted but a few seconds. He looked down at the Marlins again and crossed his fingers.

It was strange sitting on the porch by himself. He understood why Dena had insisted they spend the night rather than forcing the Muellers to fend for themselves in a situation they were psychologically ill-equipped to handle. Jason unfolded the other blanket and tucked it around his legs, then pulled the first blanket up around his throat. Dena was right…but Dena was inside, and warm, and comfortable. His eyelids became heavy.

Jason awoke to the touch of a hand on his shoulder. His first reaction was it was Isaac. It wasn't.

"Hi," Dena whispered. "Are you cold?"

"Naw. I'm used to sleeping…in an upright position…in a straight back chair…wooden…in a strange place."

"You aren't mad at me, are you?"

"No." He scooped up the Mak on the chair beside him. "Here. Sit." After she wiggled around to make sure her blanket was thoroughly wrapped around her, he said, "What are you wearing under that blanket? When we came here today, all you had on was a blouse and skirt."

"Same."

"And you're not cold?"

"Yeah, I am." She reached over Jason's shoulder and tugged at his blanket until it was around her shoulders, too. When she seemed settled, she leaned into Jason, and in a seductive tone oozing of the local maple syrup, whispered. "Can I ask you a question?"

"Sure."

"What the hell have you gotten us into, you moron? You were supposed to come back here to relax, find yourself, or rejuvenate your soul. But, no-o. Here we are, freezing our asses off holding rifles when we should be holding margaritas." Technically, what Dena was doing was whispering, but she was doing it with enough energy to power the Mueller's 12-volt generator.

Damn. Jason missed this kind of fire from Dena. "Y'know? I never expected this thing to balloon out like it did. All I did was ask one simple question. Now here we are."

"Yeah, here we are, and add one dead deputy to the mix. Look. I've only been here one day, but I've heard you talk about this David guy you used to go to high school with. Then, you evidently suspect the sheriff of having some kind of involvement in Friedel's death. Who are we supposed to trust?"

"You're not going to like my answer, but the only ones I trust are these Amish people. Problem is, they're not really conditioned to fight, or possibly even kill anyone." Jason gave a sardonic chuckle. "Not what I would consider a formidable war machine."

"Why would you think that?"

"Look at them. They're gentle. They don't go looking for trouble. All they want to do is live their lives in peace." Jason let out a deep breath while he set the Marlin on the floor at his feet. "I know what I said probably sounds like an old John Lennon song."

"*Imagine?*"

"Yeah."

"Who else do you have on your list?"

"I could make a case for a few others."

"Names, Jason." Her voice quivered from the cold.

"David Ellison is my primary focus, since his initials are paired up with Friedel's. After that, I even entertained the possibility that Isaac might be capable of killing his sister. He is very proud, overly obstinate in his beliefs, and his sister humiliated the family name. And the irony of the situation is; her death didn't have to be the result of an intentional act. Friedel could have died from the result of a heated argument. You want me to go on?"

"Yep." Every time Dena moved, her blanket kept letting in cold air, and each time, she teased more of Jason's blanket off him and around her. She always made sure the blanket was tight around her throat, and her teeth were beginning to chatter.

"You want to wear my jacket?"

"No. I'll be okay." With a lighthearted tone, she rushed in with, "Uuh…what would you wear if I did?"

"I have another jacket in the van."

"Gimme the jacket." Dena threw off the blankets and grabbed Jason's down-filled jacket so quickly, whatever body warmth Jason had managed to capture inside did not have time to escape.

"Be right back." Noticing how quiet it was, Jason slid the side door of his van open as slowly as possible and retrieved a fleece-lined bomber jacket he referred to as his *dirty* jacket—in case he had to crawl around on the ground to fix something, or to install chains. This time of year, the weather could be somewhat iffy—so said the rental agency. Jason buttoned up the jacket and settled down under the blankets next to Dena. "It's getting colder out here, don't you think?"

"Yeah. When we visited Friedel's grave, you and Mrs. Mueller mentioned a man named Jonathon Ditmann, but we never had a chance to talk about his runner-up. Did you meet with her, too?"

"Nope. Her name is Margaret."

"How do you think Margaret felt when she'd been treading water in the background, then all of a sudden, this Jonathon guy says, *Well, I guess you'll do?*" Jason was still taking a breath to answer when Dena jumped in with, "Pissed? Humiliated? Embarrassed? I know I would be."

"Sounds like a normal reaction to me. Ya know? Even though I grew up around people who just don't *talk* their religion, but openly *commit* to it—there is another side of me that can't imagine being publicly disgraced is tolerable in any religious doctrine." Jason gave a long sigh of frustration. "If anyone thinks the Amish have a corner on the market when it comes to decency or righteousness, they're dead wrong. Using a warped rationale such as that, one could make an argument that a

Catholic, or Lutheran, or Seventh-day Adventist would never commit murder."

Jason told Dena about an Amish man named Edward Gingerich, who, back in '93, did not simply kill his wife, Katie, but intensified his violence far beyond what could be conveniently labeled as a simple anger killing. Edward was convicted of knocking Katie to the floor, then stomping on her with his boots until her head had become unrecognizable mush. If that wasn't enough for him, he picked up a kitchen knife and carved her open, cut out all her internal organs and laid them on the floor next to her in a neat row.

"Can we attach this stigma to all Amish?" Jason continued. "No way. Just as we can't assign a level of certainty to any member of any religion...but it does exist. I suppose this goes with the territory—where we're forced to be realistic, no matter what we *want* to believe."

Dena glanced at the Mueller's front door. "Now you've really scared me."

◊ ◊ ◊

The sun was a mere glow on the horizon when Jason felt a nudge on his shoulder. One of the Marlins was at his feet, the other leaned against the arm of his chair. Jason's other shoulder was filled with Dena who, sometime after they dozed off, had slipped her arm through his. The smell of her hair was refreshing. He closed his half opened eyes so he could enjoy another scent of Dena. Then there was another nudge.

"Mr. Carmichael," Isaac whispered. "Are you awake?"

"Am now." At least Jason thought that is what he said. Not being a morning person, it could have come out more like, *poke me one more time and you'll be wearing your balls for earrings.*

"It's about five o'clock. I think your obligations are over."

"What time is it?" When Jason mumbled his question into his hands, which now supported his face, Dena woke up, yawned and asked the same question.

"Five o'clock," Isaac said again. "Milking time."

In the direction of the pasture where the cow had been killed, Jason watched the Holsteins, with heads lowered and swinging from side to side, plod toward their morning ritual. There were no holidays, no time off for good behavior, no managerial bonuses, no casual dress Fridays.

It was a life of pure drudgery. Eat, drink, get your tits yanked, and then do it all over again. "We made it through the night, huh?"

"Yes," Isaac said. "My mother will fix you breakfast if you would like to stay."

"That is so sweet," Dena yawned. "I have to pee."

Jason leaned down and picked up the rifles and made sure the safety was set before he leaned them into the wall behind him. "I think we'll be going, Isaac, but thank your mother for us. The place where we're staying is expecting us," Jason glanced at his watch, "but not as early as I thought. I called them last night and told them we'd not be staying there, but we would be back for breakfast." Another airy yawn found its way out of Jason's gaping mouth.

The screen door squeaked open. Framed in the doorway was Elizabeth, looking clean and polished like she'd slept standing up for fear of wrinkling her clothes. "Are you sure? Two more mouths are not a problem." She gave Isaac a stern look. "Did you ask them nicely?"

"Yes, Mother. I did."

"He did," Jason confirmed as he watched Dena squeeze past Elizabeth. Dena still wore his down jacket from last night. In the light of dawn, he noticed the shoulder seam down near her elbows and her hands were nowhere to be seen. When she waved a lazy good morning, the sleeves flapped like a pennant in a stiff breeze.

"Excuse me," Isaac mumbled. "I have chores to attend to." He did not look back.

Elizabeth frowned as her son stormed away. "Thank you for staying last night, Mr. Carmichael. I felt much safer knowing you were out here."

Jason pointed to the rifles leaning against the wall. "Keep those loaded."

Her voice shaking, Elizabeth asked, "You will not desert us, will you?"

Jason checked out a small ledge created by the header over the front porch. He reached up and rubbed the surface, hoping there were no spiders hiding there that might treat his fingers as fresh deli meat. It was dusty, but free from webs. Other than being afraid of heights, his other phobia was being taken down by a tiny creature he could never know was around until after the damage had been done. "I'm going to leave my other Mak right here. It's loaded." He slid the handgun into the opening, and backed away to insure it was adequately hidden from sight.

"Why are you doing that?" Dena asked.

"I know I'm on someone's radar. I just don't know who. If I was caught with this in my possession, I could probably be treated as just another criminal." He stood on his tiptoes to make sure the gun could not be seen by someone taller than him. "One more thing, Elizabeth. Please tell no one…and I mean no one, the gun is there."

"Not Isaac. Not Josh…?"

"No one. Please do this for me. If I'm ever going to need a gun, it's going to be where I'm staying, or here." He placed his large hands on Elizabeth's frail shoulders and looked into her eyes. "I assure you, I will do everything in my power to keep you safe. You still have the document in a protected location?"

Elizabeth nodded.

"These people want two things; the Medico-legal document, and me out of the way—and not necessarily in that order."

CHAPTER 17

Jason lied. He'd not told the Loomis' he and Dena would be back for breakfast. He knew this was going to be his fight…and now Dena's. They'd been through a lot together and Jason couldn't imagine having anyone else at his side. Had they accepted the Mueller's invitation to stay for breakfast, could it have blossomed into a routine? He needed freedom to move about, ask questions, and have no obligation to be back at any set time. Would the Muellers be safe? As long as their document remained intact and hidden, they would stand a good chance of not being gunned down as brutally as cattle in a field. There were too many others within the family who now knew the existence of the document, so whoever was determined to keep this doc from the public would have to commit absolute carnage…and to what end? It might still remain hidden. Jason hoped the person responsible for this act was leaning more toward logic rather than cold, calculated retribution.

Not being accustomed to swabbing herself off by candlelight, Dena made sure her knees were clean from the blood she'd knelt in last night. It was far more effective for her to do this in the light of day.

Jason and Dena drove into Conneaut to have a quiet breakfast together. They found a little hole-in-the-wall restaurant whose interior could have been designed by a cook from one of the obsolete iron ore carriers. The brick front had been renovated to include a much larger window to take advantage of a lake view just west of the entrance to Conneaut harbor. In its day, it was probably no more than a peep hole to check out who wanted into a place where room service was calculated by the hour. A port town, during the time when the steel industry was the prime life blood of the area, often spawned businesses catering to those who were only able to be ashore for a few hours between watches, and within walking distance.

Black and white pictures on the walls showed iron ore and limestone carriers tied up at the once thriving P & C docks unloading their valuable cargo. The Pittsburgh and Conneaut Dock Company was a major link in getting the raw material from the Mesabi ore range in Minnesota to the steel mills in Pittsburgh, Pennsylvania. Many of the pictures were probably one-of-a-kind dating from the late 1800s. A few of the more recent super carriers with their self-unloaders, all portrayed in eye-dazzling color, almost spoiled the former charm of the place—if you considered the need for sanitized hand wipes as charm. Jason couldn't help thinking of Kathleen's involvement with the museum in Vermilion. Kathleen was history. Dena is now.

A pedestal-mounted sign at the door informed customers to seat themselves. Coffee pot in hand, a smiling waitress waved them in.

Jason and Dena chose a corner booth where they could gaze across the bush-lined street and out over Lake Erie. No sooner had they picked up their menus, when Jason caught a glimpse of a familiar vehicle. When it stopped out front, Jason knew he couldn't have choreographed a better opportunity. It was David Ellison's white limousine.

The driver opened the door and David stepped out, straightened his tie and suit jacket, and had a nose-to-nose talk with the driver, who was reading something from a black book he held. Within a few seconds, two vans snuggled in behind the limo, one from the local rag and another from one of Cleveland's television stations. Jason knew a photo op when he saw one. Jason whispered, "Dena. Do me a favor."

"What?"

"We haven't ordered yet, so while David's out there strutting his stuff, go sit at the counter. We do not know each other." Jason watched as David adjusted his tie as he conferred with the driver. Then there was the last second check of his hair in the side view mirror of the limo. When the cameras were aimed and the pencils were poised, David headed for the front door. "Hurry." Jason waved for Dena to go.

"This should be fun." Dena gathered up her napkin she'd wadded up and started for the counter where a few patrons were busy devouring their breakfasts.

The front door opened with a flourish for David's grand entrance. He stepped in and surveyed the customers and surroundings in a restaurant where patrons brazenly rested their bare arms on the counter. A restaurant with no one to greet him. A restaurant where the waiters did not have a towel ostentatiously draped over their jacket sleeve. A restaurant where the help did not speak with a foreign accent. This place was far too pedestrian for the Lieutenant Governor, but if this was where the voters hung out, David would indulge them. Or would it be called pandering? Jason kept his head lowered.

When members of the media began to filter into the room, all eyes fell on the tall man, dressed as if he'd just stepped off an ad for GQ magazine, with cuff links showing exactly one inch beyond his coat sleeves. Wasting no time, David approached the counter where a waitress had been filling cups of coffee and introduced himself. In well-rehearsed jargon, he began spouting the appreciation he had for the area and its contribution to the historical significance to the state. He reached for every hand of the people at the counter first, but came to an abrupt halt next to a woman wearing a medium length blue skirt, white blouse and high heels. When she'd selected a revolving counter stool to enjoy her breakfast, the woman's skirt had risen enough to give the eye a tempting view of legs seldom seen in an establishment where there was no admission charge. "Hi. I'm David Ellison. Lieutenant Governor, David Ellison." He not only held the woman's hand, but gave it an extra squeeze.

"Hi. I'm Dena Manning. Female...and unimpressed."

"Ouch," David muttered with a forced grin, and turned his back to the camera.

Inching through the reporters and cameramen, Jason worked his way up behind his old classmate. In a soft voice, Jason said, "Blue. Buttonhook right. On three. Break. Break."

David froze. "Whoa. This could only be one person," he announced in a loud voice. "Jason Carmichael. Wide receiver. Grand Valley High School." He spun around and greeted his old classmate with open arms. "Ladies and gentlemen. This is my good friend and football teammate,

Jason Carmichael from high school. I never ever expected to see this guy again."

The cameras and photographers instantly focused on this potential by-line.

"How'd you know it was him?" a reporter asked.

"He gave me a call," David boasted. "Not just a call, but THE call when the Mustangs needed a short yardage gain." David bent over slightly at the waist and lowered his hands as a quarterback would do when anticipating the center's snap. He then began to gyrate his hips as if he now had the ball in his hands. As quarterback, his job was to spin to his right while keeping his eyes glued to Jason whose role was to go out about five yards, do a head fake to the inside, then spin to the outside to catch the well-thrown pass. It was their signature move when the team was in desperate need of a few critical yards. "That play never failed, did it, old buddy?"

"Oh, those were the glory days," Jason sighed. "Never failed."

Like a father/son gesture, David looped his arm over Jason's shoulder and whispered directly into Jason's ear. "Kathleen tells me you have some sort of crusade going on."

Jason leaned into David. "You want the media involved?"

David whispered something to the man who'd driven the limo, who, in turn, ushered the photographers and reporters aside and evidently explained why the sudden need for privacy with an old acquaintance. This only fueled the media. Intuitively, they knew the real story was *over there.*

David ushered Jason to an empty booth. When he slid in, David forced a smile and waved at the camera. "Okay, buddy. What the hell is going on with you and these Amish people?"

"You remember Friedel Mueller?"

"Yeah, yeah. She died…twenty-five years ago. Life goes on."

"I have to ask you a question. Did you ever fool around with her? Like try to get to know her…outside of your relationship with Kathleen?"

David leaned as far forward as the table would allow. "Who wouldn't? Jesus, man. That girl had tits out to here. And that ass. Damn. Those clothes she was forced to wear didn't do a very good job of hiding the goodies."

"So, did you ever score?" Jason faked a lecherous grin.

"I, David Ellison, am asked whether I succeeded at getting what I wanted?"

"Did you?"

David slapped Jason on the shoulder and burst out laughing. The sudden outburst was followed by a congenial wave at a camera. "We were close," he continued as he again focused on Jason.

"How did you ever manage that, man? I thought you and Kathleen were tight."

"C'mon Jason, old buddy. Don't tell me you never thought about getting some of that Amish pussy."

"To tell you the truth, no. We were young then, David. There was a part of me who admired Friedel."

"Under the clothes, maybe. Be straight up with me, Jason. Long legs. Nice ripe tits. She knew exactly what she was doing when she strutted through the hallways of good old GVHS. Don't tell me you never thought about what those nipples would look like." David did not have to fake his lecherous look.

Customers and the media were growing more interested in what was going on over in the corner. When they began to gravitate closer to the booth, the driver would herd them away with the efficiency of a well-trained Border Collie.

"Remember the old covered bridge on Avery Road—the one where we all carved our initials? Yours and KR—with a heart," Jason prodded.

David gave a curious nod.

"I also saw the one where you carved your initials along with FM. I kind of assumed they were yours."

"Yeah? Yours are there, too. Right with Nicole's."

"Was that one of your...?"

"Masterpieces? Yeah. Friedel was really impressed. Damn. That night we were so close. She liked riding in cars."

"She never told anyone."

"You've got to be joking, dude. Some Amish chick is going to go bragging about taking a ride in a hot set of wheels...the kind not pulled by one fucking horse. Hell, my Camaro had 375 of those."

"So? You didn't seem to think it was wrong to try to get in Friedel's pants while you were supposed to have an exclusive with Kathleen?"

"Opportunity, Jason, old buddy. Opportunity. Don't ever knock it. Did you notice the girl at the counter?" He nodded in Dena's direction. "Now that's an ass to die for."

With the unexpected arrival of a celebrity of sorts, the waitress had only managed a mug of coffee for Dena, who toyed with the cup while keeping her eyes glued on the action with the help of the well-positioned mirror. All she had to do to was cock her head slightly to the right to get a better view around the hand-printed poster listing the daily specials.

"You'd hit on her?" Down deep inside, Jason hoped he would. After knowing what damage Dena was capable of inflicting, he found himself praying David would make a move. What an item that would make for the evening news. It would probably fall under the banner of Breaking News…Lieutenant Governor, David Ellison is victim of hit and run.

"In a heartbeat." Glancing at Dena again, David whispered, "That is one world-class ass."

Jason chuckled at the thought. "If you've been talking to Kathleen, then you must know she told me you've married again."

"So?" David gave a casual shrug of his padded shoulders. "I'm only married when I'm home."

"You haven't changed much, David. Well, maybe you have. I see you've put on a little gut. Maybe you're just out of practice."

Holding a black leather-bound notebook in front of him, like a waiter would present a menu to a customer, the driver approached the table and leaned toward David. "You have a ten-thirty."

David waved him off.

"Since you admit you carved those initials at the bridge, aren't you worried some observant detective might draw some sort of conclusion as to your culpability in Friedel's death?"

"Don't try playing games with me, asshole. I know you were at Hutchinson's burial ceremony. As for those initials, that bridge is fast turning into history. And we both know, without documentation, hearsay doesn't mean shit in a court of law." David turned his head to the right and gave another generous smile for the cameras.

"Did you see me?"

"Didn't have to. I have other eyes."

Good. If David had seen him, then he would have assuredly noticed Dena, too. In all probability, David would have even bypassed Jason if he'd gotten a glimpse of Dena. "Money talks, huh?"

"God. You are so fucking naïve. I'm going to let you in on a little secret. It's not about money. It's about what money can buy...and that is power. It's all about power, Jason. It might amaze you to know I have an entire entourage of people who will buy into anything I say. I call them lemmings. They are stupid. They are shallow, meaningless heaps of biological life forms incapable of anything other than sucking air. But... they will do what I want. They will cater to my every wish. They will believe what I want. The end product is; I am their hero. I am the focal point of their very existence. Money...equals...power." David leaned back in the booth and gave a satisfied smirk. "It's a great life."

"And addictive, I see."

"Oh, yeah." His candid acknowledgement was accompanied by a lengthy sigh.

"Oh, man. I wish I'd brought my note pad. I should be writing this down."

"Fuck you." David laughed, rippled his fingers at the media, and gave them another gleaming white smile perfectly suited for a toothpaste ad.

"You don't have enough money for that. Enlighten me. First I show up and see *Keep out* signs posted all over the Avery bridge, I asked a few innocent questions, then a week later, the state of Ohio finds the funds to demolish the structure. What do you think caused them to jump-start the renovation project at this moment in time? Kinda convenient, huh?"

"What can I say? Another example of bureaucracy at its finest."

"Yeah, right. According to the State Historic Bridge Society, Avery wasn't even on their radar—something to do with insufficient traffic usage."

"Details." David tapped his fingers on the table. "It probably got bumped up for sentimental reasons."

"You've got to be joking." Jason repeated the tapping pattern David had just done, knowing it was his way of dealing with uncomfortable situations. "You must know I'm a cop, don't you?"

"I know everything." David's eyes narrowed. "What Kathleen didn't blab on about, local LE fills in the gaps. It's quite an efficient network."

"Of friends?"

David burst into a boisterous laugh. "In this business, you don't need friends. I'm perfectly at ease surrounded by all these lemmings who are afraid to have me for an enemy. Power, Jason, power." David tapped his forefinger on his temple.

A mischievous grin crept over Jason's face as he leaned forward. He waited to see if David would begin to tap his fingers knowing damn well that would be the clue to reel him in. Sure enough, after a few moments to let the fish tug at the bait, David began to drum his fingers against a white coffee mug placed upside down waiting for the next customer. "Oh, yeah? See the girl at the counter you've had your eyes on? Bet she will have nothing to do with you."

"How much?"

"If you score, I leave town."

David's eyes lit up as he glanced at Dena, who had her back to the whole circus. "I thought you were committed to these Amish people, Jason, old buddy. Sounds like you're tempting me with a chicken-shit way out."

"Score...and I'm out of your life." Jason gave him one of his confident smiles.

David slid out of the booth and in a robust voice, announced, "Ladies and gentlemen. Regretfully, due to a prior commitment, my old friend and teammate, and I must draw our long overdue reunion to a close." David faced the cameras as he strode over to the counter next to Dena. "I hope you feel the need, as I so fervently do, to have someone in Columbus, and later, in Washington, who not only hears your voices, but listens to you as well." As he babbled on, he rested his hands on Dena's shoulders.

The cameras edged closer.

Being in front of a camera was David's forte. As he captivated customers with his oratorical skills, his hands no longer just rested on her shoulder, but seemed to resemble a caress. As if in slo-mo, he pivoted the stool around and coaxed Dena to her feet whereupon he slipped his hand around her waist. "My parents came from this very county where

163

ships carrying iron ore and limestone were as common as rail cars," he continued, "and for them, God rest their souls, I will forever fight for you in every way I know how. This is my personal pledge to you." His hand slipped lower.

A few people gave a courteous, round of applause. Much like getting pity points in a game when you're getting your ass kicked and your opponent feels sorry for you.

The TV reporter stuck a mike in Dena's face while the cameraman trained his lens on her. "And how do you feel about having Lieutenant Governor, David Ellison coming here to meet with you on such a personal level?"

Dena's eyes glistened. "Golly. If you were to focus your camera on the mirror in back of me, you might catch a glimpse of what he might do to any of you if given the opportunity."

David's hand rose so quickly, he didn't know what to do with it. It kind of waved around like an airport windsock—except with diamond cuff links.

"And furthermore, Lieutenant Governor, David Ellison," Dena hissed, "you put your hand on my ass one more time and I'll pull your god-damned arm out of the socket."

This time, the customers gave a rousing round of applause, but it was not directed at David. And it was all caught in hi-def.

Jason stood in the corner and watched David storm out of the restaurant and into his limo. "Hmm. Breaking news," he muttered while giving Dena a thumbs-up.

CHAPTER 18

Mornings were pretty much planned out for Jason and Dena. It started with the traditional feast in the breakfast nook of the old Loomis B & B, followed by a private call by Dena to her son. She'd promised to call him every morning before he left for school. After the call, she would come out of her room with teary eyes and clenched lips.

Jason knew she'd been desperately trying to absorb the thoughts and beliefs Elizabeth shared with her while sitting at Friedel's grave site yesterday evening. For Dena's sake, he hoped the conversation had made an impact about her feelings of guilt. "How'd it go with your son?"

"He's okay." Dena used a wadded up tissue to dab at her eyes. "It makes a big difference to be with my neighbor and her son. They play together so much anyhow, it's like having a constant companion."

"School going okay?" Jason slowed as he entered the road leading to the Mueller farm. A lone Amish man, hunched over with his arms resting on his legs, reined the horse onto the shoulder of the road as the white van eased past.

"He gets good grades." Dena stared out her window.

Jason could always tell when Dena was in one of her moods. She had a habit of grasping the hand-hold over the door installed by GM as an assist to enter the high van. Once she'd held it, she would rest her elbow on the leather strip under the window, all the while staring out the window. Jason couldn't help but wonder why she never mentioned her husband, or even that she'd talked to him. And why was her son staying with a neighbor rather than her husband? It seemed so long ago, back in Sonora, when she'd mentioned his having a fleeting session of hide-the-weenie with a customer of his. At least he claimed it was short-lived. "Here we are."

Tied to the shade tree out front was Joshua Stoudt's carriage with his horse gulping down water from a galvanized bucket.

Taking care to raise as little dust as possible, Jason eased the Chevy down the driveway and shut the engine off far away from the horse. It looked so peaceful. He watched Dena exit the van. She always looked attractive, but for the last two days, she'd worn a skirt and feminine blouse. That was a bonus. Now it was back to basics—blue jeans and a light green cotton shirt. Before stepping out, she gave Jason a generous smile. The kind he knew meant she was going to be okay.

"Morning Mr. Stoudt. Isaac." Jason shook both their hands. "Interrupting anything?"

Isaac gave a courteous nod to Jason, and tipped his straw hat at Dena.

"A good day to you, Mr. Carmichael," Joshua said. "And to you, Dena. *Guten Tag.*"

"And a good day to you, too, Mr. Stoudt," Dena said.

"*Verstehen sie Deutsche?*" Joshua asked.

Dena tilted her head forward and chuckled, "*Ein wenig.*" She made a small gap between her thumb and forefinger to let him know she knew very little.

Joshua returned the chuckle and offered her a chair on the front porch. "We asked you here today," Joshua began, "to try to understand how close you are to finding the person responsible for Friedel's death, but we..."

"It was I who asked for this meeting, I would like you to know," Isaac said. The subtle grin and amiable expression he'd shown with Dena disappeared. "I am concerned for what good you have brought to us." Joshua started to speak, but Isaac waved him away. "Forgive me Mr. Stoudt, but we've spent twenty-five years adapting to what has happened in our family, but since Mr. Carmichael has arrived, there has been one killing of a county deputy, we have lost one of our herd, our family has been threatened, and we have every reason to believe the threats may escalate into even more violence. What do we stand to gain from all this? Peace of mind? Retribution?"

Joshua stood to reveal his full height. "This has already been discussed when we all met, Isaac." Noticeably absent was the hunched back and gentle eyes. "We have made a commitment to Elizabeth and to the Muellers, that we, as a community, wished to honor Mr. Carmichael's offer to find out who is responsible for taking Friedel from us. Who do you think you are to bring this up in such a way?"

"I am her brother."

"And I am the pastor, the elder, and I think now, probably the wiser. Maybe even the most compassionate."

"'Tis our right. Not yours," Isaac fired back.

"May I ask where Elizabeth is?" Jason said.

"She is inside doing her duties. We will settle this."

Dena leaped from her wooden chair. "Immer mit der Ruhe!"

Jason knew Dena's clenched fist meant Isaac was in for a battle. "What did you just say?" he whispered to Dena.

"I said, *hold your horses*...in German...I think, or...the Evergreen tree is resting. I'm not totally sure." She then glared at Isaac. "Did you mean that the *men* will decide what is right without consulting with Friedel's mother?"

"'Tis...none...of your concern."

Dena's eyes had become the tiny slits Jason had witnessed too many times before. "I think we should ask Elizabeth to come out here."

Isaac slowly turned to face Jason, but Joshua placed his giant hand on Isaac's shoulder and spun him around, not in a violent way, but more like the firm hand of a father trying to instill a sense of sanity into a potentially volatile situation.

"I think you should get your mother...now," Joshua said with a deep resonant, almost angry tone of voice. Even his horse stopped drinking and looked in the direction of the uncharacteristic sound.

"No," Dena said. "Let me." She peered in the screen door and called out for Elizabeth. There was no answer. She called out again, this time a little louder. Soft footsteps approached the porch.

"Dena. How nice."

"Hi. Did you know we were coming over?"

Elizabeth opened the front door and cast a nervous glance at Isaac. In a fragile voice, she whispered, "Yes, but I was asked to stay inside."

When Jason took Elizabeth by the arm to help her onto the porch, she flinched and clung to the long sleeves of her modest dress. "Are you hurt?" Jason locked eyes with Isaac for an instant, then refocused his attention on Elizabeth. "Did someone hurt you...or force you to stay away?"

Elizabeth gave a nervous nod.

Jason had just begun to open his mouth when Joshua jumped into the brew. "Let me see your arm." When Elizabeth pulled up her sleeve, it was evident she'd suffered some obvious bruising in a confined area just above the elbow. The quarter-size pattern of marks was characteristic of an arm that had been squeezed by someone...and not too gently. "Did you do this?" he bellowed out at Isaac.

"My mother has been far too lenient in this matter."

"It is not your duty to determine the amount of leniency in this matter, Isaac," Joshua commanded. "What you have done is a disgrace to your mother, and to the memory of your sister. How dare you."

Isaac picked up a hay fork he'd leaned against the entrance to the house and held the tines upward close to Joshua's face. "This is our fight, Mr. Stoudt. Our family." He then waved the fork in Jason's direction. "This man has done nothing to right a wrong. His only contribution has been to divide us. This is wrong."

When Isaac twirled the fork around so the tines were aimed directly at his throat, Jason reached inside his light jacket and, by reflex, felt for the knurling on the handle of his Mak, but realized it was still hidden in the porch's header, just above Isaac's hat. "I advise you to put the fork down, Isaac," Jason said in a firm voice. "I came here to talk to all of you, not to argue or debate." He gave Isaac a few seconds to mull over his comment. "Please."

Isaac leaned the fork into the wall and stepped away. He'd not turned around to face Jason yet before he let loose with, "And this man has also been in contact with Jonathon Ditmann, I might add. Now, he and Margaret are upset at the bringing up of old hurts. Division, not unity is what Mr. Carmichael has cast upon us." He kept his back turned to Jason.

"Isaac," Jason began. "I need you to know this. What I am doing is an investigation. And this process takes time. If there were such a thing as easy answers, Friedel's killer would have already been caught...

twenty-five years ago. No one seemed to care. I do. No one wanted to take the effort to find this person. I do. Will things bubble to the surface because of my probing around? Yes. Will these things be pleasant? Probably not. The only pleasure in this whole process will be the ending. And I intend to be here until we catch this person. I will not desert you or your family." Jason offered his hand to Isaac.

Isaac looked over his shoulder, but still faced away from Jason.

So this is what shunning would feel like. Jason kept his hand extended.

"Isaac," Elizabeth said in a fiery voice. "You honor this man's commitment. I allowed you to push me aside this morning, but I will not tolerate the memory of Friedel to be tarnished by such behavior." She reached for his shoulder.

"I have work to do." The dirt in Isaac's boots made an irritating crunching sound on the wooden deck as he stormed off the porch.

An eerie silence followed Isaac's departure. Everyone cast an awkward glance at another, and then dipped their heads. Elizabeth inched closer to Jason and slipped her arm through his. When she did, Joshua took a deep breath and offered an apologetic hand to Jason and Dena. Each sat on the edge of the porch and looked out over the field where the cow had been slaughtered. One tractor trailer in need of a muffler roared past the entrance to the farm. A solid black puff of smoke belched from the vertical chrome exhaust pipes as the driver decelerated using his engine as a braking mechanism—what police and local residents would call *Jake Brakes* in their complaints.

Tucked in behind the truck was an Ashtabula County sheriff's vehicle, its distinctive gold star glistened in the morning sun. The Crown Vic slowed as it passed the entrance to the Mueller farm, obviously ignoring the eighteen-wheeler's justification for being pulled over. Jason watched the car creep out of sight behind a grove of apple trees. Because of the distance, Jason had no way of ID'ing the driver. "I'm so sorry for what has happened this morning."

"No," Elizabeth said. "It is we who should be sorry. I allowed my son to treat me poorly this morning, but I will not allow him to treat others that way. It was inexcusable."

Dena pulled out her cell phone, excused herself and headed for the far side of the house.

It was ten-thirty. Jason watched her enter a number—time for her to call her son. When the person answered, she turned her head away and disappeared around the corner of the house. "Mr. Stoudt," Jason began. "I think it would be proper of me to offer you and Elizabeth the opportunity to back out of our agreement. You give me the word, and I will leave." There was a kind of clumsiness to his words—much like someone might feel when trying to march to a waltz.

Joshua shifted over next to Elizabeth and grasped her hands. "What do you think, Elizabeth? Shall we have another meeting with the congregation?"

Through tearing eyes, Elizabeth gazed across the fields. "I had such high hopes when you came to us, Mr. Carmichael. In my heart, I believed someone finally cared." Elizabeth's breathing seemed strained as she became transfixed with the clouds. Her eyes narrowed. "Do you know? Through billions of years, clouds become rain become rivers become oceans and then clouds again. I believe there is not one drop of water on earth that, at one time or another, has not touched every other drop of water." With eyes filled with trust, she stared at Jason. "In all this water, you gave me something to cling to."

Jason clasped her hands.

"What do we do now?" she asked.

"We talk." Jason sat sideways with one leg dangling over the edge of the porch. "You ask. I answer."

"In the meeting we held when you first came here," Joshua began, "one man introduced the idea of someone within our own community having a hand in killing Friedel." He quickly added, "It did not receive positive reactions. But what would happen if this was true?"

Jason knew that Isaac's minutes-old demonstration to willingly escalate a situation to a physical level had just resurrected a notion he'd mulled over in his mind many times, but not until this morning, did Jason take the idea seriously. "I believe there are a few members of your community who bore a serious grudge against Friedel's idealism." Jason finished with a chilly, "A crime is a crime."

Elizabeth pressed her fingertips to her lips and her eyes became deep blackened hollows.

"Ever since Ken Hutchinson's death," Jason said, "I've read in the newspaper about how a few sensationalists associate the two incidents as if they are the act of a serial killer. This is not true. These killings are twenty-five years removed from each other. This is not the work of a serial killer nor a spree killer. These killings are what a psychiatrist might deem *situationalistic* which is a word invented to define an apparent reaction to similar acts or circumstances. I believe whoever killed Friedel never meant for it to happen, but something went terribly wrong that night. And twenty-five years later, Ken Hutchinson became collateral damage."

"A twenty-five year old cover up," Dena said.

"Exactly." Jason studied her expression for any signs of stress after her abbreviated call back home. "You okay?" he whispered.

Dena forced a smile and tucked the cell in a side pocket of her jacket.

"I have to ask you this, Mrs. Mueller," Jason said. "Do you know if Friedel ever rode in a car—for fun?"

"Knowing her, if she did, she would never admit to it. Why?"

"Oh. Just a thought." Jason couldn't erase the conversation he'd had with David. He always remembered David as a pushy type, but never expected the callousness he'd encountered at the restaurant. Too bad the TV reporter covering the *spontaneous* visit in Conneaut didn't have the camera crew use a directional microphone. "By any chance," Jason continued, "when the meeting was held with your congregation to discuss my involvement, do you happen to remember the name of the person who brought up the idea that someone within your community might have had something to do with Friedel's death?"

"Yes," Joshua said. "It was the elder Mr. Ditmann."

CHAPTER 19

There were cows to be tended to, harnesses to mend, and machinery to be maintained. Isaac's day began just after sunrise with a breakfast prepared by his mother. Elizabeth's day began even earlier when she arose to make muffins, and prepare plenty of meat and eggs for her son whom she knew she would not see for hours. This was their typical day. Except for Benjamin, Elizabeth would have very little social interface with anyone.

The sun had barely cleared the grove of apple trees to the east of the farm house when Isaac gave his mother a quick hug and patted his son on the head. "Be a good lad for your grandmother," he said while running his hands through Benjamin's long blond hair.

Leaning on the sill of a side window, Elizabeth watched her son disappear from sight. From past experience, she knew Isaac would open the doors on the side of the barn that faced the fields letting in what available light there was. Her eyes became dark and hollow as she remembered so much death made especially tragic when it came long before their time.

First to go was her husband who succumbed to complications caused by pneumonia. It weakened him to the point where no one or no entity could bring him back to the vibrant hard-working man who'd been there for most of her life. Then came the news of Friedel. Weeks turned into months, and into years with no signs of serious efforts to find the truth. How Elizabeth hoped and prayed someone would step forward and offer her a sense of hope or caring. All during this time, Isaac's wife was trying to give him the son he wanted. Try as they did, something was not working for them. As time passed, they accepted the fact she would never conceive. Just when they'd given up hope, along came the good news. She would bless Isaac with a child. At this time, they didn't care whether it was a girl or boy…it would be theirs. When the time did come, it cost Isaac's wife her life. She, too, became another marker in the grove of maple trees in the back of their farm.

There was so much death for Elizabeth to cope with. It was not natural. This was not what was promised to her. All she had now was her small working farm, a son, and one grandson. Was this her blessing?

Struggling through the tortuous years of loneliness and despair, she secretly began to read some of the books Friedel had brought home. Not just the Bible…where it was preached all truth existed, but far beyond the constricting boundaries set up for her. As she began to learn more from these purportedly worthless books about science, history, and philosophy, her mind wondered if Friedel was somehow reaching out to her. Was this her blessing?

Tears trickled down her cheeks as she watched the sun take its bite of the morning dew from the handrails of the porch. Another day.

The sound of tires crunching on the dirt out front jarred Elizabeth back to now.

She looked out the front window. It was the same man who stopped by before demanding to know the whereabouts of the Medico-legal document, and he was driving the same white car. Elizabeth tried to read the numbers on the license plate, but its face was hidden in the shade. Her eyes darted toward the barn hoping Isaac would notice what was happening. A cloud of dust in the background indicated he might be towing one of his disc cultivation rigs behind a horse to prepare a section of pasture before another rain set in.

With a determined look of resolve in his eyes, the man stepped onto the porch and knocked on the door. It was not a polite knock, but a knock one might expect from a SWAT team before they burst down a door.

"You are not welcome here," Elizabeth announced through the screen.

"I'm told that a lot, Mrs. Mueller. I really want to discuss the states' document you have in your possession. This document is very important to finding out who killed your daughter."

"So, you admit she was killed? It was not an accident…or suicide… as has been suggested before."

"Look, Mrs. Mueller. Let's not make this any harder than it has to be. Don't you want to find the people responsible for Friedel's death?"

Elizabeth stayed behind the screen door with her hand poised on the latch. Whatever it took, this man was not going to force his way into her home. With her free hand, she rang the little bell she carried with her at all times. The sound brought Benjamin running. It was his assigned duty in life to come to his grandmother's side when it rang.

When Benjamin entered the room, he looked at his grandmother first, then cast a suspicious look at the stranger framed in the doorway.

Elizabeth leaned down and cradled him in her arms long enough for her to whisper in his ear.

"You sure?" the youthful voice asked.

Elizabeth nodded and eased the door open for Benjamin to slide past the stranger. "You will not touch this boy," she warned.

The man stepped aside.

"Not far enough," Elizabeth said while motioning him to move further away from the door.

The stranger held his arms up as if surrendering. "Hey. I'm not into little boys. I just want the Medico-legal document and you'll never see me again. And if you think it's any good for that kid to run for help, it ain't gonna make any difference. Just show me the document to let me know it's safe, and I'll be outta here. I just need to know you have it."

Through the screen door, Elizabeth again focused her attention on the antagonistic stranger. Then her eyes grew wide. "Benjamin. You get out of there right now," she shouted as she pushed the screen door open and forced the man to move to the side. In an instant, she brushed past him and rushed to the opened door of the white car.

Benjamin had opened the front door, climbed onto the driver's seat, and was running his fingers along the shiny metallic finish painted to resemble fine-grained wood. Using her elbow, Elizabeth nudged the car's door open further and reached in to hold Benjamin in her arms. While hugging him, she issued a stern warning about getting into other people's cars. "It is not proper," was her final and vociferous admonishment to the young boy.

"No harm done, Mrs. Mueller," the man said and offered his hand to Benjamin.

"The boy will not be touched." She held Benjamin, now essentially buried in gingham, close to her side. "It will please me if you will leave now," she announced in a bold voice.

"You may regret this decision, Mrs. Mueller."

"I said…leave."

The man returned to his car, taking time to inspect the door where Benjamin had dared crawl into. He brushed at the side with his fingertips to remove some unwanted dust, then gave Elizabeth a menacing grin.

As the man drove away, Elizabeth leaned down next to her grandson. "You did a very brave thing today, young Benjamin. Mr. Carmichael will be very proud of you."

They shared an understanding smile.

◊　　◊　　◊

"Shit. I have choices up the yin-yang," Jason grumbled. There were times when he felt guilty around the Loomis' B & B. Regardless of how they thought of their house as a business, it was still, in fact, their home. When guests rented the house, the Loomis' retreated to their bedrooms to read or watch a small TV while the guests relaxed in *their* living room on *their* overstuffed period furniture, *their* porch, and watched *their* wide-screen TV. For Jason, this was acceptable for one or two nights, but going on two weeks would certainly spawn a wound in any household. He could imagine them sitting in their cramped quarters wondering when in hell are these people going to leave? This evening, he insisted the Loomis' reclaim a portion of privacy in their home any way they saw fit.

The exception to all this was Douglas, who was more than happy to spend time in Dena's presence. Every time he entered the room, his parents seemed in awe of his cleanliness, manners, and new found appreciation for oral hygiene.

Jason and Dena sat on the steps of the B & B watching the farmer across the road maneuver a John Deere combine around a solitary maple tree in the middle of his field. The machine purred along at a slow pace while spitting out neat bundles of what looked like a long series of beige colored dashes in a brown manuscript.

With her arms wrapped around her knees, Dena said, "I've never seen you so frustrated. Are you sure you want to continue with this investigation?"

"Have to. Gave my word." He leaned forward and probed through the hair on the back of his head. After a few seconds, he moved his hand lower and dug his fingertips into the base of the neck where, it seemed, all the tension had built up. He could hear a disturbing crackling sound as he rolled his head in large sweeping arcs. "The problem is; I have no access to any data base, I have no authority to drag someone in and do a formal questioning, I can't ask a judge to issue a search warrant. And even if I did, I have too many suspects to convince a judge I'm operating at a level of confidence the law would require. I feel I've bitten off far more than my big mouth can chew."

"How sure are you the two killings are linked?"

"They have to be, Dena. Sometimes, I think Isaac may not be entirely off-base when he verbally assaults me. He's made it perfectly clear he doesn't like me, and finds my presence nothing more than an annoyance, or wedge in his society."

"But in what manual does it say you have to be liked by the person you try to help? That becomes their problem, not yours. The only thing you are guilty of is, trying to do the right thing." Dena tapped Jason on the nose and gave him one of her contagious smiles. "Remember what Elizabeth said when we visited Friedel's grave? She said you should judge someone by how they spend their free time. Think about it. You took time off to be by yourself, to help yourself heal, but you wound up placing other's needs or wishes above your own. When I see the look in Elizabeth's eyes, it is all worth it. Trust me."

"One other thing has been bothering me. Other than Friedel being killed, nothing else has happened since to tie anything together, especially when it relates to me. It started out by me seeing a set of initials. I got Ken Hutchinson involved. Now he's dead. The Mueller's dairy cow is slaughtered. That is their livelihood. Why have there been no attempts on my life?"

"Elizabeth said she prays for you. You think maybe someone is protecting you?"

"Yeah, right." Jason gazed at the green and yellow John Deere again as it made another pass in the field across the road. The farmer who owned this bad-boy could harvest more corn in an hour than the Mueller clan could in a day, but then again, the Muellers have withstood generations of hardships most could never endure. It showed in their calloused hands, and ruddy faces protected by nothing more than a straw hat. Jason was sure they'd never heard of sun screen. And how often did that John Deere break down? He focused his attention on the farm house in the distance. A large gray dish was perched on the roof pointed to the south where a communication satellite was in a holding pattern over the Gulf of Mexico. Maybe in the farmer's spare time, the family watches TV or plays video games. Hmm…spare time. "I've been thinking."

"About?"

"You. I don't have a clue where this is going…and I think it might be a good idea for you to go back home." Jason lowered his head, stared straight into the cement sidewalk leading to a picturesque white picket fence.

"Keineswegs, José."

"Huh?"

"Being with these Amish is bringing back my high school German. I kinda like it. What I said, you moron, is…No way, José." She gave a soft chuckle. "Problem with high school language courses, I can only remember the fun stuff…and dirty words."

"But…" In his mind, he mulled over telling Dena about the gunshots he was certain were meant for him, and but a few feet from where they were sitting.

"But nothing, Jason. I think you've been very fortunate. This far into the last case we worked on, you'd been shot. I didn't leave you then and I won't leave you now."

"It was your fault I got shot," Jason mumbled under his breath.

"Details, details." She slipped her arm through his. "Look at me, Jason. Do you really want me to leave?"

Jason got a far away look in his eyes when he stared across the road again. "Where should we eat supper tonight?"

"We could go back to that little restaurant in Conneaut if you'd like. Do you really want me to leave?"

"They had a pretty nice menu. Breakfasts weren't all that special, but then again, what can you do with eggs? You fry 'em and put 'em on a plate."

"The list of seafood looked pretty extensive—almost like we were eating in New Orleans. I said, do you really want me to leave?"

"I'm not a big seafood eater, unless it's really spicy. No." When he faced Dena, she was wearing the widest smile he'd ever seen, but it was the gleaming, soft look in her eyes that made him feel he had at his side the one person, he knew with absolute certainty, he could trust.

"Good. That's what I wanted to hear." The porch at the Loomis' was one of those porches most would envision on their dream list for the perfect house. It was wide and long with hand-turned spindles accenting the decorative hand moldings. Near the far end, supported by two stainless steel chains, was a wooden swing which swayed back and forth in a lazy pattern whenever a small breeze chanced through. When it moved, a tiny squeak cut through the growing darkness to remind anyone it was still available for a taste of what most would consider a memorable serving of paradise. Dena leaned against the hand rail leading up the four steps and gazed in the direction of the swing. "Can I ask you a question?"

"Sure."

"When someone comes back to a place where they grew up, I would think they would try to see if anyone is around they used to know, or date. Other than the Muellers, have you seen anyone you used to know?"

"Uuh, yeah."

"A girl?"

Jason nodded.

"Name?"

"Kathleen. Kathleen Rogers when I knew her in high school. She married David Ellison, so her name is Kathleen Rogers-Ellison now."

"So David is married to your old girlfriend?"

"No. She *was* married to him. He has moved on. They have a little girl named Jennifer. And she was not my old girlfriend. She was always David's girlfriend."

"Is she cute?"

"Jennifer?"

"Yeah, but that was going to be my next question. Is Kathleen cute?"

"YEAH. I mean, yeah."

"So. She hasn't turned all frumpy and wrinkly?"

"Not at all."

"Damn. Were you excited to see her?"

"Kinda. But not the way you're thinking...I think."

"No long, romantic nights of reminiscing?"

"No short nights, either."

"Good. Not that I was worried or anything."

In the field across the road, the farmer in the John Deere combine switched on his lights for his final run before putting it to bed for the night. Each time he'd made a pass, the sound of the diesel resonated across the road, but on this last pass, his exhaust was pointed away from the couple relaxing on the porch. It was quiet as the behemoth faded out of sight behind a large barn.

A set of headlights appeared out of the darkness from their left. Instinctively, their eyes followed the approach of the car as if it were nothing more than a local making his way back home. When the car's pace slowed dramatically, Jason remembered the recent gunshots, the slaughtering of the Mueller's cow, and how Dena stayed at his side after he'd been wounded a few short months ago. This was no time to figure out what was about to happen or a time for wishful thinking. There was only time to react. He pushed her back onto the porch and shielded her with his body.

When the car stopped next to the opened gate in the picket fence, the driver directed a flashlight at the couple on the porch through an opened passenger side window.

"I thought so," another voice rang out.

Shielding his eyes from the light, Jason yelled back, "Get that light out of our faces, David."

From inside the vehicle, a murmuring of voices could be heard, and then the light went out. Two car doors slammed shut.

David strutted toward his old teammate. "So? You set me up at the restaurant, huh?"

"You set yourself up, buddy." Jason helped Dena, who was brushing at her clothes, to her feet. "How'd you know where we are staying?"

Jason held up his hand as would a cop directing traffic. "Oh, that's right. You have followers who are more than willing to cater to your every whim. Right?"

"They're called contacts...buddy. And by the way, I was on my way back to Columbus and I thought I'd check in on you." He held the flashlight under his chin like a young child would do at a campout in an attempt to scare others. "But I see you have other ideas of how to spend the evening. Lucky you." He gave a vulgar laugh.

Jason couldn't tell for sure, but he was certain David was staring at Dena's body. "Who's the guy standing next to you?"

"My driver."

"Your bodyguard?"

"My driver," David repeated with a sarcastic tone.

"Does your driver have a name?"

"Yep."

"An-nd his name is...?"

"None of your business," David fired back.

"Could you shine the light in his face for a second? I'd sure like to see who I'm dealing with." Jason hoped the man parted his hair in the middle as Elizabeth had mentioned in their last meeting.

Sounding like he'd smoked one too many packs of cigarettes, the man managed a raspy, "Ain't gonna happen, Dude."

"Well then. I assume you're very dedicated to David Ellison?"

"Lieutenant Governor, David Ellison," Dena added with a barbed chuckle.

"What are we trying to do here, Jason? Question my driver? Question me? Let me remind you...you are out of your element. You are out of your jurisdiction. You have absolutely no business being here. I am urging you to go back where you came from."

"I do have business here. Being right doesn't have anything to do with boundaries. Maybe you haven't learned that yet. So far, all I've heard is what you want others to say. What was it you called them again? Oh, that's right...lemmings." Jason focused his attention on the driver again. "Are you one of David's lemmings? To quote your boss, they are shallow, meaningless heaps of biological life forms incapable of anything other than sucking air."

"Don't listen to this asshole," David commanded the driver.

"Do you own a rifle?" When Jason asked the driver, he received silence. "How about a shotgun? You own one...or have access to one?" Still no reply. He gave Dena one of his cocky grins. "Definitely a lemming."

"Don't listen to him," David ordered his driver. "Why don't you ask me those questions, smart ass?"

"Okay. Do you own a rifle?"

"Go home, Jason. This isn't gonna work."

"How about a shotgun?"

David folded his arms across his chest, and again held the flashlight under his chin.

"Where were you on the night Friedel was killed?"

"At the exact moment? And with whom? Golly gee, Jason. Let me see. Can't remember exactly, but she was probably doin' the Tube Steak Boogie."

It amazed Jason how crude someone could be without uttering one vulgar word, but group three nontoxic words together to form an analogy for oral sex and you're instantly disgusted, especially since the cheeky remark was added as an obvious affront to Dena. He was sure she could absorb the boorish comment. "Can you remember what time you were...?"

"All evening," David announced with a distinct air of pride.

"I bet he's a ten-second man," Dena chirped.

"Time, David. What time were you with this person?"

"A few hours, I suppose." In an obvious show of restraint, David was holding the arm of his driver who had inched closer to Jason.

"What time did you guys split up?" Jason prodded.

"You mean, what time did we clean up with some Handi-wipes?"

"Whatever," Jason fired back. "If my memory serves me right, it was a Thursday night, so we had school the next day."

"I don't recall, Jason. Unlike you, my mommy and daddy didn't dictate what time I had to be home and tucked in bed."

"The records say Friedel was killed around ten o'clock at night. You might have had your jollies, left to meet up with Friedel, and maybe exchanged words when she didn't play along with your version of a split formation."

"Records? Don't you mean record…as in singular? The only thing you have going for you, asshole, is that stupid Medico-legal document. Hardly admissible after all these years. Even if you know where it exists, someone will have to prove its validity. You're pissin' into the wind and you know it."

"It's a starting point…and you know it." Like a stand-up comic where timing is everything, Jason gauged the interval just right in order to pass close to David just as he was about to inhale. Nose to nose, he asked, "So, you admit having knowledge of the document? It must be worrying you to know it's out there, some where, some place, just waiting to point a finger at whoever killed a bright young woman just barely seventeen."

"I was simply trying to educate her, or indoctrinate her into the real world."

"Do you remember who discovered Friedel's body the next morning?" Jason asked as he returned to Dena's side.

"Some Amish kids…I think. Said they were gonna do some fishing."

Jason was sure David was perspiring. "Did you kill Friedel Mueller?"

"Fuck you, Jason. And the same goes for your chick there who set me up at the restaurant. I don't like what the papers did with that little item. They don't remember the good stuff, only the dirt."

"Did you ambush and kill Ken Hutchinson?"

"Who said he was ambushed?"

"He must have recognized the person walking toward him, David. It was chilly that evening, and there was no sign of shattered glass at the scene. Anyone with a functioning brain would realize Ken's window had to be in the lowered position. Add to that, he would have spotted anyone approaching his site. According to all reports, Ken was killed by someone who had the smarts to collect the spent shell casings before they left the scene. Whoever killed Ken had to be someone he knew or was easily recognizable through seeing numerous photos. If you were out there alone, would you let a stranger carrying a gun approach you?"

"This is getting ridiculous," David groaned.

"How about a defenseless cow at the Mueller farm? That make you feel all warm and fuzzy? I wouldn't put it past you, ya know what I mean? I remember a lot about you and high school football. Wasn't it you who took so much pride in adding a little kick to another opponent when they were down after the play had been blown dead?" Jason remembered so many times when David made sure the officials had begun to regroup the teams after a play. It was then David would add an *accidental* step to the groin or to the exposed neck just under the helmet of a rival. He'd then brag, it was all about timing and let out with one of his caustic laughs.

"You want me to...?" the driver started.

"Shut up," David fired back. "This guy hasn't got squat, and he knows it."

While walking past the driver, Jason inhaled deeply and asked, "How'd you know where I was staying?"

"Contacts, Jason. Contacts. How many times do I have to remind you? You're pretty well-known for an outsider. You might want to watch yourself...and your chick there. You are out of your league."

It was pretty much a sure bet that David was leering at Dena. David had a propensity to leer at anything with two legs and the ability to inhale. "And FYI, she's not my chick. She's my partner."

"Oooo," David sneered while turning to his driver. "We'd better be careful. Jason has a partner. A chick partner with great legs."

Dena leaned her head against Jason's chest and, in a coquettish tone of voice perfect for disarming the enemy, purred, "Golly gee, David. I kinda like being the chick partner."

Jason knew that behind the off-hand remark, a fist was clenched and ready for instant deployment.

"Hey, Jason," Dena began. "Didn't you say this guy wants to make a run for a Senator's seat...in Washington? As in D.C."

Jason chuckled, "Yeah."

"Could you imagine having this douche-bag on the Senate Ethics Committee?" Dena snickered.

Jason burst out in laughter. "Yeah, on the what-*not*-to-do side."

His voice boiling with contempt, David hissed, "Look, Jason and partner. I have more important things on my plate than to stand around bickering about history. What happened to Friedel is just that...history."

Everything around here was fine until you stuck your big ass nose into things…"

"Fine for you," Jason fired back, "but not for the Mueller family."

"Screw the Mueller clan. They don't vote. They just plow their boring damned fields every year, and then they plow them again the next year. I wish they'd join the twenty-first century."

"Did you kill Friedel Mueller?" Jason yelled out. "Or were you just as much a coward back then and have someone else do it for you?"

"Go fuck yourself."

Two cars doors slammed with a vengeance. The sounds were still ricocheting off the front of the B & B while the driver tried to crank up the engine.

Jason and Dena strode up to the still open window of the limo and peered into the shadowy interior. They knew David was fuming in the darkness.

"In the restaurant," Jason began in a well rehearsed voice designed to taunt the best, "you mentioned something about the power of your position and how others are afraid to be your enemy."

"So?"

"I just want you to know…we are not afraid to be your enemy."

CHAPTER 20

"Good morning, Elizabeth," Jason said. "We have something very important we have to talk to you about." He and Dena stood back away from the inviting front door.

"Would you like to come inside?" Elizabeth pushed the screen door open. "Fresh biscuits," she teased.

"Pass." A phone call to Dena's son each morning was on top of the priority list. It was a time for soft voices and tissues, followed by an understanding smile when she'd arrive at the Loomis' breakfast table. She would sit across from Jason and twirl her coffee cup for a few seconds before allowing Mrs. Loomis to fill it. Each time, Mrs. Loomis would slide a bowl of sugar in front of her—one of her universal home remedies she believed would cure any knotty issue in someone's life. A big slab of blackberry pie was another answer. "Is Mr. Stoudt or Isaac around?"

"No, but I can ring for Benjamin and he will fetch them." Elizabeth reached for the tiny bell dangling at her waist.

"Wait. Please don't." Jason motioned to a wooden chair on the porch. On one of the back supports, a white towel hung in a neat fold, probably placed there this morning for Isaac to clean his hands when he'd return for lunch.

"Oh, my. You sound so serious. Do you have bad news for me?" She stepped onto the porch, wiped her hands with the towel and motioned for them to sit.

Dena sat next to Elizabeth and cradled her hands while Jason paced in front of her, his face sullen and drawn. "I am glad no one is around. We hoped they'd be in the fields. We want to discuss something with you...just you."

"You aren't going to leave, are you?" Elizabeth whispered in a weak voice.

Jason pulled up another chair and sat on the other side of Elizabeth, his eyes looking deep into hers. "I, uh...I have a confession to make. As a detective, I am supposed to keep my distance from everyone until a case is solved. It's called being objective. What I've done since coming here is a cardinal sin in my business—I've treated everyone as I would a neighbor or friend."

"Is this not a good thing?" Elizabeth asked.

"No. Please forgive me, but what I'm about to say will possibly make you hate me." He studied the confusion in Elizabeth's eyes. Or was it hurt? "Most cases of murder in the U.S. are committed by someone very close to the victim. Add to that, most cases involving murder are not about money, but emotion. Highly charged emotion. When I came here, I wanted to believe the best of everyone concerned with Friedel's life. That was a huge mistake on my part. What I am going to ask of you is; I need to ask some very personal and hurtful questions...or we go nowhere with this investigation."

Elizabeth looked at Jason, and then Dena. The cheerful look on her face at the door a few moments ago had been replaced with reddened eyes, clenched hands, and a pleading look.

"Do you understand?" Dena asked.

Elizabeth gave a slow deliberate nod. "Somehow I knew, when this all began, we would be having a talk like this. In the very first meeting with our congregation, someone asked what would happen if the person who took Friedel from us, was one of us. Is that why you are here today?"

Jason gave a slow nod. "I'm sorry."

"I will help any way I can."

This was always the most difficult part of an investigation for Jason. Relating statistical data to a relative of a victim always seemed so cold and clinical, as if someone's entire life could be conveniently summed up on a computer-generated spread sheet. "One of the first priorities a detective must do is to establish motive. I need you to understand this. Do you?"

"Yes." Elizabeth's voice seemed frail, and the towel she'd wiped her hands with was now wadded up into a tight spiral as if she'd tried to wring every last drop of water from it.

"How would you describe your relationship with Friedel?" It was a delicate question to ask for Jason. Because the mind functions at the speed of light, flashbacks of his father's spin on work ethics bounced around inside his brain. His favorite story was about one tenet his father used before he'd hire someone to work in his small shop. After the interview, he'd always find an excuse to walk the man back to his car. As a young man, Jason noticed his father's peculiar routine many times, so one day he found the nerve to ask him why. In a matter of fact voice, his father said he could judge a man by the way he kept his car. If it was neat and well kept, that was a positive. If it was messy and filled with empty soda cans and debris, the man stood little chance of being hired. His father believed if the man had no respect for things he'd paid for, how could he possibly have any regard for what his employer or customer paid for?

"Our relationship was, at times, trying." Elizabeth brushed her hands across her eyes. "She read so much. I found myself admiring her courage. When the threat of shunning was introduced by the community, I cried. That is supposedly the worst punishment of all, but it did not affect her like it did others. I would describe Friedel as being on a fence. She did not totally embrace our beliefs, but neither did she seize the opportunity to explore through *rumspringa* which would have meant leaving the community and going elsewhere. She found her ability to explore other worlds through books much more satisfying. You asked how our relationship was...I would describe my role as...liberal."

"How were you informed of Friedel's death?"

Elizabeth folded her hands over her chest and took a deep breath, and yet another. Almost gasping for air, she whispered, "Isaac told us. He was up early as usual, and had taken a bucketful of grain out to one of our ailing calves. Someone stopped by and told him...over the fence."

"Over the fence? They didn't come to your home? Did he say who this person was?"

"No. Who this person was, was the least of my concerns at the moment."

"Do you recall the time of the morning?" Jason continued.

"Around seven."

"If you don't mind me asking, how is it that Friedel could leave the house late at night?"

"We had an agreement," Elizabeth whispered. "The men knew nothing of this. One evening, she asked me if I trusted her. It was kind of a strange question for her to ask. I didn't really say yes, but I didn't say no, either. She'd gone out before—but only after the men had retired for the night—and then came home in about an hour or so. Very quietly. I suppose I trusted her as any mother would want to trust their child." She glanced at Dena.

"Did she ever give you a reason for this type of activity?"

"She always came back with books. Every so often, we would talk quietly about things not associated with farming or animals…or religion. Like I said before, Friedel was a different kind of young woman. She knew there was a whole new kind of world out there, but she always stopped just short of asking if she could exercise her right to *rumspringa*. She knew if she did, she would always be thought of as a suspect."

Dena eased in next to Jason while still grasping Elizabeth's hand. As she snuggled against Jason, she gave him a not so subtle nudge with her shoulder.

Jason moved away, but not too far, and reached up into the header where he'd stashed one of the Maks. In one well-executed movement, he felt the knurling of the handle and the trigger guard. When he'd hidden it there, he purposely placed it in such a way that if the situation presented itself, he could retrieve it in a combat ready position. He also hoped no spiders were developing a fondness for the new addition to the porch.

"Did the subject of sex ever come up?" Dena asked softly.

Elizabeth nodded while casting a nervous glance in Jason's direction.

"Do you think she was ever…experimenting?" Dena continued.

"She gave me her word. We take the tenets of the *Ordnung* very seriously."

"I take that to mean she wasn't?"

"Yes. In the...uuh, developing years, it was very difficult for me to try to explain the changes within her body without discussing the reasons. Being around animals so much, she grasped the connection very quickly." Dena placed her hand on Jason's shoulder and gently spun him around.

"When Friedel went out that night," Jason continued, "when did you realize she hadn't come home?"

"I stayed up all night, Mr. Carmichael...worrying. You have to understand, none of the men—my husband was alive then—knew of her temporary periods of independence. I was afraid for Friedel, but I was also afraid for myself for agreeing to this arrangement behind their backs. When that terrible morning came and I'd not heard her stirring in her room, I expected the worse. There was no one I could call, or check with. I prepared breakfast for my husband and Isaac as usual. They went off to attend to their chores...and I waited. I stared out the window, hoping." Elizabeth blotted her eyes with the wadded up towel. "Then Isaac came running into the house." Elizabeth lowered her head into her lap and openly wept. "It was horrible."

"Mother? What is going on?" Isaac's head peered from around the corner of the house. He tapped his boots on the edge of the porch and leaned a pitchfork against the house. After removing his straw hat, he wiped his forehead with his sleeve and knelt at Elizabeth's side. A pronounced scowl punctuated the narrow slits of Isaac's eyes as if he was about to launch an evil spell.

"Good morning, Isaac." When Jason extended his hand, it was blatantly ignored as Isaac stayed at his mother's side.

"What have you said this time to cause this?" Isaac demanded of Jason.

"You will not talk to this man in that tone of voice," Elizabeth said with an uncharacteristic power in her voice.

"Can't you understand what this man has brought upon us? Nothing but pain and sorrow."

"I'm here to ask questions I should have asked a week ago." Jason excused himself from Elizabeth, grabbed Isaac's steel-like arm just above the elbow, and started to usher him a few paces away so they would be out of earshot of his mother.

After two steps, Isaac twisted his arm away in a violent motion. "I will not be led like a child by an outsider."

"Okay. I'm sorry." Jason held his hands extended out from his side to erase any semblance of a threat. "Let's just keep your mother out of this." He waited for Isaac's subtle nod before he continued. A quick glance over his shoulder assured him Elizabeth was far enough away to not overhear anything. "I assume you want to help me find Friedel's killer."

"Yes, of course."

"There are a few things I'd like to clarify. How old were you at the time of your sister's death?"

"Nineteen. What difference does this make?"

"Bear with me. How did you find out about your sister's death?"

With a sarcastic bite in his voice, Isaac began, "I was working the field out near the road. A man stopped and asked who I was. When I told him, he apologized and told me of Friedel's accident."

"Did this man say accident, and not another term?"

"He said accident."

"What time of day was this?"

"In the morning...maybe seven or eight o'clock...I think."

"Did this man wear a uniform or regular clothes?"

"Uniform."

"Did you recognize the agency? Like county, or state."

"I just remember it was a policeman. We pay little attention to outside organizations."

"What did you do next?"

"I ran back to our house and told my parents of the accident."

"How did you feel?"

"Nervous, I suppose. It was a very difficult thing to tell a mother... and father, too."

"What did you do then?"

"We walked over to the bridge. There were many vehicles there... with lights flashing."

"What were you doing about ten o'clock the night your sister was killed?"

With fire in his eyes, Isaac came nose to nose with Jason while he reached for the pitchfork he'd propped against the side of the house. At first, Isaac held it as one would hold a cherished possession, but after a few seconds, he slammed the butt end of the fork into the ground. "What are you suggesting, Mr. Carmichael?"

"I'm suggesting you answer my question."

Isaac raised the fork a few inches off the ground and shook it like a baby would shake a rattle, except this was not a display of happiness. His jaw was set firm and his breath became heavy. "How dare you come into our lives and make such an insinuation."

Jason eyed the tines of the fork poised less than an inch from his face. "I'm not making any accusations…yet. But it is interesting to see how quickly you revert to violence, or at least an indicator of it." Jason studied Isaac's trembling hand and gently placed his fingers on the handle to move it to the side. "That is the second time you used your fork to threaten me. I wouldn't do it a third time."

"Are you threatening me?"

"Let's call it a request." Backing down was never an entree listed on Jason's menu. From his many years of confronting suspects, he knew when presented with dogged persistence, many will become angry and blurt out things they'd never dream of saying under normal circumstances. Badger your way into the inner workings of the mind was what one of his earlier mentors had drilled into him. There are many techniques, but breaking down self-control was the crucial factor. His piercing eyes remained glued to Isaac's.

Isaac lowered the fork to his side.

"I'll repeat the question. What were you doing about ten o'clock the night your sister was killed?"

"If it's any of your business, I was tending to a broken wheel on one of our wagons. It is work easily done by lantern rather than taking up precious daylight." His contemptuous attitude and staccato delivery sounded much like he was swearing, but without the vulgar expletives. "I am growing tired of your verbal assaults. You have insulted me. And you are treating me as if I had something to do with Friedel's accident." He turned his back to Jason and folded his arms across his chest. "I want you off this property. Now." He was close to spitting the words from his mouth.

"You did it again, Isaac. You used the term accident. Did you exchange words with Friedel about her decision to not marry Jonathon Dittman? Did those words turn hostile? Did you feel she was defaming the Mueller name? Maybe you never intended to hurt her, but things got out of control. There were bruises on Friedel's body. The kind your own mother had when you chose to not have her take part in the decision for me to actively pursue this case. It wasn't that long ago. Do you remember?"

"I have an excellent memory," Isaac grumbled.

Dena edged close to the front wall of the house, and coaxed the fork from Isaac and held it to her side like a Roman soldier would do to guard his emperor, except the intimidating tines were pointed downward.

"Did you have a fight with Friedel that night, Isaac?"

"Yes." He cast a nervous glance at his mother. "We exchanged words, but not in the way you propose. I tried to make her understand how her actions were hurting others. She was a disgrace to us."

Standing at the corner, Elizabeth suddenly yelled out, "She was not a disgrace to me, Isaac." Elizabeth continued around the corner and faced her son. "I was proud of her. So very proud. To do something most people would not have the courage to do. She was hurting no one."

"Was it an accident, Isaac?" Jason asked softly.

Isaac glared at Jason.

"Did you see her that night? Around ten o'clock?"

"I have work to do." Again, he stormed off toward the barn…just like the last time. Before leaving, he grabbed the fork from Dena. "This is not a weapon."

It seemed Isaac's answer to everything was to walk away, even ignore it, but this very response was the direct opposite of what Jason expected of someone who'd just been incriminated in a major crime. If the confrontation with Friedel had led to violence, why didn't he have the capacity to ignore it then? Was Friedel's desire for semi-independence a slur to his own beliefs and commitments? Could Isaac have been envious of Friedel's actively seeking another plateau in her life? A place where fulfillment went beyond having multiple children…six or seven by most Amish standards, or by exploring other worlds and philosophies with an open mind. Couldn't Friedel have had both? Why was it so important to vehemently believe in only one concept of what it was to be considered…good?

"I'm so sorry for his behavior, Mr. Carmichael," Elizabeth whispered. "I was never told he'd exchanged words of anger with Friedel. I trusted him. He is my son."

"Let's hope that is all he is." Jason studied Isaac as he entered the barn. Every other time he'd seen Isaac pass one of their horses, there was always a soothing pat on the rump or an arm under the neck. This time, he passed two horses with no acknowledgment whatsoever, and the fork he carried at his side made him look like a prehistoric warrior… except for the suspenders.

Her head turned discreetly away from Elizabeth, Dena asked Jason, "Why didn't you stop him?"

"For what? He didn't admit to anything other than having an argument."

"But he lied about fixing the wheel on his wagon. He evidently followed Friedel, and it had to be a deliberate move on his part. You don't just happen to bump into your sister at ten at night on some lonely bridge."

"He never said where they had the confrontation, and besides, these medical reports list only approximate time of death."

"Oh."

During the brief discussion between Jason and Dena, Elizabeth had settled into one of the straight back wooden chairs and stared in the direction of the barn. Seeing the hurt in her eyes, Jason sat next to her and cradled her hands. "I'm sorry, but those questions had to be asked."

"'Tis not right. I never knew of such things between my children. Why did they hide it from me?"

"I think it's a universal trait, Elizabeth," Dena whispered. "It has nothing to do with being Amish or about you being a bad mother. They were young."

Elizabeth raised her head, pinched her lips and forced a smile in Dena's direction. "You're very comforting."

Jason tapped Dena on her shoulder and with his head, motioned it was time for them to go, but not before checking with Elizabeth to see if she would be okay.

Elizabeth nodded. "Before you go Mr. Carmichael, the stranger came by again."

Jason spun around. "When?"

"Yesterday morning. He was very demanding."

Jason plopped down in the chair beside her again. "So Isaac, or Joshua Stoudt were nowhere around?"

"No. I was by myself...and of course, Benjamin."

"You said this man parted his hair in the middle, right?" Jason continued.

Elizabeth nodded.

"Did this man smell of smoke?"

"I don't understand."

"Oh, Dena and I had some visitors last night. It was dark, but I edged close to this one guy so I could smell if he was a smoker or not. They have a very distinct odor. It's in their hair, and clothes. It's kind of stale."

"Uuh. No. I confronted him at the front door and noticed no peculiar odor."

"How about his voice? Was it kind of a raspy, gravelly sound?"

"No. Rather normal voice, but he was very abrasive."

"It's funny how this person shows up when he knows the men are not around. Like he has you under surveillance before he drives in." Jason scanned the area up and down the road. Small groves of elms had purposely been left standing for generations to act as a natural wind and snow break, and as a fence of sorts between neighboring farms. Perfect for concealment. "What type of remarks did he make...like threats?"

"It was more like he was issuing ultimatums. He tried to make me feel guilty by not helping find the people who killed my daughter, but when..."

"Whoa. Back up. You said he used the term people, not person?"

Elizabeth's brow furrowed. "Uuh, yes. I'm sure he said people."

Under most circumstances, Jason would have uttered a caustic, *Oh, shit*, but bit his tongue. "I can't believe this. What this guy just 'fessed up to is, there was more than one person responsible for Friedel's death. This never crossed my mind."

"There is something else about this stranger I haven't shared with you." A worried look crept over Elizabeth's face. "When he was here, I did something which may have been...not right."

CHAPTER 21

The hallways at Grand Valley High School looked very similar to the days when Jason trudged through them on his way to classes or team practices. Oh, the walls were painted a different color now, but the mosaic tile immortalizing the Mighty Mustangs was shiny and well preserved as ever.

Then there were the built-in athletic trophy cases which stared back at anyone who entered the four large front doors. A small round lock on the displays kept out would-be award hunters or conspirators from a rival school whose goal was revenge. Sitting behind the sliding glass panels were both miniature and gigantic reminders of teams or individuals who excelled at their choice of sport. Some were polished brass. Others were marble-like with a figure of the sport they represented. Inscribed on a brass plate at their bases was the title of award and of the names of the players who participated. Most cherished were the larger ones which announced a regional or state championship, but the Mustangs never seemed able to snag one of the elusive nationals.

As they strolled past the displays, Dena bent over and scanned the brass plates. "Where's your name?"

"I think the ones I was involved with are probably tucked away in the basement someplace waiting for Old Dinosaur Days."

Dena chuckled, but continued to scan the awards. "Yeah. This case isn't large enough to store all the things I'm sure you were good at."

"You're too kind. Let's go."

Voices resonated through the corridors where they blended into one homogeneous sound where not one word could be distinguishable from another, but the looks were. Jason and Dena were definitely not dressed as teachers, nor did they carry armloads or backpacks filled with what might be construed as lecture material or homework assignments.

Instead, Jason carried his small note pad and a pencil looking very much like the cocky students who never felt they had to take notes— just show up and take the test. His graying hair dispelled any thoughts of that turning into a believable scenario.

Dena drew looks of another sort, certainly prompted by intensifying hormonal imbalances. Through the crowd, the young men first caught a glimpse of her hair, confident smile, and piercing eyes, but the closer they came, the more their eyes succumbed to the fundamental force of gravity. Tight jeans would always take precedence over a face. Later, if anyone was asked what she looked like, they'd probably respond with, *Face?*

Jason smiled graciously as they moved through the crowd. He reminded himself that he'd promised they'd try to show up at GVHS between classes, but the bombshell Elizabeth introduced with the idea of more than one person being involved with Friedel's death changed his plans. He didn't care how or when he obtained information, he just wanted it.

The infamous office was still located just inside the entry doors where it'd been when he'd been a student. The smoked glass in the door had since been replaced with transparent glass panels, but the emotional pangs still resonated around in his head when he saw the word *Office*. Jason took a deep breath to shelve any feelings he had about being in trouble. He knew, just to the left as he entered the legendary room, was the Vice Principal's office—the place everyone referred to as state-sanctioned hell.

Reaching for the knob, Jason couldn't help wonder if he would recognize anyone, or would anyone recognize him? Obviously, students came and went, but teachers, administrators, and staff often made the school system their career. He opened the door and ushered Dena in first.

A young girl stood behind the polished wood counter. In a dry tone, she asked, "May I help you?"

"Yes. My name is Jason Carmichael." He flashed his Fresno County badge at her and hoped she wouldn't take time to read it. "I'm a detective and would like to know where you keep your year books dating back twenty-five years or so."

"Golly. I'm not sure we keep things that old." The girl waved to a woman wearing half-glasses slumped behind a pile of paperwork.

Without looking up, the woman slid her chair back, and in a near lifeless voice, said, "I heard. I'll take care of this." She cast Jason and Dena a curious look, but primarily focused her attention on Dena. "Didn't you used to go to school here?"

"No. Not me," Dena said. "But he did."

"Guilty," Jason whispered while looking over his shoulder at the Vice Principal's door.

"Uuh…I don't recognize you. You must have been a good boy."

"Him?" Dena burst out laughing.

"Hey," Jason shot back. "I had my moments."

"If you say so," the woman mumbled.

"Year books?" Jason asked.

"Oh, yes. We keep the last three years in here on that shelf." The woman pointed to a small ledge at the end of the counter. "Anything older than that is in the library. Do you remember where it is?"

Jason nodded and started for the door. "Thank you."

"You're welcome Jason Carmichael."

Jason spun around and saw the gray-haired woman grinning at him.

"Susan." She extended her hand to Jason. "Data entry clerk here forever." She locked eyes with Dena again. "He really was a nice young man."

"I knew he would have been," Dena said.

"You have a very attractive wife, Jason."

"Uuh…she's not my wife. She's my partner."

"Oh, my. I heard you say you were a detective, but the way you two behave, it's like you're…"

"We're partners, Susan," Jason said.

Dena pursed her lips. "He's right."

"Oh, I hope I didn't overstep my boundaries," Susan said. "The library will help you with what you need."

Classroom doors were beginning to close, so the hallway was nearly devoid of students, but there were always those few who relished pushing their way into a room just as the bell sounded, affording them a taste of momentary glory as they stood framed in the doorway...alone. Some were met with applause by their fellow classmates, while others were met with chides to, *Sit down bonehead.* Some things never changed.

Entering the library, Jason and Dena were greeted with a huge sign proclaiming, *SILENCE.* Under the word was a depiction of a mouth with a fingertip placed over the lips. It would have been difficult for anyone to not grasp the meaning. As well-intentioned as the sign was, it often fell on ears by those who believed the sign only applied to someone else.

"Good afternoon," Jason whispered to a woman gathering up books from the tables. "We're working on a murder case, and Susan in the office said you might point us in the direction of year books dating back about twenty-five years." He flashed his badge at her, too.

The woman took a quick peek. "Detective, huh?" She smiled and pointed to a line of books next to a window.

Jason waved a courteous *thank you* and scanned the rows, all of which were organized by year. He pulled out the books for 1983 through 1987 and set them on a table. When Dena eased into a chair next to him, the chair made a piercing, squeaking sound on the tile.

The woman looked over and gave a helpless shrug of her shoulders.

"Why all these years?" Dena asked.

"Gotta refresh my memory. You usually associate with students in your own class, but there's times when you come in contact with upper and lower classmen. Like I said...dredging up the past."

Jason opened up 1985 first, flipped to the page where his senior picture appeared and pointed it out to Dena.

"You were cute. And look at the hair."

"I remember hair," Jason whispered.

Dena gave a soft chuckle. "What are we looking for?" With no warning, she slapped Jason's arm. "Ooo, ooo. Show me this Kathleen's picture. The one you didn't mess around with...right?"

"Uuh. Okay and yes." Jason flipped through the pages where her picture would most likely be. She was into class politics, cheer-leading, and debate societies, so those were good starting points.

"Nice legs," Dena said while studying the cheer-leading squad. "And you said she hasn't changed much since then?"

"Huh-uh."

"You sure you didn't *do* her and just choose to keep it from me?"

"I promise. I didn't do her. Then or now…damn it."

Dena gave Jason another playful slap on his shoulder. "Thanks."

"What I'm really looking for is some guy who may have parted his hair in the middle…like Elizabeth mentioned. To me, the gating item is; Friedel had to know this person. Know her enough for her to allow him to come close to her, and other than her Amish community, this has to be it. We're not talking about a woman who was a world traveler here." Jason flipped to the beginning of the section where all the class pictures were arranged in alphabetical order. Most of the guys wore ties and were clean-shaven, while some rebels, quite obviously prided themselves with budding facial hair, sported a bad-boy look favored by many young movie actors in an attempt to make themselves appear more manly or rugged. It seemed the girls invested a little more time to make themselves look like New York runway models. Thin was *in* then, too.

"Mind if I start with 1984?" Dena asked.

"Feel free."

The only sound in the library was the faint snaps of turning pages. If there were any pauses, it was because Dena would point to a picture and wait for Jason to either nod his head in approval or roll his head from side to side. There was a lot of sideways movement for the better part of an hour.

"What would have happened if Friedel actually did graduate, Jason? Would her picture be in your year book?"

Jason flipped to the M's and pointed out an empty frame with *Friedel Mueller* under it. Jason recalled the senior year-book committee debating on what to do since she would have graduated had it not been for her death. They agreed to memorialize her with the blank box surrounded by a wreath. Under her name, *Photo unavailable*, appeared in a script font. "They don't believe in having pictures of themselves and really frown on these clueless tourists who, with no warning or permission, take pictures of them. It's really disrespectful. In their culture, a picture would be considered narcissistic."

"That must have been so sad for those kids," Dena said. "Graduation should be a time for celebration, not mourning." Dena slid 1984 in front of Jason. "Wanta take a look?"

"Yeah. I'll scan it. Nobody seem to pop out at you, huh?" He picked up 1986 and began the same routine.

"Nope." Dena picked up 1983 and flipped through to the alphabetized section. She couldn't help searching out the spontaneous pictures of Jason taken at dances or other social gatherings. She spotted one with him standing in John Travolta's famous disco pose with his hips slung out to the side and right finger pointed skyward. It was the attire that made Dena giggle. Then there were others where he was standing, in full uniform, with the varsity football team. All held their helmets in their right hands so their faces would show. She looked for his name and that of David Ellison, too. "What a scumbag," she mumbled.

"Huh?"

"Nothing." As the hour hand on the clock neared three o'clock, the pages were flipped with more vigor as if admitting this was an exercise in futility. Stifling a yawn with her hand, Dena yanked 1983 back in front of her and focused on the P's. "Look at this guy, Jason. I kinda passed over him before. Look familiar?"

Jason glanced at the name under the picture—Ted Phelps. He studied the image for a few seconds, closed his eyes and gave a slight moan. Hair parted in the middle. Unique style. *Ted Phelps*, he repeated to himself. "I seem to remember this guy. He was two years ahead of me. Give me a few seconds." Jason leaned into the picture as if trying to make a psychic connection. "If I remember correctly, there was this guy who always seemed alone. Ya' know? Musicians hang out with musicians. Jocks hang out with jocks. Nerds with nerds. But this guy hung around here even after he graduated. I remember people poking fun at him. He didn't belong."

"He wasn't pushin', was he?"

"No. I don't think drugs were on his agenda. It was more like he seemed to lose his identity after he graduated. Didn't know where he fit in, ya know what I mean?"

"He sure fits in now." The quiet woman carried an armload of books to be returned to the shelves. "Bells gonna ring in a few seconds. Kids are going to be streaming in here and quiet is not in their vocabulary."

"What do you mean about this guy fitting in?" Jason asked the woman.

"He's the county sheriff now—just like his father, he is."

Glancing at the clock, Jason said, "Fill me in."

"Back in the eighties his dad was the sheriff of Ashtabula County. Many years as I recall. The Phelps clan is a seventh generation family around here. Pretty influential."

"What's the father doing now?"

"Oh, Wayne. Probably rotting. Died about ten, maybe fifteen years ago. Buried over in Jefferson."

"You don't seem too terribly saddened by his departure," Jason said.

"Influential doesn't necessarily mean popular, detective."

"Hmm. So, this Ted Phelps is Wayne Phelps' son."

"The one and only. The kid served some time as a deputy for the county. Most people around here think Wayne was grooming his son to take over the reins when he retired. Good *bennies*, ya'know what I mean? Of course, he had to be voted in, but Wayne never let propriety stand in his way."

"Interesting," Jason whispered. "Can I get some copies of this photo...maybe some enlargements, too?"

"Can do."

The bell rang. Although the doors to the library were closed, the din cut through as if the doors were made of cardboard painted to look like wood. When the doors flew open, the sound increased dramatically. The students entering sensed they were supposed to be quiet, but the students in the hall hadn't quite grasped the idea that sounds travel.

"I'll make you those copies in a sec. Right now, I have some head banging to do."

"Kind of a take-charge lady, huh?" Dena said.

"Yeah. I guess I never knew who the sheriff of the county was when I lived here."

"Weren't worried about getting beaten up by some cop, huh?"

"Hell, no. I was more worried about getting the crap kicked out of me by the fathers of the girls I dated."

Dena gave a soft laugh as she stacked up the year-books on the edge of the table. "Are we supposed to put these back?"

"I don't think so. They like to re-file them so they're in the right location. Otherwise, the kids just jam them anyplace and the next person can't find squat."

"Speaking from experience?"

"Uuh, could be."

"Here are the copies you asked for," the lady said. They were placed neatly in a manila envelope and marked with *Ted Phelps*. All the hand writing was done using feminine, tidy characters with little swirls which gave the appearance of someone who had studied calligraphy.

"Thank you for the pics and the information about the Phelps' involvement in county history," Jason said. "By the way. I see all the books, but don't you have computers for the student's research projects?"

"Oh, we have a few in the back, but most kids have their own at home. And better quality I might add. This place is like a showroom where kids can study...quietly...away from family annoyances."

"Could we use one for awhile? I want to find out more about the Phelps family."

The woman led Jason and Dena to an area near the rear exit set aside for three computers and monitors. When Jason caught a glimpse of them, he thought he was experiencing ancient history first hand. The towers were tall, cumbersome, and probably weighed tons. And the monitors were old curved screen TVs. He was sure they were donations from someone who didn't know what to do with these behemoths once they'd acquired new, more powerful units capable of retrieving data in nanoseconds rather than hours.

"Can we do a little genealogy on the Phelps family?" Jason asked.

"Uuh. Probably not," the woman said. "When they passed the Privacy Act, some call it the Seventy-five Year Act, it pretty much limits what you can find out on line...for obvious reasons."

"What kind of info are you thinking about?" Dena asked.

"When Elizabeth said *people* rather than *person*, I want to know who these other people may be. It's a long shot."

"If you want that kind of data, ya'know where it's listed…usually? And available to anyone?"

Jason noticed the gleam in Dena's eyes again. "Tell me, oh great one."

With an air of confidence and flamboyant wave of her hands, Dena whispered, "Think obits."

"You're right. Thanks." Jason turned to the woman. "Can you find us the obituary for Wayne Phelps? Someone of his stature must have had at least a page."

The woman plopped down in the ratty chair behind one of the computers left on-line by a previous user. She entered Obituary as a search word followed by Ashtabula County. A list popped up after what seemed an hour in the modern world. Overwhelmed by the length of the listing, the woman entered a range of dates. The list shrunk… somewhat. She then entered Phelps. The list grew shorter, but because of the extensive breeding characteristics of the Phelps clan, the list still remained large. "I'm sorry, but this thing allows only so much information at a time. I have to go through so many steps."

"Not a problem," Jason said.

The woman entered Wayne. There were six people named Wayne Phelps who died in the time frame the woman had entered. "Close enough," she mumbled. One by one, she tapped the cursor to pull up the individual obits. "Let's just hope, they weren't all sheriffs at one time or another."

On the third hit, the Wayne Phelps popped up who'd died in 1999 and was listed as the retired sheriff of Ashtabula County. A picture of him in uniform, *sans* the campaign hat, appeared at the beginning of the article. Jason noticed his hair wasn't parted in the middle, but then again, hair patterns probably have nothing to do with genetics. Jason scooted in next to the woman and read through the list of surviving relatives. Listed was the son, Ted. Bingo. Jason continued down the lengthy list and then froze. Kathleen Ellison was listed as niece. That meant she and Ted were cousins. The brief conversation he'd had with her at her home in Vermilion, where she referred to her stupid cousin in Jefferson, ricocheted around in his head. She'd just told him who this other person was, and he'd blown it off as the verbal meandering of a woman who was moaning about the complexities of her life since her divorce from David. Jason sat bolt upright in the chair. "I have some phone calls to make."

"What's the haps, Jason?" Dena asked.

"I think you're gonna meet the Kathleen you were worried about." Jason asked the woman. "Can I get a printout of this obit?"

"Sure." She tapped a File/Print command. "Be back in a minute. The printers are up front...where we can keep an eye on supplies. You'd be amazed how quickly an expensive ink cartridge can grow legs."

When the woman left, Jason thanked Dena for the suggestion about the obit. "It really helped."

"No problem...partner."

Jason rested his arms on the sill of one of the two rain-streaked windows in the library. His attention became focused on a red Shelby gleaming in the afternoon sun. This was Tigre's ride. What was he doing here? The red Mustang was parked in the curved area out front where the yellow school busses routinely waited for their students. Most of the busses had left for their daily scheduled run, but two remained. The Mule was situated just to the rear of the second bus.

"Here's your copy, detective," the woman said. "I stuck it in the envelope with the pictures you wanted."

He grabbed the envelope. "Thank you so much for all your assistance." He glanced out the window again. Tigre's car was still parked in the pickup area. "I'm so sorry, but I have to run." Jason bolted for the front door with Dena hot on his six.

Over her shoulder, Dena yelled out to the woman, "He's like this some times. Thank you-u-u." Her voice tapered off as she tried to catch up with Jason.

Charging through the front door, Jason brushed aside a few students who had gathered at the entranceway and headed for the Mustang. Its polished chrome wheels were cranked hard to the left. Sounding like a monstrous dragon who'd stuck its head out of his lair to ward off intruders, the engine roared to life and the car headed for the highway.

Jason scratched his head. "What the hell?"

CHAPTER 22

"I think I know why I'm still alive." Whenever Jason was confronted with a puzzle, he liked to rest his forearms on his legs and stare at the ground. He called it his *conversation with earth* routine. Nothing at his feet moved to distract him. There were no moving cars, no pedestrians walking by, or loud noises from passing boom-boxes. It was this rite where he allowed himself the time to focus. Oh, there was the one time when just as he'd found himself in this hover mode at a crime scene back in California, an earthquake struck, but since his body was shaking at the same frequency as the earth, he had no perception of movement… until a voice broke through his personal barrier and yelled, *Get under the table, asshole.*

"Talk," Dena whispered. She, too, rested her arms on her legs while sitting on the steps of the B & B next to Jason. Every time Jason drifted into this self-examination mode, she would sit patiently and wait for him to share his thoughts with her, and then she'd make her contribution. It seemed to work for them.

"This whole thing with having more than one person involved in killing one Amish girl seems so illogical. There's a part of me that wants to believe either Elizabeth remembered it wrong, or there's more to Friedel's extra-curricular activities than anyone wants to admit. We have so many options: anger from a family or clan member, humiliation from a runner-up in a marriage decision, jealousy by a classmate, or an attempted assault by David. But because of the disappearance of the Med/Doc, it seems highly unlikely that an Amish guy…"

"Or girl."

"Yeah. Or girl—it's a two part equation. This hypothetical other person would have to have had a job at a medical lab where this autopsy was performed, or have access to medical records via a computer—highly unlikely for an Amish person." Across the road, the farmer with the John Deere combine was putting finishing touches on another section of his property. "But think about this. Friedel was teetering on the edge of *rumspringa*, right? If she did, actually, follow through with her choice, she would forever carry the burden of being thought of as a question mark in the hearts of others. She was what modern thinkers might call, a closet *rumspringa* candidate. Also a negative. So what I think is important is…we have to ask ourselves not so much what others thought of her, but what she thought of herself."

"Okay. You said you read the Medico-legal doc thoroughly, right?" Dena asked.

"Yeah."

"Any mention of sexual penetration."

"None. No mention of bruising or abrasions in the genital area. And the only mention of clothes was a torn dress—no undergarments. So, if it was an attempted rape, wouldn't it stand to reason the *perp* would home in on the good stuff and wouldn't care what was in his way?"

"Yeah."

"What I see is; if more than one person was involved, then one of them had to be a woman, or in this case, a young lady."

"How so?"

"The report mentioned Friedel's hair was not in a bun, but in fact looked as though it had been let down and brushed. If Friedel wanted to brush her hair, she could have done that in the privacy of her own bedroom. She's not going to wander off at ten o'clock at night so she can walk to the cement bridge for some personal grooming. Plus, if she had an encounter with some guy, the last thing on his list would be to brush her hair. That is something only a woman would do."

"You're right. Was there anyone who befriended Friedel at school? Especially a popular girl who might have felt threatened by her good looks."

"Kathleen was the most popular. She dated David, the quarterback for the Mustangs. They were voted Homecoming King and Queen. She could smile and any guy would buy her whatever she wanted."

"Spoiled?"

"You might say."

"Who was second in line for the guys' stamp of approval for Miss Popular?"

"That would have been my girlfriend, Nicole Carsten."

"Seen her lately?"

"Haven't seen nor heard from her since I left for California after graduation."

"Doesn't mean she wasn't involved at the time," Dena said in a matter-of-fact tone. "Women are strange creatures—if you haven't noticed."

Jason smiled and nudged his elbow into Dena's side. "Sometimes in a good way."

"Thanks. Then, evidently, Friedel was what, maybe third on the list?"

"Unofficially. Most guys respected her beliefs and just kinda let their hormones coast along in neutral."

"So. Between Kathleen and Nicole, who stood to lose the most if say someone, like David Ellison, had put the moves on Friedel and the student body found out about it?"

"Kathleen."

"She gets my vote, too." Dena took a deep breath. "Now, I'll add one other item...Ken Hutchinson. If more than one person is responsible for Friedel's death, what are the odds that one female, an outsider, would somehow pair up with an Amish guy—or vice versa?"

"Why would you ask that?"

"Because you seem to be homing in on Isaac. I don't see a connection there. I see people who may not agree with what Friedel was doing, but not enough to kill her, plus kill a deputy to silence him twenty-five years after the fact. To be honest, the investigation would have ended much quicker had this person killed you." She took another deep breath and offered an airy, "Sorry."

"Because of the initials at the covered bridge, I was really homing in on David, and thought maybe there was some connection there. David's good at playing people against each other. Maybe he preyed on those suspicions and anxieties."

"Friedel's death was an act of passion. Ken Hutchinson's was a cold-blooded case of a cover-up. Someone is running scared."

"Someone with a lot to lose."

"Someone with a family name to protect, possibly?"

Jason pulled the photo copy of Ted Phelps from the manila envelope. Sifting through the obits, his eyes fell on Kathleen's name again. He recalled her tone of voice when she so nonchalantly mentioned a cousin she had in Jefferson. The voice and attitude was too casual, almost callous. This was probably one of those circumstances where someone spends time with others at holidays, not so much because they want to, but because they're expected to. So much for the sociological conditioning associated with being nothing more than a biological coincidence. "Someone who may feel their family stature justifiably places them above the law."

"You may not feel comfortable with this...partner...but I think we need to talk to this Kathleen. Do a little more prying into her inner *chi*. Woman to woman."

Jason grinned. "Any ideas...partner?"

"Ooo. Ooo, I have a cramp in my leg." Dena leaped to her feet. "Gotta walk it out. Gotta walk. Gotta walk."

"Here, let me..." Jason reached for her arm.

"Gotchya." Dena plopped back down. "Sometimes, you are so easy."

"Well, did you ever think that maybe I care about you?"

"Really?"

◊   ◊   ◊

The branches from Kathleen's willow tree drifted in long sweeping arcs in the evening air, looking very much like long silky feathers trying to paint a portrait on the ground beneath. A lawn rake, its tines bent and a little on the rusty side, leaned against Kathleen's wrought iron fence.

Jason drove past the house and continued around the block so Dena could get a feel for the area. Every house appeared well-maintained except one, which seemed to fit the universal trait of every block in the

US. No matter how many rules were set up for communities, one person seemed to slip through the cracks and would take great pride in letting everything dry up, break up, or generally die. And it was always this house that received the most attention when visitors happened by. Few notice the beauty of the face, only the pimple.

The white van pulled to a stop across the street from Kathleen's house. In case she was checking out her window, Jason wanted Dena's presence to be a surprise for Kathleen for as long as possible.

The front door opened. Kathleen was framed in the doorway, her blonde hair pulled to one side and wearing a generous smile, along with a tempting dress one might wear to a nightclub on a Saturday night's let's-see-what's-out-there fishing expedition. Then she spotted Dena. Her eyes darted from Jason to Dena and back again. The smile became forced.

Dena scooted under the low hanging branches of the willow tree while Jason brushed some aside so he could pass below them.

"Hi. I didn't realize you were bringing a guest." Kathleen clutched her hands to her neck to hide the ample display of cleavage.

"Hi. This is Dena."

Kathleen accepted Dena's outstretched hand. "Welcome to my home. Are you the one visiting from California?"

Oh, oh, Jason muttered to himself. Spontaneity was one of Dena's enduring qualities, as was her propensity to shoot barbs at anyone who struck her wrong, much like what one might expect to follow the low rumbling snarl from an agitated dog. Kathleen's use of the term *visitor* would not go down easy, when in all doubt, she knew exactly who Dena was. Jason was ninety-nine percent sure Dena would fire back with a curt, *No. I'm a hooker still trying to collect for last night.*

"Actually, I'm Jason's partner."

Whew. Jason pried their hands apart. "Can we go in?"

Kathleen stood back away from the door and with a sweeping arm motion, invited Dena in first. When Jason passed her, she reached for his hand and gave it a tender squeeze, but let go as Dena caught a glimpse of her actions.

"You're decoration is simply lovely, Kathleen. I have to ask you; did you do this all by yourself?"

"Yes. This is my first house as a single mom…and no husband to critique my choices."

"I like it. It's bold…in a feminine way. Thanks for having us over."

"My pleasure."

My displeasure is what Jason thought as he studied Kathleen's obligatory smile and icy stare. Maybe he'd made a mistake when he called asking if he could pay her another visit. But if he'd been honest, would Kathleen have agreed? This was no time for niceties. If nothing comes of this visit other than eliminating another possible suspect, or at least an accomplice, then there might come a time for healing, but for now, this was business. He was glad Jennifer was not here. "Can we sit down?"

"Oh. Where are my manners?" Kathleen said. "Can I offer you something to drink? Coffee, tea, bourbon?"

Dena chuckled. "No tequila shooters?"

"I can do that," Kathleen said with a reciprocal chuckle and softened smile. "What brand do you like to drink? I have Cuervo gold, Cazadores Añejo, Cabo Wabo."

"Ooo. The good stuff." Dena smiled.

"I never had Cabo Wabo before, but I just thought the name looked so funky." Kathleen looked at Jason. "You?"

"Cabo is fine."

"Cabo it is." Kathleen gestured to the sofa that faced the window. "I'll be right back." On the far wall of the living room, she opened a drawer in what looked like an antique sewing cabinet and pulled out three shot glasses with pictures of Great Lakes' ore carriers painted on them. "These are some of the best sellers at the museum." Under the felt lined drawer was a swing-out shelf where an array of liquors could be stored. The Cabo Wabo was off to the side, and opened.

"I don't remember seeing that when I was here last time," Jason said.

"Wasn't. Needed a pick-me-up and I happened upon this at a local furniture store and I thought, how perfect."

"It works," Dena said. "You would never know what it was, and all the good stuff is just steps away. I'd like one of those in my living room."

"One problem. No place for ice." Kathleen started for the kitchen.

"Who needs ice," Jason said. "Bring those glasses."

The three sat on the couch. Jason sat side-legged next to Dena. Kathleen sat at the far end facing the varnished oak coffee table which served as a platform for pouring the shots. For the first round, each tapped their glasses together and raised them in a toast to the past. Cabo went down go-o-od. Within seconds, a second round was poured.

"Ooo. Ooo, I have a cramp in my leg." Jason leaped to his feet. "Gotta walk it out. Gotta walk. Gotta walk." He stumbled away from the couch and rubbed the inside of his right leg. "Crap. I get these every so often."

"Don't bend your leg," Dena warned. "Just keep putting weight on it."

Jason bent a little at the waist as he tried to walk around the confines of the living room. With every step, he reached for the back of the couch, or a sturdy piece of furniture, all the time, moaning.

"There's not too much room in here," Dena said. "Maybe it'd be better if you stretched your legs outside."

Jason rubbed his inner thigh again and let out a long groan. "Maybe more Cabo."

"No more Cabo, you big dummy," Dena said. "Take a walk. Do you want me to come with you?"

"I think I can make it on my own." His hand was poised on the front door handle to steady himself. "You guys gonna be okay?" His voice sounded as if he was going to faint.

"We'll be fine," Dena said as she tapped her glass against Kathleen's.

Dena and Kathleen stood at the front window and watched Jason duck under the branches of the willow tree. Before he opened the gate in the fence, Jason bent over and rubbed his inner thigh again. In a few seconds, he was out the gate and disappeared down the street behind the neighbor's shrubs.

"I hope he'll be okay," Kathleen said.

"He'll be fine. He goes through this every time he doesn't eat for an extended period of time—like an hour." Dena reached over, poured herself another shot of Cabo Wabo, and then offered another for Kathleen.

Kathleen slid the window curtain back in place and plopped down next to Dena.

"Jason tells me you have a little girl."

"Yeah, we do. Or I do. Name's Jennifer. You?"

"Naw. My husband and I haven't figured out what causes them yet."

Kathleen let out a bold laugh. "I didn't think I'd like you, but... you're okay." She clinked Dena's glass. "Isn't this better than visiting with those Amish people all the time?"

"Yeah, but they're okay once you break past the odor barrier." Dena lifted her glass and downed another shooter.

"I know what you mean. They do all that physical work and God knows they never take a shower until when? Maybe Sunday before church."

"It's a wonder some people choose to procreate."

"On purpose," Kathleen added with a light laugh. "Like, don't they have sense of smell?"

"You don't like these people very much, do you?"

"They're good farmers."

"You know, we're looking into the Friedel Mueller case, don't you?"

"Yeah. Jason said something about that before...before you came here."

"I was supposed to come here for fun and what do we do? Go pissin' into the wind. It's so frustrating." Dena offered Kathleen the bottle.

"What have you guys found out?"

"Not much. Twenty-five years is a long time. They didn't keep track of records like we do now. It was pretty much tree-based. If a doc is gone, it's pretty much gone forever. But...Jason knows of one document," her words were beginning to slur, "that still exists. This could pretty much determine the outcome of his whole...entire...complete case." Dena twirled her finger around in the air. "Am I re...repeating myself?"

"Does he have it?"

"Naw. The Mueller woman has it hidden someplace. Won't say where. Kinda stubborn, she is. But Jason thinks he has a way around this little problem. He's very clever, you know?" Dena downed another shooter, laughed, and slouched into the back of the cushy leather sofa.

"Yeah, I do. So. You're married?"

"Yep. A lot of years. Too many years."

"Are you and Jason…ya'know…messing around?"

"No. Did he tell you how we met?"

"No."

"He was the one who helped me find my brother's killer. It was sad, and good at the same time. I owe Jason…big time. Family means a lot to me."

"Me, too," Kathleen whispered.

"Other than your daughter, do you have family here?" Dena's eyes were at half-staff and her head bobbed like one of those dolls some people place in the rear windows of their cars.

Kathleen now joined Dena by leaning against the backrest of the couch, the bottle of Cabo clutched in a death grip. "Another?"

"Why not?" Dena said and then positioned her glass under the tilted bottle. "Don't spill any of this stuff, girlfriend."

Kathleen carefully poured another round for Dena and herself. "Family, you asked. Yeah, I have family here…one cousin. My parents live in Florida. Don't socialize with them very much anymore."

"Do you miss them?"

"My parents or my cousin?"

"Both. Either."

Kathleen took a slow sip of the tequila. "Sometimes family is not a good thing."

"Wh…what do-o-o you mean?"

"It obligates you. It paralyzes you."

"Sometimes, don't you think it's better to have friends rather than family? Then you don't have to *feel* these obligations are screwing up your life." Dena grabbed the bottle from Kathleen's hand and waved it in the air. "Em-mp-ty."

"I have more." Kathleen used the backs of the same chairs Jason had used to steady himself to maintain her own vertical position on her way to the *faux* sewing cabinet. It was a precarious maneuver, but she managed. "You were saying?"

"Oh. I just asked if family meant more than friends or vice versa."

"I think you're right, Dena. It's kinda like politics at the most basic level. You do what's right for the family without regard for what's morally right. Decisions suck. And you live with this."

"You made bad decisions? I can't believe that girlfriend. You graduated from where?"

"Kent State."

"A great school. Did you go there right out of high school?"

"Yeah. My parents had the money and wanted me to have a good education. Get a good jumpstart at a career. Make a future for myself. All the right reasons."

"Kinda like Friedel, huh? She wanted a good education. Even if it was just a high school diploma."

"For sure. What happened to her was a shame. And she was so beautiful. Her skin was flawless. She could have made it outside the appalling confines of the Amish culture."

"Yeah. It's a shame," Dena continued in a dreamy voice. "Kinda reminds me of my high school days. I was on the timid side. Afraid to get involved, make friends, ya'know? So I just hung out with myself, eventually got married, did the whole pot and pan thing. I would never challenge anyone. I suppose some thought of me as weak and fragile. There was never anyone around to protect me."

"What do you think you would have done if someone tried to attack you...ya'know, like a physical assault...or worse?"

"Ooh...probably scream my lungs out...run...I don't know. I was just lucky I guess."

"Yeah. You were." Kathleen stared out the window. "Wonder where Jason is."

"He'll be okay. Like I said, he gets these little spasms in his legs, but he walks it off. Sometimes it takes a little longer than usual. I have to say, you were a very beautiful girl in high school. Were you ever attacked?"

"Never had to worry." Kathleen held the bottle of tequila in the air signifying the universal gesture of asking if anyone wanted more. Without waiting for Dena to respond, glasses were filled again. "David was my protector, my hero...until he started...fucking around. Forgive my language, but I seemed to have lost my sense of ladyhood...is that a legitimate word?" Her words were becoming more slurred, too.

"Anyhow, he started to expand his social networking skills. In the back seat of his Camaro. Bastard."

"Anyone in particular? Or a crap shoot?"

"I take that back. I don't know for sure, but someone told me he'd been seen with Friedel. Talking...in the parking lot...after the school busses had left. Long walk home for a farmer's daughter. And I bet he knew it. I bet he planned it. Guess where it went from there, girlfriend?"

"So, you don't know anything for sure, but you attended college together. Got married. Had a daughter."

"Go figure. Chalk up another bad decision for Team Kathleen."

Dena noticed Jason staring in the front window. With a discreet wave of her fingers, she motioned him away. "You keep talking about bad decisions. You seem like an in-control type of person. Cut yourself some slack. It's been a long time."

"Some things are never supposed to go away. Some horrible things. I tried to be nice."

"What do you mean? To David?"

"No. To Friedel. I tried to get her to open up...ya'know...like confess to me she was interested in David. Then I could kick her ass."

"Did she...open up to you?"

"Kinda. Once I met her after school when David was at practice. Talked about girl things. Tried to steer the conversation around to boys, and David in particular. She said something to me that day... really made me realize how controlled these girls were. Did you know, they can never cut their hair? All they can do is brush it and curl it up in a bun. Cover it up with a black prayer covering. What a waste of beautiful hair."

"So?"

"We talked about hair. My hair, and how good it felt to have someone else brush it, and take care of it. Toners, conditioners. Ya'know, like at a beauty shop. She'd never been to a beauty salon. So one day, I offered to brush her hair for her. She thought it would be a nice gesture. So we met, late once. Really late."

"Did she show up?"

"For sure. But just as we were getting started, someone else showed up." Kathleen peered into the bottle of amber liquid and rolled her head around. "Isn't there supposed to be a worm in here?"

"Rumors." Dena twirled her fingers like a mother would do when asking their child to continue, but Kathleen resumed her hollow, emotionless stare into the half-empty container, seemingly mesmerized by the motion the liquid made as the bottle swayed from side to side. "Were you guys afraid?"

"Oh, no. This guy..."

A loud sound on the front porch startled the two women. Jason waved through the window and mouthed, *I'm okay.* A few seconds later, the door swung open and he limped in. "Kinda tripped over a lawn chair. Sorry. Did I scare you guys?"

CHAPTER 23

"Boy. I was doing so good until you bumped into the front porch furniture." Dena had a death grip on Jason's arm as they crossed the street. "I was thi-i-is close. But, no-o. You had to go get all kinda clumsy. You aren't hurt are you? I wouldn't like it if you were hurt…again. I don't like my partner to be hurt."

"How did it feel to drink your way through an interrogation?" Jason helped Dena up on the curb so he could unlock the door. He first propped her with her backside into the side of the van, but when he let go, she buckled and, with the spontaneous effect of gravity, began to do a slo-mo downward. He beeped his opener as quickly as he could and caught her before she became one with Mother Earth.

"I was this close to finding out what happened that night, but no-o. Mr. I've-got-a-cramp had to discover patio furniture. By the way, Mr. Gotta-walk-it-out, you were good. Really good. Almost too good. I thought you were gonna turn into a drama queen."

"Here. Let me help you in." Jason tucked his head under her arm so he could hoist her into the passenger seat. With her back firmly against the rear of the seat, he reached for the seat belt and tried to locate the latch mechanism.

"I don't need no stinkin' seat belt. Ya'know? If you hit something and the car stopped, ya'know, like really quick? It wouldn't do any good. Ya'know why? I'll tell you why. 'Cause my body would just flow around it. Ya'know, the body is what…ninety percent water, or something like that? Well, Mr. Stubbed-my-toe, right now, I feel like I'm one-hundred percent water mixed in with a little tequila. So this stinkin' seat belt isn't gonna do squat. My body will just blen-nd around it and hit the windshield and splat…there goes Dena. Another bug on the windshield. Yes sir, boy. Splat."

"You're not going to go splat. Here. Scoot your butt over so I can fasten this belt." After a few seconds of tugging and pushing, Jason managed to snap the latch shut, and reach into the rear compartment for a spare towel…just in case. She accepted the towel with all the grace of a mama Grizzly with PMS. When he hopped into the driver's seat, all he could see of Dena was her face buried in the towel. There was no convulsive movement, so he figured she was okay for now, but who could know what bouncing down the road would bring.

On the way back to the B & B, there were no conversations or progress reports regarding Dena's spontaneous interrogation methods. Their goal had been to determine who the last person was to see Friedel alive. This would be a critical element of the investigation to unravel. Any hope of gaining insight into this elusive ingredient was pretty much in a holding pattern. Talking of holding patterns…Jason kept glancing at Dena to make sure she could make it from one storm drain to the next. His plan was to pull up next to one if an awful gurgling sound began to emanate from within the wadded-up towel. Once outside the city limits, a ditch would have to do.

◊   ◊   ◊

"Are you okay this morning, my dear?" Mrs. Loomis asked. With a light touch, she stroked Dena's hair and shoved a cup of coffee under her nose. "I wasn't sure if I should make you breakfast or not, so it's up to you." Mrs. Loomis backed away, crossed her arms over her ample chest and stared down at Dena like a compassionate mother might do to her beloved offspring…just before she lit into the youngster with a tirade of stern reprimands.

"I'm okay," Dena muttered, her voice sounding much like she was talking through a megaphone filled with gravel.

"Coffee is fine," Jason whispered. "Maybe we'll go for a little walk. Dena and I are good at taking care of each other."

Through swollen eyes, Dena glanced up at Jason, offered a frail smile and moaned, "Yeah, we are, aren't we." Then her head hit the table top with a resounding thud.

"Let's forget breakfast this morning, okay?" Jason asked the Loomis'. "The last thing Dena needs right now is the smell of food. It might conjure up bad memories, or worse."

Mrs. Loomis hung her iron skillet on a decorative wrought iron utensil rack suspended over the breakfast island. It swung back and forth for a few seconds creating a lazy shadow. She waved her arm at her husband like a wagon-master in a western movie. "Maybe we should leave these two to themselves."

"We appreciate the gesture," Jason whispered. "We'll see you later this evening." After the Loomis' left, Jason sat next to Dena in case she started to slide off the chair again. The hot mug in his hand felt good and he inhaled the steam as if it was an inhalant capable of breaking up clogged toilets. He'd gotten very little sleep the night before. The drive back to the B & B was border-line routine. Except for an occasional burp from Dena, there had been no emergency stops at storm drains or roadside ditches. Better yet, there were no telltale lava flows down the side of the van. It wasn't his van, but he cared little for the thought of having to endure the boorish smirks from others who would know, without a doubt, that within this van, someone in the recent past had performed a Technicolor belch.

A moan broke the silence. "How did I get to bed last night?"

"'Twas me, fair maiden."

"Did you brush my teeth?"

"No."

"I always brush my teeth before bed." Dena raised her head and peered at Jason through half-closed eyelids. "I suppose I should thank you. So-o. Thank you." Her head became somewhat more stable and less like a bobble doll. Bracing her hands on the edge of the table, Dena pushed herself into an upright position. "I can do this." A few deep breaths were followed by another attempt to stand. Success. "Coffee? Aspirin? Sledge hammer."

The mug of coffee Mrs. Loomis had poured for Dena was sitting on the table in front of her, still steaming. "Here," Jason whispered.

"Oh, goody, it wasn't just my imagination" She slumped back down in the chair, cupped the mug, and inhaled just as Jason had done earlier. "I feel a lot better. Thanks."

"You sure?" Mrs. Loomis not only made her coffee hearty, but hot as well. Her technique was to fill the empty cup with boiled water while the coffee was brewing, then pour it out just before filling the cup with coffee. Jason flipped through the morning issue of the Cleveland Plain Dealer. An article caught his eye.

"Positive."

"How much do you remember of last night at Kathleen's house?"

"Test me. Just don't do it loudly."

Jason studied the determined look in her eyes. In a staccato delivery, he began, "What was the first thing you noticed when you walked into Kathleen's house?"

"Cleavage."

"Second thing?"

"Rails missing going upstairs. Somebody could fall."

"Anything else?"

"Furniture faced front window. Definitely a *faux pas* in interior design. For that size room, it cut down on available floor space leaving little room for serious entertaining. Her leather sectional should have been…"

"Okay, okay." Jason chuckled at Dena's mischievous grin. "We're good for go."

"Told ya."

"By the way, your leg cramp idea was a good ploy to get me out of the way yesterday. Just thought I'd toss that in."

"Told ya."

What Jason and Dena needed was a ruse to coerce Kathleen to openly admit she had a cousin in Ashtabula County at the time of the killing. By the obit, they knew he existed, but knew of no motive for what happened and why. And what role, if any, this person played was up for grabs, but Elizabeth's relaying of the conversation with the stranger and his use of the term *people* rather than *person* was underlined in his pad. What did this stranger know?

More times than not, when you want to find out some things, plural, about others, you have to find out something about how they feel about themselves first. A surveyor, or psychiatrist, would call this a benchmark. It allows the interviewer a point of reference.

Timelines were another critical element to their investigation. By his own accounting, they knew where Isaac was, but then again, lying is a universal trait and has no ideological borders, especially when the liar's own life may be in jeopardy. Jason flipped through page after page of potentials, but the word *people* gnawed at him. Would an Amish man team up with an outsider? And to what end? Would two Amish men conspire to eliminate a prospective embarrassment to their community? One might consider it, but two? And did it have to be only men who were involved?

With his ever-present notepad at the ready, Jason asked Dena to give him a general rundown of the conversation she'd had with Kathleen.

"Okay. Where to start. Let's see. First off, when we started talking, Kathleen used the phrase, *Those Amish people* in kind of a derogatory context. When people openly set themselves apart, what they're divulging to others is a certain amount of hostility or contempt toward that target group. It's a common trait associated with a superiority issue."

Jason flipped to a new page and kept writing.

"She once referred to them as good farmers, as if that was something to be ashamed of. I have to admit I was baiting her a little."

"That's okay. There's a difference between baiting a suspect and leading a suspect. We want answers."

"Good. One thing I steered clear of was the mention of my son. It just came to me in a flash. I thought if the subject came up, we'd turn into the quintessential soccer moms and jabber about children."

"Counter-productive. Great choice. Did you call Dave this morning?"

"Yeah. I mustered up the strength to appear normal, but I cut it short and told him we'd talk more tomorrow. It took almost everything out of me. I love my son so much."

Jason touched her hands. When he did, Dena grasped his hands and stared deep into his eyes. There was this softness again, this feeling of vulnerability. He continued to hold her hands. Why did she blatantly exclude any mention of her husband? This wasn't the first time Jason wondered about this. Was she keeping a secret from him? In a soft voice, he asked, "Uuh. Anything else you found interesting about Kathleen?"

"Yeah. She started out with a comment about how much nicer it must be for us to not be visiting with those Amish people all the time? This struck me as odd. How did she know we were talking to them so often?"

"Could be she's privy to inside information." His eyes became focused on the year book photo of Ted Phelps and the peculiar way he parted his hair.

"Then she rattled on about how family obligations paralyze her—like she'd been pressured to support *family* regardless of morals."

"Interesting."

"I tried to steer the conversation around to Friedel—ya'know, to see what her thoughts were at the time. She didn't actually 'fess up to this, but she admitted to trying to cozy up to Friedel with girl stuff—hair to be exact—to determine if she'd been approached by David. If she had, Kathleen said she was going to kick her ass, and this, I believe was the night Friedel was killed. Kathleen acted a little edgy when this came up."

Jason cast Dena a scowl. He knew there were turning points in any investigation, but this involved a woman he'd searched out, enjoyed several suppers with, seriously contemplated a physical relationship with, maybe even more, and visited with her daughter and showed her how to wash dishes more efficiently. "You sure?"

"No, but all the signs were leading in that direction." Dena took a sip of her now lukewarm coffee.

Jason wrote slowly, as if convincing himself to make these details official. "What else?" he asked in a calculated tone of voice.

"After Kathleen confided in me about being with Friedel, she said some guy showed up. Didn't have a chance to pursue this any further because that's when you moved a sizeable piece of garden furniture with your toe."

"My bad."

"Actually, she didn't say *guy* from the get-go, she said *someone else*. It was later when she said *guy*. When I asked if she was afraid of him, she started to say no, but by then, you were in the living room. We were both hammered. You were pretty much a blur."

"I remember. All during this time, did she ever ask you any questions? Like trying to pry information from you."

"To be sure. I mentioned the legal document. She grabbed hold of that like a schoolboy with the latest issue of Playboy. She wanted to know who had it. I told her the Mueller woman. Was I wrong?"

Jason stared out the window until a bird lit on the clothesline just outside the rear of the house. A few sharp chirps jolted him back to reality. "The fact that she was interested means she's been in contact with someone who does care. This could work in our favor."

"Phew. I did something right." Dena let out a long airy sigh.

"You did so many things right. I'm glad I left you two alone." He glanced at his note pad again. "Let's go over a few things. You said Kathleen said *someone else*, right? And later mentioned a guy...whom she was evidently not afraid of...which meant she must have known him."

"If it was Isaac, don't you think she would have used his name rather than *some guy?*"

"Exactly, but that's assuming she knew Isaac. It's pretty much a given that Kathleen didn't socialize with the Mueller family, so Isaac would have been a stranger to her. So, if it had been Isaac, and knowing Kathleen's condescending attitude toward the Amish, she would have said, *some Amish guy*. But let's say, for a moment, it was David. Don't you think she would have used his name? I've never heard her talk of David as a *him* or *another guy*. She leaps at every chance to use his name because it gives her the fuel to spit his name out like a rotten vegetable... which he is, by the way."

"Easy, big guy."

"Did she ever mention having knowledge of David giving Friedel rides in his Camaro?"

"Didn't think to ask, but the mere thought of her contemplating kicking Friedel's ass would indicate she was capable of waging mini-warfare."

"Yeah, and the newspapers are full of where border skirmishes wind up."

His note pad, now closed, was pushed to the side. Jason rose and stretched his arms upward. At his height, he could almost touch the ceiling. Coffee cups, cold to the touch and no longer enticing were moved to a plastic drain board next to the sink. Mrs. Loomis made a special point to remind them she would do dishes. That was part of the deal. No one argued with Mrs. Loomis when it came to household chores. The little clock over the window chimed twice, reminding everyone another hour had passed.

Jason picked up the Plain Dealer and flipped to page two. "Wanta hear something interesting?"

Dena nodded in the direction of the newspaper.

"There's a columnist who seems to be a bit of an activist." Jason scanned this morning's spread. "Been writing a series of articles dealing with government waste."

"Like that's news?"

"Not the point. He's into local corruption. National politics deals with trillions of dollars, but the locals are just as irritated about where their thousands of personal dollars go." He shoved the folded paper across the table to Dena and leaned on the counter over the sink and gazed out the window where the bird had lit on the clothesline a few minutes ago. In those fleeting seconds he'd watched the bird, he realized it had chosen that perch for a reason and, in fact, had a decision to make. Jason became this bird.

Because its metabolic rate is so high, a bird has to consume six times its body weight every day just to stay alive. So what prompted the bird to fly in any particular direction? The bird didn't have the option to flip a coin and let fate decide where to go. Down there on the ground somewhere was what a fisherman would call bait. The further Jason dug into Friedel's death, the more he realized those initials on the wooden beams of the Avery Road bridge were nothing more than a veneer and had no intrinsic value except to post a storm warning in hopes someone would notice something was wrong. The real bait was the Medico-legal document. It was time for Elizabeth's treasure to come out of hiding and crawl along the ground and wait for the bird.

"Why did you want me to read this column?" Dena asked. Her voice had the same soothing effect as the sound of an owl late into the night.

"I've been following this guy's column the last few days. He's on the verge of being front page material...just hasn't had the right vehicle."

"And?"

"It's one thing to be concerned where tax dollars are going, but quite another when a member of LE is killed and the spokesman for the county maintains it's being treated as a probe. I am convinced… we find Ken Hutchinson's killer and we find Friedel's killer. And Ken's death has been down-played by the county from the get-go, both in the Plain Dealer and the Ashtabula Star Beacon. This should be a full blown effort to find the killer, not a friggin' probe. If we can persuade this guy to cooperate, he'll furnish the rain for someone's parade. Sound like a plan, partner?"

"Yeah, except for one thing. This guy's a page two journalist. Why did you home in on him instead of someone with a front page track record?"

"Guys on page two are hungrier."

CHAPTER 24

"This isn't going to be a fun visit, is it?" Kathleen ushered Jason and Dena in. Unlike yesterday, her hair was a little on the unruly side, and the door to the faux sewing cabinet had been left open. The empty bottles of tequila sat unattended as did the glasses she and Dena used to polish off some very expensive alcohol. Instead of cleavage, this afternoon she was showing saggy bags under her eyes.

"No, it's not," Jason said. "We have some talking to do."

Kathleen eased onto the sofa and cupped her hands over her face. "Jennifer is next door, so don't go yelling. Promise me."

"We promise," Dena whispered as she sat down next to Kathleen.

"Remember the first night I visited with you?" Jason asked.

"Yes."

"Remember the gunshots out front?"

"Yes."

"Those were not coincidental, were they?"

"No. I suppose not."

"I believe those gunshots were a warning. At first, I thought they were a warning to me to get out of Dodge, then after they happened again where I was staying, it came to me, Kathleen. Those were not directed at you *or* me, but to you *and* me. And you knew it, didn't you?"

"I didn't know what to say, or do, Jason. And Jennifer was here. I will do anything to protect her. I always have."

"After I contacted you at the museum, did you call Ted Phelps? And just so you know where I stand, we know he is your cousin. So, I'll ask you again. Did you let him know I was snooping around?"

"I hoped you were doing more than snooping around, Jason. I needed you. I needed some part of my past to be right." She kept her face buried in her hands. "Jennifer is the only part of my past that's right. Whatever happens, she has to know that about me. I never want her to feel I've let her down."

Dena inched closer and looped her arm over Kathleen's shoulder.

Jason pulled up a dining room chair and faced the two women. "The night you met Friedel at the bridge to comb her hair…was that the night she was killed?"

"I didn't mean for anything to happen to her." Kathleen grasped Dena's hand. "I know I told you I wanted to kick her ass if she was fooling around with David, but down deep, I knew it wasn't about her, it was about David. And yet David and I continued our relationship as if nothing ever happened, and I married him, and we had a child together."

"Just before Dena and you bought the bullet last night, you mentioned someone showing up. Who was that person?"

"I…I, uuh didn't know what to do. I knew I'd done something wrong and was being punished."

"It wasn't you who was punished, Kathleen. It was Friedel. For doing something as innocent as having her hair combed by another person. For her, that must have been like going to her first dance, or having her first kiss. Who was this person?"

"Teddy." Her voice was barely audible and her entire body began to quiver. "He wasn't supposed to be there. No one was supposed to be there."

"Why was it so important for Friedel to let down her hair so you could brush it?"

"I was seventeen. I was supposed to be the popular one, but when she walked by, all the guys would stare at her, and I could see the looks in their eyes. Guys don't hide their feelings too well, especially when their tongues are hanging out." She made a vain attempt to laugh. "I'm sorry. I thought if I could convince her to leave the Amish community for a while—they have a word for that—"

"*Rumspringa*," Jason and Dena said in unison.

"Whatever. If I could persuade her to do that, she would have to leave the area and I wouldn't have to contend with her anymore. I did not want her to be hurt, just leave. Is that something to be ashamed of?"

"I wouldn't be overly proud of it," Dena said with a distinct bite in her voice.

"Did you ever tell your cousin about a report Friedel's mother has in her possession? Given to her just after Friedel was buried."

"No, yeah, maybe. I can't remember."

"Did you know about this report at all?"

"Yeah, like an autopsy...something like that."

This report was so critical to prove Friedel's death was not an accident. The locations of bruising and abrasions were not the result of a simple fall, and Jason recalled talking to Ken Hutchinson about this after Elizabeth let him read it. Departmental policy dictated every deputy fill out a daily report of their activities. This would be standard practice in any jurisdiction. Included in Ken's details would be the mention of this report, so Jason concluded it was not important whether Kathleen had access to this information or not, only that she knew about it, and if she did, who else, other than the sheriff, was in the loop to know about it? "Why have you hidden this information from the authorities all these years, Kathleen? Twenty-five damned years for the Muellers to not know what really happened to their daughter. How would you feel if it happened to Jennifer?"

"I was scared. I didn't know what happened until the next day."

"Exactly what happened the night your cousin showed up at the bridge?" Jason asked. "I want a blow by blow."

"Like I said. Friedel and I agreed to meet there. It was a warm autumn night. It felt good. She removed her prayer cover and took the clips out of her hair. When she shook her head, her hair fell down to her waist. It was beautiful. We talked girl talk for awhile, then I started to brush it. She said she brushed it every night, but it wasn't the same. She always had to fling it over her shoulder. Said it felt good to lean her head back and let her hair fall naturally. That's when I started offering her some ideas of what it would be like if she wasn't...drowning...in the Amish culture."

"You don't like the Amish very much, do you?" Jason asked.

"They have their place."

"Okay," Jason continued. "Your cousin showed up. What did you do then?"

"It surprised me. I knew he hung around school even after he graduated just to get a look at her. Tried to offer her rides home, but she refused. I have no way of knowing how he knew we would be at the bridge that night. Maybe it was just plain luck."

"Maybe he'd been stalking her," Dena offered.

"How long had you been at the bridge before he showed up?" The intensity of Jason's voice began to rise.

"Ten, maybe fifteen minutes probably."

"Where did the Phelps family live at the time?"

"In Jefferson. His father was the sheriff…back then."

"So, by pure coincidence, this guy from Jefferson just happens to drive by the concrete bridge halfway across the county…at night…and this didn't tickle your intellect?"

"He was family. You trust your family. We spent holidays together. What was I supposed to do?"

"Ask him what the hell he was doing there," Dena fired back. "Ask Friedel if she wanted to go home, for Christ's sake. You probably had a car there, right?"

Kathleen gave a nervous nod.

"What did your cousin say to you when he arrived?" Jason asked.

"He said *Hi* to us, but what he really meant was, *Hi, Friedel.* He reached for her, like he wanted a hug, but she backed away."

"What happened next?"

"He kept looking at her. Without even turning to look at me, he told me to go home." Kathleen was shivering as if she'd been outside for too long. It was a total body shiver. "So I drove home."

Jason shook his head in disbelief. So often in his life, he recounted the difference between ignorance and stupidity as if someone told another person to jump off a ten-story building. If a child did it, that would be ignorance, but if an adult jumped, that would be stupidity. Jason looked at this woman he'd reminisced about for so many years and marveled at how fortunate he'd been to have her make choices that did not include him. "So, your cousin shows up outta nowhere late at night...and you voluntarily leave him alone with Friedel?"

"Uh-huh."

"Did Ted Phelps somehow force you, or bully you to leave?"

"No."

"When you got home, did you tell anyone what had happened? Ya'know? Like your parents or someone who could have driven back there to help...possibly save a life?" Jason's voice was taking on a tone he seldom used except in the most reprehensible of circumstances.

"I kinda snuck into the house. I wasn't supposed to drive my parents' car for a week."

"Where were they?"

"A fundraiser. At the community center."

"How'd they get to and from the fundraiser?"

"They had three cars. Actually two cars and a pickup."

Jason leaned forward, propped his arms on his legs and stared at Kathleen, then at Dena, then back at Kathleen. He noticed that the more Kathleen spoke, the further Dena inched away from her. What had begun as sympathy had evolved into repulsion. The façade was down. Barriers had become transparent. Lipstick and short skirts no longer mattered. "So? When did you first hear of Friedel's death?"

"Same as you, Jason. Over the school PA system."

"Almost true. Yeah, they broadcast a message over the PA, but what the message dealt with was the call for a special assembly so *admin* could have all the students together at the same time. It was the school's principal who made the announcement on the stage. Were you shocked, or disturbed by the news that the person you'd seen the night before was dead?"

"Well, yeah. The first thing I thought about was if Teddy had anything to do with it."

"When did you contact Teddy?"

"I didn't have to. He contacted me...before I left for school. Remember, his dad, Wayne, was the sheriff at the time. I guess his department was closest to the scene."

"What did Ted say? Did he have any explanation for what happened?"

"He swore to me he had nothing to do with it."

"When was the next time you saw Ted in person?"

"Oh, a week or so later…at a birthday party for Wayne."

"How did he appear? Confident? Scared? Nervous?"

"Same Teddy. Cocky. Strutted around like he didn't have a care in the world."

"Any unusual marks on his face or arms?"

"Yeah. He did have a scratch on his jaw. Right below his ear."

"And this didn't trigger any reaction from you?" Jason continued. "You didn't confront him about what happened that night?"

"We, uuh…we talked in the corner once. Again, he swore he knew nothing about how Friedel died."

"And you believed him?" Dena asked in a voice laced with sarcasm.

"What was his spin on what happened?" Jason continued.

"He admitted he tried to make out with her, but she fought him off. So, he got all pissed and drove home."

"Teddy admitted she fought?"

Kathleen nodded. "Teddy wouldn't lie about something as serious as this—at least that is what he said."

"I can't believe this," Jason fired back. "A guy admits he put the moves on some girl in a desolate location late at night. She evidently wanted no part of it and used the only option open to her, and that was to fight back. Good old Teddy shows up a week later with a scratch and you bought this line of bullshit?" Jason stared out the front window at the willow tree, its branches swaying to a gentle breeze. "Did he say if anyone else just happened to stop by the bridge that night?" Jason tried to keep his sarcasm to a minimum. Keep it analytical he kept reminding himself.

"Yes, I mean no. He said when he left, there was no one else around."

"To your recollection, during a family get together, did the topic ever come up?"

"Yeah. Teddy's family always wanted to hear the latest gossip, but his father always insisted we let the police do their job and everything would work out. My parents subscribed to the Star Beacon at the time, and we never read much about it in the paper, either."

Jason raised his head from his note pad where he'd been feverishly taking notes. In situations like his, rather than trying to spell everything out, he'd abbreviate or use partial words and fill in the blanks later. He called it the Carmichael shorthand method. It got him through college. "Kathleen. There's not a cop in the civilized world who wouldn't arrest you on the spot as an accomplice to murder." He took a few moments to look through his note pad to watch her squirm. "You know there is no statute of limitations on capital crimes, right?" He didn't wait for her anemic answer. "What you did was not abetting, you were a flat out collaborator in Friedel's death. When the local prosecutor takes charge of this, and we will make sure he does, you will be joining good old Teddy behind bars."

Kathleen burst into tears. After blowing her nose with a tissue, she continued in a shaky voice. "Oh, my God. I never thought it would come to this. I wanted to tell someone at the time, but Wayne kept telling me to keep my mouth shut. Believe me, Jason. I never intended to hurt her. She was my friend."

Jason paced around the silent living room. The only sound was from an occasional sniffle from Kathleen, who kept looking to him for support, sympathy, or a possible way out. Dena had now distanced herself from Kathleen and offered no looks of condolence as she'd done earlier. Jason hoped Jennifer would not come barging in from Beth's home next door. He had no way of knowing what Kathleen had said to her or for how long she was to stay away. What would her mother say to her if she did? Had Jason been back in his jurisdiction, he would have called Child Protective Services to pick up the minor child and escort Kathleen away. But this wasn't California.

Jason also knew a prosecutor would have a tough time proving *intent* in a court of law without irrefutable evidence. This fact would hold true anywhere. With his fingers laced together, Jason stood staring at Kathleen. A furrow developed on his brow. He wanted closure for the Mueller family. He wanted to see a look of peace on Elizabeth's face knowing her daughter's killer had finally been caught...after twenty-five pain-filled years of staring at Friedel's cold, clinical report describing bruises, abrasions, and their locations. It wasn't a picture she could cherish. What Elizabeth had was an antiseptic depiction of a human being. Her human being. Jason had a decision to make.

"Look, Kathleen. I'm going to give the opportunity of a lifetime, and you have only one chance to get it right. Answer these questions for me. Are you willing to keep this conversation we had today on the down-low, and by that I mean you talk to no one except Dena or me? You will not contact your cousin or any other family member, David, no media, no attorney, no one?"

Her eyes now swollen nearly shut, Kathleen muttered a weak, "Yes."

"Will you furnish the authorities with a written deposition about what transpired the night Friedel was killed?"

"Yes."

"If I can come up with a strategy to flush your cousin out into the open, will you help Dena and me carry out the plan?"

"Yes."

"Congratulations, you passed." There was no smile on Jason's face welcoming Kathleen into the winner's circle. "I hope you realize, Ted Phelps will have dual charges brought up against him—for Friedel and Ken Hutchinson."

"Yes. I...uh, I thought maybe he had something to do with that, especially after I told Teddy about you and Ken working together."

"You didn't really have to do anything in those regards. Your cousin is the one who assigned Ken to work with me."

"What can I expect if I cooperate with you, Jason?"

"We, Dena and I, will try to have the charges against you lowered to abetting at worst, or total immunity at best. You may well serve time, but not the same amount as your cousin. There is always the possibility that the prosecutor will not allow you to come out of this unscathed. Are we clear?"

"What about Jennifer? Does she have to know?"

"For Christ's sake Kathleen, she's old enough to read and watch TV. I don't see a way around her not knowing. It's best it comes from you."

"I'm so sorry for all this." Kathleen buried her face into her hands again. A tissue dangled from her moist fingers.

"One more thing," Jason whispered. "If I can, I'd like to get you and Jennifer enrolled in the Witness Protection Program. I don't know whether or not it's possible."

"What?"

"Understand this. Your cousin has killed two people. What in the hell makes you think you're so special that he's not going to come after you? Family? Family doesn't mean jack to this kind of guy. Ted Phelps has the position, the means, and the incentive to track you down, and it will all look official. Any LE agency in the country would cooperate with him to find you. I will try to use my contacts back in California to locate a safe house for you out of the Cleveland area. Usually, these arrangements are facilitated by the U.S. Marshall's Service. I will furnish you with a disposable cell, and that is the only way you will communicate with Dena or me. You will not use the cell for anything except to receive my calls or to call me. No extra calls...period. Understood?"

"I suppose."

"Understood?"

"Yes. Yes, I understand."

"When I first came to visit you, did you call your cousin or did he contact you?"

"I think the first time, I called him. From then on, he began to contact me." Kathleen took a few moments to dab her eyes and blow her nose. "This relocation means what? Jennifer will no longer go to school? I don't understand. Can't you just confront Teddy? Get him to confess or something?"

"Pathological liars like him are methodical and well-rehearsed. He would have an answer for anything we'd toss at him and we'd have no way to prove anything without your testimony. It would amount to nothing more than a fishing expedition. And he'd go home and enjoy a good night's sleep...right after he devised a way to eliminate his final threat...you."

Kathleen pinched her lips together so tightly, they began to take on an ashen hue. Her eyes darted between Jason and Dena as if somewhere in those piercing looks, there would be a sign of compassion or empathy. She was met with indifference. "When does this all take place?"

"I have an idea, but for now, I think you are safe here. If your cousin calls, don't act any different than you normally would. Tell him you have something in the oven and cut it short. If you have any doubts, you call us, and we'll be here." Jason plopped down next to Kathleen. "You were seventeen when this happened. You were neither a child nor an adult. You made bad decisions. You did something to get yourself grounded. You took it upon yourself to entice Friedel to stay out of the picture because she was a threat to your popularity. You disobeyed your parents who trusted you and in effect, stole their car for the evening. You met a person who trusted you and you let her down. You trusted a young man just because he was related to you. You drove away because he told you to, and that very act caused a young woman to die a violent death. Do you get the picture? It was always about you, and now it's time you did something to correct this wrong. Do I make myself clear?"

"Yes, Jason. God, I don't know what I'm going to tell Jennifer."

"Can she stay with David? Ya'know, tell her dad wants to be a bigger part of her life."

"In other words…lie?"

"It's a choice you have to make. What's it going to be?" Jason watched Kathleen wad up a tissue around her ring finger and pull at it until it snapped, then look at her image in the living room mirror. What was once a beautiful face had, within an hour, evolved into a haggard old woman who seemed to depict the *before* picture in a cosmetic ad.

"And if I do nothing?"

"What?" Dena hissed. "We've been sitting here all evening giving you every break we could think of. And now, for your own convenience, you're going to turn your back on doing something right for a change. Let me tell you something…girlfriend. If it was up to me, I'd bring your sorry ass up on murder charges and let some slick lawyer help you wiggle your way out of it. But you know what you would lose either way? You'd be plastered all over the news, both local and national. You'd lose your daughter. You'd lose your career. You couldn't buy a loaf of bread on credit. And then there's the part of life called the future…girlfriend. Just because you weren't convicted of murder now, doesn't mean you and your cousin couldn't be retried later due to some loophole in the prosecutor's legal tactics. You are an eyewitness to a capital crime. That is the best weapon in a prosecutor's arsenal. Do you really think your cousin is going to let you live to testify against him in a second trial?" Dena stood nose to nose with Kathleen. "You're out of high school, Kathleen. Act like it. Do what's right for a change."

"Who do you think you're talking to, Dena?"

"Ya'know?" Jason fired back as he held Dena's arm, which was in a cocked position. "Mrs. Mueller has tried so hard to do what Friedel would have wanted. She's had three confrontations with either your cousin or his surrogate and has withstood those threats. A few days ago, with the help of her grandson, Mrs. Mueller did a very brave act. Dena and I will tolerate no more self-serving crap from you. That's it. We're out of here." He flung his jacket over his shoulder and started for the door.

Dena fell in behind her partner.

"Wait, wait. I didn't mean what I said." Kathleen tugged at Dena's arm and drew her back toward the sofa. "I'll, uuh…I'll talk to David."

◊ ◊ ◊

On the drive back to the B & B, after staring out the window at cornfields, pastures, cows, and rows of maple trees with their leaves beginning to turn color, Dena asked, "I don't understand something."

"What?"

"At Ken Hutchinson's gravesite, we saw David and the sheriff together and they looked rather…cozy. Why would you suggest that Kathleen contact him? Wouldn't David jump at the opportunity to contact Ted Phelps and let him in on the skinny?"

Jason smiled one of those confident smiles where he knew he had someone by the short hairs. "David Ellison is a politician. The last thing he would want is to align himself with someone who would put him in the loss column of a popularity poll. Trust me, Dena. If Kathleen follows through with her promise to contact David, he will distance himself from Ted Phelps and maintain that distance. If he has the sheriff on speed-dial, the next button David would punch is the erase key."

"Oh." Dena leaned over toward Jason and whispered, "So, what is this plan you have in mind to flush out Teddy?"

"Plan?"

CHAPTER 25

The new Plain Dealer building in Cleveland was not even a publisher's wet dream when Jason walked these streets. In place of the old stone-faced structure he remembered, there now stood a brick-red, four-story building with a narrow white canopy—looking much like a caricature of a nurse's cap perched on the head of a candy-striper. Its top floor with ceiling-high panoramic windows seemed perfect to accommodate the upper echelon. And it did contribute a bit of visual enrichment to an otherwise drab downtown area.

On this dreary morning, Jason and Dena decided it best to wear something other than their traditional attire which screamed of casual. Instead, Jason sported black slacks and a blue pullover shirt with a white turtleneck underneath. He even wore a belt.

Dena wore a modest skirt with high heals. It wasn't the same skirt that had captured David's attention at the restaurant in Conneaut, but then again, she had the ability to capture everyone's attention even if she wore a World War II pup tent. As they entered the lobby, men smiled while women offered their why-can't-I-look-like-that glare.

Rather than hopping on the elevator, they climbed the stairs to the second floor where they arranged to meet with the journalist who'd been prying open doors never intended to be opened. At least that seemed the consequence of the few who now cowered behind those massive barriers. Nothing like having the barrel of a rolled up newspaper pointed at you to make you reconsider a few choices you've made.

The high heels Dena wore created a high-pitched clicking sound in the cement-lined stairwell. When they paused at the top, it took a few seconds for the sound to stop reverberating inside the gigantic vertical tube. Jason opened the door to let Dena enter first.

Cubicles. A world of cubicles. Some large, some no bigger than the squeeze-in closet in a low-priced condo. Working one's way up in this environment would mean getting a cube where you could actually turn around without breaking out in a sweat. All were colored beige. How unfortunate if your favorite outfit was beige, too—you might be counted absent for the entire day.

Jason stopped a girl carrying an armload of envelopes. "Could you direct us to Ian Stewart's office?"

She giggled. "Down the aisle there. Look for the cube with all the Dilbert cartoons pinned to the wall."

Jason spit out a, "Thank you," as fast as he could since the girl was about six feet away when she finished her sentence. The last glimpse he had of her was a delicate wave of her fingertips directing them down the corridor to their right.

Dena scanned the area. "You're a detective. Fetch."

Jason stuck his nose into the air and took a long sniff. "Follow me."

Just as the girl said, there was a partition to a cube festooned with Dilbert cartoons. It would have been hard to miss. Jason scanned the topic of the day that Ian opted to post. Most dealt with the pointy-haired boss who remained forever clueless. Jason poked his head in the medium sized cubicle. "Ian Stewart?"

"Yes," the voice said, yet to turn around.

"I'm Jason Carmichael, the detective you talked to yesterday. And this is my partner, Dena Manning."

Ian spun around. Late twenty-ish, Ian evidently failed the how-to-dress-like-a-professional course in college. A framed diploma from Northwestern University in Illinois hung over his workstation alongside an advanced degree in Journalism, also from Northwestern. Wild eyes peeking out from under reading glasses were his outstanding feature, and gave one the feeling they were being examined under a microscope. "Hi. Sorry for the mess." He removed a stack of papers from his one and only guest chair and piled them on…more papers on top of his desk. "I don't have a lot of room to sit, so do the best you can."

Jason offered the chair to Dena while he leaned against the partition. She accepted with little options other than to curl up on the floor wearing her abbreviated skirt. Jason plopped down on the floor facing Dena. Good choice. He was beginning to appreciate Ian's surroundings. "The reason I called yesterday was to…"

"You explained that to me yesterday on the phone. I'm on the clock. My editor doesn't know I agreed to anyone coming up here. But what you said intrigued me. Want coffee? Tea? What's in the envelope?" His eyes widened even more.

Ian's face was becoming distorted. Jason wondered if he'd made a bad choice for two reasons—one was if this guy really earned those degrees and two, did he have a hatchet buried in amongst all this debris? "Like I said yesterday, I am a detective working on a twenty-five year old murder, but I firmly believe the person who did this also murdered an Ashtabula County deputy a week ago. I have very little to go on in the murder of the Amish girl, but…"

"Is this about the Hutchinson fiasco?"

"Yes, it is."

"Wait here." Ian used one hand on the side of the cube and the other on the desk to leap-frog over Dena's outstretched legs.

Ian actually exhibited the grace of a gymnast as he landed halfway out into the corridor. Jason gave Dena a curious look, and then checked the hallway. "Weird."

Dena nodded.

They waited, and waited. The offer of some sort of beverage began to sound better to Jason and Dena while they passed apprehensive looks back and forth.

When Ian rounded the corner, he tucked in his shirt while clenching a folder in his armpit. "That went better than I expected." After flinging the folder on his desk, he did the same leaping motion, but in reverse, he'd done to exit the cube. It, too, was graceful, and he landed in his seat like he'd practiced this move countless times before. "Coffee? Tea? Aspirin?" he rattled off.

There was an instant assimilation of energy between the three. It was as though Ian was the conductor and Jason and Dena were the choir. They found themselves staring in anticipation at this maniacal figure with wild eyes. Jason wondered if he would have the same blasé reaction had he met Ian in a dark alley. "I think we're fine for now. Thank you."

"Okay," Ian began, "here's the deal. My boss, the editor, is a woman...name's Shauna Delrosso. Not just any woman, but a woman on a mission. She abhors governmental corruption of any kind at any level, and especially by those agencies whose charter it is to protect us. Once she sets her mind on an issue, she won't let go until...sure you don't want any coffee? Anyway, she won't breathe easy until it's settled. The PD covered the death of Deputy Hutchinson of course, but what struck us, me and the editor, as strange and uncharacteristic of police procedures was...there was no follow up. To date, everything we get is page-two fillers."

"Yeah, we noticed..." Jason said.

"Every time we contact the Ashtabula County Sheriff's Department, we are told they are probing into this guy's death." Looking directly at Jason, Ian fired off, "You're a detective, right?"

"Yeah, but I'm out of my jurisdic..."

"Whenever a cop gets popped, the police are all over it, right now, ya'know what I mean? In one of our staff meetings, Shauna wanted to know the reason the media is being aced out of the equation. We've seen more ink dedicated to road kill. Anyway, I held up my hand really quick. I wanted this one—might even get my own column if I'm lucky. She decided to give me a shot, but I still have other subject matter on my list. Wanta know how I landed this job?"

"It did cross our minds, but..."

"For my Masters at Northwestern, I wrote a rather rebellious dissertation dealing with the fine line between probative journalism and what I called spick and span journalism. It received a lot of attention because it included the boundaries we all are forced to adhere to...by corporately owned members of the media. Most often...am I boring you?"

"No," Jason said, wishing he had a recorder so he could tape this guy and play him back in slo-mo. "In fact we..."

"Good. My paper jiggled the Jello. My profs told me I'd never land a job with my attitude, but you know what? I didn't care. Actually, I did care, but not for the same reasons corporate wants. Anyway, the editor here at the PD got wind of me and liked my style…and here I am. Anyway, this Hutchinson situation has been on the editor's tickler list since the funeral. As a detective, have you dug up anything?" Ian pulled a small recorder from his top drawer and spun it around to face Jason. A tiny red LED let everyone know this thing was alive.

"As a matter of fact, we have." Jason shot a quick look in Dena's direction wondering if he was really going to get to finish an entire sentence before being interrupted by Ian. "When I first came to the area, I started looking into the death of an Amish girl about twenty-five years ago. In so doing, I hooked up with Deputy Hutchinson and he told me the sheriff gave him a temporary assignment to look into the dormant case. We were just starting to make some headway before he was killed."

"I didn't know anything about an Amish girl. Go on."

"That's it. I don't think the sheriff wanted anyone else to make the connection either. Before he died, Ken Hutchinson told me about their budgetary cutbacks. They used to have an Internal Affairs group, but it was dismantled because of the force reduction. Bottom line is, if you want IA now, you get Sheriff Phelps. Rather convenient, wouldn't you say?"

"Indubitably."

"I know it's your column, but it's important in this type of investigation to proceed in a logical way, and by that I mean, the two crimes cannot, I repeat, cannot, be openly related as far as the public is concerned. There are two critical aspects to bringing this guy down. One; there has to be no reference to me or an unspecified investigator who is involved in this inquiry. Sheriff Phelps is already aware of my presence, so the second stipulation is; this article I'm asking you to publish will concern only the perceived cover-up of Hutchinson's death. It has to be presented in such a way that the PD is asking why all the perceived secrecy. Make him understand he is not immune from being under a microscope. My goal is to make him nervous and flush him out into the open. Only then can we stitch the two killings together."

"Sounds like you've already written the column for me."

"Not really. It has to be in your words and your style, but since you brought it up, I did come up with a lead-in for the article." Jason pulled an eight-and-a-half by eleven sheet of paper from his envelope and handed it to Ian. "Whatchya think?"

Ian read it once, then again, looked up to the ceiling and chuckled. He had one of those infectious laughs a comedian might hire to sit in the audience. "You sure you're not looking for a writer's job here?" He scanned the paper again. In addition to the stipulations they'd just discussed, it read, *In today's world, the initials SPF would most likely be associated with the government-mandated rating for sunscreen, but if you work as law enforcement at the Ashtabula County Sheriff's Office, SPF would stand for, Serve, Protect, and Forget.* "You've given me a good launching pad. Understand. Every copy I write will have to go through Shauna Delrosso. I can't make any promises pertaining to what she might redline."

"I was afraid of this. So what I'm going to do is make your editor an offer she can't refuse."

"Which is?" Ian asked.

"We all know the media's primary goal is exclusivity. So here's my proposal. If you agree to my terms, I will ensure the Plain Dealer gets exclusive coverage of bringing this slime ball down." Jason knew Ian was a page-two teetering on the edge of page-one. Gone was the edgy gleam in Ian's eyes. This rogue who believed in unfiltered truth gave way to a feral posture crouched for the kill.

"You know?" Ian began. "With what you've told me today, I could still write anything I want and if my boss gives me a thumbs-up, it'll be in tomorrow's PD."

"Yeah, you could," Dena said as she locked eyes with Ian. "But just to let you know. You're approaching this proposal from a short term perspective. You might sell a few more papers…tomorrow, but I'd be willing to bet if you play by our rules, there'll be a more personal advantage in store for you. At the end of a long hard day, would you rather haul in the bait or haul in a world class Great White?"

Ian scratched what little facial hair he had. "If this sheriff actually did kill his own deputy to keep him quiet, and if this sheriff knows about you, why are you still alive?"

"Ahh, that's our trump card my friend. We have the potential to gain access to DNA samples…and an eye witness."

"Whoa. You never told me you had an…"

"An eye witness? No, we didn't. So sorry."

"You still haven't answered my question. If you are a *known* to Sheriff Phelps, why are you still sucking air?"

"That's where the eye witness comes in." Jason gave a raised eyebrow—the universal gesture for, *any more questions?*

"Wait here." For the second time, Ian demonstrated his Olympic quality prowess as he vaulted across Dena to exit his cube. This time, the armpits of his shirt were visibly stained with perspiration.

Minutes passed. Jason and Dena cruised adjacent hallways. Not far, but just enough to poke their noses into cubes just to see what a newsroom looked like in the real world. The cubes seemed to have one interior designer who specialized in beige. Beige partitions, one or two tacky plastic chairs, one computer, one computer chair, one land-line phone with a small plastic gizmo clipped to it so the user could cradle the phone between their shoulder and ear, and one coat hook clipped over the rim of the partition. The only dash of color was from the brightly colored push-pins which held clips of news articles pinned to the partitions. The contrast of color was almost blinding. Ian's head crept up over the tops of the cubes looking much like the man in the moon, except with reading glasses. His strained voice called their names accompanied by a frantic hand wave.

Ian was already poised behind his work station when Jason and Dena arrived. "My boss has one question. She wants to know how certain you are about Sheriff Phelps' involvement in both murders?"

"Unless something catastrophic happens to my eye witness," Jason said, "one-hundred percent."

CHAPTER 26

The windows of the van were rolled down to let in much wanted fresh air after being closed up while parked on Superior Avenue in bright sunlight. Although September was almost over, there were remnants of the humidity which neither Jason nor Dena was accustomed to.

"Boy. You seemed pretty sure of yourself back there when you promised Ian one-hundred percent on bringing good old Teddy down." Dena cocked her head to the side to get a better look at the height of some of Cleveland's downtown buildings.

Rather than taking the direct 322 route back to the Windsor area, Jason opted for the scenic lakeside route. Who could resist the chance to visit a few of his or her favorite beaches when they were teenagers? The Pacific Ocean had tides and currents and heavy swells whereas Lake Erie had waves, varying from small to sizable depending on the time of year, wind speed and direction. Those things didn't seem too terribly important back then. Seeing Nicole or Kathleen in abbreviated swimsuits was. When they arrived at the Geneva State Park area, Jason pulled in so they could walk around.

Before they could enter, an Ashtabula County vehicle gave them a short chirp on the siren and flashed its lights. Jason eased to the side of the narrow road. Through his rearview mirror, he watched the person who appeared to be just sitting there staring straight ahead. Under most circumstances, the officer or deputy would approach the suspect vehicle from the passenger side if in a high traffic zone, or from the driver's in a safer zone. Jason thought a two-lane road blacktop with no one in sight would qualify for a driver's side contact.

The door opened. Once outside the Crown Vic, the deputy positioned his campaign hat precisely level on his head just like a trainee at a military facility would do...until they graduated from boot camp and began to think how much cooler it would be to cock their *cover* down until the brim almost touched the eyebrows. With his hand on his hip, the deputy approached the driver's side and snuggled in close to the van. Standing just to the rear of the center post of the van, the deputy said a robotic hello and asked for Jason's driver's license and proof of insurance.

Jason glanced at the deputies name tag. It wasn't T. Phelps. This was good. The first and last time he'd seen the sheriff was at Ken Hutchinson's burial service, and that didn't really count since the only view he had was in his side view mirror and the person had his hat on and head lowered. The only giveaway was the four stars on his collar.

Out of necessity, when Jason reached for his wallet, he leaned over and reached down to remove it from his back pocket. The deputy backed up a step and rested his hand on his holster which was unsnapped.

Dena had already retrieved the rental agreement papers from the glove box and handed them to Jason. "Here."

Jason nodded thanks and handed the deputy what he'd asked for.

Without a word, the deputy returned to his vehicle. Jason knew he was checking for any outstanding warrants or traffic violations. At least in theory, that's what he was checking. Jason kept an eye on him through his side-view mirror. From around the corner leading to the main road, a second vehicle approached with its light bar activated. As it inched past the van, the driver kept his head down and made no eye contact, and then pulled in front of Jason's van close enough so Jason couldn't move forward. Jason watched as the driver sat with his back to the action. The door never opened.

"Here's your documents, sir," the deputy said in the same robotic monotone. "Everything appears in order. I notice you're from out of state. Are you visiting or passing through?"

"Visiting."

"Anyone in the immediate area?"

"Yes."

"Would you please step outside your vehicle?"

Dena grasped Jason's arm for an instant. It was her way of showing her concern without saying anything that might be interpreted as confrontational. Jason gave her an understanding, but quick smile and opened the door. As he stepped out, he eyed the person in the forward car, who'd yet to move. "You are aware I am a detective from California."

"Would you turn around, spread your arms and place your hands on the side of the van," the deputy instructed.

Jason did as he was told.

The deputy patted him down. When he finished, he said, "I notice you're wearing a shoulder holster. Do you have the weapon in your possession now?"

"No."

"Would you mind if I check inside the van."

"Go ahead, deputy."

The deputy looked at Dena and asked her to step out, also. When she did, he then asked her to stand next to Jason.

By the look in his eyes, Jason knew this guy was contemplating a pat-down of Dena. God, he hoped not. If he even came close to the good stuff, she'd have him in a finger lock before he could count to one. She'd twist his arm behind his back while putting pressure on his bent fingers, and make sure his face was sucking paint on the hood of his car. She'd deal with legalities later. The deputy ducked his head for an instant as if checking with the driver of the first car and then backed off his assessment of Dena.

The deputy's head never disappeared from sight. Jason couldn't be sure, but he was fairly confident the deputy was only feeling around under seats and recesses in the side panels.

"Clean," the deputy said as he backed away from the van. "I advise you to not wear anything you don't intend to use."

"Are we free to go?" Jason asked.

"Yes, sir."

"May I ask why you stopped us?"

The deputy never acknowledged the question. He simply waved a good-bye. The front car pulled forward so Jason had room to drive off.

Both cars remained in place until Jason could no longer see them in his rear-view mirror.

"Do you think Kathleen contacted Phelps?" Dena asked as she stared out the back window of the van.

"I'd like to think no, but then again, I've been wrong about certain people lately, haven't I?" He checked his mirror again to make sure they were out of sight.

"Do you think the guy in the other car was Phelps?"

"Yes. He's not stupid enough to exit his car and confront me. He left that up to his deputy."

"I didn't like that guy," Dena hissed. "It was like he was catering to Phelps, not serving the public."

"He was young. Maybe his first gig. Who knows? Anyhow, I'm glad I stashed my Maks elsewhere." Jason pulled into one of many vacant spots where there were picnic tables available. They chose one that faced the lake. "Let's go over some stuff. See what you think."

"The first thing I'd like to know is," Dena began, "do you trust Kathleen…after what's just happened?"

"Categorically, no. And without her testimony, we don't have squat. Actually, we could have more if we were in a position to demand DNA evidence be collected from under Friedel's fingernails. But even science isn't as valuable to a prosecutor, or more importantly, convincing to a jury, as someone who's been there, done that."

"So, you don't think she's gonna bail on us? Call good old Teddy and stay in his good graces?"

"I don't think so, Dena. We made the point that her time is limited. So, I can't believe she would try to take sides with someone who, she must now know, is a multiple killer. She'd have to be totally stupid to take his side."

"Wanta hear my spin about what I heard from Kathleen? Yeah, you do. Well, there're two things actually. First off, she was worried about her daughter. This tells me she is concerned for someone other than herself. We both know David is a total ass. Maybe she is worried that Jennifer will be forced to be with him and his new poster wife." Dena gave nonchalant shrug of her shoulders. "It's a mom thing."

"Let's hope this *mom thing* helps her make the right decision. You said there were two things you wanted to say."

"Yeah. Take this for what it's worth, but I believe Kathleen is the reason you're still alive. She admitted talking to her cousin, and I think one of the topics of conversation was you. She didn't want anything to happen to you. Maybe she didn't come right out and say, don't kill him, but made it clear you were someone special to her—kind of a subtle threat. This is why I believe we should have faith in her to do the right thing for a change."

"Hmmph. Makes sense."

"Oh, oh. I have another thought."

"That's three things you..."

"Quiet. I'm on a roll. What we really have to concentrate on is momentum. We have to move fast, before Kathleen has time to change her mind. Rather than trying to enroll Kathleen and Jennifer into the Witness Protection Program, which may take more time than we can afford, let's arrange to have them stay at some place local—some place Phelps might not expect."

"Good idea," Jason said. "Hotels are too obvious. A few phone calls and his credentials would mean a death warrant. If we use our credit cards, he already knows our names."

"Exactly. What about the Loomis'?"

"Teenage son. Blab city."

As if by divine intervention, they turned to each other. Both knew the perfect place for Kathleen and Jennifer.

◊　　◊　　◊

"Good morning, Mr. Stoudt," Jason said. On the way up Joshua's driveway, Jason scouted the layout of the farm and in particular, the location of the communal phone. It was situated in a handmade shed about three feet square just inside the fence line near the drive where any member who needed it would have easy access. The little wooden building was crafted to look like a lighthouse complete with glass panes at the top to represent the multiple lenses. The panes also served to keep rain from pouring in. A narrow door was located at the rear of the lighthouse onto which was attached a door handle fashioned from a weathered tree branch. This little building housed the only wire which entered the Stoudt farm. Like his other Amish neighbors, everything else was either manually operated, horse drawn or, if necessary for refrigerated milk storage, powered by 12 volt DC produced by diesel generators.

"And a good morning to you, Mr. Carmichael." Joshua reached for Jason with his leathery hand, then removed his broad-brimmed hat for Dena, said a courteous, "*Guten Tag*," before putting it back on.

"*Tag*." Dena beamed at the thought of Joshua addressing her in German.

"We have a big favor to ask you," Jason said. "It concerns someone who is an important witness to what happened to Friedel. This person and her daughter have to be kept safe, isolated, and near a phone if necessary. With someone we can trust to tell no one else...and this includes members of your own congregation. It is imperative no one knows of their presence."

"And this place would be here?"

Jason nodded. "Do you have the room?"

"For Friedel and Elizabeth, we will make room. *Sicherlich*—for sure."

"Have the police ever visited your farm?"

"No."

"Do they even cruise by just to check if everything is okay?"

"Never. We are a solitary people. We communicate very little outside our congregation."

"Good. I'll give one more chance to back out, because if it's too much trouble, we can find some other..."

"*Nein. Nein.* If it will help, I am very willing. There is no question in my mind. How long will these people be staying?"

"If everything goes according to plan, Saturday morning."

Dena gave Jason a short look of surprise.

"Before you make a commitment, I have to warn you there is an element of danger involved."

"How so?"

"There will be one woman and one young child...about eleven. Here is the situation. It will be mandatory for them to stay inside, out of sight." Jason glanced over Joshua's shoulder toward the rear of the house. "If they want fresh air, they can go onto your back porch...no further. No back yard, no side yard—definitely no front yard. Nowhere."

"Am I to be their *Wachhund*?"

Glancing at Jason, Dena whispered, "Watchdog. I think. Or maybe Water Spaniel. I'll go with watchdog."

"No. I will make sure they understand this before we bring them here. And I would like to bring these people here at night...probably nine o'clock or so. Any problem there?"

"No. Does Elizabeth know of this arrangement?"

"Not yet. And she will only know about Saturday, not about these two people who are staying here. I do not want to expose her to any more danger than is necessary."

"Then, it is settled," Joshua said in a firm voice.

CHAPTER 27

The smell of Mrs. Loomis' coffee drifted not only throughout the kitchen, but upstairs as well. Her ritualistic approach to their budding business was to rise first to prepare freshly brewed coffee. Inside her cupboards, she was proud she was never caught with anything which had *powdered* or *instant* as part of the product description. This was followed by prepping morning meals, and making sure the table was set for their guests. Of course, the Cleveland PD was neatly folded to one side of the place settings.

Although the Loomis' B & B underwent a complete renovation a few years ago, the contractors left just enough of a gap beneath the doors to allow the coffee to announce itself each morning. It seemed like a plausible excuse at the time. Jason appreciated this unintentional feature much more than a complimentary bedside alarm clock. Every morning when he'd wake up to the aroma of coffee, he was tempted to tap on Dena's wall to make sure she was up and about, but knew this was her special time to be with her son, even if it was by her cell. And it was getting more difficult to ignore the fact that her bed was right next to his...separated by a wall—a well-insulated wall for obvious reasons.

When he showered, he was aware how cost effective it is to construct bathrooms facing each other in adjoining suites. It had to do with what plumbers would call risers—the pipes that bring water to each site. Knowing this didn't help him since, as he would stand with his head buried under the jet of hot water, Dena might be standing just a few feet away doing the same thing. Go pour yourself some coffee, Jason, he'd remind himself over and over.

He was always the first one at the table. It gave him time to scan the PD, even read the comic section. He loved *Zits*—a strip about a quirky teenage boy, and his allegedly clueless, misunderstood parents. As Jason read it each morning, he had a constant reminder named Doug who could have been the inspiration for the strip.

This morning, his first goal was to find out if Ian's editor had enough garbanzos to set his plan in motion. As he unfolded the newspaper, he hoped he would see the name Ian Stewart listed under the lead-in for an article. It wasn't. Ian Stewart was listed under the banner headline.

The lead line was exactly as Jason had written it. The beginning amounted to a scathing reprimand for treating a member of LE with no more respect than one would a common rodent. The middle section contained a listing of the times and examples when the Plain Dealer's reporters and columnists had tried to contact the sheriff, but were categorically dismissed by staff or by Phelps himself. The words *arrogance* and *apathy* found their way into multiple sentences. The article ended with a challenge for Sheriff Phelps to be more candid with the community in which Ken Hutchinson served. Jason made a mental note to contact Shauna Delrosso and thank her.

This was Tuesday's paper. Time for him to contact Ian again about the second reason to take more jabs at the sheriff, but he didn't want it to be tomorrow's paper. It would be better for a Friday release. Give time for Phelps to stew about his self-generated predicament, but not too much time to think about what to do about it.

◊   ◊   ◊

Ian was floating when Jason and Dena walked in. What had been an abundance of optimism yesterday had morphed into euphoria. Ten copies of the front page fluttered from his partition, pinned there with brilliant red push pins. His name was highlighted by a yellow marker on every copy. A little sign hung at the top saying, *Autographed copies available for an additional fee.*

Jason and Dena paused at the entrance to his cube.

"Sign doesn't say how much," Jason whispered behind Ian's back, who seemed buried in another project.

"Guys. Glad you're here." He grabbed their arms and whispered back, "Don't tell anyone, but for you two…ten big ones." His twenty-seven inch flat screen looked surprisingly narrow in comparison to his smile.

Jason reached for his wallet. "You take plastic?"

"Sit." He performed the same routine he'd done yesterday by relocating papers, notebooks, and clipboards to the top of his cluttered desk.

Dena snagged the chair.

Jason claimed the floor right in front of Dena. "Congrats on the article."

"You've got to be kidding. This was much more than an article. This was friggin' headlines, man." His eyes grew wide and the maniacal look returned. "I got tanked last night."

Remembering how Dena managed to pry information from Kathleen, Jason hoped he would not be on the receiving end of Ian's celebration. "We want to thank you for you cooperation regarding this first salvo against Phelps. Have you had any feedback on the piece yet?"

"Have we. Our editorial department has been inundated with a flood of e-mails. They've been forwarding them to me and Shauna. Seems we made a dent in someone's armor."

"Let's hope we can do more than inflict minor damage to this guy. I've set up a probable date for a showdown with Phelps for this Saturday. Is there a chance we can go over my thinking with you?"

"Yeah, but not right now. Shauna wants to meet you." He punched in four digits. "Hi, it's me. The detective is here." During a slight pause, Ian exited out of the program he'd been working on. "Great. Thanks." Ian turned to face Jason and Dena. "She wants to meet you two."

A few well chosen pictures on the walls of the cube stoked the interest of Jason and Dena. One was of Ian at a younger age while in college. He was standing with a small group, all of whom had some sort of mugs filled with liquid. By their looks, it had to be beer, and by those same looks, they'd been at it for quite some time. Ian told them it was taken during semester break before they all began their post grad work. "It was an exercise in academic fortification," he explained.

"Good morning," a feminine voice said. "I'm Shauna Delrosso."

When Shauna entered, Ian leaped to his feet. The last time Jason remembered someone reacting this quickly was when Jason was in the Navy and someone yelled, *Attention on Deck.*

Her hand was already aimed at Jason. A quick greeting was exchanged and she did the same for Dena. She handed business cards to Jason and Dena. Her gray skirt and matching jacket was accented with a blue blouse with every button, buttoned. Around her neck was a pearl necklace—the kind that wraps and wraps until the wearer runs out of neck. "Very interesting piece this morning." There was a sly gleam in her eyes. "Would you agree?"

"Yes. I'd like to thank you both for keeping these articles independent of the other." Jason waved another manila envelope in Shauna's direction. "It is imperative Phelps believe these two articles have no bearing on each other."

"What I was getting at Jason, was the lead-in. Are you sure you're not looking for a job?" Shauna leaned against the partition and tugged at the necklace. The mischievous gleam evaporated into a more serious look. "I got the gist of the message from Ian yesterday. That's why I shifted gears. If I may: when I took over here, my philosophy was and still is, if someone is killed in Washington DC, we are saddened, but not as much as when our neighbor is killed. One is a statistical reaction whereas the second brings it down to the gut level. We have been asking for some input from Sheriff Phelps for quite some time regarding the Hutchinson situation, so I will speak for Ian and the Plain Dealer when I convey our appreciation to you and Dena for forcing the issue." She waved her hands around in a quick circle. "Enough sociological meandering. I was told you have a secondary motive for using the Plain Dealer as a launch site."

"Yes, we do." Jason pulled out another piece of paper. Included on this list, done in bullet form, was a series of facts dealing with Friedel, her age at the time, school, background, goals, relatives, favorite color, or anything he and Dena could come up with. Jason handed it to Shauna. "This last article pertains to an Amish girl who was killed twenty-five years ago, we believe, by Ted Phelps when he was about nineteen."

"That means he will be tried as an adult," Shauna added.

"Good. My goal is to force Phelps into a face to face with me and the victim's mother on Saturday, and I would like one of your reporters to be present, plus it would be great if we could capture it all on video."

"Ho hum. Just another day," Shauna yawned. The gleam was back. Glancing at the notes on Jason's paper, she said, "I see you have this pretty well thought out."

"It has to be done in this order, otherwise Phelps might smell a connection between the two articles. I'm hoping this morning's piece will make him more receptive to showing up on Saturday, especially since he will know the media will be there, and by that, I mean the PD—exclusively."

Shauna asked Ian to turn his recorder on. The tiny recorder was out in a second and the LED flashed, *go*. "For the record. Go through these steps for us." As she spoke, Shauna made sure the recorder was facing Jason.

"Okay," Jason started. "In the article, you will refer to me by name, and I am a private investigator from California. Secondly, Jason Carmichael read the article in today's PD and Jason Carmichael understands the strains of an understaffed law enforcement agency. Third; Jason Carmichael is offering to meet with him personally this coming Saturday to turn over a valuable medical document which may help in the investigation of Friedel Mueller's death. And as a bonus, add Carmichael as well as his partner will be returning to California after the exchange."

"No mention of Deputy Hutchinson's death?" Ian asked.

"No," Jason said. "He has to think these are still considered separate issues. He may have his suspicions, but we don't want to fuel those notions."

"Yesterday, you said something about having an eye witness," Ian said.

"This should definitely NOT be part of the PD's article. This is our trump card. Dena and I discussed this at length. We want to blindside this guy so he has no recourse other than to make an immediate response. If he's gonna crumble, this is where it'll happen."

"You do have this well thought out," Shauna said. "How can we get in touch with you if we need more data?" Shauna asked.

Jason gave her and Ian his card which listed his cell phone number after the Fresno County Sheriff's number.

"Why is Saturday morning so important anyhow?" Ian asked as he shrugged his shoulders. "I don't see the connection."

"One thing I learned while working with Deputy Hutchinson was; unless there's a catastrophe in progress, Phelps routinely takes Saturdays off."

"So?" Ian said.

"Dena and I want to be reasonably assured he will show up in his personal car rather than a county Crown Vic."

CHAPTER 28

"Why?" Jennifer asked. She'd just walked in the door after school. Her customary routine had always been to check in with Beth next door before going home. Once Beth gave the okay for her to go home alone, Jennifer was trained to signal her by raising one window blind, usually in the dining room, before she did anything else. It was not unusual for Beth to stop in to *chat*, as she called it. Long ago, Jennifer had figured out the purpose of the chat, but welcomed the company until her mom arrived home. Shortbread cookies were never part of the agreement, but nevertheless, a small plateful was always in sight.

Kathleen knelt down and hugged her daughter. "Jason thinks it would be good for us to go away for a few days, honey. There's something we have to do and we can't be here until it's over."

"What about school?" Jennifer eyed the other woman in the room.

"Jennifer, this is Dena Manning," Jason said. "She's a good friend of mine, and she wants to help us."

"Hi." Dena extended her hand.

For all the bravado she often portrayed, Jennifer was still the shy little girl who stood beside her mother and peeked around the corner at the rest of the world. She took Dena's hand and made a motion similar to a smile, but came across more like a facial exercise one might learn at a day spa.

"If we're going to go someplace," Kathleen said to her daughter, "we should probably go pack a few things. We're going to have fun and we're going to learn some things I bet you never knew."

"I suppose, but what about school?"

"I've already talked to them and they said it was okay. Do you know what your teacher said about you?"

"Miss Cooke?"

"Yes. She said you are way ahead of some of her students and she is proud of you."

"I like science the best."

"Miss Cooke said she will miss your cheery face every morning, but she will just have to suffer through the next few days without you."

"Could I stay at Beth's? I've stayed there before."

"You know what?" Dena said, her eyebrows raised and full of excitement. "I bet if we look at this as an adventure, you'd be all for it. Am I right?"

Jennifer gave a tentative nod.

"Because it *is* going to be an adventure." Dena squatted down next to Jennifer, but made no effort to draw her closer. Much like training animals, her philosophy was; she had to wait for them to come to her. After a few moments of quiet girl talk, Jennifer knelt down next to Dena. There was a hint of a real smile by Jennifer, not the phony show-them-you-have-teeth ritual.

While Dena and Jennifer were doing their bonding, Jason motioned Kathleen aside. "I want you to know how much the Muellers and the Hutchinson family will appreciate what you're doing."

"I'm worried, Jason. There are so many things going through my mind now. Terrible things. What if Teddy finds out what we're doing? What if he finds out where we're staying? Would he really try to kill me…us?" She shot a nervous glance at Jennifer. "Will your plan work? What if it doesn't? What do I do with the rest of my life if this fails? Who's going to believe us? I've been living with this for twenty-five years. Maybe I'm not as strong as I thought I was."

"You are strong, Kathleen. It was the weak you who was keeping quiet all these years."

"Hmm. Sounds good in theory."

A few soft giggles drifted from across the room where Dena and Jennifer were lying on the floor leafing through a fan magazine featuring Miley Cyrus on the front cover.

"I, uuh…I promised this family we'd be there around nine," Jason said. "This may sound cold, but it's getting kind of late. Can we pack you guys up? Remember, it's just for three days."

"And it's local?" Kathleen asked.

Jason held Kathleen's hand and guided her over to Jennifer.

"Jenn, honey. We have to pack a few things. I'm sorry, but we have to leave." Kathleen grasped Jennifer's hand and helped her to her feet. They disappeared up the steps.

"You think Jennifer will be all right?" Jason asked Dena.

"We had a little talk. She'll be fine."

Together, they checked the house to make sure windows and doors were closed and locked. Before locking the back door, Jason looked into the garage to confirm Kathleen's car was secure. When he came back, Kathleen and Jennifer were standing next to their luggage. Jennifer, one suitcase and a backpack presumably full of books. Kathleen had one very large suitcase and a smaller bag probably for toiletries. Jason didn't care. They would all fit in the van. Dena was poised at the front door.

"Shall we?" Jason said.

The drive to the Stoudt farm was understandably quiet. Even though they'd driven this area many times, it wasn't the same this time. Kathleen and Jennifer weren't going to their home, they were going to someone else's home. Jennifer looked confused. Kathleen looked worried. The little pep talk she'd had with Jason had evidently worn off since the scowl on her forehead widened and her lips were clenched. At one time when Jason glanced at them in his rear view mirror, he thought Kathleen was on the verge of throwing up.

Driving under these conditions had an effect on Jason, also. He thought that if he drove too fast, it would seem he would appear happy and having a good time, almost cavalier in attitude. But if he drove too slowly, it might seem as if he was driving a hearse in a funeral procession, or leading cattle to slaughter. He tried to find that magic in-between speed where they would arrive there on time, and Kathleen wouldn't have a chance to change her mind.

When they arrived at the Stoudt farm, Jason dropped Dena off at the entrance and asked her to stay in the vicinity of the lighthouse. If any car happened by, she was to note whether it slowed as it passed, or in the worst case…stopped. She could use the little door Joshua had constructed to hide from passersby.

"Evening Mister Stoudt," Jason said. "These are the people we talked about." He then introduced each one to Joshua and his wife, who greeted them like royalty.

"We're sorry to be of any inconvenience," Kathleen said while prodding Jennifer to let go of her leg and greet their hosts.

Jennifer was occupied looking around the Spartan room with but a few candles lit, and walls that looked strange. She couldn't have known it, but these walls were movable so they could accommodate a large congregation when church services or meetings were held at their home.

"This is no trouble for us, my dear," Mrs. Stoudt said as she smoothed her apron with her hands. Her white prayer covering had the appearance of freshly fallen snow. "We welcome any chance to help Mr. Carmichael in his search for truth. It is the least we can do."

"We have a room set up for you," Joshua said. "I hope you don't mind, but you will be sharing a bedroom."

Jennifer tapped her mom on the leg. When Kathleen bent down, Jennifer whispered, "They don't have a TV."

"Aah. I have excellent hearing young lady." Joshua bent down next to Jennifer. "But we do have animals, and lots of food. Do you like biscuits?"

Jennifer gave a shy nod.

"And how about fresh berry preserves?" Joshua continued as he rubbed his substantial tummy.

Much to the delight of Jennifer, Jason quickly waved his hand in the air at the thought of biscuits and fresh, sweet, tasty, preserves. Jennifer's smile broadened. Or maybe it was the thought that this amiable bearded man wearing coveralls might really be Santa Claus in the off season.

"I don't want to rush things, but we do have to hurry," Jason said. "Dena's out by the road to take note of anyone who drives by, and my van is parked out front. Kinda suspicious this late at night, you know what I mean?"

Joshua agreed.

Jason pulled a disposable cell phone from his pocket and handed it to Kathleen with the reminder she was not to use it except to call him, no exceptions. The land-line out front was to be used only by Joshua or his wife. Training the Stoudt's to use a cell would be a little problematic in candlelight.

When it came to horses, Jason was well aware of how the imagination kicks into overdrive when a child sees a horse. The first thing that pops into their minds would most likely be to envision themselves aboard this magnificent creature. Their hair would be blowing in the wind. They would hear the sound of the horse panting, and admire the mane as it flowed up and down as they galloped through grassy fields. Those images would have to be put on hold. Joshua agreed to bring one of his horses as far as the back porch and let Jennifer feed him, pet him, or sit on him, but the ride part would be saved for another, more joyous visit.

Jennifer made Mr. Stoudt agree by doing a pinky-swear. He'd never heard of such a thing, but with Jennifer's guidance, he performed it flawlessly.

There was a tap on the door.

Joshua peeked through the window and swung the door wide. "Dena. How nice to see you this evening."

"Hi. There's been no traffic to speak of, and I can barely make out the van in the dark, so I thought I'd come up and say hello."

"You're just in time," Jason said. "We were about to button this up."

"May we offer you some water or tea?" Mrs. Stoudt said. "I think we can indulge ourselves just this one evening and entertain our guests." She looked to Joshua for his approval.

"I think Mr. Carmichael is correct," Joshua said. "We do not want to draw attention to ourselves any more than is necessary."

The last view Jason and Dena had this evening was Jennifer holding her mom's hand in a room softly lit by three candles. They were facing away from the front door listening to Joshua. He picked up Kathleen's large bag in one hand, stuffed the toiletry bag under his arm, and then hoisted Jennifer's suitcase with his spare hand. Jennifer carried her own backpack. All faded from view up the narrow stairway. Except for Mrs.

Stoudt, the room was empty. In turn, she blew out each candle and followed the others. Everything was now dark.

There was a part of Jason who wanted to stay with the Stoudt family to make sure everything would be okay. There were other parts of him who wanted to stay with Elizabeth for the same reason. These would be a long two days.

CHAPTER 29

Sleep is supposed to be one of the bodily functions designed to rejuvenate the body and mind. With every investigation, there was this special time just prior to putting the final piece of the puzzle in place where Jason would lie down and stare at an inanimate object...usually the ceiling. No matter how much effort he'd put into fitting the pieces together, there was a nagging feeling the last part would be a rebel...something to look up at him and torment him when it refused to slip into the only remaining location on the board. It had to fit.

The problem was, this was a puzzle of his design. He couldn't return it to the store and demand his money back. Counting ceiling tiles or repeat patterns in wallpaper never offered him much of a diversion since all those were history. His purpose was to manipulate the future. There were two important contacts Jason had to make tomorrow. One was to Ian to verify the contents of his article for Friday's Plain Dealer, the other...Ted Phelps.

Jason hoped Ian would compose a gripping article—persuasive enough to lure Phelps into exposing himself. He also hoped Shauna would not change her mind, especially if another more heinous incident were to occur. When he was within his jurisdiction, Jason had all the information at his fingertips through the coordinated efforts and data bases of every LE agency in the country, but who would he contact when the perp was a major player in local law enforcement?

Jason looked at the wallpaper again. The repeat pattern was thirty-six inches.

◊   ◊   ◊

Thursday's paper was devoid of any mention of Phelps, Ashtabula County, or Ken Hutchinson. In its place, the front page dealt with the upcoming senatorial races, complete with brief statements from all the candidates and the obligatory polls. The appearance of David Ellison's name on the ballot would have come as no surprise to Jason, but the voters were spared his entrance into the political arena this time around. Maybe there was hope for Ohio. Nowhere on the front page was Ian Stewart's name mentioned. Jason flipped to page two, and then page three. Upon seeing no mention of his name in the entire issue, he punched in his extension. After a courteous greeting between the two was exchanged, Jason asked if everything was still a *go* for tomorrow?

"I had second thoughts after you left, detective. If I were reading these similar articles, and if I were a tad suspicious, I might detect a conspiracy of sorts. That's why I thought we should put Shauna Delrosso's name on tomorrow's copy rather than mine. And rest assured, she and I discussed this and agreed I will receive credit for it, but it will be between us."

"Ya'know? When I was there Tuesday and you read my lead-in, you asked me if I was a budding writer." Jason offered a little chuckle. "Now I have to ask you, are you a budding detective?"

"I have my moments. Look, I don't want to blow you off, but I have another assignment I have to compose in…one hour. So, your article, which includes your offer to relinquish the Medico-legal doc, was written from a standpoint of offering Phelps a chance to redeem himself in lieu of my piece in Wednesday's edition. Secondly, I will be at the Mueller farm early Saturday as we discussed, plus I will bring a staff videographer and his trusty shoulder-mount. Beyond that, I have to get my butt in gear and get this piece done."

As Jason was taking a breath to say thank you, he was interrupted by a dial tone.

◊   ◊   ◊

Thursday was a what-if day for Jason and Dena. He'd ask a question, she'd respond, and then they'd reverse their roles. Everything had to line up. One missed cue or one raised eyebrow could put the screws to their entire plan. After they felt they'd wrung this out as much as they could, they visited with Elizabeth so Dena could get a quick sewing lesson.

When Friday morning arrived, Jason woke up early, pulled on a pair of Levi's and added a pullover to his minimalist wardrobe to cut the chill. He peered out the living room window at a dilapidated gray car delivering the morning Plain Dealer as it rumbled down the road. Its rusty fender wells gave testimony to the years of service it had seen on roads where salt was the primary ingredient for keeping ice and snow at a minimum. The car slowed at every farm house. If the house was set far off the road, there was a white plastic box attached to a post where the newspaper could be shoved in. If the house was closer to the road, the driver would do a hook shot any NBA player would love to have in his arsenal. The Loomis residence fit the hook shot delivery system. The paper had not stopped skidding across the porch when Jason was out the door.

There it was on the front page—Ian's challenge to the sheriff to rectify any mounting ill feelings between his department and the general populace. And just as Ian had suggested...the article bore Shauna Delrosso's name in lieu of his own. Class act.

A quick shower, followed by breakfast kept Jason entertained for what seemed hours. His watch became an anchor to him, as if it was jerking him back to the reality of how time drags when you want it to be in passing gear. He didn't want to make this call too early. He wanted Phelps to arrive at headquarters, perform his daily routine, get briefed by the night shift about what had gone down the night before. He wanted him to sit with his cup of coffee and scan the PD and Star Beacon which was on his desk every morning as was his standing order.

Dena arrived at the table with Doug not far behind. The lad could not have been more obvious had he dangled a huge sign from his belt buckle proclaiming, *Have boner- Open in case of emergency*. Whenever Dena made a move, he would check her out. Jason knew his seventeenth birthday was nearing. Maybe he would buy him a bib.

Jason read through the article once more before checking the time and reaching for his cell. "Good morning, Sheriff, this is detective Jason Carmichael calling."

"I figured I'd be hearing from you today."

"Did you read this morning's Pl...?"

"Plain Dealer. Yeah."

"Look. I don't particularly agree with how this journalist portrayed a branch of law enforcement. We both know we sometimes have no choice but to keep the media at arms length so they don't reveal too much, and then we wind up taking it in the shorts. More than one case was blown by some over-zealous reporter out to make a name for themselves."

"Uh-huh."

"I feel my partner and I have done about all we can to resolve this Friedel Mueller case. I assume you know about the Medico-legal doc that Elizabeth Mueller has in her possession?"

"Yeah?"

"When I started on this case with the help of Ken Hutchinson, I found a set of initials on the old covered bridge over on Avery Road. Those started out to be my original clues. Turns out those initials don't mean squat. It's the doc Mrs. Mueller has that is so crucial to finding out what happened to Friedel. The report is well documented as to bruises, lacerations, and their locations. Without this report, anything about how Friedel died would be up for grabs, so, before we head back to California, I've convinced Mrs. Mueller to turn this over to you."

"Really."

"It's the only physical reminder she has of her daughter. She has treasured these pieces of paper all these years. When your investigation is over, she would like it back."

"When are you going to bring it in?"

"To your headquarters?"

"Yeah."

"That's just it, Sheriff. I had to do a hard sell on Mrs. Mueller to even get her to agree to let this document out of her sight, even if it is only temporary."

"What's so important about tomorrow? Can't this wait until Monday?"

"We've booked reservations for a flight back to San Francisco."

"I'll see what I can do."

CHAPTER 30

Like any good director, Jason showed up for the Broadway opening hours ahead of time. He had one shot to get it right and was determined to leave nothing to chance. The part of the script he had no control over were the reactions of some of the major players, who, up to now, knew their roles, but this would be a test in improvisation. At least, this was the plan, but with no dress rehearsals, no wardrobe checks, or script rewrites, this had all the potential to become the inaugural flight of an Amish bomb destined to make front page news.

Joshua was asked to keep Jennifer and Benjamin at his farm until this operation was put to bed. The only major on-stage players for the opening scene were Elizabeth, Isaac, and Jason until Phelps showed. Dena would stay inside with Kathleen until the confrontation with Phelps was in gear.

Last evening, Jason and Dena worked out a few verbal cues and hand gestures that would signal her on what to do with Kathleen. First on their list was a wave to warn her to keep themselves away from the front of the house should gunfire erupt.

Try as he might, Jason had no luck in convincing Isaac to absent himself from his mother's side during the pending philosophical collision of ideologies. The only concession Jason could get Isaac to agree to was; he would not be armed.

Ian and his crew of one rode to the Mueller farm in Jason's van to keep as few cars as possible off the site. Sometimes hopping up and down to keep warm, they sipped designer coffee they'd picked up in Cleveland before meeting up with Jason at the Stoudt farm.

Elizabeth sat in her favorite chair on the front porch huddled under a shawl and a scarf pulled tightly around her face to protect her from the morning chill. She gave a subtle wave when Jason asked if she was going to be okay. Isaac stood at her side, this time with no pitchfork in his hand.

Note pad in hand, Jason strolled back and forth surveying the scene. Tucked in between the pages of the note pad was a sealed white envelope, and under his shirt, he packed the Makarov he'd hidden in the front porch header over a week ago. It felt comforting to have the weapon there.

A few minutes after ten, an Ashtabula County Crown Vic drove into the driveway. Rather than proceeding directly to the front of the house, the car paused and activated its light bar. From the distance, Jason could not make out who was driving. The car inched down the dirt driveway and parked under the beech tree. In seconds, the door opened and a uniformed county deputy stepped out and positioned his hat squarely on his head.

"I was told you have something for Sheriff Phelps," the deputy said in a practiced delivery.

Ian and his videographer stepped toward the deputy.

Close behind was Jason. "I do. Where is the sheriff?" Jason took note of his ID tag—B. Forrest. It was not the same one who'd stopped him in Geneva.

"This is his day off. He asked us to pick up…whatever it is you have of his."

"This was not the agreement we had," Jason said. "Sheriff Phelps was asked to be here in person. And secondly, what we have is not his. It belongs to this woman." He pointed in Elizabeth's direction.

"Sorry, sir, but I'm just doing as I was told." Forrest held out his hand as if he expected Jason to hand over…whatever. "Who are these people," he asked while pointing at Ian and the videographer.

"They're from the Cleveland Plain Dealer and are here to document what was supposed to go down this morning."

"Excuse me." The deputy disappeared inside his vehicle.

Jason watched Forrest through the window as the deputy contacted what was probably Dispatch back in Jefferson. He was glad the PD was capturing this on video. It would reveal the reason why the word *arrogance* was emphasized in the first article Ian had written about the Hutchinson case.

Forrest remained in his vehicle. About ten minutes passed before another county car pulled into the Mueller's driveway, its light bar was also flashing. As it neared the porch, Forrest waved him to park in front of his Crown Vic. Both stood talking quietly amongst themselves before the second one approached Jason. He wore the stripes of a sergeant.

"I understand we have some sort of problem here," the sergeant said.

Jason eased in front of Ian, who was busy notating the situation into a small tape recorder. "The problem is," Jason started as he glanced at his name tag, "Sheriff Phelps and I had an agreement for him to meet us here this morning. He made no mention of having a day off, and we do expect him to honor his agreement." Jason leaned closer and stared at the sergeant's ID again—W. Hottstetler.

The sergeant held his hand up in the direction of the cameraman. "Turn that thing off," he said.

Ian looked into the sergeant's vehicle and told the videographer to keep it rolling.

"I said, turn the camera off," Hottstetler ordered. There was a definite crescendo in his voice.

"Is your Dash-cam activated?" Ian asked the sergeant.

"Yes."

"So, what you're advocating is you reserve the right to video us," Ian continued, "but we have no right to video you? Hmm. Interesting concept." Ian again motioned the videographer to keep filming the confrontation.

"Look, gentlemen," Jason said as he stepped in between Hottstetler and Ian. "We have a situation here, not because of what you were told, or what the reporter is doing, but because your sheriff evidently refuses to honor the commitment we made yesterday. It's that simple. You get your boss here or we just ask you to leave."

"We will leave when we are told to leave," the sergeant said.

"It's up to you, Sergeant." Jason faced Isaac and Elizabeth. "I guess we have a clear demonstration of Sheriff Phelps' spin on integrity. Isaac, if you have chores to tend to, you can go. I think we're through for now."

Isaac chose to remain at his mother's side.

The videographer kept his Sony Camcorder alternately focused between the deputies, Jason, and the Mueller family.

Isaac helped his mother to her feet and guided her to the edge of the porch which was now in direct sunlight. As Elizabeth made her way across the porch, he whispered, "This will be better for you."

Hunched over and clutching Isaac's arm, Elizabeth sat in the high-backed wooden chair he'd moved for her. She clasped the shawl and scarf tightly around her shoulders and face again, and then waved a frail *thank you* to Isaac.

"So where is this envelope we were supposed to pick up?" Hottstetler asked.

Jason waved the nine by twelve inch envelope in the air. "Right here." He then took a seat next to Elizabeth. "We can wait."

During the ensuing silence, the deputies looked at each other and in a subtle way, shrugged their shoulders. Isaac took a few steps toward the barn, but returned to the porch. Elizabeth raised a hanky to her nose. Jason hummed the theme to Springsteen's *Born in the USA*.

"You know?" the sergeant said. "We could simply order you to hand over the envelope."

"You've gotta be joking," Jason fired back. "You know damn well you can't order us to hand over something this woman has volunteered to give your boss. This deals over. You guys can leave."

In a voice loud enough for all to hear, Ian turned sideways in what was surely a well-choreographed maneuver to ensure the camera's point of view would include the county vehicles in the background while he spoke into his microphone. "Well, there we have it ladies and gentlemen. This did not turn out as well as we had hoped. What was supposed to be a breakthrough in a twenty-five year old murder case involving an innocent young Amish girl has been callously swept aside by a sheriff who finds his day off more valuable than unearthing a critical piece of evidence and possibly finding her killer. This is Ian Stewart reporting from the Mueller farm in Windsor, Ohio." When he made a slashing motion across his throat, which indicated the videographer was to stop recording, Ian faced away from the deputies and his lips curled.

As diminutive as Ian seemed, Jason was beginning to think of him as the Pit Bull of journalism.

The deputies went back to their cars, leaned against a fender and began to talk amongst themselves. After a few hand waves and exchange of words, Hottstetler climbed back into his car and keyed his mike. He also switched off his light bar and waved out the window for Forrest to follow suit. As if frozen in time, everyone stayed in their places.

It was Elizabeth who broke the stalemate.

In a bent over position next to Elizabeth, Jason announced, "Mrs. Mueller would like to know if anyone would like a glass of water." He stood tall and in a louder voice, added, "This includes the deputies." He then waved at them, effectively inviting them to exit their vehicles.

Forrest emerged from his Crown Vic and looked to his sergeant for approval. He received none.

Hottstetler then exited his vehicle and in a brazen show of force, unsnapped his sidearm. "I've contacted Sheriff Phelps. He's ordered me to seize this document by any means at my disposal. Now, I'm asking you one last time...turn that envelope over to us." His hand rested on the butt of his sidearm.

"Now see what you've started?" Jason said to Hottstetler. "All we've asked for is some acknowledgment from Phelps that he gives a damn. Are you sure you want to initiate a feud in front of a reporter and have it in tomorrow's headlines?" Jason watched the sergeant remove his hand from the gun.

Hottstetler backed away from the confrontation and keyed his shoulder-mounted transceiver. "Dispatch. This is Hottstetler again. Inform the sheriff the situation has turned belligerent. These people are adamant about having his presence here...now."

A gravelly voice came back with, "Tell them I'll be there in about thirty, and they better damned well follow through with their promise."

When Jason heard the growling voice, he pictured Phelps hovering over the dispatch crew in Jefferson, listening to what was developing at the Mueller's, and had, most likely, been feeding them with what to say. Jason found it pathetically amusing for Phelps to demand a commitment to follow through with a promise when he'd done everything possible to ignore his own promise. The word *arrogance* bubbled to the surface again. "How long?"

"Thirty minutes," Hottstetler replied.

Had Jason chosen one word to represent the scene at the Mueller's, it would have been *reenactment*. Both deputies returned to their cars and conversed with each other just like before, while Jason, Elizabeth, and Isaac remained on the front porch. All this time wasted and for what?

Thirty minutes passed with no sign of Phelps. Jason kept checking his watch in full view of the deputies. It was his way of showing them they were on the clock. Just before noon, a white Lincoln Town Car entered the driveway. Rather than driving through the dirt, the car stopped just inside the fence near the main road. The occupant, dressed in the black shirt and gray tie of the Ashtabula County Sheriff's Office, stepped out. The colors were different, but for Jason, the black stripe down the outer edge of the gray trousers was reminiscent of the Marine Corps' blood stripe. Jason held his breath as he watched the figure place his hat squarely on his head as if he was conducting a formal departmental inspection.

The closest Jason had ever been to the sheriff was at Hutchinson's funeral, and that barely counted since Phelps kept his head lowered as he passed the van, and the hat basically obscured any facial features Jason might have noticed. This was going to be interesting. The sheriff seemed to be in no hurry to cover the distance from the road to the house.

"Okay. What's the problem here?" was the opening salvo from Phelps.

"Good afternoon, Sheriff, I'm..."

"Jason Carmichael. I got it. So what's the problem? I'm here. I'll take the document and we can call it a day." He held his hand out like a child at Halloween.

"It's not that easy, Sheriff. Mrs. Mueller has two requests before we turn this document over to you." Jason gestured at Elizabeth sitting on the porch. "Mrs. Mueller has had a visitor three times in the last two weeks, the first two, he requested this document, the last time, this individual demanded the document. Have you ever been here before?"

"I'm not about to answer any of your questions...detective." He glared at Ian and the videographer. "And get that thing off me."

Ian ignored the comment.

"It's a simple question, Sheriff. Yes or no?"

"No. Satisfied?"

"Well, there is the second condition we have to deal with," Jason said.

"And what do I have to do now?"

"Remove your hat."

"What?"

"We have reason to believe you, or someone who looks like you, has made some rather threatening demands to Mrs. Mueller."

Phelps leaned forward and whispered in Jason's ear. "Go to hell."

"Did you get that?" Jason asked the videographer.

The cameraman gave a quick nod and thumbs-up.

"Isn't technology great?" Jason gibed Phelps. "All we're asking is for you to allow Mrs. Mueller to see your face. Is that asking too much?"

"What this woman thinks is of no concern to me, Carmichael. I'll give you ten seconds to turn that envelope over to me or I'm outta here."

"Okay then. At least face Mrs. Mueller so she can determine if you are the one who's been paying her these unwanted visits. Will you do this for us?"

Phelps gave a heavy sigh and did a half right.

Elizabeth stared for a moment, and then leaned forward to take a closer look. While she clutched the scarf over her face, she squinted, then slowly raised her arm and pointed to Phelps.

"You sure?" Jason asked.

Elizabeth made a slicing motion to her cheek and nodded again.

"What the hell is going on?" Phelps bellowed. "Some old woman points at me and I'm guilty?"

"How did you get that scar under your jaw?"

"Listen, damn it. I'm not here to be questioned by some do-gooder from California. It's none of your damned business where I got a scar. I have one on my ass. You wanta see that one, too, you moron?"

"No, but thanks for the offer." Jason glanced at Ian while holding the large envelope up for Phelps to see. "So? This report will be of some value to you...in finding the person who killed Friedel Mueller?"

"It would be helpful."

During the drilling of Phelps, Jason noticed the looks on the deputies' faces. If he was reading them correctly, they were growing concerned as to where their loyalties should be—to the sheriff or to a principle. "I was wondering, since you claimed you've never been here, would you agree to have your Town Car searched?"

"What? Are you out of your fucking mind? Who do you think you are?" Phelps glared at the deputies who'd yet to make a move to support him.

"It's a legitimate request," Jason continued. "We're here. Your car is here, and your car bears a striking resemblance to the car Mrs. Mueller said was driven by the person who has been hassling her." He pulled a sealed business size envelope from his rear pocket. "In my hand, I hold a description of an item of interest. With your permission, I would like to hand this to your sergeant and have him inspect your car. When he is finished, we will open this envelope together. If he does not find what's described in here, I will let you do anything you want to me, no questions asked. Throw me in jail. Beat the crap out of me. Anything. What do you say?"

"You have no right to inspect my car."

"No, but your deputies do."

"Carmichael. I'm losing my patience with you. I'm about ready to beat the crap out of you on principle alone."

Jason focused his attention on the deputies. "Are you gentlemen familiar with the Supreme Court's ruling in United States versus Johns of 1985...ironically, the same year Friedel Mueller was killed?"

"No," they both replied.

"Here's the deal," Jason began. "If that Town Car is lawfully under police custody, the area in and around the passenger compartment can be searched without a warrant if it is deemed possible that a specific item could exist. It's called probable cause." He held the envelope high in the air. "What's in this envelope defines probable cause...and you can not get any more specific than what's described inside. What do you say? Inspect or not?"

"I know that ruling, Carmichael. It only applies if the person has been arrested."

"Damn, you're right, Sheriff. So you intend to hold me to that constraint?"

Phelps nodded.

"Okay. On camera, you are unwilling to waive that proviso in hopes of rectifying a gross allegation by me, and at the same time, possibly gain an opportunity to hold me up for public ridicule? Damn, I really admire your tolerance. If I was accused of something, and I knew I was innocent of any wrongdoing, I'd say, have at it, dude." Jason watched Phelps' face grow redder by the second. He knew if this was a bar or back in high school, one of them would wind up on the deck.

"You want to search my car? Go ahead." Phelps flung his keys at Jason.

In turn, Jason handed the keys to Hottstetler. "Just so I'm not accused of doing a bait 'n switch, I want you to have this." He handed the sealed envelope to the sergeant. "Open it when you come back here."

With the white envelope stuffed into his rear pocket, Hottstetler headed out the driveway, but not before casting a nervous glance at his boss.

It was evident to Jason the deputy was concerned not only for his job, but his career as well. If this went south, he could be blackballed from any other job in law enforcement. Not so much officially, but as in advertising, word of mouth could become his worst enemy. Little clouds of dust spurted up as each step was taken in the dry soil.

Hottstetler slipped on a pair of latex gloves before opening the passenger's side door of the Lincoln Town Car. Knowing from here on out, he would be working upside down, he placed his hat on the car's hood. All anyone could see of him was his rear end pointed skyward. As he emerged from the passenger's side, he held his hands outstretched to the side indicating he'd found nothing. He then proceeded to the driver's side and began the routine again.

This time, his body was hidden from view, much to the consternation of the videographer, but Ian prodded him to keep rolling.

It didn't take long before Hottstetler backed out and held something over his head. As he approached the area in front of the porch, he

275

slapped at his trousers to rid himself of any residual dust. "The only thing I found was this old rag." He started to hand it to Jason.

"I don't want to handle that," Jason said. "For the record, would you give us a general description of what you've found and where you found it?"

"Oh. It's a cloth of some sort," Hottstetler began, as he suspended it between his hands, "Blue. Kind of plain. Sewn around the edges. Less than a foot square. This article was found stuffed under the driver's seat of Sheriff Phelps' Lincoln. How much more do you want?"

"That will be fine. Thank you. Now, you can please place it in an evidence bag."

Forrest opened his trunk and retrieved a paper bag, but before handing it to Hottstetler, he marked the date and time on it.

"Good," Jason said. "You can place the evidence in the bag now."

The camera was aimed at the finding.

"So you found a rag in my car. So what?" Phelps bellowed out.

"Sergeant Hottstetler," Jason said. "Would you please open the sealed envelope now and read what's on the paper."

Hottstetler removed his gloves and slipped his finger under the glued flap, tore open the envelope, and held a letter size piece of lined paper in the air.

"For all those present, would you please read what it says?" Jason's voice had mellowed.

"It reads," Hottstetler began. *"My name is Elizabeth Mueller, mother of Friedel Mueller. On September 20th of this year, a man approached me for the third time to hand over a document to him. I do not know or trust this man, nor did he properly identify himself. I was afraid of him. He always came when the men were in the fields, so I believe he was watching my every move. I knew I had to leave something of value in his car to prove he was here. I asked my grandson, Benjamin, to do a very brave thing this day. The man left one of his doors open. I whispered for my grandson to climb into this man's car. When I went to get him, I pretended to scold him. As I gathered him into my arms, I shoved one of my most cherished possessions—a handkerchief made from a remnant of Friedel's wedding apron— under the seat as far as I could reach. It is blue, and about twenty-five centimeters square. I hope someone will find it. It is the only thing I have to hold that was hers. It is signed, Elizabeth Mueller."* In a slow, methodical move, Hottstetler folded the note and reinserted it into the envelope.

Phelps blurted out an obscene chuckle. "A rag? A God-damned rag that could have been there for years?"

"Tis not a rag, you contemptible ass," Elizabeth yelled out. She then covered her mouth in shame for uttering what, to her, would probably be considered an obscenity.

"Carmichael, I should have arrested you weeks ago."

"On what grounds, Sheriff? We just proved what you really are—a liar."

Phelps lunged at Jason.

Jason spun him around and used his own momentum to drive him headfirst into the hitching post.

Through a bloodied nose, Phelps yelled out to his deputies. "Arrest this man. Arrest this son-of-a-bitch. Nobody fucks with me."

"Is that what you told Friedel Mueller twenty-five years ago?" Jason yelled back. "When she wouldn't let you have what you wanted? Huh? Was it?" Jason kept grinding Phelps' face into the wooden post. "And what did you say to Ken Hutchinson before you shot him?"

"I'm ordering you to arrest this man," Phelps shouted at his deputies again. "Arrest him or I'll shoot your fucking asses right here and now."

Ian was kneeling down in the dust motioning the videographer in Phelps' direction. "Ooo. This is gonna be good."

"You could beat up a woman," Jason shot back, "or ambush a man who trusted you. But you know what? You don't even have the allegiance of your deputies without having to threaten to shoot them so they'll do what you want."

The deputies un-holstered their weapons and pointed them in the general direction of Phelps. It wasn't the conventional tactic they'd been taught when confronting a hostile, but then again, they'd never been conditioned to assume an offensive stance against their superior officer—a potentially bad career move.

Hottstetler ordered Jason to release Phelps saying he would assume the responsibility to escalate this grilling any further. His voice remained firm, but his gun still targeted the sheriff...kind of.

Not knowing, with any certainty, just how deep their loyalty was for their boss, Jason surveyed the scene and fired back with, "Unless you can prove you have no prejudice in this case, I intend to pursue this matter as I see fit."

"I don't have to prove anything to you," Hottstetler shouted. "We represent the law here, not you."

"You're right," Jason said, "but unless you want to take me out on camera, I suggest you wait for what comes next."

"I'll give you thirty seconds," Hottstetler said. "When that's up, you damned well better know, I'm not letting this turn into a circus."

Jason yanked Phelps to his feet, pushed him backward into the tree, and jammed his forearm across Phelps' throat.

Dena opened the screen door and stood at Elizabeth's side looking very much like...Elizabeth. Yesterday afternoon had been spent altering one of Elizabeth's dresses in haste hoping whatever happened today would tempt Phelps to take Elizabeth hostage in a moment of desperation. That was Plan A. Dena was prepared to stand in for her if the situation presented itself. The plan was for her to remain seated and disguise her face with a long shawl. The only outstanding feature they couldn't mask was the choice of shoes. Where Elizabeth wore lightweight, plain black shoes, Dena had no choice than to wear her New Balance running shoes. If she tucked her legs back underneath her long dress, maybe they wouldn't be so obvious. It didn't go down exactly the way they'd planned, but at least Dena had her chance to face off against him. Dena approached Phelps like a Panther homing in on an evening meal and stared into Phelps' soulless eyes. With a flick of her fingers, she flipped his hat off. It landed at her feet. "Elizabeth. Is this the man who has been contacting you?"

"Yes. The hair. I recognize the hair...and the evil eyes." Elizabeth returned to the porch, but never took her eyes off Phelps.

"Ya know?" Jason said. "Technology has changed so much in the last twenty-five years. That handkerchief your deputy just found under your seat will have Elizabeth Mueller's DNA all over it. And I'd be willing to bet if we were to exhume Friedel's body, we would find DNA evidence under her fingernails when she fought for her life." He studied the scar under Phelps left jaw. "Care to make a wager?"

"You haven't got shit, Carmichael. No one is ever going to believe you."

A shaky voice broke through the awkward silence. Plan B kicked in. "I think a jury might find me *very* convincing." Kathleen stepped onto the front porch, stood for a moment, then inched closer to her cousin. "Twenty-five years, Teddy." Rather than the tentative voice she'd used when debating within herself about what to do when confronted by Jason and Dena, she now spoke with a steady, firm voice laced with resentment.

"Shut up, Kat." Phelps' voice echoed across the fields. Being pinned to the tree by Jason's arm was the only thing that kept him from pouncing on his cousin.

"No, I won't. This has to be over," Kathleen continued. "I can't take any more of your lies, and your father's lies. It was all lies. I tried to believe you and your father, but I was too young to do anything about it. I've grown up, Teddy. Maybe you should, too."

"Kathleen," Jason said. "Are you willing to testify as to what happened the night Ted Phelps met up with you and Friedel Mueller at the cement bridge on 322?"

She nodded.

"We need to hear you say it," Hottstetler added.

"Yes." There was a pleading look in her eyes as she focused on her cousin. "You badgered me all my life, Teddy. No more. I will testify against you. I will testify about what you said to Friedel and me that night."

"Kat. I'm warning you." His eyes narrowed as he glared at her. Using the tree as leverage, Phelps took another lunge at Jason. This time, he succeeded in gaining enough distance between himself and Jason that he could take a swing.

"Freeze," Hottstetler yelled out as directed his gun at the sheriff.

"Fuck you." Phelps grabbed Kathleen's arm and yanked her toward him. In a split second, his forearm was around her throat and he pressed his gun to her temple.

Dena shielded Elizabeth's eyes with her hands and herded her back inside. In defiance, Isaac stood his ground with his arms folded across his massive chest.

Jason pulled his Mak out of his shoulder holster and pointed it at Phelps. This time, the two deputies made their first serious career commitments by training their weapons solely on the sheriff. Gone was the tentativeness. "You're outgunned, Phelps. Give it up."

"Nobody insults my family, especially this bitch."

"Don't make this any worse than it already is," Jason warned.

"Sheriff Phelps. It's Sheriff Phelps, you asshole. I'm still the sheriff."

"In theory…Sheriff," Jason said as he repositioned himself so if he had to shoot, the occupants inside the house would not be in the line of fire.

"Sheriff. Drop your weapon," Hottstetler called out.

Kathleen's eyes seemed to be floating freely in her head. They pointed up, then down, or toward anyone who could free her from her cousin, who had increased his grip on her throat—to the point where she began to gag.

Everyone seemed in a heavy breathing mode. To the right of him, Jason saw Isaac reach up into the gnarled branches of the Beech tree and retrieve one of his Marlin rifles. "Shit." He'd promised Jason that he would be unarmed during this face-down, and at the time, Jason couldn't conceive him purposely stashing a weapon in the tree. Before he had a chance to shout out, Isaac lowered the rifle and was taking aim directly at Phelps' head. Under most circumstances, when someone cocks a lever action rifle, it is done with two quick snaps, but Isaac, his eyes now narrowed into tiny slits, made two slow, deliberate snaps—the kind that rang of hatred and retribution. Jason lowered his voice to a whisper. "Isaac. Don't do this." He waited.

Phelps pivoted around so his face was hidden behind Kathleen.

As Elizabeth started to make a move in her son's direction, Dena coaxed her back.

Squinting his left eye as he sighted down the barrel, Isaac barked out, *"An eye for an eye,* the Lord said." His voice had a deep, intense rumble like that of a cornered animal.

"This is not right, Isaac," Elizabeth said. "The Lord also said, *Do not repay anyone evil for evil.*"

Isaac kept his rifle trained on Phelps.

This unexpected turn of events forced Jason to signal Dena to inch closer to Isaac from his blind side. The motion of Jason's head and eye swing was subtle, but she read him well.

Jason trusted her, and kept his eyes and Mak trained on Phelps.

Dena eased closer to Isaac. In a soft, soothing voice, she whispered, "Doesn't the Sixth Commandment condemn the killing of another human being?"

"This is not a human being," Isaac shouted. "He is an animal with earthly lusts and it cost my sister her life. He must pay."

"He will pay, Isaac," Dena whispered. "Jason and I promise you this. The two deputies promise you this. Phelps will pay for what he's done to your sister. Do you trust us?"

"I trust in my Lord to guide me."

In an attempt to take advantage of the growing distraction, Jason saw Phelps move his foot in an attempt to reach one of the county vehicles. Seeing the painful look on Kathleen's face, Jason hissed, "Don't make another move, Phelps. I won't hesitate to take you out."

"What is the difference?" Isaac cried out. "Have I not the right to redeem myself in the eyes of the Lord?"

"To what end?" Dena asked softly.

"I must do what is right. I was not around to protect my sister."

Dena eased in front of the barrel of the Marlin and gently lifted it. In a soothing, velvety voice, she murmured, "You cannot protect her anymore, Isaac." She gently lifted the barrel high and waited a few seconds. "Please."

Control the situation was the fundamental objective Jason had drummed into him years ago when he chose his career path. Know who the players are. Know their probable responses. Know how they would probably interact with each other. Know what weapons might be used. Be prepared for at least one surprise and always have an exit strategy.

Jason started this whole confrontation with a script of five actors. Two of whom represented the media. Kathleen was to be his trump card and would wait offstage until the final curtain would fall on Phelps. He hadn't counted on two more deputies whose allegiance would be questionable at best. He hoped to persuade Isaac, and his propensity for violence, to stay out of sight, but Isaac was adamant about not leaving his mother's side. Jason accepted this as understandable since Isaac admitted feeling a sense of inadequacy about not being able to protect his sister twenty-five years ago. The list was growing.

At least the elder Stoudt and his family agreed to remain safe at home and oversee Jennifer.

Jason did have two options at his disposal…at the beginning. Plan C was introduced on the fly when Isaac produced a weapon he had every intention of using. Losing control was not routine for Jason and he hated himself for what was happening. But here he was, facing a multiple killer. Not a serial killer. Not a spree killer, but a killer of circumstance. Where one makes one horrific blunder and years later, commits another to cover it up. Regardless of how others perceived him, Jason felt he'd made the right choices. He'd tried the official route through an alliance with Ken Hutchinson, but this one futile attempt to play by the rules cost Hutchinson his life. Whether or not anyone liked his methods, Jason started this and would finish it anyway he saw fit. He had to regain control and see this through to the end. What else could possibly happen?

From behind the group, the roar of an engine cut through the mayhem. Yelling and screaming commands were no competition for the snarl of the powerful V8. In a quick glance, Jason verified who was behind the wheel. It was Tigre. Crap. There was no Plan D. What the hell was Tigre doing here?

Deputy Forrest motioned the car away.

The pumping of the accelerator and resultant din only increased with each wave of the hand.

On the front porch, Dena kept her arms around Elizabeth. Jason motioned her to step back.

"Get that car out of here," Phelps commanded. "He's in my way." Still holding Kathleen in a death grip, Phelps made a move toward the road.

The videographer kept swinging his hi-def camcorder wildly between the two scenes while Ian crouched behind a picnic table flipped on its side.

The car kept up its steady fluctuation between idle and seven grand. Idle, seven grand, idle.

"I said get that car the fuck out of my way." Phelps began a slow side step in the direction of the lead county vehicle. "Keys in there?" he shouted at Hottstetler.

"Yeah."

"How far do you think you're gonna get, Phelps?" Jason demanded. "Out the driveway? A mile down the road? You know damn well you have nowhere to run. Let Kathleen go. Let her walk over to us."

"Please end this, Teddy." Kathleen choked the words out. "This has to end."

"You want it to end?" Phelps hissed in her ear. "I'll tell you how it's gonna end. If I pull this fucking trigger, you're gonna die just like that fucking Amish bitch. That's how it's gonna end...for you."

The Shelby Mustang kept up its unsettling growl. Then it stopped cold. Except for heavy breathing, there was no sound until footsteps approached.

Jason watched Tigre swagger toward the group. Tigre had a way of walking where, with each step, he would dip his lead shoulder, then repeat the process with his other foot. At his side, he carried an intimidating Smith and Wesson .44 magnum revolver—the model favored by Clint Eastwood in his movies. His gait was one of determination, commitment, cocky confidence, and his piercing eyes were focused solely on Phelps. There was nothing else in his world at this time other than Phelps.

Hottsteler called out for him to stop and drop the weapon.

Tigre was operating with tunnel vision. His glare never wavered as he neared Phelps and Kathleen.

"Shoot this son-of-a-bitch," Phelps yelled out. "That's an order."

"Don't anyone move," Jason shouted. "No one is to fire on this man, do you understand?" When no one replied, Jason repeated himself... louder.

"Yes," came the cautious reply of the deputies.

Tigre stood nose to nose with Phelps. "This how you guys do business? Shi-i-it. This how Tigre do business." He breathed on Phelps' face. "You one sick mother-fucker. You stand there hidin' behind some woman. I don't hide behind nobody." He pressed the revolver under Phelps' chin. Even from a distance, one could see the indentation it made. Anyone with any common sense would have been in dire need of a massive amount of toilet paper if they had the misfortune to be at the business end of this handgun. "Let me introduce you to Dirty Harry, mother-fucker. You gots two choices. From where I stand, you cap this woman…you got no place to hide…you die. If you try to cap me…you die. You ain't that quick. So what's it gonna be? You either let this woman go…or we pick up what's left of your head with a vacuum cleaner."

Damned if Tigre didn't do what every member of LE hasn't been tempted to do at least once in their career. The deputies kept their guns trained on Phelps, as did Jason.

Slowly, Phelps raised his right arm in the air and let the gun pivot within the finger guard so the barrel pointed skyward. He then dropped it at his feet. His other arm which had been wrapped around Kathleen's neck loosened. And never had he taken his eyes off the magnum jammed into his chin.

With his Mak still pointed at Phelps, Jason inched closer and kicked the gun out of reach. "Hands in the air and back up two steps, Phelps," he said in a snake-like tone. Phelps did as he was told. "Now keep your hands in the air and turn around." As Phelps obeyed the command, Jason reached for Kathleen's arm and pulled her away, and in the same flowing movement, steered her toward Deputy Forrest. A quick glance let him know she was safely out of Phelps' reach.

Dena moved to Jason's side. "May I?"

Jason grinned. "Sergeant Hottstetler. Would you mind if my partner cuffs this douche bag?"

The deputy handed her his links. "You guys deserve this. Have at it."

Dena reached over Phelps' left shoulder and grabbed his wrist, then twisted the arm behind his back.

She was just about to snap the first cuff on when Phelps yelled out, "No cunt is gonna hook me up."

He didn't realize he'd just made his last mistake. When he started to spin around to face off against Dena, she grabbed his arm, did a fast twisting motion which effectively immobilized his arm. In the same split second, she twisted his fingers backward. With the agility of a soccer-style NFL place kicker, she planted her left foot and, with her right foot, swept his feet out from underneath him and drove his face down into the dirt.

"I'm the sheriff," he yelled. "Have some respect."

"You're getting all the respect you deserve," Dena hissed as she placed her knee between his shoulder blades, placed one cuff on him, and then repeated the process for the other arm. When she felt the last snap, she got off him, grabbed the cuffs, yanked Phelps to his feet, and shoved him towards Hottstetler. "He's all yours. And don't forget, this slime ball is responsible for killing one of your own."

"Ted Phelps," Hottstetler began. "I am placing you under arrest for the murder of Friedel Mueller and Ken Hutchinson."

Over the sound of Hottstetler reading Phelps his Miranda Rights, Forrest told Jason, "Whew. I'm glad she's on our side." He then faced his soon-to-be ex-boss.

"Me, too." Jason smiled and curled his arm around Dena. "Good job, partner."

In all the commotion, no one noticed Tigre and his Mustang had vanished.

CHAPTER 31

Yellow barrier tape was strung from oak tree to oak tree and to each side of the Phelps' residence in Jefferson. Because of the nature and magnitude of the crimes coupled with the public figure involved, it took Sergeant Hottstetler little time to contact his Chief Deputy, who, in turn, attained a search warrant for the house. And the judge who signed it didn't care that he was dragged off a golf course.

Phelps was booked into the holding cell in Jefferson. Due to his legal status, Phelps was kept isolated from the general inmate population in fear he might be confronted by someone he'd just caused to be incarcerated. The result may have caused the time span from trial to death sentence to be reduced from years to seconds.

Jason and Dena were asked if they cared to accompany the forensics team as they dissected Phelps' life. It was a no-brainer.

The all brick house looked like it had been featured on the front of a home improvement magazine. The lawn was manicured and the bushes perfectly rounded and equally sized. There was a gently curving sidewalk leading to a minimal porch. The curved sidewalk was not the shortest route, but to the eye, must have been more graceful and pleasing. All the wood trim around doors and windows were painted an antiseptic white.

Jason and Dena were handed latex gloves before being ushered in by Hottstetler. Inside, Mrs. Phelps sat on the couch while being consoled by a female deputy. Tissue paper was in abundance as were tears and shaking hands.

"You've gotta check this out," one member of the crime lab team whispered, keeping his eye on Mrs. Phelps. He led them down the narrow stairs into the basement. Three lights spaced about eight feet apart dangled from the floor joists. The separation caused multiple shadows as the group moved about the area. He focused his flashlight on two cardboard boxes jammed into a corner. Both boxes had been opened.

Wearing his protective gloves, the crime scene coordinator reached into the first box and pulled out a form not used for many years. It was the same as the one Elizabeth cherished. "We're going to test these for prints, but ya wanta see something interesting?" He held up two different docs. "We're going to recommend an exemplar test for Ted Phelps. There's handwriting on these docs, but they don't seem to be from the same person."

"Remember Kathleen mentioned Ted Phelps' father when she was begging him to call it quits?" Jason asked.

"Say no more," Hottstetler said. "I see where you're going with this. Good old Teddy kills Friedel. Lies to his dad..."

"Wayne," Jason added.

"Wayne knows all the signs of a liar, but nevertheless proceeds to protect his son."

"Misuse of power," Jason said.

"To say the least," Hottstetler added. "Accessory after the fact would be more appropriate."

"Like father, like son," Dena said. "What's an exemplar?"

"We ask Ted Phelps," Hottstetler began, "since his father is dead, to write something, over and over. We use that sampling to determine who made these notations on these docs. Or, if we prefer, we could examine samples of his handwriting at headquarters. Either way, we nail his pompous ass. And I'm sure, somewhere in the archives, we will find records of Wayne's handwriting."

"It looks like Ted and his father were collectors of sorts," the coordinator continued. "It boggles your mind, doesn't it? They've created a mini-museum down here dedicated not to the good they'd done, but to the evil."

"You guys want to see what else is in the cardboard museum?" Another evidence technician moved the second box closer to the group and opened the interlocking lids. On top was a 9mm Glock. "We're already running *latents* on this. Seems the serial number is recorded elsewhere...as in the evidence room at headquarters. Seems Phelps checked himself out a seemingly untraceable piece. Seems he thought he had all the time in the world to replace it." He held it up to his nose and sniffed. "Seems this puppy has been fired recently."

"Seems Teddy Phelps was living in denial," Dena said.

"You have the bag with Mrs. Mueller's handkerchief, right?" Jason asked.

"Sure do," the coordinator said. "That was ingenious."

"Sure was," Jason added. What he kept to himself was the little discussion he'd had with Elizabeth after the stranger's second visit.

As Jason and Dena left the Phelps' house, their last vision was Mrs. Phelps leaning on a window sill looking at the back yard. Like the front yard, its grass was neatly trimmed, as were the bushes. Her shoulders were hunched over. "He liked to make things grow," she sobbed.

◊   ◊   ◊

"Welcome. Welcome. Welcome," Ian shouted from across the room. Whoever thought of him as mousy or ordinary sorely underestimated his drive. Multiple morning editions of the PD hung from every partition of his cube. There wasn't one open space which didn't have a copy in case someone didn't happen to notice.

"We just wanted to stop by and tell you how much we appreciate your cooperation in reeling a dangerous killer in," Jason said.

"Hold on." Ian punched an internal extension number on his landline. "They're here," was his abbreviated message.

Within seconds, Shauna Delrosso appeared with her arms outstretched so wide that had the corridor been a tad narrower, she'd have broken both wrists. She gave Jason and Dena an industrial strength hug. "You guys. I just love you guys. This exclusive got us so much attention, you wouldn't believe it."

"It's even been picked up by the AP," Ian bragged.

"And national television coverage, too," Shauna continued. She regained control of herself by fluffing up her hair as if she'd just stepped out of a shower. "Okay, here's what's happened...in one day. Ian has..."

"I've been invited to speak with a few power players in New York. Every day, there are numerous murders in this country. If all of them made news, we'd have to cut down every tree in the world to print it, but when a member of law enforcement commits multiple murders, it grabs everyone's attention. Our video has become gold."

The next hour was spent with four people huddled in a cramped cube going over every detail of the copy Ian had written with Jason's attention-grabbing lead-in, and the well-choreographed script Jason and Dena designed to make sure all the hooks were set before anyone jerked on the rod. From an outsider's point of view, it would have sounded like a meeting of the mutual admiration society, and ironically, it was.

"Do not roll your window down," Jason warned Dena. "And keep your eyes straight ahead if someone glares at you." He eased the white van through the neighborhood where he'd happened upon Tigre. There was something about this man that Jason couldn't wrap his head around. Why had he showed up at various times throughout the investigation? How did he know where he and Dena were staying? And what was the impetus for his impromptu arrival at the Mueller farm two days ago? And why did he leave when he did? Was he on a wanted list and afraid to stick around after he'd taken care of business his way? Jason drove slowly in case he got pulled over again. The Cleveland Police Department was justified in the previous stop—white guy driving a clean white van in a predominately black section of town known for having its own set of rules. If you didn't like the rules, leave. Simple.

Jason swung around the corner where he'd first seen Tigre and his boys. At first, there was no sign of him, but the bright red Shelby Mustang was on the street, its windows rolled down as if defying someone to steal it. Across the street, a dilapidated Plymouth pulled out leaving a convenient slot for the van. Jason pulled into what was supposed to be an entrance to a private garage, but was piled high with black plastic garbage bags. He eased ahead as far as he could, and then backed out into the street to get a clear shot at the spot. When he finally coaxed the van into the cramped spot, he said, "Stay put." He opened his door, let his legs dangle out, and stared across the street at the Mustang.

One ragged man carrying a plastic grocery bag weaved down the street next to him. When he spotted the occupants of the van, he furrowed his brow and crossed the littered street. After several steps, he turned and looked back at the van, continued on, then turned and repeated the process. Jason wondered if this was one of Tigre's lookouts.

The door across the street opened. This was the stoop where he'd first seen Tigre. The door stayed open, but for awhile, no one came out. Maybe someone was letting in some fresh air. A minute passed and an image came out. It was Tigre. Jason remained in his seat and looked at him.

Tigre plopped down on the blackened cement steps, folded his tattooed arms over his knees and stared at the van. His stare was not of anger or hatred, but more like apprehension.

With a near imperceptible rippling of his fingers, Jason acknowledged Tigre's presence.

Tigre nodded in return. Not appreciably, but just enough to let Jason know he could come across the street. "No matter what you see, don't get out of this van," he told Dena. "With Tigre in sight, no one would dare make a move on you."

"Hi," Jason said.

"Yo." Tigre leaned against the soot-stained bricks of his building. "Whutchu doin' here, man?"

"Friendly visit?"

"Ain't no such thing in this neighborhood."

"Where are your friends?"

Tigre rubbed his hands over his face. It was like he was washing his face, but with no water.

"None of my business, right?"

"Uh-huh."

"Well. I just wanted to see you again and say thanks."

"For?"

"The groceries."

"If you're thinkin' of returnin' them, I got me a no return policy." Tigre gave a short sardonic chuckle. "But you know better than this, so let me ask you a question Jay-sohn. Why you pick me?"

"Hmm. Fate maybe. I don't know. I saw you sitting there. I thought you could help me out."

"You mentioned my father. I don't like nobody mentioning my father."

"Is it any of my business why?"

"My mother hooked up with some white guy and they had me. Then they leave me when I was fifteen. I guess I didn't count for shit. They went on a vacation out to California. Never came back."

"I remember you stayed with your aunt."

"Yeah. Then she ups and dies."

"I'm sorry."

"Not your fault, man. My aunt told me they were killed…or some shit like that. Went hiking out in the mountains was something they dreamed of doin'. That's why I don't like nobody doin' a throw-down on my father. It's all his fault."

"I won't say anything more about your father. I promise."

"Good." Tigre took a deep breath.

"I know you like to be called Tigre, but what's your real name?"

"Why?"

"Just wanta know, I suppose."

Tigre said nothing. He gazed up and down his street. This was his territory, his home, his entire life—all summed up on this block.

"Okay. I get the message." Jason stood to leave.

"Arthur. Now you happy, Jay-sohn?"

"I'm a rather curious kind of guy, and I think you are, too. Am I right?"

"Could be."

"Why did you do what you did the other day…at the farm?"

"Shit needs doin', I do it."

"What you did was against the law, but don't think it wasn't appreciated."

"I don't give no shit about the law, man. I be the law. And just to let you know," Tigre cast another anxious look up and down the street, "I ain't never dropped nobody."

Jason reached for his hand.

Tigre refused when two of his lieutenants, one of whom had to weigh in at no less than three-hundred pounds, rounded the corner.

"I am curious. Why would you want to help someone you didn't even know?"

For an instant, Tigre's eyes softened. "You did." He then sprang to his feet and struck a defiant pose as his friends drew closer. "Play with me Jay-sohn. Either I *dis* you or your ass be theirs. Don't go trippin' on me." He gave Jason a serious poke in the chest and backed him against the Shelby.

"Bye…Arthur."

"Arthur Triall," Tigre said softly, then yelled out loud enough for everyone to hear, "Don't you give me no shit." He then went nose to nose with Jason and whispered, "My mother's name was Cynthia. My white boy father was Virgil. Hated the name he always told me, 'cause it sounded like virgin." Tigre stared at the grimy cement at his feet. "Yeah. Good old Virgil Henry Triall." He spun Jason around and slammed him face first into the Mustang.

"So what did he like people to call him?" Jason threw up his hands as if he was trying to defend himself.

"He went by his middle name a lot. He wanted to be called, Hank." Tigre grabbed Jason by the back of his collar, yanked him backward for an instant, and then pushed him into the street.

The lieutenants were now standing at Tigre's side, arms folded across their chests and legs spread wide eagerly waiting for a retaliatory strike from Jason signaling their chance to pounce in for the kill. The three-hundred pounder with a shaved head was slamming his fist into his open palm.

Casting a nervous glance at the seven or eight hundred pounds of attitude facing him, Jason put his hands to his side and walked away. Behind him, jeers were hurled so all within shouting distance would know Tigre was still *Da Man*. Jason climbed back in the Chevy, revved up the engine and left no doubt to any observer that he was running scared. In his side-view mirror, he saw Tigre's two friends making taunting gestures with their handguns while kicking street debris in his direction. Tigre stood motionless in the middle, watching.

"What the hell happened back there?" Dena asked.

"Remember on our last case, there was a guy who always seemed to appear out of nowhere?"

"Hank?"

"You're not gonna believe this."

◊   ◊   ◊

The District Attorney wasted no time filing charges against Phelps, if for no other reason than to demonstrate, to what had become a national disgrace, the counties ability to resolve the situation quickly. There would be no special treatment, or no lengthy time delays. The Phelps family already had a high-powered attorney in their back pocket and was making demands, all under the pretext of Phelps' years of dedicated public service. The general consensus on the news and local papers was, *poor, poor, Teddy*. It seemed the populace had grown tired of special treatment for the privileged few.

Jason and Dena were called in to the county court house to formally make their statements, as were Elizabeth and Isaac Mueller, and of course, the prime witness, Kathleen.

The chief deputy under Phelps had been appointed the interim sheriff and assumed control very quickly and efficiently. News conferences were held to let every branch of the media ask their questions. Naturally, Ian Stewart was honored with a front row seat at every airing.

As Jason and Dena exited the court house, they saw David Ellison facing cameras, reporters, and an array of microphones. The pedestal-mounted microphones were from the major networks. All others were handheld by eager journalists chomping at the opportunity to ask what they perceived were penetrating questions.

"Thank you for allowing me to share my observations with you today," David murmured into the mikes clipped onto a wooden podium. A voice called out for him to speak louder. He clenched his lips and his voice became low and serious. "I'm sorry. This series of events has struck me to my very core. I, like all of you, thought I knew Ted Phelps. Turned out we were wrong. It wasn't until a few weeks ago when I started having my doubts, and called for the aid of an old friend who might be able to help me find the truth. Together, we plunged into a full blown investigation and devised a plan where we could flush out the vicious ambush-style killing of Ken Hutchinson and the killing of one of our Amish neighbors twenty-five years ago. I could never have completed this task without the help of this old friend. All I can say to all of you here today is, I feel humble just to be able to be a part of the solution."

Another voice yelled out, "Where is this detective friend of yours, Mr. Ellison?"

"Oh, please call me David. This is no time for formalities." David scanned the area.

"I hope this prick doesn't ask me to say something in response to this bullshit," Jason whispered to Dena.

"If he does, be creative, partner. I have faith in you." There was an unmistakable gleam in her eye.

"There he is," David yelled out as he pointed to Jason and Dena, who were trying to make it back to the van. "Come on up here, buddy. These kind people want to know more about how we accomplished all this."

Jason and Dena inched through the crowd who began to applaud. The closer they got to the podium, the more people moved out of their way. They felt like they'd become Mr. and Mrs. Moses at the parting of the sea. He and Dena stepped onto the platform where David stood acting out his self-righteous, humble drama.

"Everyone, this is Jason Carmichael and his lovely partner…Dena." He stopped quickly when he realized he didn't know her last name. "Would you care to say a few words about how we accomplished what we set out to do for the people of the great state of Ohio?"

Holding Dena's hand, Jason eased toward the mike and looked at this pathetic piece of crap and in a booming voice, announced, "No."

◊   ◊   ◊

The drive to the Mueller farm was filled with laughter about the look on David's face when Jason made his impromptu speech. Jason and Dena were confident the remark would make more headlines across the nation than would David's lengthy garbage-laden rhetoric whose transparent objective was to capture votes.

"Can I share something with you?" Dena asked in a dreamy voice.

"Certainly."

"I think it's time I told you why I came here to be with you." Her voice weakened, not in volume, but in intensity. "He's done it again."

"Uuh. Who?"

"Clay. My husband." Her eyes reddened and there was a slight quivering in her lips. "About a week before you called, I caught him. I went to his office to have him sign an authorization slip for a field trip for our son. The door was locked...and it was two in the afternoon, so I hung around out front. I saw him come out of the storage room with another woman. And he saw me."

"I'm sorry. If you don't want to talk..."

"That's just it, Jason. I want to talk. I have to talk. It was like before. He said he felt nothing for her. When you and I talked back in June about the other time, I said I could accept it if he'd felt something for her, but he didn't. He didn't feel anything for her. If something happens, there has to be a reason, Jason. Just give me a reason."

Jason liked the first look he'd seen a few moments ago, but she did not deserve this look. Her eyes seemed to sink deep inside her cheek bones. "I don't know what to say, Dena."

"Do I seem callous when I say it wouldn't have had the same impact on me if he'd actually fallen in love with someone else?"

"People change. He may have been this way when you met him, but you were looking for something different in him—something different from your parents—a sense of stability, if I remember correctly."

"My parents were habitual gamblers, and all through my teens, and even before, Jerry and I had to fend for ourselves while they were off on another quest for the sure thing. What I was looking for was substance."

Jason couldn't help but reflect on their encounter with the pot growers in the mountains, and how Dena stayed at his side when it would have been so easy for her to run for help while leaving him weak from the gunshot wound, or at the mercy of some nocturnal prowler looking for an easy late night snack.

Her voice wistful, Dena continued. "The anxiousness to be in love and somehow fill a gap was my fundamental mistake. Where does it say you have to be married by twenty, or thirty...and have children... and a white picket fence? Wouldn't it be better to wait to find that one special person who you know will be there for you, no matter what? Maybe it might come when you're twenty or thirty, or forty. Who cares, just get it friggin' right."

"Where would you draw the line?"

"What do you mean?"

"At what point do you put a stick in the sand and draw this line? The first person, the second, the tenth?"

"The person you were meant to *be*, will emerge from chaos. Think about it, Jason. If you were born into money and privilege, it would be like living in the biblical perception of Eden. Wouldn't it be boring? If all you had to do was wake up every morning, and all your food would be waiting for you, there'd be no work to do. You could go shopping, to parties. Everything would be at your disposal. The sun would always shine. You'd never experience the thrill of a lightening storm. You'd have no reason to be something—to make something of yourself—to be productive, or make a contribution to the world. And in the end, what would we have? A world full of Paris Hiltons." Dena tapped her fingertip to her temple. "Chaos builds character. Goodness comes from not assuming you are as good as you can be, but from trying to be better."

"In other words, Eden should not be a verifiable place, but an unachievable goal."

"Exactly. Kind of like finding the last digit of pi."

"Do you think you could ever find near-perfection?"

"I believe I have experienced chaos, and from it, someone did come into my life."

As they neared the entrance to the farm, they were met with a sight neither could have imagined. There had to be at least fifty carriages lined up alongside the driveway. In each, a man and woman sat. The women clapped delicately while the men tipped their hats to Jason and Dena. As the van passed slowly by, Dena began to well up. She couldn't reach her handkerchief fast enough. After the van had passed each carriage, the man and wife climbed out and walked to the house.

On the lawn in front of the porch, picnic tables were set up complete with roasted chicken, fried sweet potatoes, mashed potatoes, gravy, applesauce, local cheeses, cold-cuts, pies, and homemade lemonade. Jason scanned the table for what he'd grown accustomed to—Elizabeth's now famous biscuits and blackberry preserves, the kind where little seeds find refuge in the spaces between your teeth.

On the front porch, Elizabeth stood like a regal queen overlooking her domain. Isaac stood at her side as he'd done so many times before, except this time he carried no pitchfork. She waved frantically as the van pulled up near the hitching post. When Jason stopped, she and Isaac came to them and gave each a warm hug. Dena used one of her tissues to dab at Elizabeth's teary eyes. This was followed by a little laughter and another hug.

There were no long-winded announcements like at the courthouse. Everyone knew the purpose of the festivities, but that did not deter most from stopping by and introducing themselves.

Conspicuously absent were Kathleen and Jennifer. Joshua explained how, after the confrontation with Phelps and the ensuing questions directed at her by deputies, she chose to take advantage of what might be her last chance for free time, and spend it at home with her daughter. "This will be the beginning of a painful journey for her. I wish she would have chosen to stay with us. We welcome anyone who would do what she did for not only the Muellers, but to set an example for us all." Joshua took a healthy swallow of his lemonade and then with a wide-eyed expression on his face, said, "She called for transportation with a tiny little phone."

"It's called a cellular phone, Joshua," Isaac said with a big grin.

Sitting shoulder to shoulder, Jason and Dena absorbed the scene. Platters of food were passed around. Children ran and played tag. No one told them to, but at one point as if on cue, all the children stopped what they were doing, filled a galvanized bucket with water and saw to the horses' needs. All the while, petting the animal and sharing what were probably a few guarded secrets.

As one more person joined the table, people scooted closer. Without realizing it, Jason and Dena were jammed into each other. Each time they'd look at the other, there was a comfortable exchange of smiles.

When the celebration began to wind down, Jason and Dena pivoted on their benches and leaned back into the table and looked at trees, fields, and animals, all cared for with a hefty measure of respect. They chose to stay close to each other even though the table was being cleared. Isaac joined them.

"Young Benjamin. Please come here," Isaac said in his authoritative voice.

Benjamin did come running, but instead of sitting in his father's lap, he reached up for Jason to hold him. Jason obliged without hesitation.

"Benjamin," Jason whispered. "I want you to know that you are a brave young man to do what you did the other day to help your grandmother and me. Did climbing into the man's car scare you?"

"No-o."

"Did anything scare you?"

"No-o."

"Why?"

"Because...I am a BIG boy." He threw his arms up in the air and watched to see if everyone was laughing. They were.

Members of the congregation stopped by to shake hands with Jason and Dena one last time before departing. Most offered the excuse they had a long trip to make before sundown, which made sense when their transportation didn't have headlights and a two-hundred horsepower engine.

Isaac patted Benjamin on the head and asked him to go find his grandmother. When the lad left, Isaac pulled Jason and Dena aside. "I wish to apologize for my behavior toward you. There is no excuse for what I did and said. You had nothing but the best intentions." He offered Jason his hand, then embraced Dena. When Isaac hugged Dena, she moaned as if every bit of air was being expelled from her body. "I'm sorry," he said.

"Not a problem," she gasped. "Do it again."

All shared a robust laugh.

Wearing her formal cape over her dress, Elizabeth explained she thought of today as a special day to honor two people who were thought of as members of the family. "Before you go, would you like to join me at Friedel's grave? I hate to end such a festive occasion with such a sad request, but it would mean a lot to me...and Friedel."

"We were going to ask you if we could visit with her," Dena said, turning to Jason. "Weren't we?"

"Thank you, my dear." Elizabeth grabbed Dena's hand and started for the pasture in back of the house.

Four people waded through the fields towards Friedel's marker at the edge of the woods. It was quiet. Even the Holsteins seemed to respect the solemn procession by moving aside.

"I did not visit Friedel yesterday," Elizabeth said in a soft voice as they approached the wood marker. "I wanted us all to be here together."

She knelt down and placed her hand on the name, carved so intricately by Jonathon Ditmann.

Dena was the first to kneel next to Elizabeth. On her other side, Isaac removed his straw hat and knelt, too. Jason stood for a few seconds until Dena tapped him on his leg and motioned for him to kneel.

"I don't want to take up your time, but there are some things I think Friedel would want to hear."

"We can take as long as you'd like, Elizabeth," Dena said.

"Friedel. There are some very special people here today. One of them is an old classmate of yours named Jason Carmichael. He has a good friend with him named Dena Manning. Of course Isaac and I are here, too. All these years, we've agonized over what happened that awful night. With the help of Jason and Dena, we now know. So, if you can see us or hear us, I want to let these people know how special they are to you, to me, and to our community. Sometimes people leave a place in spirit, but if we are so lucky, they find their way back. And that is what Jason did, if only for a brief period of time. It is like the old covered bridge we used to drive over, now condemned because the wood is deemed rotten and can no longer carry our loads. Jason carried a load for us, and like the aged timbers, there are those of us who believe the inner heartwood will always remain strong and true. And Jason is our bridge."

Dena buried her face in Elizabeth's shoulder.

"One more thing," Elizabeth said softly. "I know Friedel can see all of us with her beautiful blue eyes…but especially Jason and Dena, and she is whispering, *Thank you.*"

Jason snuggled in behind Dena and Elizabeth and rubbed both their shoulders until he felt he could add something to this commemoration. "Would you mind if I added something?"

"Friedel would love to hear from you," Elizabeth whispered.

As Jason began to speak, he stayed behind the two women and continued to hold their shoulders. "We all seem to grow according to some grand scheme, but as we grow, we should never grow apart."

Dena squeezed his hand.

"And I think that is what I have done. Until I came back here for a visit, I'd forgotten this person who I shared hallways with, and an occasional sandwich. Part of growing is allowing others into your life, and here's what I regret. I regret never sitting with you and talking—just talking. I regret never visiting your home to experience your family and what was important to you. I regret never slowing down to the speed of a horse and buggy. I regret treating life as one would when skimming over the tops of waves rather than appreciating what's in the trough. So what I will promise you is this; I will follow your example and slow down enough to see what is in front of me." Then he squeezed Dena's hand.

Four people huddled together on their knees under maples beginning their annual cycle of shedding off what had served a purpose to make room for those to come. The strength they felt came not from muscle or training, but by bracing the other.

Evening set in and the shadow from Friedel's marker was growing longer. Jason and Dena were invited to remain as long as they liked, but they had a van to return before catching their flight. Saying good-bye was not easy for any of them, so as one good-bye stretched into another, Dena slipped her arm through Jason's and whispered, "Come on. Let's go home."

THE END

Epilogue

Ted Phelps was indicted on first degree murder with special circumstances for the killing of Deputy Ken Hutchinson. With the special circumstances addendum, he would be eligible for the death sentence. For the death of Friedel Mueller, he was formally charged with voluntary manslaughter. The DA felt he had no choice since it would be purely speculative at best to determine what exactly caused her death. Phelps may have initiated it, but for a jury to be convinced, it might come down to the reasonable doubt dilemma. Better to take the given than to let this slip through the system on a technicality. Under further scrutiny by the forensics team, the ghoulish boxed museum in Phelps' basement contained more damning evidence. The 9mm Glock had indeed been illegally acquired out of the locked evidence storeroom and had been fired. A ballistics test on the weapon was compared with the striations on the bullets found in Hutchinson's side and head and were confirmed to be from the same gun. Papers found in the boxes dating back to when Friedel was killed were dusted and found to contain both Ted and his father's prints, which meant Wayne Phelps had willingly taken on the role of an accessory after the fact, but since he was now deceased, there was little to do other than publicly condemn the act as an unconscionable abuse of power and position. Ted Phelps is being held in solitary confinement in Lorain, Ohio for his own protection.

In return for Kathleen's willingness to turn states evidence against her cousin, the state dismissed all charges of culpability in the death of Friedel Mueller. Kathleen maintains her position as curator of the maritime museum in Vermilion and has added more mockups of lake freighters for visitors to stand on and dream.

Because of Kathleen's contribution to turn state's evidence against her cousin, coupled with so much damning evidence found in the Phelps home, Elizabeth and Isaac Mueller were pleased to find out the state was not going to ask for Friedel's body to be exhumed for DNA analysis.

Outraged by the audaciousness of Sheriff Phelps' presentation of the American flag to Ken Hutchinson's family at the burial ceremony, they did not want to display the tainted flag in their home, but didn't know what to do with it. They decided to donate it anonymously to the Boy Scouts. The new sheriff promised to replace it with an unblemished flag.

Mrs. Phelps sold their home, reverted to using her maiden name, and moved to a condo in Euclid overlooking Lake Erie.

By the insistence of Shauna Delrosso, Ian Stewart was rewarded with a larger office. It didn't have a window overlooking Superior Avenue, but it did have three cushy guest chairs, each with a holder for coffee, water bottle, or gin. He was not one for taking taxis every place he went, so when he was offered a lucrative position with a New York paper for his aggressive investigative reporting, he chose to stay where he felt comfortable.

The Loomis' were pleased with the extended revenue afforded by Jason and Dena's stay, but were also happy to regain their private living quarters. And Doug continues to take showers and engage in acceptable oral hygiene in hopes another Dena would show up on their doorsteps.

Jason's two Makarovs found good homes with Isaac and Joshua who said they might use them to scare away deer during the corn's growing season. As much as they cherished and respected life, they needed the corn to sustain their Holsteins.

On occasions, Jennifer visits with Joshua Stoudt's family and gets to ride their horses. Technically, they are work horses and not riding horses, but no one has told Jennifer or the horses. Her favorite is named *Kamerad*, which means Pal in English. And she wants to learn German when she reaches high school.

Tigre and his gang still sit on the grimy front stoop overlooking his Mustang.

Jason was mildly depressed when the only thing he could find David Ellison guilty of was being a total ass, but did take considerable pleasure in seeing David's first bid for one of the senatorial posts of Ohio be so vehemently rejected by the voters. Jason liked to think his condensed endorsement on the court house steps contributed to the downfall.

And as for Jason and Dena. Well…